With my thanks and gratitude to:
Anna Majcherczyk, Jozef Kowhan, Maria and Bohdan Stropek and Janina Gendek, whose accounts of personal wartime experiences have inspired and compelled me to write this book.
Michael for his tireless research.
Liz for all her practical help.
My colleagues at the Leicester Writers' Club for their patient listening and constructive criticism.

For Anna and her generation
so that their wartime experiences,
imposed on them by their oppressors,
should not be forgotten.

STOLEN YEARS

STOLEN YEARS

Kazia Myers

Matador
9 Priory Business Park,
Wistow Road, Kibworth Beauchamp,
Leicestershire. LE8 0RX
Tel: 0116 279 2299
Email: books@troubador.co.uk
Web: www.troubador.co.uk/matador
Twitter: @matadorbooks

ISBN 978 1789015 485

British Library Cataloguing in Publication Data.
A catalogue record for this book is available from the British Library.

Typeset in 11pt Adobe Garamond Pro by Troubador Publishing Ltd, Leicester, UK

Matador is an imprint of Troubador Publishing Ltd

PART 1

JUNE-AUGUST 1940

CHAPTER 1

4th June 1940

"They're here," I whispered. Something shrank inside me.

I watched them through a chink in the curtains, two German soldiers striding towards our door. It was inevitable now. And yet, from the turmoil in my mind, came one last desperate thought. Perhaps the order had been withdrawn. Perhaps they were messengers of a last-minute reprieve.

I turned to my mother. She was wiping her eyes.

"My little Aneczka!" She threw her arms around me, and held me tight. I felt her shudder with suppressed sobs. I did not want to let go of her, but I had been warned. They did not tolerate delays.

I bent down to my sisters, Alina and Marysia, clinging to each other with wide-eyed anxiety. I hugged and kissed them in turn.

The fierce banging made me recoil, but I had to be strong. I forced my legs forward and opened the door. They were big men, towering above me, their rifles slung over their shoulders, their helmets like skulls gleaming in the early morning light.

"Anna Myszkovska," one of them spoke. Deep, guttural, voice, his tone like an accusation.

"That's me."

"*Du kommst mit uns!* You're coming with us."

I felt a movement behind me.

"Sir, have a heart!" my mother spoke up. "She's barely seventeen. Look at the size of her! Like a sparrow…"

He waved her off with impatience, raising his voice to me,

"*Schnell! Schnell!*"

I picked up my canvas bag, packed with a few belongings the night before, and I hurried outside.

The morning was like any other summer morning just after dawn, dewy grass, long cool shadows cast by the trees and remnants of mist rising from the ground. To me it looked unreal, as if I were seeing it for the first time.

As we approached the village green, the soldiers' close presence straining every nerve in my body, I experienced fleeting relief at the sight of other young people already aboard an open army lorry, a group of about twenty, most of whom I knew well. Their voices died down when they saw us coming. The village official licked the tip of his pencil and wrote something briefly on the wad of documents before handing them over. His gesture was precise, marking clearly the moment of demarcation. His responsibility was over for now.

I lifted my bag to Michal, my older brother's friend and then climbed up the high single step to outstretched hands waiting to hoist me up. The soldiers climbed up behind me, pulled up the metal tailgate by the chains, bolted it in place, then sat down on the two wooden stools, resting their rifles against their thighs.

"*Geh!*" one of them ordered and we were off.

The sudden jerk unsteadied our legs and made us grope for support. We sat down against the sides of the lorry, well away from the guards. No one spoke, no one commented on the jolts and the shakes as the lorry's wheels bounced along the stony track. Only the birds twittered, twittered like mad in the lush growth between the houses. There was no one about but I noticed curtains twitching and the odd silhouette in the windows as we passed by and out of the village.

The silence filled me with unease. Strange how glad I was of the closeness of my brother's friends, Michal, Franek and Staszek, who had been fixtures in my life for as long as I could remember and had treated me with the bossy superiority reserved for younger sisters. Normally I could barely tolerate them.

The ride made my flesh wobble and my bones feel loose, but when the lorry mounted the smooth surface of the main road to Krakow, the transition was barely noticed. Our attention was caught by an extraordinary sight. A convoy made up of hundreds of vehicles, lorries, buses, vans, horse-drawn carts and carriages, all packed with young people, was heading towards the city.

The two soldiers, who until this moment, had sat silent and still like stone statues, began to stir. Their eyes studied the road beyond our transport with guarded alertness, while they spoke in low tones out of the corners of their mouths. A hesitant murmur rose within our group, lifting the oppressiveness that had travelled with us like additional baggage.

"What does this mean?" I whispered to Michal, stretching my neck to see better.

Michal whispered back, "We are their workforce. Crazy, isn't it? While they're too busy fighting Hitler's war."

"But why such crowds?"

"More hands, less work. Six months, we've been told."

"I don't want to be going at all," I said.

"Who does? Your brother got wise just in time."

"And look where that got me!" Bitterness welled up inside me. I felt a twinge of guilt. I should have been pleased with his timely escape. Michal nodded.

"Don't hold it against him. How was he to know they were going to pick on his younger sister?" It was easy for Michal to be so forgiving. He was not the one forced to take his brother's place.

Our group consisted mainly of young men. The few girls present had been picked from all-female families, as mine had become, having been stripped of all its young men. They were all older and bigger than me.

Michal nudged me again.

"Think of all the fun we shall have at Christmas. And the New Year."

I could not think of that now. Six months could have well been six years away. Besides, my older brother Vladek had already been gone eight months working at some remote German farm and there had been no news of his return as yet.

"I hope you're right," I said with no conviction and kept my gaze fixed on the distance, but Michal placed his fingers under my chin and made me look at him. His hair was flattened with brilliantine. No doubt he thought that was stylish. He smiled.

"Don't look so glum, Darkeyes. It doesn't suit you."

I jerked away my face, irritated by his familiarity.

"What's there to be happy about?"

"Come on, Anna," his tone was gently reproachful, "we can't do much about that," his sideways glance indicated the two soldiers behind us, "but in here," he tapped his head, "we must never give in!"

He was right, I admitted reluctantly, but I did not need him to tell me how to feel. The only interest he had shown me in the past was when he teased me and had made me bad-tempered. Why this sudden concern now? Did he think he could replace my older brother?

"I can manage, thank you," I said, and pretended to watch the swallows flying in circles above us.

I waited for the last bend on the familiar road, beyond which lay hidden my favourite sight. Krakow, my city. I loved the unchanging skyline. I knew the shape of every building, every tower, every church spire, as they all shot upwards, each from a different level, as if competing for dominance. From the highest hill in the city rose the WawelCastle, once the residence of kings, now the headquarters of the SS Governor General.

Krakow was where I was going to live one day. I was already a good seamstress, and my fine embroidery easily matched the best in the shops of great repute. I often daydreamed of dazzling them with my talents and of being offered a job in one of the high fashion houses. Now, this war had got in the way! How long would it be before my dreams and plans became real?

Station Square, when our lorry arrived there after countless stops and starts and long waits in between, was a river of humanity, its currents shaped and directed by continual arrivals and departures of vehicles. There was a waft of sulphur fumes in the air and a milky haze hung about, fed intermittently by billowing emissions of steam.

Our lorry stopped level with the station entrance, a lofty archway with ornate stonework. Our two guards jumped down first and shouted, *"Schnell! "Schnell!"*

We all scrambled down, holding onto our bags and were hurried along and pushed towards the waiting train on the nearest platform. One could not see the ground for the crowds nor the end of the train, lost in the distance. The lettering on our carriage read: "Wien" in bold blue capitals edged with gold.

"Where are they taking us?" Michal wondered aloud.

We had not been informed of our destination in advance, only given a promise of a chance to write home once we arrived.

The space on the coach allocated to our group of twenty consisted of two wooden benches and the floor in between. I waited till the boys and the girls older than myself filled the benches before I sat down on the floor with the rest. It was a tight squeeze. I found myself wedged between Michal on one side and his friends Franek and Staszek on the other. There was no room for our bags except on our laps.

"This is fun!" Michal said, his face a centimetre away from mine. I caught a whiff of his cheap brilliantine and a smell of yesterday's stew trapped in the fabric of his shirt.

"We'll suffocate even before we leave," I complained and stretched my neck for fresh air from the window above me. Thick steam rolled in making me duck and press my face against my bag.

"Rest your head on my shoulder," Michal offered.

"I'll manage, thank you," I replied. I was not his girl. All I needed was more room and clean air.

Staszek leaned forward, risking the loss of his space between Franek and the bench's wooden leg.

"What's a little discomfort for tough nuts like us?" he said, contorting his elbows on top of his bag, catching glints of sun in his white-blond hair. "Just think of all that money we're going to bring back."

I did think of that and of how much the assurances given to us would materialise into real rewards.

"I was perfectly happy where I was," Franek said. He had been an apprentice in motor-mechanics. His spiky thinness made me think of grasshoppers. He sat squashed, his bent long legs pushing up his chin, his dark hair falling behind his ears.

"I just want to get up and go. Even if I have to walk all the way home."

"I'll come with you," I put in quickly.

"Don't leave us," Michal raised his palms in a mock gesture of begging that made me smile, despite my mood. His cheeks lifted and I noticed amber flecks in his brown eyes.

He said, "Now that we've all agreed to stay, let's take bets on our destination. South or west?"

We were sent to Vienna and arrived there that evening after what seemed like a month in hell. To begin with, our train did not leave Krakow till mid-morning. In the heat generated by rising temperatures, overcrowding and pervasiveness of steam our clothes soon turned to damp rags. The boys got up, pulled off their shirts and used them as towels, much to the annoyance of our privileged companions, seated on the benches, who could not avoid inhaling all the odours generated by this activity. I stayed put, with my back pressed against the wooden frame, helpless against the sweat that gathered in every hollow in my body before seeping into my dress.

There were shouts of relief when the whistle's piercing sound jerked our train into action and the journey began. I stood up with the boys to watch the buildings fly by and green fields come into view, but all I could think of was my mother and the growing distance between us.

Our legs got tired after a while and we all sat down on the floor, sticky and compressed. I was surrounded by naked torsos and arms. Franek's ribcage stood out in ridges underneath his skin. Staszek's soft flesh had retained some of his childhood plumpness. Michal was lean and muscular, his large hands hardened by work. On his left shoulder there was a small brown mark. I closed my eyes but I could not shut out the heat and the sickly smells of caged humanity.

Incredibly, I slept. I had only become aware of that, when I was woken up by someone tapping my shoulder.

"Get up, Anna," I recognised Michal's voice, "we are all getting out."

Groggy from my sleep, I followed everyone out of the carriage, along the narrow passage to the outside door that had been left open. One by one, we jumped down onto the rail track.

We were in the middle of a forest. This was the first of our stops for toilet purposes. The guards, with their rifles pointing upwards in readiness, spaced themselves out along the side of the train, while others followed us through the bracken into thicker growth. It was a simple matter for the men, not so for the girls. Unable to shake off our intrusive minders, we walked away in groups and formed small, outward-looking circles, fanning out our skirts to screen the girl in the middle, as one by one we took turns. The fresh forest air and the breeze blowing through my dress around my legs sent shivers of relief all over my skin.

After a short break there were shouts and orders and we were herded back onto the train. The journey continued like a blur of passing landscape, forests, villages, towns, more stops. The heat had blunted my appetite. I took a bite of my cheese sandwich but it felt like sawdust in my mouth when I rolled it around, unable to swallow. I marvelled at the boys' ravenous appetite as they raided their bags for every last bit of bread, sausage, cheese and boiled egg. I saved my food for later.

It was about seven in the evening when a wave of excitement reached our carriage. We were approaching Vienna. The descending sun was still bright in the west, but where our train began to slow down, the thick forest was already in shadow, deep and dark below the bursts of light in gaps between the branches.

Suddenly I became aware of a silence in our carriage. Franek and Staszek must have felt it too, for they stopped talking and looked uncertainly at Michal and me. People around us were getting up to their feet, but no one spoke. Their attention was fixed on something beyond our windows. The train was barely moving now. Our little group stood up and we craned our necks above the shoulders of those next to the window.

Then I saw it too. At first I could not understand, I could not absorb what it was that I was looking at. The shock, when it came, hit me like a whip, like an all-illuminating flash.

There, only a few metres away from the rail track, were three bodies hanging from the branches of a pine tree. They were limp and perfectly still. Their dark shapes were barely visible against the background of gathering dusk, but for three features. Startling in their whiteness. Three elongated necks, strangely curved in the grip of three thick nooses.

I covered my face with my hands and screwed my eyes hard, till all I could see were red concentric circles, forming, spreading, fading into infinity.

I felt an arm on my shoulder and I knew by the whiff of brilliantine that it was Michal, as he hugged me to his chest.

CHAPTER 2

Our overnight accommodation in Vienna was a vast empty warehouse on the station site near some sidings where carriages were brought in for repairs and cleaning. The space allotted to our group was six rubber mattresses pushed together to form one layer on the concrete floor. There were hundreds of us, young people herded together, but no sound rose above a stifled murmur. We watched, tense and furtive as the armed soldiers, on their night shift, walked up and down the central area that had been left clear for them.

Dusk was falling outside. The tall sliding doors made of corrugated iron had been pushed back and left open. Naked bulbs hung from the high ceiling casting pale light that made us all look jaundiced. Franek and Staszek were sitting beside me. They were unnaturally quiet. Michal, on my other side, leaned his shoulder against mine.

"Christ almighty!" he whispered, "I'm still shaking. I can't believe what I saw!"

"I can't think of anything else either!" I whispered back. The image of the three dead bodies hanging from the tree was like an engraving cut deep into my mind.

"No one deserves to die like that!" Michal's whisper was intense, "they did it to frighten us, Anna. Leaving them exposed like that, where everyone could see."

I raised my head a fraction and glimpsed a sea of bowed heads. I shivered and felt my throat tighten and my eyes become prickly and a sensation in my stomach like the prodding of a hundred fingers.

"I mustn't cry," I told myself, clenching my fists and fighting fear with the sharp pain of my nails jabbing my palms.

The sudden rattling, metallic sound at the door made me jump and only when I saw what it was I unclenched my fists and allowed myself to sit upright. Dozens of trolleys were being wheeled in and pushed to equidistant points around the hall. They carried huge iron pots each, aluminium mugs and large bowls stacked with bread rolls.

We were organised into fast moving queues and given each a mug of potato soup and a bread roll. The woman who served our group had greasy hair that hung like pieces of wet string around her face. Her plump hands were rough, covered in scratches and cuts, and there was grime embedded underneath her nails.

"Well, what do you think of that?" Staszek regained his voice as soon as we sat down to eat.

"I'm trying hard not to think at all," Franek said, "but I have to say the soup is passable."

It was. I surprised myself to find I could eat at all. I used chunks of bread to retrieve cubes of potato from the base of my mug.

"I wouldn't mind some more," Staszek was the first to finish and smacked his lips like a cat. But there were no second helpings. The trolleys had been removed with hurried promptness.

"I've got some food," I offered. I had not eaten any of the sandwiches that I had prepared that morning. God, was it still only the same day? It felt like a time from a distant past.

I pulled my headscarf out of my travel bag and spread it on the concrete floor before emptying on it the contents of my food box. There were ham and cheese sandwiches, a couple of tomatoes and a jar of sweet gherkins.

The boys' faces brightened up, but with remarkable control they held back.

"Go on," I said, "have it between you. It will go to waste in this heat."

Michal slid his hand up the sleeve of his shirt and from a secret pocket brought out a miniature penknife. He cut all food into three precisely equal portions. Cutting the two tomatoes required some calculation, but Franek and Staszek agreed not to fight over small differences. They did not waste time and set about their food with nervous haste.

"Best not to attract attention," Staszek winked, flexing his back over his few provisions on the floor.

He need not have worried, for we were of no interest to anyone amidst the general commotion and clatter in the collection of the aluminium mugs. At the same time, fear had made us wary. Only the guards knew all the rules, and only they could decide if we were breaking them.

Michal saved half a sandwich for me.

"Last chance," he said.

I shook my head.

"Eat it. And hurry. We need to tidy up." I wished for nothing more but to have a wash and to go to sleep. To lose consciousness, to forget everything.

Our two guards approached us with shouts of *"Aufstehen! Aufstehen!"* We jumped to our feet and followed them outside. It had grown dark now, transforming the passages between the buildings into black holes. I clutched Michal's hand, holding back against each uncertain step, feeling as if I were walking a tightrope over the edge of an abyss.

We were marched to an area behind all of the buildings. To my relief it was still lit, minutes before the compulsory blackout. There in the dim light of a few bulbs dangling from an overhead cable, stood a row of about twenty wooden huts. They could have been termed almost pretty in their doll-size proportions, but this momentary illusion was drowned in an overwhelming stench. Gut-wrenching, eye-stinging, gagging stench. I placed my hands over my mouth and nose to hold down the impulse to retch. Some others, less fortunate than myself, were attacked by racking spasms of revulsion, strong, merciless, forcing them to throw up their just-eaten meal. I was aware of splashes against my legs and feet, but the soldiers hurried us along and the three-quarter darkness made it difficult to detect what had stuck to my sandals. My new white canvas sandals. Bought with the money I had been saving for months.

Again, we were ordered and organised into long queues, one by each hut. I slipped in between two older girls and waited my turn, trying hard not to listen to the sounds amplified by the hollowness of the cubicles. Groaning, retching, slurpy noises of diarrhoea. I looked sideways at one of the soldiers, at his features half-hidden by his helmet, and I had an urge, a terrifying urge, to slam my fist into his perfect mouth, to break his delicate nose. But all I could do was to stand with the others, quiet and helpless against the brutes who had robbed us of our dignity.

"Please, guardian angel, let me be quick." I invoked the help of my imaginary protector, as I watched a girl stagger out of the latrine holding a handkerchief to her mouth.

Inside, the floor space to stand on was covered by two parallel planks, one on each side of the oval hole. I placed my feet on them, firmly, wide apart. The moment I pulled the door shut I was plunged into total blackness. Panic gripped me, freezing my movements, making my thoughts run wild. What if my foot slipped? What if I fell into the hole? What was that ferocious buzzing? Just the blue-bottles or something worse? Something unspeakable at the bottom of the pit?

With all my strength I hit the door open and gasped for air. It was just as putrid as the stink inside.

"So quick? Already?" It was Natalia, an older girl from our group.

"No. I haven't been yet," I cried, panting. "Please, I beg you, stand guard at the door and hold it open for me. Just a little. So I can see what I'm doing."

The boy behind Natalia popped up his head over her shoulder.

"I can help you," he grinned.

Natalia gave him a sharp nudge with her elbow.

"Very funny! Get lost!"

She stood with her back to the door, allowing a chink of light inside the cubicle. I could just about distinguish the black shape of the hole and the lighter outlines of the planks. I spread my feet wide apart, well away from the treacherous edge, only to discover, with a pang of dismay, that this position made it difficult to pull my knickers down to a safe distance from the imminent stream. What was I going to do? Not go at all? That was too risky. Would I last all night?

"Please guardian angel, help me!" I had an idea. "Natalia," I said, "I've got to hold onto the door frame. Don't shut the door on my hand, will you?"

Natalia took a moment to digest this.

"What are you doing, Anna?"

"Please! I beg you!"

I heard the boy behind Natalia shout.

"Get a move on! This isn't a bloody beauty parlour, but a shit house! We are all…" He stopped in mid sentence, and I guessed Natalie gave him another thump.

Balancing both my feet on the narrow doorstep, I held onto the doorframe with all the might of one hand, while with the other I pulled down my knickers and stepped out of them, contorting my legs and feet with all the concentration of a circus performer. One slip and I would have ended in the quagmire of excrement at the bottom of the pit. I stuffed the knickers down my neckline and slowly, very slowly arranged my feet again, wide apart on the two planks. The relief when it came made me weak with happiness. I pondered over the power of such small things, when, a few minutes later, I stood guard at the latrine door for Natalia's sake.

We all washed in the water from the hoses that were normally used for washing down trains. There was a row of them attached to a long brick wall and the boys took delight in splashing themselves and others, having undressed to their underpants first. A few brave girls took off their dresses and bathed in their underwear. I was not one of them. Getting my dress wet was the least of my worries. I rinsed my mouth, my face, my neck, and with a wet handkerchief I wiped my armpits, ridding myself of the stickiness accumulated through the day.

I did not dare touch my sandals, but kept them on my feet as I hosed them down with a strong jet of water manipulated by my thumb. In the near total darkness I could only hope that all remnants of vomit had been removed.

Afterwards, having moved out of the way for the next person in the queue, I crouched down pretending to adjust the buckle on my sandal. Assured that no one was looking I used the soaked hemline of my dress to wipe the perspiring, itching, stinging flesh between my legs. It made me feel better straight away and when I looked up, I was infinitely grateful that I was not the girl walking ahead of me, with blood stains spreading into the wet fabric of her dress.

We felt our way back in total blackout, by linking our hands in a chain and following the contours of the buildings, till we reached the lofty iron doors of the warehouse. The doors had now been pushed back together, leaving a slit just wide enough for us to slip through.

Inside, the darkness was lifted at the edges by the dimmest of lights emanating from squat table lamps on the guards' desks, dotted around the vast hall. We were frog-marched to our set of six mattresses and ordered to sit down by our belongings. Finding enough space to lie down in became a problem straightaway. No amount of our combined ingenuity to make ourselves fit somehow, like pieces in a jigsaw, could produce that extra room for the odd elbow, or shoulder or knee, and the tiniest shift of position sent a wave of unrest across our communal bed.

"This is mad," I said to Michal, "I'm moving onto the floor."

"No, Anna," his face was centimetres away from mine, in the dark, "it's you who's mad. How will you sleep on the bare concrete?"

"Just watch me," I whispered back, which was silly, because it was too dark to see anything at all.

I sat up, rummaged through my bag, pulled out my cardigan and lay it flat on the floor next to our mattress. I curled myself on top of it, drawing up my knees so that my calves would not touch the dusty surface. I used my travel bag for my pillow, feeling all its contents, especially my shoes. This seemed like a good moment to slip on my knickers. As soon as they were half way up my legs, I manoeuvred them in place through the thin cotton of my dress.

"Hey, what's all that wriggling for?" Staszek whispered, "Are the fleas biting you?"

"They must be yours," I whispered back, "I don't cultivate them."

I heard Franek snort.

"How's your royal bed, then? Any room for us?"

"Make your own," I answered back, thinking, "and see how it hurts your bones." I had never imagined that the floor could be so hard. I had slept on the grass, I had slept in the hay, but this was torture.

"Anna," Michal leaned over, "how about if we make a thick layer for us both to sleep on, with all our clothes piled together?"

He surprised me so much with his suggestion that I did not think to argue. I did not have the energy to question his motives. I was miserable. I longed for just a touch of comfort to enable me to sleep.

On top of my cardigan we used Michal's jacket, his jumper, his trousers and my other dress to form a kind of a giant cushion, big enough for the two of us. We lay down next to each other, careful not to touch. Close up to us, Franek and Staszek did the same amidst sighs of approval from the rest of the group.

I closed my eyes and willed myself to sleep but all I could see were three bodies. Hanging. Stark clear. Terrifying. Persistent. I opened my eyes and stared into the blackness that was heavy with the heat, stored all day underneath the corrugated iron roof above us. My dress was dry now but smelled like a dirty old towel. My sandals were stiff on my feet, but I dared not touch them for fear of contaminating my hands. I convinced myself that my socks were an adequate barrier to protect my feet against the unspeakable germs ingrained in my footwear.

All around me there were murmurs and sighs. I thought of the evening back at home, the fragrance in the air, the song of the night jar, the frogs' chorus down by the lake, as I listened to Franek and Staszek whispering to each other their dreams of the future, after the war. It was so strange, lying down next to them, and next to Michal, my brother's friends, whom I had never liked very much. It was strange, that I no longer found them that bad.

"Are you awake?" Michal's whisper surprised me. He had been so still I was certain he was asleep.

"My throat's very dry," I said, thinking at the same time, "and the floor is killing my back and the heat is bursting my head and I want to get out of this hell and just go home!"

"I've kept something for you," he said.

I became aware of his hand searching for mine, then I felt something like a pebble drop into my palm.

"Pop it in your mouth," he said.

The cherry flavour, as it spread, was heaven on my tongue. I knew the sweet to be like a red transparent marble with a creamy swirl running through it, and I moved it around my mouth extracting the juicy sweetness slowly, prolonging the pleasure, holding back the impulse to crunch it all at once.

"It's magic! Thanks!" I said, overwhelmed by his generosity.

"It's no big deal," Michal whispered, "I'm doing this for Vladek. Can't let him down, can I? It's the least he'd expect me to do for his kid sister."

Just the sort of thing he would normally say. Why did I expect more? So I did not tell him that just for a moment I thought he had a heart.

My big brother Vladek had been gone eight months now, working on a farm in Germany. Our little brother Joseph, only twelve, had cried so much that Vladek had to take him along too. After our father's death, the two had become inseparable. It suddenly occurred to me that they too must have endured a journey like ours. I could picture Joseph anxious and bewildered holding onto Vladek desperately, and Vladek putting on the brave big brother act. There had only been one letter from them. They were both well and working very hard. No mention of their return.

I wondered what was awaiting us the following day. Hundreds of images passed through my mind. I pushed them all away, just hanging on to one: a sprawling farmhouse, sleepy in the afternoon sun, with cows in the meadow, chickens in the barn and pigs rolling with contentment in their mud bath. Perhaps, once we got there things would be all right. Perhaps…once I got rid of the heaviness in my heart and the tight knot in my stomach.

Later, it seemed like the middle of the night I was woken up by shouting voices. I raised myself and winced at the stiffness that had set in all my joints. People around me were lifting their heads, alarmed by the commotion. I held my breath and watched in the dim light two soldiers dragging away a boy, his limp body slumped forward. Another boy was sobbing aloud and waving about his arms. He was restrained, then punched before being dropped to the ground. He did not get up, but remained sprawled on the floor, moaning softly. Something tightened in my chest and I felt pain shoot up to my temples.

"I'll find out what's happened," Franek volunteered, when the soldiers walked away. He crawled like a caterpillar the few metres between our groups. The sounds of retching and throwing up close by made me hug my stomach, as I lay curled tight.

Franek came back with this story:

"There are these two brothers, Jan and Czes. Czes has had stomach pains all day. Real bad ones. Jan thinks it's the appendix. The soldiers have taken Czes away, but they won't let Jan come as well."

"Where have they taken him?" I asked.

"God only knows."

16

My companions became quiet and I lay down and tried hard not to think of Jan's anguish and Czes' pain.

The shrill alarm of the wake-up call hit me like a physical knock and made me sit up before I was fully awake. At the same moment the tall corrugated iron doors were pushed back flooding the hall with blinding sunlight, though it was only half past five. I squinted to protect my eyes and pressed my hand against the stiffness in my neck. My lower lip was tingling like the pricking of needles. I licked it feeling the bump of a cold sore. All around me there were lethargic stirrings, hushed grumbles and stifled yawns.

"How's the princess this morning?" Staszek teased as he and Franek began to roll up their clothing to pack it away. "Felt the pea under all your mattresses?"

I was not really in the mood for joking, but before I could think of a retort, Michal came to the rescue.

"Never slept better!" he said with feeling, rubbing his back with both his hands.

"I'm glad somebody did!" Franek said, shaking out his shirt and folding it in his bag. "The sooner we get out of this hell hole the better!"

He did not have to wait long. The order of the morning was carried out with military discipline and unrelenting haste. A supervised visit to the latrines, even more revolting in the all-revealing daylight, than the night before, and a quick wash at the outdoor hoses was followed by breakfast. This was distributed from the trolleys and consisted of a jam bread roll and coffee made from roasted millet grains. It tasted smoky and bitter, but slid like honey down my parched throat. We were also given two bread rolls each to save for the journey.

We sat with our belongings ready to go. My once elegant navy cardigan, with silver buttons and a tie belt, now looked like an old badly steam-pressed garment. I thought of Aunt Julia and felt a pang of guilt. She had spent hours knitting it for me and I had used it for a mattress. I rolled it up and hid it inside my bag.

Franek and Michal could have done with a shave, I noticed. I did not like their stubble, it gave them a sinister, menacing appearance. Staszek was lucky with his blond colouring. As he moved there were glints of gold on his face and his hair shone like a halo against the daylight framed in the open door.

Suddenly, teams of white-coated people streamed through the entrance and with energetic strides walked up to their pre-arranged spots around the vast hall. Some – the doctors, I guessed – had stethoscopes hanging from their necks. The nurses, in pairs, carried light trestle tables and a few people carried chairs and leather bags.

As soon as the medical teams organised themselves at the makeshift desks, orders were shouted out around the hall for the groups nearest to the centre to get up. Our group was approached by a woman who spoke to us in Polish.

"*Rozebrac sie! Do pasa*! Undress to your waist!"

This was so unexpected, no one reacted at first.

"Undress to your waist, I said!" she shouted this time, and as she did so, our two guards raised their rifles and made a step towards us.

After that, it felt as if I were in a trance, as if I were somewhere else looking down upon myself going through some strange unrehearsed mime. Automatically, I untied my long hair and dividing it at the back I brought it forward over my chest. Underneath its cover I unbuttoned my dress down to my waist, slipped it off my shoulders, and left it to hang around my hips. Then I took off my brassiere. Holding my arms crossed over my chest, I stood with my head bowed, not daring to look sideways, for fear of seeing my friends' enforced nakedness, their stricken faces, their humiliation. My eyes stung with the shame of my own nakedness in such a public place.

There were no quips from the boys, none of their usual silly talk. No one spoke. The only voices heard were those of the doctors, when they questioned us individually, after we had been examined by the nurses first.

My hair and my armpits were checked for lice, then the nurse, in her white glove, prodded my breasts, looked inside my mouth and inside my ears.

"Next!" she shouted with unconcealed impatience, while directing me to one of the many queues awaiting the doctors' decision to rubberstamp our fitness for hard work.

I hid behind a tall boy with spiky elbows and protruding shoulder blades, and after a while I dared myself to look up. What I saw reminded me of a painting I had seen once in a library book about famous frescos. If I remembered correctly, it was called *The Last Judgement*. It was full of naked bodies. The memory of that scene and the reality surrounding me filled me with dread.

I became aware of new queues forming around the hall and as I watched closely, I realised that the boys were being sent to the barbers to have their heads shaved. This was a job done roughly, with great speed, leaving uneven tufts springing in all directions from the bare scalp. A few feet away from me I heard someone cry out. I turned to see a girl being led by an irate nurse to the barber's chair.

"I give orders here!" the nurse was shouting in Polish, as she pushed the girl onto the wooden seat and stood over her till the man set about his task. The girl clutched her blouse to her bare breasts with one hand, and with the other covered her face. Her long brown hair fell to the floor in handfuls like skeins of silk, till all that was left of her crowning glory were a few wisps on a pale scalp above a tanned face.

My heart shrivelled and my stomach contracted as I watched her misery, and though gratitude that such fate had somehow omitted me, touched my soul, I felt no joy. Only a sense of injustice. Of violation. Of utter helplessness.

The doctor was a middle-aged man, with shiny black hair, stuck down flat with brilliantine, and wearing glasses so thick they made his eyes appear like two distant dots. He listened to my chest and back before fixing me with his faraway gaze. He spoke to me in Polish.

"You're not very big for farm work."

I knew that. Was he expecting me to comment?

"When was your last period?"

I told him.

"Not pregnant then?"

My face turned hot and crimson. What sort of a girl did he take me for?

"I'm not married," I said, deliberately frowning.

His thin mouth twitched.

"So who's been kissing you then?"

My lower lip, by now, felt like a rubber ball stuck to my face. I had an urge to tear it off, but in fact I could hardly bear to touch it, so taut was the membrane over the swelling.

"You're fine," he said, finishing writing his notes. "Next!"

When I got back to my belongings the boys were already there. I did not recognise them at first. With their shaved heads they looked like escaped convicts.

"So, you've been spared," Michal's smile was half-hearted and his movement uncertain as he stroked his bare head.

"Not quite," I answered, sitting down on the mattress with my back to them. I slipped on the top part of my dress and buttoned it up, before tying back my hair. Then I stood up to take a second look at them.

"Could be worse, couldn't it?" Staszek said, his dimpled face looking like a baby's, now that all his blond hair was gone. "Hey, just think of all the time and all the shampoo we'll be saving!"

"Brilliant!" Franek rolled his eyes, "this would have never occurred to me!" Without his hair he looked even thinner. He turned to me. "And what do you think about us, Anna?"

What did I think? I thought the rats' teeth would have done a better job than the barber's scissors. I saw three boys before me with haircuts intended to ridicule them, their heads partly shaved, partly sprouting hedgehog bristles. They had that pitiful, somehow battered look, as if they had just escaped an attack and a robbery. They reminded me of my little brother Joseph, when he was hurt and cried and needed to be comforted. But these were big men. They did not need my sympathy.

"I think," I said, forcing a painful, lop-sided smile, "that before long your hair will grow again. Remember Samson in the Bible?"

Incredibly, their faces brightened up.

"Hey, why didn't I think of that?" Franek exclaimed. I was expecting sarcasm from him, but when I looked into his sunken eyes, they appeared to shine.

It was later, when we were crossing the various sections between the warehouses and the sidings, each group escorted by their armed guards, that we were suddenly stopped in our tracks by a scream so torn with pain, that it felt like a blade going right through me.

There, on the side, by a stack of wooden crates stood a rough trestle, with its top covered by an untidy pile of old sacks. Beside it was a boy shouting and fighting off two soldiers who were forcefully restraining him.

"That's my brother!" he was crying out, "that's my brother! And you've just left him to die!"

I guessed this was Jan. Somehow he disentangled his arm from the soldiers' grip and pulled back the sacks.

Then I screamed too, and immediately clamped my hand over my mouth.

On the trestle lay Jan's brother, Czes. The angle of his head and his lifeless arm hanging over the side explained everything.

"Let me go! Let me go!" Grief and desperation made Jan hysterical. "Let me take him home!"

He was crying now like a child, big, racking sobs. He started kicking out. One of the soldiers hit him on the head with his rifle. Jan fell to the ground, his face spattered in blood. He did not move. The soldiers yanked him up by his arms and dragged him away out of sight.

We arrived in Sankt Veit late evening that day, our group and about sixty other young people. The original crowd had been first divided into smaller groups in Vienna, and again in Klagenfurt and sent to destinations all over the region.

We were marched with impatient haste to the cattle market situated at the side of the station square. My fleeting, hurried impressions were those of a main road, lined with parked vehicles and horse-drawn carts, tall three-storey buildings, long red banners with black swastikas hanging down from top windows, an orange glow of the setting sun reflected in the panes. The boys were immediately separated from the girls and each newly formed group was enclosed in a cattle pen for inspection by the waiting farmers.

I found myself with girls older and bigger than me. I strained my eyes not to lose sight of Michal, Franek and Staszek, who had been led away to the far side of the square, but they were continually obscured from my view by people milling around them. I began to feel anxious. This was the moment of our separation. I prayed that I would be picked with someone I already knew. I looked out for Natalia, but she was already being led away with another girl.

The first few minutes were very busy, then rapidly, the market square began to empty, with carts and motors setting off. The only people left now were remnants like myself, too small, or too thin to inspire confidence in our ability to work hard.

A farmer of about fifty with a weathered face and piercing black eyes approached my enclosure. He looked hard at me, then at my only companion, a big girl with a hump on her left shoulder. He pondered briefly, shook his head and turned his attention on the only boy in the adjoining cattle pen. The boy's shaved head and his bare arms were covered in a red, blotchy rash.

The farmer poked the boy's chest with his stick.

"Ausziehen!" he ordered gruffly.

The boy pulled off his shirt, as he was told, revealing more of his bad skin. His muscular chest and his strong hands however must have appealed to the farmer, because he crooked his finger saying, *"Komm mit mir."*

He gave us one more look then appeared to hesitate. He returned to my female companion and with his rough hands squeezed her arms then her good and her bad shoulder.

"Accident," she tried to explain in German. "Now, it is good."

He used his stick to lift her skirt, and after allowing himself a long stare at her sturdy calves and thighs, he nodded and pronounced, *"Gut. Du kannst auch mitkommen."*

He turned to me and made me flinch as his big hand came out towards me. But he only pinched my arm, shook his head and decided, *"Nicht* gut!*"*

I watched them walk away across the now almost deserted square, a girl with a deformed shoulder, a boy with blotchy skin, and their new boss, forced by necessity to make his reluctant choice. There was no sign of my friends, Michal, Franek and Staszek. I felt suddenly bereft.

I sat down on the dusty ground, hugging my travel bag to me and wondered what was going to happen if no one showed interest in claiming me. What were the soldiers going to do? Now that their duty was almost over, they paced impatiently up and down the path underneath a clump of trees, checking their watches, stopping to talk to the few remaining farmers.

My mouth was dry with thirst, my cold sore had developed into a pea-sized blister, my white-print dress was now the colour of the grey cloth I used for wiping floors at home. I was ready to give up half my life to be transported home, to my mother. A sudden, stupid hope sprang in my mind. Perhaps they would simply send me back? If no one wanted me.

I looked towards the soldiers. They seemed unaware of my solitary presence. Perhaps... Another wild thought, perhaps... I could crawl away unseen. And hide. And under cover of darkness start my journey home.

I was so absorbed in plans of my escape that when I heard my name being called, I thought I was dreaming.

"Anna! Anna!"

The voice was familiar, and the figure running towards me was like a messenger from heaven.

CHAPTER 3

The crazy sight of him, legs and arms flying, head bobbing up and down, his grimy face lit up with excitement, made me cry out. Not with derision, but with a strange, overwhelming joy. I got up to my feet and waited, ready to embrace him, ready to hug him, that indifferent, ordinary boy, whom I had never liked very much.

But Michal stopped at the barrier of my enclosure panting and trying to catch his breath.

"Anna, I think we've made him understand. I think we've managed to explain that you are one of us."

He pointed to the man coming towards us, flanked by Franek and Staszek. The farmer was about forty, with thick, greying hair and a long scar across his left cheek and upper nose, bearing testimony to his days at the front.

"*Herr Holtzmann,*" he said in a deep voice, pointing to himself, "*Komm Anna, Komm mit mir.*" He said a lot more, none of which I could understand. I could only guess there was need for me too on his farm.

He exchanged formalities with the guards, then led us to his black van. Franek was allowed to sit in the passenger seat, while we three – Michal, Staszek and I – climbed in through the back. My anxiety left me. I felt a lightness, and comfort in my friends' company. Even the old sacks layered on the metal floor gave me the feel of a soft carpet. Before long the swaying of the vehicle and the droning of the motor, combined with my total exhaustion, lulled me to sleep.

Michal woke me up later, when we arrived at Herr Holtzmann's farm. I scrambled out of the back door of the van and in my half-awake state registered vaguely a wide cobbled yard, surrounded by numerous buildings and barns, set amidst rolling hills and pine forests. Everything was outlined with an almost daytime clarity, so bright was the moon that night.

We followed Herr Holtzmann across the yard, then through a door in the main building and found ourselves in the kitchen. Though dimly lit it was visibly a spacious room with a number of doors leading to other parts of the house. Above one of the doors hung a large framed photograph of Hitler. A girl was standing at the stove and stirring the contents of a large pot. We stopped at the door, a little uncertain, but she turned round and greeted us in Polish.

"*Witam*. Welcome. I'm Maryla. Come closer, come. Sit down at the table."

We dropped our bags onto the floor and followed her request, gathering round the table, made of chunky, solid pine. Her boss gave her instructions in German before addressing us.

"*Gute Nacht,*" he said as he made his way out through one of the doors.

Maryla smiled and with a sweep of her hand, invited us to sit down. Her wide-set eyes caught the light briefly. She had a thin heart-shaped face and two long plaits. I noticed Staszek looking at her with interest, his optimism apparently undeterred by his ravaged appearance.

"Everyone's gone to bed ages ago," Maryla explained. "We all get up at dawn to work. When you've eaten, I'll show you to your rooms." She pronounced the word "rooms" as if it were something amusing.

"Is there anywhere I can wash my hands?" I asked.

"There is the kitchen sink," Maryla pointed to the far corner, "I'm afraid that's the only washing place we've got."

It was a deep, trough-like sink, designated for all manner of washing: pots, pans, as well as muddy boots and heavy soiled items that needed soaking. It was empty now and I was glad to quench my thirst with the free running water, wash my sticky hands and splash my face. My cold sore hurt like a nail driven through my lip. The boys did the same, all of us using the same dirty towel that we found hanging on the side of the sink. We sat together round one end of the table and Maryla placed a large bowl before us. She gave us a spoon each.

"I'm afraid we don't use plates or bowls here," she said, "We are allowed one big bowl between us."

"Why?" I exclaimed. I found such a notion quite odd. Off-putting, in fact.

"Regulations." Maryla gave me a meaningful look, which I did not understand. "There are lots of them, you'll see."

I placed my hand over my swollen lips worrying over its effect on the boys, but judging by their hungry, eager expressions, I could see their concerns were different from mine.

"What the hell!" Staszek said. "It could be worse! At least there's food on the table."

It was a thick lentil broth, and together with wedges of brown bread, it proved desirably welcome at the end of our long day. We huddled together, careful not to spill the contents of our spoons between the bowl and our lips, while all the time I tried really hard not to think about the invisible deposits on our four spoons being washed away in our communal soup.

Maryla sat down with us, broke off a piece of crust and chewed it as we introduced ourselves and haphazardly described our long journey. We told her of the terrible things we had seen. She placed her finger on her lips and pointed at the far end of the kitchen.

"Walls have ears," she whispered. We nodded in tacit understanding and lowered our voices.

"Those three bodies," Michal whispered, "I can't get them out of my mind."

"And those two boys, Jan and Czes…" Franek shook his head, "and none of us did anything…"

"And what could you have done?" Staszek asked. "You saw what happened to Jan when he tried to fight them."

"Listen to me, boys!" Maryla interrupted. Her voice a barely audible whisper. "You'll see lots more. Horrible things. And you won't be able to do anything. That's how they like to show us who is in control. We have frequent visits. At random. To keep us on our toes. My best advice to you is stay out of sight. Don't stick out. Don't get noticed. They can find fault with anything they please. Arrests and beatings are commonplace…" Maryla's earnest expression left me in no doubt that she was warning us of a terrible truth. I was bewildered.

"But we are their workforce," I reasoned, "surely they must be glad we're here…"

Maryla gave me a pitiful smile.

"You'll see for yourself, Anna. We count for nothing. We're just their slaves."

I clutched onto the "six months" promise.

"But we've been told the work is seasonal!"

"Yes. All four seasons. Indefinitely." Maryla's quiet statement was like the final turn of the key in a prison door.

We all fell silent. I felt sick. Six months was imaginable. Beyond that was black infinity stretching out before me. I looked at the boys. Their rough shaved heads made me think of medieval penitents, their grim expressions offered me no joy.

"I've built my hopes of the future on my earnings here," Franek said.

Maryla got up, as if to clear the table.

"I'm sorry to be the messenger of bad news, but for us here your arrival is a godsend. There's so much work, and not enough hands. We work from dawn to dusk."

"So how long have you been here?" Staszek asked.

"Six months, almost exactly. We were rounded up in a street, Bazylka and I. She's my sister. We were packed onto a train. With hundreds of others. We had nothing with us. Just the clothes we stood in. It was January. We nearly died of the freezing cold."

Suddenly I did not feel so unfortunate.

"I'm glad you didn't," Staszek's cheeks dimpled, catching Maryla's attention. "So who else is here?" he asked.

"Bazylka is the cow girl. There's Ludwik and Stefan. They work in the fields. There are two older men, Johann and Max. They are Austrian. The regular workers here. And I'm the swineherd." She gave a mock bow.

Staszek stood up beside her.

"I'll have you know," he said, "that it has always been my secret dream to be a swineherd. I shall be delighted to be Maryla's assistant."

He made us laugh despite the oppressive mood.

"It could be worse, couldn't it?" he shrugged.

"I was quite happy with my life at home," Franek said.

Michal looked at me sideways.

"As long as we're together," he whispered. Normally, I would have been annoyed at his presumption, but strangely now, I felt comforted by his veiled reassurance. I nodded and briefly brushed his arm with the side of my face.

"Shall I show you where you're going to sleep?" Maryla asked. "It's in the barn. Across the yard. You'll have to be quiet. Ludwik and Stefan are already in bed."

While the boys collected their belongings, she turned to me.

"I'll be back in a tick. Then we we'll go to bed too."

When they were gone I cleared and wiped the table, washed and dried the spoons and the single bowl, then in the same sink, under running water I washed my dust-blackened feet.

"Where do you normally have a wash?" I asked Maryla when she returned.

She stifled a yawn.

"There's no bathroom for us workers. There's a bowl we can fill and take into our room to wash in, or go to the tap in the yard. But the best is the lake, Anna. I'll take you there tomorrow. Now let's go to bed or I'll drop dead, I'm so tired!"

She looked at me closely.

"Have you got any cream for your lips?"

I shook my head.

"I've got nothing. Nothing at all." I should have been better prepared. I had imagined it all so differently. I had imagined buying things here, with my own earned money.

"I've got some Vaseline," Maryla said, leading me to what seemed like a passage on the other side of the stove. It turned out to be a tiny room spreading out into two deep alcoves, with beds pushed inside them. One bed was already occupied.

"That's my sister, Bazylka," Maryla whispered, pulling out a bag from underneath her bed. She rummaged inside it and produced a small jar.

"It's not a cure, but it will help a little." I wanted to hug her.

"I owe you," I said, spreading the greasy jelly over my cracked lips. The cold sore was barely touchable.

"I'll come to you when you get paid," Maryla grinned, adding, "I'm only joking. Now let's get some sleep."

It dawned on me then that we were to sleep in Maryla's bed. Together. Sharing the one mattress.

"You must be ecstatic to have a lodger in your bed," I whispered, slipping out of my grubby, smelly dress.

We undressed to our underwear and climbed into bed, I with great longing to rest my weary body at long last.

"It's not often we have our beds just to ourselves," Maryla whispered in the dark. "There have been other girls."

"What's happened to them?"

"One became pregnant and was sent home. The other ran off with a rebel Austrian boy."

I tried to imagine that. It was like listening to a fantasy. Nothing seemed real. My own life stopped feeling real. Was it really only two days ago that I had left home? Two days packed with confusion and fear and shocks and images, too many for my battered mind to assimilate, to make sense of. I lay with my eyes closed, invoking my mother's face, yearning for her closeness, willing everything else to disappear. Then, mercifully, I slept.

I woke up with a start and at first I could not make out where I was. It was daylight. Two faces were peering down at me. I recognised Maryla. Next to her stood the fattest woman I had ever seen. She was old, she had strong coarse features, grey hair that had come out in long wisps from her plait, and a tent-like dress that hung loosely from her shoulders.

"Anna, it's time to get up," Maryla was saying. "This is Frau Holtzmann, the boss's mother. She needs you to prepare breakfast for the workers. They will be coming from the fields at eight."

"What time is it?" I asked, sitting up, already feeling the pressure to hurry.

"Half past five."

Maryla spoke to Frau Holtzmann in German then she turned to me. "Can you get ready in five minutes?"

We waited for Frau Holtzmann to move out of the way. She swayed heavily, her fleshy arms wobbling, her expansive hips undulating against the fabric of her thin dress, then I slid off the bed, and together with Maryla, dashed off at the speed of demented bees.

Five minutes later, as ordered, I was ready, having splashed my face at the outdoor tap, rinsed my mouth, thrown on the first thing out of my bag and tied my tangled hair on the nape.

Frau Holtzmann was waiting for me in the kitchen, her big bulk supported by a stool near the table.

"Anna!" she raised a finger and pointed at the stove. I looked inside the big pot. There was a heap of buckwheat ready for boiling. I guessed she wanted me to cook it. I salted it, poured water over it and left it to simmer.

"Anna!" Frau Holtzmann pointed at the cupboard. I opened it to find a row of jars filled with a variety of grains: barley, yellow lentils, green lentils, dried beans, dried peas and lots more. I looked at Frau Holtzmann wondering what she wanted me to do. She spread her sausage fingers and counted them.

"*Eins, zwei, drei, vier, funf. Funf, Anna, funf!*"

I counted the jars. The fifth one contained roasted millet grains. Frau Holtzmann mimicked drinking actions. I guessed she wanted me to brew them for coffee substitute.

Under her further instructions, that were part exclamations, part mimicry, part repetition of words that I could only attempt to guess, I prepared two breakfast tables.

On the workers' big table I was directed to cut brown bread and leave a jar of plum jam, two knives, eight spoons and eight aluminium mugs. The smaller table, pushed against the wall, was to be set correctly: three bowls, three plates, three earthenware mugs and three sets of cutlery. I was shown the pantry door and instructed to fetch butter, ham and cheese. My stomach rumbled as I inspected the row of hanging sausages and cuts of smoked bacon. The shelves were stacked with bottled fruit, preserves and jams.

At home I would have cut a piece of sausage and chewed it as I continued with my chores. Here, Frau Holtzmann's watchful eyes made me nervous of my own thoughts. Now and again, as I swept the floor and washed and wiped all surfaces, I sent a friendly smile in her direction. A little lopsided, where the blister had burst and where the spot was hardening into a scab. Frau Holtzmann did not acknowledge my well-intentioned attempts, not with the slightest change in her dour expression. I dared myself to pluck up courage to speak to her. I could only communicate in Polish.

"Frau Holtzmann," I said, pointing to her unbuttoned dress at the back, "shall I do it up for you?"

She did not object when I stood behind her and did the simple task for her, that she was unable to carry out herself.

"Anna," she half turned, twisting a long strand of hair around her finger, *"meine haare kammen!"* She pointed to a drawer in one of the dressers, and when I pulled it out, there were her chrome-plated combs and brushes, and a blue ribbon.

I loosened her hair, brushed it all together and plaited it tightly, tying the end with the ribbon. I brought the end of her plait forward, over her shoulder where she could see it, and pointed to it and to her eyes, willing her to understand that the colours matched. To my surprise there appeared something like a flicker of warmth in her face.

Just then one of the doors was pushed open and a woman walked in. She was followed by two small children, a toddler wobbling on his feet and a girl of about four. Frau Holtzmann's face was transformed. Her eyes and her lips smiled and her hands beckoned impatiently. The little girl ran up to her with shouts of *"Oma, Oma!"* and buried her face in the old woman's enormous lap. Frau Holtzmann stroked her soft, curly hair but was unable, despite attempts, to bend down far enough to kiss her. I watched the little boy toddle uncertainly on his chubby legs and grasp a fold of Frau Holtzmann's voluminous dress for support. His balance teetered and he sat down with a thud, an ecstatic smile spreading across his face.

"Mein kleiner Engel," Frau Holtzmann said, stretching her arm so that her fingertips could caress his face.

But the younger woman, who I guessed was the children's mother, bent down and with a show of annoyance prised the children away, talking all the while, saying things I did not understand, things that dimmed the light in Frau Holtzmann's face.

She turned to me and introduced herself, making it clear who was the mistress of this house.

"Elise Holtzmann, *Herrin Frau*."

She did not look like the farmer's wife. She was slim, dressed in a straight navy dress with a white collar, and her feet looked small inside their neat, high-heeled shoes. Her hair was crimped tightly around her face.

Keeping her children close to her, she took out of the dresser a white porcelain platter, went inside the pantry and a moment later came out with it laden with bread, butter, cheese, ham and a jar of fruit preserves. Before she shut the parlour door on us, I glimpsed an opulent interior with velvet drapes, velour armchairs, a crystal chandelier and a mahogany table with a top surface as shiny as a mirror.

I could think of no one that I knew surrounded by such wealth. I could not imagine what I'd do amidst such splendour. I'd be afraid to touch anything, let alone sit in one of the armchairs and do normal things, like knitting or darning old socks.

My unguarded lapse into daydreaming was interrupted by Frau Holtzmann. She was talking rapidly, her voice was raised, her face was flushed. I could not tell if she was shouting instructions or venting her temper. Anxiety gripped my stomach. She picked up her brush and comb and hurled them at the parlour door. The noise that cut through the air was like a gun blast. I stifled a scream and for a moment everything was quiet. Then she half turned to me, and though I did not understand her words, I knew what I had to do. Holding my breath I approached the parlour door. It was flung open and Elise Holtzmann stood before me, her delicate features set hard, her stare chilling. She took in the scattered objects on the floor, shouted to her mother-in-law then slapped me across the face. The unexpected attack caught me off balance and sent me reeling to the floor, at the same time as the door closed with a bang and she was gone. A pain like a stab pierced my lower lip and caused my eyes to water. I felt a warm trickle on my chin and automatically touched the scab to stop it bleeding.

Frau Holtzmann was shouting again, but somehow I knew I was not the cause of her anger. I picked myself up, put away her brush and comb set, and at the sink I cooled my face with running water. The old, dirty towel from the previous night was still hanging at the side, but even in my agitated state I felt revulsion at the thought of using it. I made signs to Frau Holtzmann of my need to go to my room. There, sitting on the bed, I buried my face in my own clean towel. Sweet Jesus, Sweet Mary, what kind of a hell-hole was this? What had I done to be punished this way? I pictured the elegant, cruel Elise Holtzmann, her cold eyes staring down at me, and I knew I could never make myself like her. More than at any other time since leaving home I longed to be with my mother. The need was like a physical ache.

Then Frau Holtzmann called me. I put away the towel, checked my scab and went back to her. Miraculously, she had moved herself off the stool by the table to another one by the sink. She was talking a lot and pointing to a large enamelled bowl that once had been white, but was now chipped and had grey rings beneath the rim. She was also pointing at her feet, which she had taken out of her slippers. Her toes, the colour of plums, looked like miniature balloons, squeezed at the base.

I did not need explaining what she required me to do. I filled the enamel bowl with water, warming it with a small amount from the boiling kettle, then I lifted Frau Holtzmann's heavy feet off the floor and lowered them into her foot bath. I could not help wondering if this was the bowl used by everyone. I longed for a dip in the lake.

With her feet soaking, Frau Holtzmann became quiet and pensive, but then, in the distance voices were heard. The work force was coming down for breakfast. She said something to me and pointed at the towel by the sink. I spread it out to show her the state of it, but she only shook her head and made hurrying, impatient movements.

Holding my breath, I dried her feet and got rid of the water just as Maryla came in from the yard with another girl.

"This is my sister, Bazylka," she said.

Bazylka was older, taller and with her fuller figure looked mature. I found that and her ready smile strangely comforting.

"Glad to see you," she said, taking her place at the table, "we need more people."

"Don't use the towel," I whispered to Maryla, "it's filthy."

"We've already washed at the tap," Maryla said, "come, I'll give you a hand with the breakfast."

Frau Holtzmann shouted to us, *"Ihr musst mir helfen!"*

We helped her heave herself off the stool and sit down at the small table set for three.

The room filled with people. Herr Holtzmann headed straight for the parlour. Two older men sat down by Frau Holtzmann.

"That's Johann and Max," Maryla said, stirring the buckwheat, while I brewed the coffee, "they are the old regular workers."

My three friends came in, Michal, Franek and Staszek. They waved and smiled in my direction. I was not used yet to their hairless, slightly comical appearance. The sudden shock made me smile back.

"Two more to come," Maryla said. "Here's Ludwik."

Ludwik had curly black hair and dark skin and he reminded me of a gypsy boy who used to come to our village. I warmed up immediately to his friendly smile.

The last person to come in was Stefan. For a split second it felt as if everything had stood still. My heart beat faster, something flipped over at the pit of my stomach. He was the most beautiful boy I had ever seen.

CHAPTER 4

He was the perfect Aryan type. A tall, athletic frame, long, graceful limbs, blond abundant hair and truly blue eyes. Hitler's blueprint for the ideal human being. He reminded me of the Angel Gabriel on a painting in our church at home. When he smiled in my direction something strange happened to me. It lasted barely a moment, but it left me shaken and weak and confused all at the same time. Maryla nudged me to pick up the bowl and place it in the middle of our table. There was also a smaller bowl and a jug of milk for Frau Holtzmann's table.

I sat down next to Stefan, as luck would have it, on the only unoccupied seat. His warm, bare arm brushed against mine with every spoon-dig into our communal bowl, making my skin tingle, yet I was unable to move away my arm, so tightly packed we were around the table.

Amidst the general, hushed banter, Stefan asked, "How's it going on your first day?"

It took me a moment to realise he was addressing me.

"A bit of a shock," I answered truthfully, feeling a blush spread across my face.

"We all felt that at first." He gave me a sideways glance. His long eyelashes, I noticed, should have adorned a girl.

"Tell me it gets better," I said, willing him to continue talking to me.

"No, I'm afraid it doesn't. Nor do you get used to it. You just learn very fast to grow a tough skin." He gave me suddenly his beautiful smile. "Don't worry, Anna, you're not on your own. We've all got each other. Tell me…what's happened to your face?"

I clamped my lips together, desperate to cover my ugly scab, but he shook his head saying, "No, I mean your left cheek. It looks as if you've ran into a wall."

"Oh that!" I said looking over my shoulder, but Frau Holtzmann was busy talking to Johann and Max, "I got caught in a cross-fire. It seems that the two mistresses Holtzmann are not the best of friends."

"You'd think they'd keep up appearances at least in front of the house guests," Stefan joked, but before he could say anything else, the parlour door opened and Elise Holtzmann walked in. I saw Herr Holtzmann sitting at the elegantly set table with his two young children. A heart-warming, domestic scene. A picture of fatherly love.

It was quiet in the kitchen, even at Frau Holtzmann's table, while Elise fried bacon and eggs for her family. The aroma was the most seductive smell I had experienced for a long time. It was only after she was gone that all the banter was resumed.

"Maryla," Staszek said, making a face at his plain bread and jam, "when do we get eggs and bacon?"

"We'll get cheese and ham at lunchtime," she feigned excitement, as if describing a feast.

"I only want eggs and bacon!" His tone was that of a reasonable person with very few needs.

"Then I suggest you join them in the parlour. Go on, brighten up their day!" She gave him a most charming smile.

"Maryla," he reproached her, "you're being cruel!"

"Realistic," she corrected him, biting into her slice of plain bread.

I felt a hand touch mine. It was Michal, stretching his arm across the table.

"Are you all right, Anna? It was strange this morning, without you there..." His brow was furrowed. Did I detect concern in those brown eyes of his? The boy had feelings, after all. I gave his hand a friendly squeeze.

"I'll survive," I assured him, "we Krakowians are made of tough stuff, aren't we Michal?"

He seemed to like that. His frown dissolved in cheerful agreement.

Our frugally simple breakfast was over quickly. I wanted to hang onto the warmth of our companionship that made me feel closer to home, a little while longer, but the boys had to go. They began getting up when suddenly two men walked in and stopped in the middle of the room.

"*Halt!* Stay where you are!" one shouted. He was an armed policeman, a big man with ruddy complexion. His companion was a slight, slender man, meticulously groomed, but there was something chilling about his perfection. I disliked him on sight, his clean regular features, his sleek hair, his attire that was all black.

"Gestapo," Maryla whispered in my ear.

The policeman looked around and shouted an order, which I did not understand. This signalled to Stefan to walk to the parlour door. He knocked discreetly. We waited in heavy silence for Herr Holtzmann to appear. There was no sound, nor the slightest movement even on old

Frau Holtzmann's table. Johann and Max were staring at the wall.

When he emerged, Herr Holtzmann held his scarred face high, his body straight and tall, looking down on his visitors with a hint of arrogance, as if he were the master in charge.

"*Stefan, bleib hier bei mir!*" he said, keeping his gaze fixed on the two officials, and it soon became clear that he needed Stefan to interpret for us.

We, the newcomers, Michal, Franek, Staszek and myself were ordered to stand up. The two men stared hard at us as if memorising our faces, then the policeman began to talk, in an aggressive, intimidating tone, with Stefan translating in a calm, quiet manner.

"You have been brought here to work. Any deviation from carrying out your duties or breaking regulations will be severely punished. Individually and as a group. Think of your friends before you transgress. Herr Holtzmann is your absolute boss. All your activities inside and outside the farm will be conducted with his knowledge and his permission. You will guard his possessions and all his livestock on this farm with total dedication. Any theft, however trivial, or attempted abscondment, will be punished with arrest and imprisonment. You are forbidden, except in work situation, to have any contact, whatsoever, with our own people here. As a constant reminder of your subordinate position and for immediate identification you will wear your badge on every item of your clothing at all times."

He could say what he liked, I thought, simmering with defiance, but to me, the bright yellow "P"s displayed starkly on my companions' shoulders would always be the mark of our solidarity.

The two officials spoke briefly to Her Holtzmann, then the Gestapo man clicked his fingers at Stefan. His face remained expressionless as he enunciated each word precisely.

"We make frequent visits. We expect nothing less but to find things in order. At all times. Is that understood?"

We said *Tak* in Polish, yes it was understood, but through Stefan the man insisted that we said "*Jawohl mein Herr, Ich ferstein.*"

I disassociated all this from Stefan, the useful but hapless medium for conveying the enemy's message, and watched his face with fascination, storing his beauty in my mind for times when he was not around.

The Gestapo man studied each one of us with unnerving slowness, before his slit-eyed gaze fell on Staszek. He beckoned to him to come forward, and when Staszek did so he raised his hand and with his long, bony fingers he grabbed hold of Staszek's ear and gave it a sharp twist.

Staszek yelped and we all winced. Staszek's face became bright red. His hand shot up protectively over his ear.

"Bastard!" he muttered under his breath. The big policeman slapped his face while the Gestapo man looked at him in disdain. He ordered Stefan to translate.

"There's an old saying, The nail that sticks out must be hammered down. Remember that!"

He walked out of the room, his black coat swinging behind him like a cape and his henchman close on his heels. We remained still, paralysed with fear, and it was only when Holtzmann made the first move that it seemed as if the blackness began to lift and the sun began to shine again. He fetched a card box from the cupboard and gave out each one of us a tied bundle of white felt badges, with purple edging and a bright yellow "P" embroidered boldly on them.

"Sew these on tonight," he instructed through Stefan.

My mind was feverish with questions and my chest was bursting with outrage as I dashed about the kitchen, completing my chores under Frau Holtzmann's watchful eyes. She was like a fixture stuck to her stool. Finally, she let me go, after what seemed like hours, making signs at the clock to indicate that I should be back by twelve.

Like a bird, freed from its cage, I flew across the cobbled yard, past the barns, past the stables, past the cowsheds, towards the source of the chicken sounds. I found Maryla cleaning out the coops and raking the ground inside the wire-fenced enclosures. I regained my breath and blurted, "Maryla we must talk. There's so much I want to know. I need to know. I've got thousands of questions."

She carried on raking as she spoke to me in a lowered tone.

"Later Anna. In the barn. It's better in there. Out of sight."

She had let out the chickens. About a hundred of them, to feed freely in the orchard.

"Won't they fly away?" I asked.

"No. They always come back. They know what's good for them."

Maryla had prepared large containers of boiled vegetable peelings, mashed and mixed with grains and shredded greens. She scraped the chicken mess off the ground and together with the sawdust, she shovelled it into the wheelbarrow.

"Where shall I take it?" I was eager to help.

"There's a cesspit at the back of the farm. That's where we throw all the animal muck."

And so we worked together till the job was done, Maryla collecting the dirt, and I disposing of it. The stench in the heat was overpowering. It stuck in my nostrils, I could taste it, I could smell it on my skin, it emanated from my clothes. I soon discovered what heavy work the simple task of pushing a loaded wheelbarrow could be. My palms were sore and red. My arms and my shoulders felt as if they were pulled apart. Sweat trickled down my face flooding my eyes, salty, stinging. Instinctive reaction made me wipe it off and smudge my face with the dirt stuck to my hands. I was a walking, stinking mess.

"Can't we stop for a second?" I asked, when I could not bear it any longer.

"You can, but you never know when Holtzmann is watching. He can pop up, just like that, when you least expect it." Maryla carried on raking.

"Isn't he in the fields with the boys?"

"He's all over the place. Making sure we all pull our weight."

Maryla did not stop, so I did my best to keep up with her pace.

Later, we washed our hands at the tap in the yard, cooled our faces and drank the cold water with the urgency of addiction, before tackling our next job inside the barn. It was easy work, searching for eggs laid among the bales of hay.

"I'll show you the boys' room," Maryla said, taking me up the open wooden stairs to a platform beneath the rafters. All they had were bare mattresses on the wooden floor. The heat was stifling now, but at the same time I could imagine the deadly cold of the winter months.

We filled our baskets and when we could not find any more eggs Maryla led me to the furthest corner in the barn, where we hid behind some bales.

"We can talk now," she whispered. "We can pretend to be counting eggs."

The tea-like smell of the hay and the semi-darkness in our sheltered spot gave a semblance of safety for a short while.

"It's about this morning," I whispered, "I can't get it out of my mind. What they said. And what they did to Staszek."

"Spitz and Blitz." Maryla said. "That's what we call them. After their aircraft. They always swoop down on us like that. Out of the blue. To give us a fright. We are nothing more to them than slaves, Anna. Just slaves."

I was shocked that she was so matter-of-fact.

"Is there nothing we can do?"

"What would you suggest? Escape? We've thought of it a thousand times. But where would you go? It's all enemy land. You saw for yourself what happens to rebels. Could you take that risk?"

"But…" I was incredulous, "is this it now? For the rest of our lives?"

She shook her head. Vigorously.

"You must never say that, Anna. Never! Our time will come. You'll see."

"What if they win the war?"

"Then," her smile was defiant, "we'll be so well trained we'll be able to tackle anything."

That was not what I wanted to hear.

"This place gives me the creeps." I told her about Elise Holtzmann and her strange behaviour before breakfast.

"The two women can't stand each other," Maryla explained, "Elise is only here by default. She is a town person, really, not a farmer's wife. Holtzmann's been put in charge of the farm until the owners return from the war."

"How come?" It was a strange arrangement.

"Holtzmann's German. He's done his bit in the last war. You've seen his face."

"He must have only been a schoolboy then!"

"Not that much younger than our boys!"

"Does she do anything at all, Elise? I mean in helping out with the farm work?"

"Only indoor things. She has three regular women from Eberstein. They bake bread together. They make dairy products. They process various meats. They make jams and bottle fruit in season. She's also good with the needle. She can spin wool. From our sheep."

"Really? That's just the sort of thing I'd love to do." My mood suddenly lifted.

"Don't get excited," Maryla gave a short laugh, "she would never share anything with worms like us. Unless," she made a funny face, "you wriggled somehow into her affection."

"God save me! Maryla! I'd rather wash old Frau Holtzmann's feet ten times a day!"

Maryla giggled. And then I giggled too. And though nothing had changed, I felt as if Hope had passed by.

It was a long day. When I hit the pillow that night, I no longer felt like myself, a seventeen-year-old, vigorous, bubbly, bursting with the impatience and with the optimism of youth. I felt like a lump of battered flesh wrapped around aching bones. The morning seemed like centuries ago.

After our joined efforts in the chicken pens, Maryla and I helped Bazylka to milk the cows. Twice. Before lunch and again before the evening meal. There were thirty cows: some docile, yielding their milk willingly, some aggressive, kicking out and hardening their udders against my touch. My hands, unused to such marathon of repetitive actions, began to seize up with cramps. It was painful clenching them, it was painful trying to loosen them with shakes. I was weary with the irritating scab on my lower lip that pulled the skin and made it bleed every time I forgot myself and smiled.

We stored the milk in metal churns, two of which Maryla and I carried to the crossroads, a kilometre away, from where the army truck collected them regularly, morning, noon and night. My shoulders felt dislocated, my arms a metre long, my hands almost touching the ground as we hurried back to our unfinished jobs. We cleaned and lined with hay the pigsties, the cowsheds and the stables. The cows were left in the fields for the night, but the pigs had to be hosed down and locked securely inside their pens.

In between these duties I assisted Frau Holtzmann in preparing the meals; she gave the orders and I did the work. Lunch was easy; sliced brown bread, ham and cheese and water. For the evening meal we had a vegetable broth. I peeled and diced all vegetables: potatoes, carrots, parsnips, turnips and onions, last autumn's vegetables, crinkly and shrivelled with age. The fine broth they produced was a wonder achieved by slow and patient cooking that matured the flavours as they blended together.

And then, at long last, at seven in the evening we were absolved from our duties for the day. I felt as if I could not make another move, another step, yet I longed to take a dip in the lake, to wash away all grime and sweat and pain.

We picked up our towels and our clean underwear, Bazylka, Maryla and I, and we walked to the woods on the slope of the nearby hill.

"Do the boys come to the lake too?" I asked, struggling to keep up with Bazylka's long, purposeful strides.

"They do, but they wait, till we've finished first. Don't worry, they won't peep," she assured me.

"They only tried it once," Maryla laughed. "Bazylka hid their clothes to teach them a lesson. They had to wait till dark before they crept back inside."

"Ludwik? And Stefan?" This made me chuckle. I could just picture them, two white ghosts darting between the trees, desperate to hide.

"They look such sensible lads," I said.

"They are now," Bazylka agreed. "This place makes you grow up fast."

God, didn't I know that! After just one day I felt worn and old.

We walked along the mountain stream to a plateau half way up the hill. There on the plain, surrounded by moss-covered rocks and grassy banks was a pool, its waters cleansed constantly by the waterfall. Maryla's lake.

"This is heaven!" I exclaimed.

"It is. One of the few places that keeps us sane," Bazylka said.

We undressed to our knickers, modesty preventing us to bare all. Bazylka and Maryla did not look like sisters. Maryla, closer to me in age, was also similar to me in size, with thin limbs and a flat chest. Bazylka had the body of a mature woman. I envied her, her breasts and her hips, which somehow had retained their roundness despite the months of hard work. No wonder the boys had been tempted to spy on her.

We lowered ourselves into the pool. The icy water took my breath away. I jumped up and down several times, before being able to immerse myself long enough for a thorough wash. I swished my hair through the water and rubbed my scalp till it squeaked.

Afterwards, when I dried myself, dressed and plaited my damp hair, it was bliss to lie back on the warm, soft ground and just stare at the sky, high above the treetops, while I waited for Bazylka and Maryla to get ready. Such small things. So much joy.

"Do we ever get any time off?" I asked.

"Sunday afternoons. About three hours," Maryla said, buttoning up her blouse, "but only after we've seen to all the animals first. The boys help us out usually. This gives us more time to do things together."

"What sort of things?"

"Once a month we are permitted to go to Treibach. To buy the few things we need."

"What about church on Sundays?"

"That's not allowed."

"Not allowed?" I was astounded. "What, even though they are Catholics, and we are Catholics, and we are not allowed?"

"No," Bazylka made an expressive face as she folded her towel, "we might contaminate the congregation."

"Who needs them, anyway?" Maryla said, "I can pray in my head any time any place. There are lovely walks in the woods. We've already found places where there will be blackberries and bilberries and edible chestnuts in season. But the best thing is getting together with the other lot. From the other farm. Just over the other side of the hill."

"Really?" I raised myself on my elbow. "How come Herr Holtzmann allows that?"

"It's a mystery. Amazing, isn't it?" Bazylka agreed, gathering her things together.

"We make the most of it, while it lasts," Maryla said. "There's this boy there, Bruno. He plays a mouth organ. Anything you like."

"Like tunes to sing to?" I asked.

"And dancing tunes. Waltzes and polkas. It's good fun. I promise." I sat up and felt a smile creep into my face. Little miracles happened all the time.

On our way back we met the boys going up to the pool. Their talk was as animated as their energetic strides, which made me wonder if they had found a cure for tiredness after a gruelling fourteen-hour day. We exchanged pleasantries in passing. I scanned Stefan's face for a flicker of interest, and when he caught my eye and smiled, something skipped inside me.

"First day nearly over," he said pleasantly, as if implying that things could only get better now.

"And tomorrow's exactly the same," Ludwik laughed. His teeth were impossibly white in his swarthy face.

"You're a barrel of laughs," Bazylka scolded him, "if you've got nothing cheerful to say, don't say anything at all. And you three," she jabbed the air with her finger in front of Michal, Franek and Staszek, "bring your badges later. We'll sew them on for you."

"Yes, boss," Franek saluted her, making us all laugh.

We sat at the kitchen table lit up by a paraffin lamp and sewed on my badges first. Bright yellow embroidered "P"s. My aching fingers were clumsy with the needle and what normally would have been a leisure activity was now a difficult task. It was quiet but for muffled distant sounds in the part of the house where Herr Holtzmann and his family had shut themselves off from the rest of us. The old Frau Holtzmann had retreated for the night to her room on the ground floor.

Now was a moment, I thought, that made our escape appear tantalisingly possible, but even as the thought crossed my mind, I knew this was nothing more than a fantasy. Escaping together would draw too much attention. Where would we hide as a group? Escaping singly was not an option either. The consequences for those left behind were too frightening to contemplate. I kept my thoughts to myself as I watched my two companions sew, their rough, cut fingers moving fast, putting aside my ready garments: two dresses, two blouses, one cardigan and a light raincoat, all clear-marked with a bright yellow "P".

The boys joined us later – Michal, Franek and Staszek – bringing with them, into the paraffin-tainted atmosphere, a breath of freshness, a fragrance of pines, of the mountain stream. Their shaved and scrubbed faces shone like polished wood.

"Aren't the other two coming?" I asked, listening for footsteps out in the yard.

"Ludwik is nursing a painful shoulder," Michal said. "He needs to rest it. When he can."

"It's an excuse," Maryla said, "he likes to be alone. He writes notes to his girl every night and sends them in a bundle at the end of the month when he can afford to buy a stamp."

The swarthy gypsy? With black flashing eyes? I was surprised. My perception of him changed in an instant. No one had ever sent me love notes.

"And does she write back, his girl?" I asked.

"We keep telling him she does," Maryla said. "We also tell him it's not her fault that her letters never get through."

I pictured him writing by torchlight, underneath the rafters, and I made a wish for him. That his wishes would come true.

"And what about Stefan? What's he doing?" I asked, my hearing sharpened for outdoor sounds.

"Who knows?" Staszek winked and nudged Franek. "He was just going out for a walk in the woods, as we came here."

A walk? In the woods? In the dark? What did it mean? Maryla raised her eyes from the sewing and I saw a look pass between her and Staszek.

"Did he tell you?" Her tone was cautious.

Staszek smiled and shrugged.

"He didn't have to. Some things you just know. There's a girl on the other farm, isn't there?"

Maryla put her finger to her lips.

"Walls have ears," she whispered.

"What girl?" I asked. I felt my stomach contract.

Bazylka looked up.

"Best not to know, believe me Anna. The less you know the better for you."

My mind was spinning.

"You talk in riddles. Please tell me Bazylka."

She considered me for a moment, then leaned over and whispered, "It's what Staszek has guessed. We all know that Stefan is seeing someone, but we don't talk about it."

"Is there a regulation against loving? Is that forbidden too?" I could not stop myself.

"Anna," Bazylka placed a hand on my shoulder, "when you've been here for a while you'll notice all sorts of things. But for your own safety you keep things to yourself. All right?" She gave my shoulder a sisterly squeeze.

So that was that! I'd lost him already. Why was I feeling this way? Let down, rejected, when I had never owned him in the first place? Stupid, stupid, stupid me! My eyes stung with disappointment and shame. I forced myself to listen to my friends' accounts of their first day on the farm. They had been cutting and storing grass for silage. There were two more fields to be done before the rain came. They would have to hurry.

When the last badge was sewn on we were all ready to go to bed. Staszek and Franek went on ahead, but Michal lingered in the doorway. It was dark now except for the moonlight bouncing off the cobbles in the yard, and I could not see his face in the dark, only a flat silhouette of his head and shoulders.

"Tell me Anna, that you're all right," he whispered, "or I'll worry."

This surprised me.

"Why would you worry about me?"

"Because it's damn hard work, isn't it? For a slip of a girl like you."

"You don't have to worry about me. I'm growing muscles. In record time."

He turned his face slightly and I saw all the contours outlined in pale silver. He looked up at the moon.

"It's the same moon that's shining on our village right now. Doesn't it make you feel closer to home?"

He could have read my thoughts and my feelings. This evening was full of surprises. First Ludwik. Then Stefan. Now Michal.

"That's exactly how I feel," I said. "When the wind blows on my face I think of the washing flying on our line at home. The pines in the wood today reminded me of the trees at the back of our house. Even the chickens here make me homesick. They make me think of my four red hens. And you, Michal, you always make me think of Vladek."

His face was in shadow again. I could not read his expression, but I thought I detected a hint of gladness when he said, "Really? You say such funny things."

He gave me a light pat on the head and was gone.

I bolted the door and in the dark felt my way across the kitchen to our narrow recess behind the stove, undressed and slipped into bed beside Maryla.

"I could sleep now for a hundred years," I whispered.

"Don't do that. We need you in the morning. Is Michal sweet on you?"

It took me a second to absorb her words.

"Goodness, no, Maryla! He'd want someone his own age. And besides, I've certainly never fancied him."

"I only asked," she said with a smirk in her voice.

I was too tired to protest. I felt my body grow heavy with sleep as my thoughts dissolved into nothingness.

CHAPTER 5

Herr Holtzmann did not work on Sundays. Johann and Max had a day off and our boys were free from the work on the fields. They helped us to feed the animals, milk the cows and clean all the sheds, stables and barns. By two in the afternoon we were ready to visit our compatriots on the other farm.

Sitting on the bed next to Maryla, I brushed my wiry hair as flat as I could manage, plaited it at the back, twisted it upwards and tied it all together with a red ribbon. The ribbon was Bazylka's and Maryla's envy. They tied their hair with knitting wool that could be bought for one *pfennig* a bundle, because it had been eaten by moths and could not be knitted into a garment. Unless you spent hours tying the bitten ends together.

Bazylka and Maryla had only one blouse each, the blouses they had been wearing at the time of their arrest. The constant use and the frequent washing in the stream had weakened and greyed the fabric. The cuffs were frayed and there were holes on the elbows.

"If only we could get some material," I said, "I could cut out and make you new blouses. I promise! As fashionable as anything from Paris."

"Anna, we've thought of that a hundred times!" Maryla said, wiping her cracked shoes with a damp rag. "But there's nothing, not even a length the size of a handkerchief that we can afford after we've bought the most necessary things."

I would not give up.

"Couldn't we ask Frau Holtzmann for some old sheets or curtains?"

Bazylka smoothed down her faded skirt that had been navy once.

"Frau Holtzmann has no say in this house," she said. "No doubt you've noticed. And would you really want to ask Elise?"

There must be a way, I thought. With regret, I decided against putting on my other dress, the one with a print of tiny red flowers that matched my ribbon perfectly. I dressed in a skirt and a blouse instead. Grey and white. I felt excitement and anticipation of something wonderful about to happen.

The boys were waiting for us in the yard, scrubbed and clean-shaven. Michal, Franek and Staszek had managed to level off the uneven tufts on their heads with some old scissors that I had found in the kitchen. Beside them, Ludwik's black curls looked mockingly abundant. There was no sign of Stefan.

"Is he not ready yet?" I asked, careful not to sound too interested.

"He's already gone," Staszek said, smiling to Maryla.

Of course. To his girl. He could not wait. I felt something twist inside me. I had hoped – I had imagined – walking with him, talking, enjoying his attention just for a while. I did not ask for much.

A voice from the house made us look back.

"Anna! Anna!" It was Frau Holtzmann filling the doorframe.

"I wonder what she wants now," I said, already dreading her interference.

Since my arrival, it seemed that I had become indispensable to her every need. I was ordered to help her wash, dress, undress, brush her hair, lift things for her, fetch things; her demands were endless. Her bossiness peaked usually when Elise was around. None of my efforts seemed to satisfy her.

Maryla came with me to interpret Frau Holtzmann's instructions.

"She wants you to stop behind till Herr Holtzmann and his wife get back from their shopping. She doesn't like being left on her own with the children."

My heart sank low. I could not believe it.

"I've no choice, have I?" I looked at Maryla helplessly.

"I'll stop with you," Maryla offered.

She was a saint, but I shook my head.

"No Maryla, you go. I'll catch up with you later."

She hesitated only a moment.

"Just follow the stream, Anna. The path veers off to the right at the top of the hill. You'll hear us long before you come down on the other side."

I nodded and saw Michal approach.

"Has anything happened?" he asked.

I told him. All this under Frau Holtzmann's watchful eyes. Her dour expression did not change. Nor did her stance.

"I'll stop with you," he said. His brown eyes were direct and earnest. He made me smile.

"Come off it, Michal. And what would you know about minding babies? Go. I'll join you later."

He appeared reluctant to leave, but the others were calling to him and to Maryla.

"Go!" I repeated.

I followed Frau Holtzmann, pyramid-like and wobbly, across the parlour to the other open door that looked out onto a cultivated garden with flower borders, decorative shrubs and a lawn. She lowered herself into an armchair by the door, next to a perambulator in which the little boy, Bernard, was sleeping. His sister Gaby was building castles in the sandpit, her curls blending with the colour of the sand. I crouched beside her and handed her containers of varied shapes and sizes, showing her how to expand her structure with towers and solid rectangular blocks. She enjoyed this and chatted incessantly exposing her little white teeth in her wet, dribbly smiles, totally unpuzzled by my lacking knowledge of the German language. I helped her make a garden around her castle with buttercups and daisies, distracting her away from the geraniums in the borders.

Frau Holtzmann snoozed in her armchair, and I listened all the while for the sound of Herr Holtzmann's van, counting all the wasted minutes. I pictured my friends on the other farm, their defences lowered, their laughter unforced, their tension relaxed as they enjoyed their much-awaited Sunday recreation.

I could not help but think of Stefan. And of his girl. How lucky she was to have met him first. But I was lucky too, I reminded myself. He lived on our farm not hers, and I could see him daily. He called me "Aneczka", diminutive of Anna. Only my mother called me that. He had told me things, about himself and his family. He had just begun his architecture studies when the war broke out. His two younger sisters were dispatched with haste to the relatives in the country. His parents were arrested for 'subversive activities' and taken away. Nobody knew where.

"But I'll find them, Aneczka. One day all this will be over!" He spoke with conviction, such that made you believe every word he said.

He sat next to me at mealtimes, usually, and entertained our group with guarded but pointed anecdotes that made us look over our shoulders nervously as we suppressed our amusement. He thought up grand names for our limited variety of broth.

'Steamed maggots a la Madame Holtzmann' was Frau Holtzmann's speciality on the days I was needed elsewhere. She was not particular about food hygiene and the old ham that she chopped and mixed with the cabbage stew had regular traces of mould and of worse things.

One evening we found plump white maggots floating on top of our communal bowl of soup. It just so happened that Herr Holtzmann was still in the kitchen with us, having stopped to talk to Johann and Max at their separate table, with their separate meal that had been cooked for them by Elise.

"Herr Holtzmann!" Stefan called out, "can you explain what this is?"

I thought Stefan was brave. I thought he was reckless. I was expecting an outburst of rage. But Herr Holtzmann came over and studied our bowl with solemn concentration. I never saw him smile. He picked up a spoon, skimmed the maggots and put them in his mouth. I averted my eyes to stop myself being sick. I heard him say, "Be thankful for your food. I've eaten rats in the trenches to stay alive."

I heard a car approaching, a distant drone of the engine, and sure enough, to my great relief, Herr Holtzmann's black van appeared from around the bend. Gaby stopped playing and ran up to the gate. She climbed up the first rung, her chubby little fingers holding tight, her neck stretched to see over the top. I came up behind her and picked her up so she could see her parents arrive and wave as they alighted with their bags of groceries.

Elise in her flowing muslin dress moved in long hasty strides. She stopped only long enough to give Gaby a peck on the head. She did not look at me. She never did. She made me feel invisible. Non-existent. She ignored her mother-in-law, who was now awake, and rushed off inside the house.

Gaby was a bubbly chattering yo-yo; I could hardly hold her. Her outstretched arms, her bright eyes, her gurgling smiles were all directed at her father. He came up to us and, taking her, acknowledged me with a nod and a wan smile that barely touched his eyes.

"*Gehen Anna.*" He waved me off, then as I turned to go, every nerve in my body taut with the impatience to leave, he called me back.

Please God, don't let him stop me.

I turned round. He was holding out half a slice of honey cake. I was astonished.

"*Danke, Herr Holtzmann, danke shone*," I blurted out, accepting it from him. I forced myself to walk away as calmly as my inner tension allowed. The moment I was out of his sight, I took a bite of the cake, slipped the rest into my side pocket then I shot forward like a bullet from a gun.

I ran without stopping across the yard, across the field, across the wild meadow and continued my pace even when I reached the wood, even when I knew I was hidden from view by the trees and the thick growth of shrubs and ferns. The path along the stream was now familiar ground. I felt safe here. I stopped to catch my breath when I reached the pool. I sat down on the soft mossy bank and rested my arms and my throbbing head on my raised knees, panting and inhaling deeply the heady sylvan scent around me.

When the buzzing in my ears stopped and my heart settled, I thought I could hear voices, indistinct, remote, above the murmur of the stream. I got up, looked around and listened. There was no doubt someone was there, just behind the thick growth, about twenty metres from the main path. My first thought was that my friends must have changed their plans.

Automatically I started walking in that direction, pushing aside lush fronds of bracken, quickening my pace, ready to shout out, to tell them I had made it after all.

Then I stopped. I could hear a girl's voice repeating the same name over and over again.

"Stefan... Stefan... Oh Stefan... Oh..." It was like sighing, but not the sad kind of sighing. It was like sighing with wonder and contentment.

Suddenly I felt I should not be there, but I could not move, I could not breathe. My heart was thumping again. Slowly, very slowly I lowered myself and crouched, anxious to move away unseen. I could not bear the thought of being discovered. Eavesdropping. On Stefan and his girl.

I lay flat on my stomach, my face almost touching the ground. After a second, after eternity, I lifted my eyes. There, right before me, in the surrounding growth was a natural gap, a space like a tiny porthole making it impossible for me not to see. What I saw hit me with shock and incredulity. I was witness to an act that I had only ever pictured in my imagination, but had never been able to work it out. It appeared such a strange thing to do. It was baffling why anyone would want to do it. The very thought of it made me blush with shame. And here was Stefan and his girl enjoying the unspeakable.

I could not see her face. It was turned away and obscured by Stefan's hair. She was calling out his name. Her voice was heavy with emotion. Wistful and happy at the same time, as if she was drowning in pleasure and pain. The sound of it did strange things to my skin. I felt a crawly kind of sensation all down my spine. I was riveted. I could not take my eyes off them.

She moved her hands up and down his naked back, caressing him, pressing him to her, cradling his weight between her bare thighs, moving in rhythm with his thrusts.

I shut my eyes tight to stop myself watching. I had to get away. Fast. I was committing a sin. God, how would I ever be able to confess this terrible thing. Watching a lewd act. Between a couple who were not even married.

I began to crawl backwards at first, stopping with every move, checking that I had not been heard, my heart and my pulse ready to explode. When my feet touched the pebbles on the path, it was like stepping onto a safe shore of an island after a hundred-mile swim.

There was no stopping me now. I ran as if all the dogs in the neighbourhood were chasing me. On the top of the hill I fell to the ground to catch my breath. Here the trees were sparse, letting in the fresh, breezy air, cooling, soothing my hot face. Distant laughter echoed upwards from the valley. I got up and saw Michal coming up towards me. Relief swept over me. And gladness. It was like coming home.

He waited till I walked down to his level, in dappled sunlight that made patterns on his shirt, on his face, making parts of him glow, making me notice how his growing hair softened the contours of his head, how his cheeks lifted when he smiled.

"And what's happened to you?" he asked, eyeing me up and down, "you look as if you've been dragged through a haystack!"

It was only now, as I wiped sweat off my hot face, that I noticed earth and grass marks on my white blouse and down the front of my skirt.

"Goodness! I don't believe it! All I did was rest on the ground for a minute. After running all the way!" I lied, rubbing the marks with my sleeve. "What about you? Where are you going?"

He shrugged and stuffed his hands in his pockets.

"I thought I'd come up and meet you on the way."

This surprised me.

"But what if you didn't? What if I was still stuck at the farm?"

"Then I'd be stuck with you, wouldn't I?" he laughed, his brown eyes twinkling with amber flecks. "Don't worry, there'll be other Sundays."

We started walking down together. I remembered the honey cake.

"Stop!" I said. "And hold out your hands."

He looked mystified. I moved my skirt around to get to the side pocket with ease, and then very carefully, as if I were handling filings of gold, I emptied the crumbs into his cupped hands.

"You'll never guess! A reward from the master himself. Sorry it's in bits. It'll taste just the same."

He smiled in anticipation and held out his hands for me to taste first. I was suddenly aware of the pink mark just below my lip, where the scab had come off. I covered it up with my fingers.

"Don't be silly," he said, as if reading my reservation, "it's not contagious and you look perfectly fine. Now tuck in!"

We took turns dipping our tongues into the soft, aromatic heap of crumbs that tasted of sweet spices and cinnamon. Michal made exaggerated noises of contentment that made me laugh.

"Mmmmm…Mmmm…" I joined him.

"Anyone listening to us," he grinned, "would think we were making love."

I froze. How could he possibly already know where I had just been? "What are you saying?" I cried.

He gave me a puzzled look. "Anna, I'm only joking! Hey, relax!"

He licked off the last few crumbs, wiped his hands against his sides, then grabbing my hand, he shook it limp and loose before doing a few windmill circles with my arm.

My anxiety ebbed. I giggled.

"That's better," he said, "now let's go and have some fun."

We found our friends and the group from the other farm gathered inside a semi-circle, marked out with logs around a clear-swept patch of ground at the edge of the forest, from where the farm buildings could be seen in the middle distance.

Only two were sitting down. Ludwik and the boy playing the mouth organ. I guessed that was Bruno. All the others were dancing in pairs to a lively polka tune, their pace like a mad gallop. My spirits lifted. The atmosphere was so carefree. Who would have thought there was a war going on?

"Come on, Anna," Michal called, encircling my waist with his arm, "let's not waste any more time," and before I could protest, he grasped my left hand, lifted it high and we were off, hurling ourselves into the fast rhythm, our skipping feet barely touching the ground.

I laughed. I was happy. My joy surprised me. Something strange stirred inside me every time Michal's strong arm held me close.

"We didn't have to wait till the Christmas dance, after all," he teased, his face the only focused object in a whirring background. He was being cheeky suggesting that my expectations were the same as his. But I did not mind. All I was aware of and totally given into was the intense pleasure that took me outside the nightmare of the last few days.

We changed partners with every dance, a polka or a waltz, to give everyone a turn. Discounting Stefan, who was absent, and Bruno, the musician, there were six boys to five girls. I did not like it when the girls had to choose their partners. My shyness held me back then worsened my predicament when I had to make a choice between the last two remaining boys. I wanted to be fair, so I danced half the time with each.

I noticed Staszek and Maryla were oblivious to turns and somehow managed to end up together in every single dance. A girl called Agata from the other group, with her hair neatly combed in the fashionable roll, spent much of the time around Michal. He appeared to enjoy her attention, and they laughed a lot each time their bodies bumped as they whirled around. Bazylka danced with Franek. One could tell by their controlled and graceful movements that they were both accomplished dancers. I remembered now Franek talking of his visits to his older brother in the city, where dance halls were the big attraction.

Bruno stopped playing and pointed to his red mouth that looked as if it had been rubbed with sandpaper.

"Five minutes' break," he pleaded.

We all sat down on the logs except for Michal and Staszek who appeared to be trying to resolve an argument.

"But I'll feel a right prat," Staszek was protesting, "standing in front of everyone, and singing on my own."

"No, you won't!" Michal was adamant, and then turning to us he said, "We all want to hear Staszek sing, don't we?"

We all shouted "Yes" and clapped in advance. Spreading his hands in a show of good-natured resignation, Staszek said, "Don't blame me. Blame him!"

He began with *Oczy Czarne*. "Black Eyes". I loved that song. I fancied it had been written specially for me. Staszek's voice was resonant, gently vibrating, as if charged with emotion. It made my hairs stand on end. I had heard singers like him in the big churches in Krakow. And occasionally on the radio when I went round to my friend Slava's. Hers was the only family in the village who owned a radio. But I had never heard Staszek sing before.

He sang a medley of light-hearted songs, one of which was particularly amusing about a boy with two pairs of interchangeable legs, long and short, for all occasions. We laughed and clapped, and Staszek bowed, his cheeks pink with pleasure. Maryla gazed at him entranced, and I had to admit, with a sudden discovery, that he was worth gazing at.

Then Franek surprised me too. The tall, lanky, undernourished-looking Franek, my brother's pal, apprentice mechanic, whose dream was to own a "Sokol", the motorbike with the roar of a lion, the speed of a cheetah and the lightness of a hawk. I knew all this, because he and Vladek talked of nothing else, as if their Sokol was the only dream worth living for.

As soon as Bruno began to play again we stopped talking. The melody of the tango, with its exciting, irresistible rhythm, set us all humming and tapping our feet.

Franek stood up, drew himself to his full height, then performed a few moves that were intended to express the smouldering passion beneath the cool exterior of his precise steps and poses. The boys chuckled and nudged each other, but he gave them a theatrically disdainful look. The girls watched him as if bewitched. He stopped before Bazylka and bowed, but she shook her head vigorously and protested. "I'm no good, Franek, really!"

He got hold of her hand, nevertheless, and pulled her up gently.

"You'll be brilliant with me. Trust me."

Their bodies fused and parted in a series of steps, twists and turns. The boys whistled. The girls shouted them down. I sensed a curious magic around us. In the air. In the rhythm of the music. In the moves of our two dancers. In the smiling faces. In the shining eyes. I felt a strange, warm feeling at the pit of my stomach and when Bruno finished playing it was like the end of a dream.

We all clapped and called for more, but Bazylka returned to her place on the log, blushing and panting, leaving Franek to absorb all the ovation into his expansive bows.

A voice behind me made me jump.

"Bravo! Bravo! Valentino and Rambova! Encore! Encore!"

It was Stefan. He stepped over the log and sat down beside me.

"How's Aneczka?" His gaze was direct and friendly, as usual. I did not think I would be able to look him in the eye, but I did. And the extraordinary thing was that nothing about him appeared to have changed. He looked the same as always. For a second I doubted myself. But only for a second. No, what I had seen earlier had been real enough.

I looked around to see who his girl was, but there was no female addition to our company. That puzzled me.

"You missed all the fun," I said. Pointedly.

"I've had things to do." He looked down and began to tap his foot to the beat of the well-known song. *"I have a date at nine tonight."*

"What sort of things? Or shouldn't I ask?" This was pushing it a bit.

He did not answer straight away. He looked at me briefly, lowered his gaze then spoke quietly.

"It's no secret, Anna, in our group, that I have a contact who provides me with outside news. How else would we know what's going on out there?"

I was taken aback, not by the content of his words (that came later) but by the glibness of his explanation.

"So what's the news?" I tested him.

He seemed to hesitate before replying.

"I was going to wait and tell everyone on the way home. But since you ask, it's not good news. The British have withdrawn from Dunkirk. Paris is preparing for the German invasion. If the British and the French are defeated, what's going to happen to us?"

He was serious. Suddenly I felt silly. Petty. The magic was gone.

"What's going to happen to us?" I repeated his words, sensing tension return to my stomach.

"We need a miracle, Anna."

I followed his gaze and saw Franek walking towards us, but Franek was looking over and beyond my shoulder. I turned round when he went past us. Well away from our group there stood a girl between the trees, too far for me to see her face clearly. I watched Franek talk to her in his sign language, making it plain he was inviting her to join us. She shook her head and slowly walked away towards the farm. Stefan was watching too. He was very quiet.

"Who is she?" I asked.

"Lilli. Lilli Steinfeld. The farmer's daughter."

"Franek's not got much luck with her, has he?" I said willing the lightness to return to our talk.

"He is wasting his time." Stefan sounded tense. "She is not allowed to mix with the likes of us."

CHAPTER 6

I met Lilli Steinfeld a few days later. She came to our farm with a basket, its contents carefully covered with a white cloth. Exchange of goods among the farmers was a common practice, a way of getting around general shortages.

I was washing the farm tools that we had been using with Maryla: shovels, rakes, forks and the wheelbarrow. They were plastered with chicken and pig muck and needed some forceful scrubbing under strong water pressure. The pungent spray settled on my face and arms and saturated my clothes.

I turned off the tap as she walked by, then resumed my work, watching her, envying her deep blue dirndl dress and her pure white blouse with puffed-out sleeves, that was a reflection of her own cleanliness, of the smoothness of her fair beauty, of the wholesomeness of her appearance. I was Cinderella drenched in sweat and muck. She was the beautiful princess. My throat tightened. My mouth tasted bitter. No introduction was necessary. I knew it was her.

I thought of Stefan. With her. Since Sunday afternoon I could think of nothing else. Why had he got himself involved with an Austrian girl? Knowing all the dangers. All the possible consequences? How could he be so reckless? And if, as he had hinted, she was his contact with the outside world, what did that make him out to be? A user, exactly the sort of boy my mother had warned me against, a boy who dumped you as soon as you gave into his pleas and promises. I preferred to believe, much against my own dreams, that his love for Lilli was genuine. How else could I continue to admire him?

Lilli came out of the kitchen door a few minutes later. She walked straight towards me. I turned off the tap and watched; puzzled, expectant. She stopped right in front of me, with her back to the house, and pushed out her foot.

"There's dirt on my shoe. Wipe it off."

I understood every word in German and was so astonished by her demand, that without a second's hesitation, I pulled out a rag from my side pocket and crouched down. She bent down at the same time. I felt something being slipped inside the neckline of my blouse. Our eyes met and she smiled. The briefest smile.

"Welcome Anna," she whispered, "I'm Lilli. I'll help any way I can."

She straightened and I made a show of buffing her shoe for the benefit of Frau Holtzmann, who I knew would be spying on us from the kitchen window. And sure enough, as Lilli walked away, I saw the old woman from the corner of my eye, but all she would have seen was Lilli giving orders to a servant girl.

I gathered the washed tools, placed them in the wheelbarrow and pushed the lot inside the barn. There, behind the screen of bales, I withdrew the secret gift from inside my blouse. Wrapped in a small handkerchief with a pink embroidered rose, was a slice of soap. The uneven, ridged sides indicated that Lilli had cut a piece from a large block. It was not the snot-coloured carbolic soap, but silky cream, smelling of jasmine. I inhaled and inhaled till I felt dizzy with its scent. Something inside me changed. All my bitter thoughts were gone. But as I thought of Lilli now, I began to fear for her safety.

In our group existence, it was difficult to find moments of privacy, but one morning Stefan limped inside the barn, when I was searching for eggs among the bales. His right trouser leg was stained with blood. I put down the basket and ran up to him.

"God Almighty, what's happened to you?"

He sat down on the nearest bale, saying, "It looks worse than it is. I stepped on some barbed wire. It was hidden in the ditch. My leg went right through the coil."

He pulled up the trouser leg to above his knee exposing deep punctures and scratches in the skin, some still bleeding.

"Holtzmann has sent me down for some iodine. The wire was rusty. God knows how long it's been there."

I jumped up, ready to dash off and fetch things from the kitchen, but he grabbed my hand.

"I've got iodine upstairs. In my bag. Can you bring it down? Second mattress on the right."

I ran up the wooden steps, looked for his belongings, rummaged through his bag and found a white-enamelled metal box with a red cross on it. I rushed back and sat down on the floor at his feet. With a wad of crushed gauze I dabbed the orange liquid onto his cuts. I winced more than he did.

"Bazylka should be doing this for you," I said. Bazylka had been a student nurse in her real life.

"You're doing a grand job, Aneczka. I wouldn't want anyone else." He had a way of making me feel special.

After I had checked his leg right down to his toes, he relaxed, sat back and rested on his elbows.

"Don't go yet," he said, "I've got to wait for this to dry a bit."

"We'll be in trouble if we're caught. I mean doing nothing." I looked nervously towards the open entrance.

"And who is likely to catch us?" he smiled, with a hint of mischievousness. "The master's in the fields. Elise is busy baking. And Frau Holtzmann…well…" he rolled his eyes.

"It's not just them… Spitz and Blitz…" anxiety was already gripping my stomach. The pair made frequent, random checks, keeping us in a perpetual state of uncertainty and nervousness.

"Aneczka, relax! We'll hear their car first. We'll have plenty of time to hide." How did he stay so calm?

"All right," I conceded, picking up my basket and placing it beside me in readiness, "I'll stay for a minute, but I'll stand just here."

Time was precious. If I were to say anything to him of my fears regarding him and Lilli, and our group, I had to say it now.

"Stefan…" He looked up, his gaze like a physical, warm touch. "I know about Lilli and you. No one's told me. I guessed."

He kept looking at me as if trying to read my thoughts.

"It's a big risk for everyone…" my voice trailed off.

He remained quiet, and for a moment I thought he would refuse to discuss this with me, but when he spoke his intensity startled me.

"Anna, Lilli and I love each other. The very moment the war is over we shall get married. It is a big risk, I know. I can well imagine what you must think of me, but don't judge me too harshly. We're very much aware of the dangers, to everyone. We're always very careful, believe me."

He waited for my reaction, his expression persuasive, his eyes pleading, and I did want to be happy for him, to be able to say something cheerful, encouraging, but I felt crushed.

He stood up, pulled his trouser leg down and clasped my hand.

"Aneczka, please understand. Besides, there are things in life worth risking everything for."

I missed him the moment he left. Would anyone ever love me as much as he loved Lilli?

It had been raining all morning. Nothing stopped for rain. The boys worked in the forest, felling the trees and cutting the trunks into shorter lengths. Bazylka, Maryla and I continued with our regular chores around the animals, our clothes dripping with water and dirt, our feet soaking inside our muddy, squelching shoes.

I envied Elise and her two women baking indoors in the warmth. I envied Frau Holtzmann perched on the stool by the sink. I would have done any jobs for her, if only for a few minutes I could get out of the rain that beat against my face like a hundred tiny whips.

"The milk is ready!" Bazylka called out to us from the entrance to the cowshed.

Maryla and I lay down the fork and the rake beside the pigs' fence, washed our hands at the tap and ran, jumping over the puddles. It was steamy and warm inside the cowshed. I envied the cows standing dry in their pens, chewing lazily their cud. I did not want to leave.

"You can take these two churns," Bazylka had put them to one side, "and I'll take the rest to the dairy."

We picked up our containers, looked at each other like those condemned to death, and stepped out into the rain. I could hardly see where I was going. Step by tortuous step we made our way down the sodden track, our feet slipping and scraping against uneven ground. I summoned up all my concentration into a prayer, begging my guardian angel to stop the rain. But he was somewhere else that day.

My shoulders began to ache as if pulled out of their joints, my stiff fingers felt welded to the metal handle, and when I could not bear it anymore, I dropped my heavy load to the ground and sat on top of it, on its flat metal lid.

"Maryla!" I cried, no longer caring that she could see my tears, my defeat, "I'm totally done in. I shall die if I have to make another step."

She sat down beside me, on top of her milk churn. She looked as if she had been dragged out of the river. Her breathing was laboured.

"We mustn't give up Anna. Look always for the bright side!"

Her brain was affected, I was certain of that.

"Bright side!" I cried. "We're drowning in this blasted bloody deluge and you talk of bright side! Grrr…" I growled like a rabid dog.

"Anna, just think, the sooner we get this done, the sooner we'll get back for lunch. Think of the warm kitchen."

She was so reasonable, so bloody reasonable!

"Lunch!" I shouted above the rain, "I'm sick of their lunch! I'm sick of their smelly cheese! I'm sick of their green ham, of their maggots, of their stale bread. I'm sick…sick… SICK!"

I stopped shouting. A car was coming our way. We could not see it through the thick greyness of the rain, but we could hear the engine. We jumped off our milk churns and pulled them to the verge.

The black car, like a phantom, materialised from the mist and pulled up beside us. Spitz and Blitz got out, wearing identical black rainwear, cloche hats and long capes.

"What have you got there, girl?" Spitz, the policeman, approached Maryla.

I understood every word. In the Holtzmann household you learned things fast.

"You know, Sir. It's the milk. For the army," Maryla's voice was small and polite.

"You're lying!" He lowered his face. He looked menacing. "I want to see. Open it, girl!"

"But Sir…" Maryla made a gesture indicating the rain, "the milk…"

"Open it!" he shouted.

She unscrewed the large metal cap, and he peered inside, letting the rain from his hat and his collar drip inside the container.

"What's hidden at the base?" he demanded.

"Nothing, Sir. Nothing. Just milk. For the soldiers. Straight from the cows."

Maryla wiped the rain off her face with both hands. Spitz took a step back and with his booted foot kicked the churn right over. We stood, as if turned to stone, unable to stop the white flow spread all over the grass.

Blitz, the Gestapo man, stood motionless on the side and said nothing.

The policeman turned to me.

"What about you? What have you hidden there?"

I felt a massive jolt inside my stomach, as if all control had gone, as if all my organs had turned to water and were about to rush out of me. I clenched my buttocks with all my might, desperate not to disgrace myself.

"Milk, Sir," I managed in a rasping voice. The rain dripped from my hair down my face.

He turned to his companion.

"Time for us to go."

Just as suddenly as they had appeared, they climbed inside their car, turned it around and drove out of sight in seconds. Maryla raised her fists.

"God! How can you watch and not do anything! I want to kill the bastards!" Her voice soared to the highest pitch before being drowned by the downpour.

"Maryla! I've got the runs!" was all I had time to shout as I jumped over the ditch to crouch behind a bush. I felt better straight away. Maryla had been right. There was a bright side to everything. The soft wide leaves of the foxglove that I used for wipes, the immediate, natural, cleansing shower from above.

I returned to Maryla. She was stamping her feet, punching the air and swearing, shouting words I had not expected her to know, not a young lady from a good home, a girl, who in her real life had trained to teach young children.

"Maryla," I put my arms around her and hugged her tight, "bright side, remember?"

She became still for a moment then her voice mimicked mine, "What bright side?"

We giggled and I released her.

"Come on, Maryla, One churn is lighter than two."

We hurried to the crossroads and back again to repeat this task with the second churn, in time for lunch, in time for the collection by the army truck. As Bazylka was in charge of the milk distribution, no explanations were necessary to anyone else. Another ray of light in our black day.

"Spitz is a stupid man," Bazylka said. "He's digging his own grave. It's only a matter of time."

I would have preferred instant retribution.

CHAPTER 7

Ludwik was mad about sport. In his real life he had been studying engineering. He also ran, sprinted, swam, rowed, played tennis and did other things, which I could not picture in my mind, as I had not heard of them before. In our little village, where unemployment and food prices had always been the main concern, sport did not figure high on our list of priorities. Except for the volley ball, but that was the boy's territory. Girls helped to cook and to sew and to make things for the home.

One evening, after all our chores for the day had been done and after we had all taken our cleansing dip in Maryla's lake, we did not rush back to the house, but stopped in the meadow, where a few logs had been left at the edge of the field. It was bliss to throw ourselves onto the warm grass, to do nothing at all, just to wallow in the soothing calm of the balmy evening.

Ludwik stood up in the middle of our circle, his face animated as if his thoughts were trying to burst out.

"Hey, listen everyone! What we all need is a little entertainment. How about if I organise a sports evening?"

The boys' reply was to snort and laugh. We girls were more subtle than that. Our mere expressions told him what we thought of his idea.

"No, really!" he protested. "Come on everybody, this could be such fun!"

"I've had enough exercise all day," Michal said, "I feel as if my brain's detached from my body."

"Franek, what about you? You'd be so good in the high jump!" Ludwik persisted.

Franek lay flat on his back, his long grasshopper legs bent, one on top of the other, one foot kicking the air, as he chewed on a sorrel leaf.

"Staszek?"

"I'm perfectly happy here," Staszek replied, rubbing his back against the log and sidling up to Maryla.

"You're such weaklings!" Ludwik complained, "I bet the girls have more go about them!"

"We certainly have!" Bazylka agreed. "But not for squandering on your schemes!"

Ludwik turned around, slowly nailing us one by one with a severe stare.

"You'll all be queuing up to join me soon. Just watch this!"

He threw himself into a handstand, made a few hand steps, then let his body bend over in a perfect arch. He repeated this several times, adding headstands and cartwheels.

"You're making me dizzy!" I laughed, envying him his energy. My body felt as if it was made up of a thousand aching bones and joints. Every move made me wince inwardly. Michal was sitting next to me. He was rather subdued.

"Not tempted, then? To join Ludwik's academy of sport?" I teased.

He sighed heavily.

"If I had the energy to do anything at all, then I'd like to do something practical."

"Like what?" Bazylka asked.

He pulled himself up slowly, brushing against my arm.

"I miss doing woodwork. I'd love to keep in practice, if only I had some tools."

"And what would you make?" she asked again.

"Just little things to begin with. Decorative boxes, flower tubs, small seats, maybe. At home we made everything. Any furniture you could think of, my brother Jacek would design and make it for you. He's pretty good. I'd say the best carpenter in the region."

His words sounded like a boast, but I knew he was telling the truth. When Michal's father died, his oldest brother took over the family business, trained his three younger brothers in the trade and built up a reputation for excellent work.

"Mmm... I am impressed!" Bazylka's praise was genuine, "I'll know who to consult when I furnish my house. I also need a good shoe-maker." She wriggled her toes visible through the holes in her battered shoes.

"Don't we all!" Maryla sighed. Her shoes were held together with string.

Ludwik was taking a rest from his self-imposed gymnastics in the middle of our circle. He was now timing Stefan, who had not been able to resist Ludwik's challenge after all, and was doing a headstand.

"They need their heads testing!" Bazylka declared.

"No, actually, headstands have been proven the best remedy for poor blood circulation," Ludwik retorted. "You should try it yourself sometime, Bazylka!"

I found it all amusing. Besides, I never tired of looking at Stefan. My knowledge of his association with Lilli did not diminish the pleasure I experienced when he was around. His good looks were a constant source of fascination for me and his easy manner had a way of lifting my anxiety, which sat like a heavy brick on my chest, even when I slept.

I stopped resenting Lilli. It was easier than I had imagined possible. She was an invisible presence that made herself felt only through the gifts she smuggled for us, or through her regular reports of the radio news that kept us in touch with the outside world.

It was not the sort of news we wanted to hear, but each new blow hardened our resolve not to let go of our belief that one day things were going to change. France had surrendered to the Nazi invasion, while Hitler approached Mussolini to become his ally. Together they planned to take over all neighbouring nations and to create a fascist Europe under German rule.

"They've still got the British to reckon with," Stefan would remind us with an optimism we were all desperate to share. "There's talk of the commonwealth forces heading towards Britain. The Australians and the New Zealanders. And another thing, the Free French are forming an army under General de Gaulle in London."

These little snippets of hope were like a few grains of sugar thrown into a cauldron of bitter brew, especially when news from Poland was nothing more than glorified accounts of the German victories over the Russians, as both sides pushed against each other on land that was not theirs, crushing whole communities in their wake.

"Not long now before our first shopping trip to Treibach," Michal said. "I can't wait to buy that box of tools! What about you, Anna?"

I laughed.

"I just want a bucket of hand cream," I said, noticing his hands were as rough and scratched as mine. The worst pain was around the nails, where the cracks were open and raw, making the slightest touch feel like a splinter. Every night Bazylka sneaked in a blob of butter, which we shared between us and rubbed into our hands as we lay on our mattresses in the dark.

"But really, if I had lots of money," I continued, "I'd buy pieces of lovely material and make beautiful clothes." I stopped. My dreams could not have been of any interest to him. But he seemed to watch me closely, his lips curled in an indulgent smile.

"That sounds very clever and very complicated." He spread his fingers. "My big hands could never do such fine work."

His hands were solid yet well shaped. They looked capable, protective. Strangely, I found them attractive, but I did not tell him so.

Dusk was falling. All a little stiff – even Ludwik – we walked back to the farm and parted company with the boys when we reached the yard.

I was startled to see Herr Holtzmann waiting inside the kitchen door, like a shadow at first, transforming into solid form as he stepped out towards us.

"My wife's brooch is missing," he said without preamble. "Has anyone seen it?"

My understanding of the German language grew rapidly in the first month at the farm, but not all the words were familiar.

"What's missing?" I asked Maryla in Polish.

"Her brooch."

The implication of his words sank in with oppressive dread.

"What's it like? We need to know what to look for," Bazylka asked.

"A silver flower with garnet petals. I must look through your belongings. My wife will not be satisfied till I've searched everywhere."

We went inside, locked the door and drew the blackout curtains, before lighting the paraffin lamp. Bazylka placed it high on a shelf from where it threw its pale yellow light into our alcove.

"Empty your bags on your beds," Herr Holtzmann ordered.

We did as we were told, knowing all the while, and knowing that he knew it too, that this exercise was pointless. He shone his torch through our belongings, our clothes, our underwear, our few items of toiletry, then he crouched down and looked under our beds. There was nothing there, I knew, except the bare floor tiles and the rough wall.

He stood up.

"I shall not report this to the authorities," he said, "but only because I cannot afford to lose my workers. But paytime is two days away. I shall suspend your earnings, till the brooch is found."

When he was gone, we turned out the light and climbed into our beds.

"The bastard!" Bazylka whispered in the dark. "He knows damn well we did not pinch the blasted brooch. For Christ's sake, where on earth would I be able to wear it? To milk the cows?"

I felt Maryla's movements beside me. She was sniffing and rubbing her eyes. I wanted to comfort her, but I could not think of anything convincing to say. I found her free hand and gave it a squeeze.

"Let's sleep on it. There's nothing else we can do right now."

But I thought hard and prayed, before I slept. I bargained with my guardian angel.

"Just listen to my hands," I told him, rubbing my palms together, "like a pair of graters." I need that cream badly. You've got to help us!" In my mind, I traced all the farm buildings, barns and outhouses and tried to imagine where Elise could have been. First thing at dawn, I'd go looking.

I found Elise's brooch where I should have looked in the first place. The morning sun lit up the ruby petals with a red glow. I restrained myself from picking it up. I wanted Herr Holtzmann to see for himself. I caught Bazylka and Maryla on their way out to begin the first chores of the day.

"I've found it!" I could hardly contain myself as I told them where. "I'll be right back, as soon as I've seen Holtzmann."

Their wide-eyed relief was a joy to see.

"You're an angel," Maryla said, looking down at the leather shreds attached to her feet. "Can it be really possible that I shall have my new shoes, at last?"

Old Frau Holtzmann was not up yet, so I set about preparing breakfast while listening for Herr Holtzmann to come out of his part of the house. He looked severe, as always, when he appeared but that did not put me off. For once, if only briefly, I felt in control.

"I've found your wife's brooch," I said.

His face remained set.

"All right, give it to me, and I shall forget this has ever happened."

"It's outside," I said. His eyebrows moved a fraction and then he followed me out of the kitchen, round the main building to the other side, where his well-kept, flower-decked garden offered a pretty view from the parlour window. I stopped by the low wooden fence and pointed to the sandpit.

Gaby had constructed a miniature garden made up of wilted daisies and dandelions. A few forbidden geraniums were stuck in a random pattern around Elise's brooch with its crimson garnets. Herr Holtzmann looked hard at it then at me.

"Gaby loves making gardens," I said, hoping for a sign of warmth in his face. He did not smile.

"This is a set-up. Anyone could have done it."

"Yes," I agreed, "but the truth is none of us did. Just ask Gaby."

He shook his head.

"Go. Enough time wasted."

On Saturday night we all received our monthly wages. Twelve marks each. Bazylka and Maryla asked for their shoe coupons, which, together with our food and clothes coupons, were being hoarded by Elise. Herr Holtzmann raised his eyebrows. I felt a touch of threat in that slight change of expression and wondered if my friends had pushed their luck just a trifle too far. But Bazylka was undeterred.

"Our shoes are falling apart," she pointed out the obvious. "How are we to work?"

"We shall be getting clogs for all of you soon," Herr Holtzmann replied.

"Clogs?" Bazylka made it sound like something disgusting.

"That's right. Clogs. They are hard wearing. Ideal for work."

"Please Herr Holtzmann, I need shoes. Just normal shoes." Exasperation had crept into her voice.

He said nothing, just went away and after a while we heard raised voices behind the parlour door: Elise's high, hysterical pitch, his commanding low tone and then silence.

"Sounds as if it shall be clogs after all," Maryla whispered.

But Herr Holtzmann returned holding out the small paper stamps, like a monarch bestowing treasures upon his serfs.

CHAPTER 8

The little town of Treibach lay four kilometres from our farm. It was dominated by the Schloss high up on the hill, with its adjoining church and administration buildings, an excellent vantage point for the Gestapo. From there, the valley could be observed into the farthest distance with its network of country roads leading up to dwellings scattered on the hillsides.

We walked briskly in twos, Stefan and Ludwik leading. Once we left the shelter of the forest and crossed the field to continue along the rail track, we were helplessly exposed. I was racked with fear. We had been constantly warned against drawing attention to ourselves, but here, there was not one tree, not one bush to screen us from spying eyes. It was only when we reached the first row of houses and blended in with the shadows that I felt a moment of relief.

It was Sunday afternoon. The town appeared deserted, and the odd person we happened to come across, would hurry away with a sudden change of direction, as if we were lepers. The buildings were dressed in long dark-red banners, forming a sombre backdrop to black swastikas on white discs. The face of the *Fuhrer* looked down from every window and *"Heil Hitler"* posters were plastered on all doors.

The approaching sound of marching boots behind us heightened my anxiety. I wanted to run, to get off the street and hide inside Herr Neuman's shop, but the soldiers caught up with us and a shout ordered us to stop. There were only two of them, yet their raised guns had immediate effect. My chest tightened and I found it hard to breathe.

"What's your business here?" one of them asked.

They knew very well our business, but Stefan explained with controlled calm.

They ordered us to stand against the wall. I felt a pounding in my head and a ringing in my ears. I pressed my palm against the wall for support.

They made a step forward and came so close I could see the sweat run down in rivulets on the face nearest to mine. A whiff of stale tobacco rose from his shirt as he lifted his hand towards me. I flinched, but all he did was to run his fingers over my left shoulder where the bright yellow "P" had been sewn on.

"Open your bag!" he ordered.

Even in my petrified state I was able to think how silly his order was. The floppiness of my cloth bag made it quite clear that nothing was hidden inside.

We were all checked in a similar way, then one of the soldiers shouted, "Go!"

We were the only customers in Herr and Frau Neuman's shop. Shopping trips from the neighbouring farms were staggered over the month, so that the workers would not be tempted to form a crowd. Though I had been used to shortages even before the outbreak of war, the sight of empty shelves hit me with disappointment, sinking deeper my mood. The only objects displayed on the shelves were printed card cut-outs advertising cigarettes, a French perfume, a lavender soap and a lipstick to make your lips as glossy as Marlena Dietrich's.

"Don't be put off," Maryla whispered. "There's a magic door behind the curtain. They keep everything there. Anything you ask for."

I liked the old couple on sight. They were both grey and slightly roundish with the kindly appearance of patient grandparents, but even this impression could not abate my nervousness. Not straight away. Only when they started serving us with the same practised politeness, that they must have treated their real customers with, I calmed down and began to rehearse in my mind the names of the things I needed. When my turn came I asked for soap (they only had carbolic), toothpaste, (that was a round solid chalky block), washing flakes (grated carbolic soap), shampoo (that was iodine-orange), aspirins and Vaseline. All this came to six marks and fifty pfennig, over a half of my monthly allowance. I asked for a small towel and safety pins. Cut up into narrow strips, it would be made into washable, reusable sanitary towels. This set me back another two marks fifty. I had three marks left.

"Frau Neuman, have you any cotton material for sewing?" I asked.

"Three marks fifty a metre is the cheapest I've got. Dishcloths. That's all it's good for," Frau Neuman shrugged helplessly.

"What about old curtains?" I tried, "for three marks?"

She shook her head, but then her cheeks lifted, softening the creases around her eyes.

"I've got a bag of off-cuts. All sizes, all colours, all weights."

She disappeared behind the curtained door and I waited while Herr Neuman served the boys.

She came back with an old pillowcase stuffed like a sack.

"Fifty pfennig, if you want it," she said, lifting it over the counter.

"If I want it?" I felt insane with happiness. I added, "And knitting wool please."

"There's only the moth-eaten wool." Frau Neuman's lips turned down in apology. "Fifty pfennig a bundle of ten balls. Some are better than others. It's just your luck."

And so, for my month's hard labour, I earned my toiletries, a bag of off-cuts and a bundle of moth-eaten wool. I had two marks left.

A nagging thought surfaced in my mind, a thought of winter boots and stockings and vests and woollens. I pushed the thought away and prayed I would be home by then.

Bazylka and Maryla needed shoes badly. Theirs had fallen apart, before their monthly savings of a mark or two could accumulate enough to buy new replacements. They did not hope for much, just some cheap sandals. Anything would be better than the leather shreds tied to their feet. Or so they thought. They did not expect just one style and one size for all.

Bazylka looked bewildered as she studied the chunky brown lace-ups that were three sizes too big for her feet.

"They make the size uniform," Frau Neuman explained with an air of resignation. "Cheaper to produce. That's what they say. It's the army now who get all the attention."

"But what if our boys need shoes?" Bazylka tried to reason. "What if this size is too small for them? What do they do with their toes? Chop them off?"

Frau Neuman managed an indulgent smile.

"There's a simpler way. They'd just have to cut off the tips of their shoes."

Bazylka rolled her eyes.

"How can I walk with these boats loose around my feet?"

"Stuff them with rags," Frau Neuman suggested.

There seemed no choice.

"How much?" Bazylka asked.

"Fifteen marks."

"Fifteen?" Bazylka and Maryla exclaimed together.

That settled it. The ugly shoes were way beyond their means.

"Clogs it shall be then," Maryla forced a thin smile.

It was at this point that we were all silenced by a commotion outside in the street. Herr Neuman rushed to the door and locked it.

"This buys you time, if need be," he whispered, stepping back, while we stood still and watched through the narrow gaps between posters of the *Fuhrer* stuck to the windows, that would have normally been adorned with displays.

An army truck had come to a halt on the opposite side of the street, its engine running noisily. A group of soldiers spilled out of its open back, ran up to the wide courtyard entrance of the building and with the butts of their guns began to hit the oak gate with such force that it sent echoes down the street. After a short while, the gate appeared to be pulled back from the inside. The soldiers pushed against it and ran into the yard.

It was so quiet in the shop. I could not even hear my friends' breathing. I felt an arm rest on my shoulder, protectively, and I let it stay there because I knew it was Michal. I stood still, letting him stand close to me, our sides touching, aware that the fragile, fleeting comfort was needed mutually.

There was more shouting outside. A man and a woman and their two young boys, maybe five and seven years of age, were being marched out of the courtyard towards the back of the truck surrounded by raised guns as if they were criminals. The woman tripped on the metal steps and fell to the ground. The man bent down to assist her. The soldiers nearest to them, like a pack of jackals, attacked with punches and kicks. The little boys were distraught. Their screams cut through the core of my being.

I could not watch. I closed my eyes and pressed my palms against them, feeling Michal's arm tighten around me. I waited till the cries of the victims and the shouts of the oppressors subsided, till the truck's doors were banged shut, till the revving of the engine died in the distance. When I opened my eyes all was quiet in the street outside.

"I suppose we'd better finish our business," Herr Neuman's voice was eerily subdued.

Later, when we were all ready to go, Herr Neuman said mysteriously, "Follow me," and led us towards the curtained door.

"May God keep you safe." Frau Neuman clasped her hands on her ample chest and watched as we filed out.

There was no magic cave behind the curtained door, just a dark passage with other doors indicating other rooms or storage spaces. We came outside into a sunlit backyard where Herr Neuman advised us, "Take the side street to your left. It will lead you out of town, into the woods to a path that goes straight to your farm."

We thanked him and followed his instructions, moving with great speed till we were out of town. We crossed the main road and the rail track beyond, where we could see the tall thick ferns spreading out from the forest.

We carried on till we reached a clearing that looked safe in its diffused light within a circle of dark pines. As if by pre-arrangement, though no one had uttered a word, we threw ourselves onto the mossy ground and heaved a sigh of relief.

Nobody spoke for a while, then Franek said, "I'd give anything for a fag!"

All cigarettes had been finished on the train journey to Klagenfurt. It now seemed like centuries ago.

"Me too," Michal added. "It's a nightmare! And we've not been able to do anything!"

"I'd love to smash their ugly mugs to smithereens!" Staszek said, clenching his fists. A month on the farm had reduced him to the skinniest boy in our group.

Ludwik pushed his fingers through his tangled curls as if he was going to pull them out.

"I just want to kill them!" he declared.

I felt the same. I wanted instant retribution. I was shaking with helpless rage. It was hard thinking normal thoughts when two frightened little faces were peering inside your soul. A shadow fell upon our Sunday afternoon.

"Listen everyone!" Bazylka's commanding voice made everyone sit up. "Just to remind you. We've got exactly one hour and thirty seven minutes left of our free time!"

Somehow, her words broke the tension and the boys began rummaging through their bags, examining their purchases, with the excitement reserved for priceless treasures.

Stefan got up. Until now he had been very quiet, lost in his own thoughts.

"I've got to go," he said, with his eyes cast down, his tone asking us to understand.

Ludwik jumped up to his feet and raised his arms as if barring the way.

"Stefan, you're mad! Surely not after what's just happened!"

They eyed each other, unblinking, tense, the beautiful blond god, and the dark-skinned athlete.

"Please Ludwik, don't do this," Stefan spoke quietly, "I've got to go."

"No!" Ludwik gripped Stefan's shoulder, "I won't let you!"

Stefan remained still, his hands by his sides.

"I don't want a fight, Ludwik. They've got their victims for today. Why would they come looking for me?"

Ludwik threw his hands in the air.

"Why? Listen to him, folks! He's asking why? Why anything? Why this bloody war? Why this shitty existence? Stefan, they don't need a reason! And you're already in a hell of a mess! You seem intent on suicide!"

Bazylka got up and stood between them with the determined stance of an older sister.

"Stop it boys!" she said sternly. "We can't afford divisions in our group. We've already got an enemy. We've got to stick together, do you understand?"

"I understand all right," Ludwik retorted, "but does he?"

I sided with Ludwik this time, despite my weakness for Stefan in all other matters. His wilfulness was placing us all in danger.

Bazylka touched Ludwik's arm, her movement gently placating.

"Imagine yourself in his place," she said quietly.

"Hell! Bloody hell!" Ludwik nailed Stefan with his stare, "Do you think I want to spoil your fun? I'm concerned for your safety, you idiot!"

"That's right, call me names, if it makes you happy," Stefan said calmly, "I've got to go."

"What you need is a good thrashing!" Ludwik narrowed his eyes, but then suddenly his tone softened. "Go if you must, but come back in one piece!"

Stefan grabbed Ludwik's hand and gave it a hearty shake before picking up his rucksack and disappearing in the bracken.

All chatter resumed. I made a half-hearted attempt at small talk with Michal, who had been sitting quiet beside me.

"So did you get your box of tools?" I asked.

His solemn expression relaxed into a self-deprecating smile.

"I'm a big spender," he said, "I'm afraid, all my money's gone. Not a hammer, not one chisel. Not yet. But next month, maybe. What about you?"

"I've got two marks left," I said with mock smugness.

"I'll know where to come for a loan, then," he teased.

"Only if you convince me first that you can be sensible with money."

"You sound like my mother," he said and I threw a handful of moss at him.

Maryla moved up to me.

"I can't wait to see what Frau Neuman has stuffed into that sack of yours," she said.

I untied the string and shook out part of the contents onto the grass. All three of us girls plunged our hands into the soft mound of cut fabrics, some as small as a handkerchief, some a quarter metre wide.

The patterns and the colours were all different, some weaves heavier and coarser than others, but all the pieces were cotton. That was good. In an instant I knew how to make use of them.

"I just love the colours," Maryla said with childlike joy.

"But what will you do with these scraps?" Bazylka asked. "Dress dolls? Make finger gloves?"

"Make us new blouses!" I said triumphantly. "It's easy! We've just got to join the pieces together first, like patchwork."

"But that will take months!" Bazylka was already disheartened.

"Not if we do it together, in the evenings. I might even…" Another idea occurred to me in my excitement, but even as I thought of it, I knew my audacity bordered on madness. "I might even ask Elise for her sewing machine."

The sisters did not bother to hide from me the pitiful look that passed between them.

CHAPTER 9

I waited for the right moment to catch Elise. That was not easy. She hardly ever came into the kitchen when we were there. When she did, she showed no signs of noticing us, three girls, an act she had practised to perfection. As we swept, cleaned, washed up and dried, she weaved her way around us with feline grace, avoiding all contact, as if we were a disease. No wonder. The farmyard smell trapped in our clothes and intensified by the heat in the kitchen must have assaulted her delicate nose like the stench from the sewers.

Usually, she waited till we were out of the way, gone to tend to the animals, before she brought in her two helpers, women from Kappel, to start their daily jobs of baking, cutting and marinating the various meats, bottling peas, beans, beetroot and shredded cabbage as the vegetables were harvested in stages.

By lunchtime, when we returned, she and her helpmates were already gone to start the afternoon in the dairy. I could only imagine, with a twinge of wicked amusement, how stressed she must have been in her efforts to keep herself and her children away from the rest of us, in a household of fourteen people when we were all present.

One evening, she surprised us, and no doubt herself, by walking into the kitchen earlier than usual after the meal. She may have been distracted by Herr Holtzmann, who followed close behind, leaning his head forward, intent on finishing his account of the meeting with the SS, which all farmers had to attend by order every week.

Her momentary hesitation was perceptible to experienced eyes like mine. I spared her further discomfort by stepping forward to take the tray of dirty plates from her hands. At the same time I heard Bazylka's whisper above the sink, "Now! Ask her now."

My heart began to pound as I braced myself against Elise's displeasure. I raised my gaze above the tray to her averted face.

"Excuse me, Frau Holtzmann," I said, in a voice that did not sound like my own, "is there any chance I could borrow your sewing machine?"

I put down the tray by the sink with controlled slowness before daring to look at her again. The shock in her face could not have been more pronounced if I had slapped her.

She turned to her husband.

"Is that girl speaking to me?"

Herr Holtzmann confirmed in a tone reserved for mollifying fractious children. I shot him a glance, searching for a spark of humour in his scarred face. There was none.

"Then tell her," Elise turned her neat, slim back on us, "tell her, I've nothing to say."

She walked out with her long skirt swishing around her high heels.

"Please, Herr Holtzmann," I put in quickly, clutching at my last chance. "Please let me have the sewing machine just for one evening. I've got one at home. I'm used to it. I wouldn't break anything. I promise."

I thought his gaze softened a little and for a brief second I anticipated the joy of being granted my wish, but he only shrugged saying, "You heard my wife. It's her sewing machine. I don't make decisions for her."

That night, after all the chores of the day had been completed, after we had scrubbed all the grime off our bodies and loosened our hair to dry, I brought out my bag of material scraps onto the dimly lit kitchen table and spread out the rainbow array of colours and patterns before Bazylka and Maryla.

"What now?" Bazylka sounded disgruntled, yet she could not stop running her fingers through the pile, picking out the greens, that would have gone well with her auburn hair.

"We shall not be beaten," I said. "We shall sew by hand."

"You're mad, Anna," she replied. She made it sound like praise. Already she was laying the pieces together, like fragments of a jigsaw.

"This is like finding jewels in a rubbish dump," Maryla exclaimed, her large eyes lighting up her peaky little face. She was selecting pieces in all shades of blue. I looked for reds and pinks. Suited to my dark hair.

"We need to cut them and trim them into neat shapes," I said.

There was an old pair of scissors kept in one of the drawers among a jumble of cut string, odd balls of wool, used envelopes, pencils and nibs, a few nails and tacks.

The scissors were useless. As each of us tried them in turn, the blades merely chewed the material and the two rings on the handle left deep, painful dents in our fingers.

"Just as I thought," Bazylka said, rubbing her fingers. "This whole idea is crazy!"

"I'm not giving up!" I said, feeling my stubbornness set in, "Michal will fix them for us."

It was a dark night, with the stars like pinpricks on a black cloth. Once my eyes were able to distinguish shapes, I made my way to the barn and slid in through the gap between the two halves of the door.

"Michal!" I called out, just loud enough for the boys to hear me, high in the loft.

Their talk stopped and soon I heard creaky footsteps coming down my way.

A torch shone suddenly lighting up Michal's face like a mask with distorted features. He switched it off when he reached me. I explained my problem, aware of his closeness through the feint scent of the field dust and horses.

"Nothing to it," I heard him say. "A drop of oil and the whetstone is all we need."

He took the scissors, clasped my hand and led me outside.

"Hold tight," he said, walking confidently straight ahead into what seemed to me like a void. I held tight, glad to have him so close, amazed he could see anything at all.

Inside the shed, where all farm machinery was stored, Michal gave me his torch to shine while he oiled the pivot and sharpened the blades.

"Try now," he said.

I cut through the air with fast satisfying snaps.

"They're like new!" I exclaimed, overwhelmed with gratitude. The pleasure in his face made me want to hug him, but all I could say was, "Thanks a million! Now we can really get on with our job."

Strangely, when he had walked me back to the kitchen door, I was reluctant to let him go.

We stayed up late; Bazylka, Maryla and I, cutting our selected pieces into rectangles and squares to be joined later like patchwork.

My second rummaging through the drawers produced another discovery, a sewing box. The thread on the spools was yellow with age, but my main concern was how to charm old Frau Holtzmann into letting us use it.

In the morning, after I had helped Frau Holtzmann to wash her dough-like feet in the rust-stained bowl with chipped enamel, and cut her toe nails with the newly sharpened scissors and brushed her grey hair into a neat plait and complimented her on her black dress with daisies, I said, "Excuse me, Frau Holtzmann, I need some thread and a needle."

She scratched her head in a distracted manner, as if thinking was an effort, then she looked towards the chest of drawers where I had found the sewing box the night before. She said, "It's years since I've made anything... It's my eyes, you know. And my fingers...they're not what they used to be. Look in there." She pointed. "There should be a box with all the things you need."

I brought the box to her and she opened it.

"Take what you need," she said, "I can't see myself sewing again."

I could not believe my luck.

"What about Frau Holtzmann, your son's wife. Won't she mind?"

Old Frau Holtzmann's expression hardened. She shifted position to upright, defiant.

"Elise has her own things. The kitchen is mine. No one's going to tell me what I can or can't do with my own things!"

Our patchwork, designed to end up as T-shapes for the fronts and the backs of our blouses, was slow work as we sat up late each night, sewing by hand. My fingers were not as nimble as I willed them to be. My broken nails scraped against the material and the thread caught painfully in the cuts in my chapped skin, making me drop the needle, making me want to scream with frustration. Some evenings, I had had enough and was ready to give up, then I'd look at Bazylka and Maryla plodding on, Bazylka with a trifle less patience than her sister, immersed in quiet talk, as if they were still at home, and I knew I had no choice, but to plod on with them.

Some evenings the boys joined us and livened up things, lifting my dark mood, making the work appear less tiresome. Franek kept us spellbound with his ghost stories, and promised to show me, when we returned home, the exact spot where a girl drowned because of her broken heart, and where each year, on the same night, her ghost rises from the water.

Ludwik's accounts of foreign lands, strange customs and exotic animals made me dream of travel. He had already travelled as a child with his father, who was an engineer, and had been contracted to build bridges in places that I had only heard of in geography lessons at school. No one travelled from our village at home. Only to Krakow, only for a good reason. Travel was for people outside our existence. In our lives a regular dinner on the table was deemed good living, a job in service considered a stroke of immense fortune and an item, any item of new clothing, bought for Easter Sunday was a joyous achievement to be shown off in church before everyone.

Michal had an old deck of cards. Each time I happened to look his way he smiled. Why had I thought him to be such a pain at home?

He, Franek, Staszek and Ludwik would play poker or pontoon some of the time, while Stefan gave us accounts of the latest news, obtained in secrecy from Lilli.

One evening he came with this news:

"It's all about Hitler. How great and mighty he is. How his armies march on undeterred. Across Europe. To Africa. To the East. God knows how much of this is true. The latest is that the German bombers are blitzing Southern England and Wales."

The boys stopped playing.

"It's propaganda. The usual stuff," Franek said, rubbing his chin.

"What, a lie on this scale?" Staszek was not convinced.

"Who's to stop them? Who's to check what they're up to?" Franek argued.

We were all quiet thinking about it.

"Listen," Ludwik broke the silence with forced cheerfulness, "Britain's not an easy target. What, with her colonies and the States on her side?"

I felt a whisper of movement around the table, like a sigh of hope and relief.

"Do you think so? Do you really think so?" Maryla put down her sewing and clasped her hands as if in prayer, her anxious face seeking confirmation.

"You'd better be right, Ludwik, or God help us all," Bazylka said, wincing as she pricked her finger.

I shivered. I did not like her talking like this.

"Bazylka, you said yourself, many times, that it's only a matter of time…"

I wanted her to say it was going to be all right. I needed her reassurance that God was watching over us, that we would come to no harm. That soon the war would be over with the Germans totally defeated.

But she just sucked her finger, silent and thoughtful

A few days later, Stefan came with the news that Hitler had ordered Luftwaffe to destroy the British airforce in preparation for invading Britain.

Cut off from the world as we were, there was no way of verifying this news. I thought constantly of my mother and my sisters and missed them with a pain so physical, it felt like a heavy load pressing on my chest. I waited each day for their reply to my letter, but as no one else in our group received any post, I made myself believe that one day a sackful of delayed letters would arrive all at once for everyone.

One morning, when I was cleaning up after breakfast, alone with the old Frau Holtzmann, I plucked up courage to speak to her. As usual, she sat on a stool by the sink and dried the crockery that I washed, her bulbous fingers lethargic, her ample dress covering her enormous thighs and falling in folds to the floor. My German was not fluent but I was able to formulate simple phrases.

"Frau Holtzmann," I said, "I miss my mother, my family. When can I go home?"

She lay down the tea-towel in her wide lap and lifted her dull eyes.

"I don't understand," she said, "Go home? What do you mean, go home? Your place is here, with us."

I shook my head.

"No, Frau Holtzmann. Here is where I work. But I have a home. With my mother, with my sisters. When can I see them? When can I go?"

She considered this for a moment.

"No one can tell you that."

"But just give me some idea," I persisted. "Is it a month? Six months? A year?"

A spark of animation crossed her face, as if suddenly she needed to explain something that I did not understand.

"No Anna, not a month, nor six months. That much I can tell you. And afterwards, who knows? When all Europe becomes one Reich we shall need to keep our workers more than ever."

Later, when I found Maryla in the barn, I could not hold back my grief any longer. I wept into my rag that I carried around with me for wiping muck off my hands between jobs. It smelled of bog, even though I washed it every night.

Maryla put down her basket of eggs and sat beside me on the bale, her thin arm comforting on my shoulder.

"Slaves! That's all we are to them!" I sobbed, "There's no escape for us!"

"That's silly talk, Anna!" Her sharp tone, so uncharacteristic of her, made me stop and look at her. She had fire in her eyes. "What do they know about the future? What does anyone? Things can change overnight!"

I wanted to believe her. I blew my nose and stuffed the rag inside my pocket.

"I'd rather die than spend my life in this hole," I said.

"Shhhhh…" She placed her hand over my mouth. "Don't talk of dying. I forbid it!"

That evening we were given our clogs. Herr Holtzmann handed them out after supper, after all our daily chores had been done. Size five for us girls and size nine for the boys. They were made of thick, shaped wood with a brown leather top.

We rushed out into the yard to try them on. Mine were hard and stiff, unlike the pulped, mud-coloured sacking on my feet that was all that remained of my once-white sandals.

"It's like walking on stilts!" Bazylka declared, not overjoyed.

"How will I dance in mine?" Maryla joked, balancing her thin legs on the slippery insteps, like someone walking the tightrope.

"Who needs clogs for dancing?" Staszek cried, kicking his off and taking Maryla with him in a few impromptu polka steps.

They laughed and fooled around, drawing out our smiles, our amused glances, and for a few brief seconds I was back on the green, in my village at home.

"Bazylka!" Maryla was breathless. She dragged Staszek to her sister. "Have a look at this! What's best for a wasp sting?"

She held up Staszek's hand and we all gathered closer for a better look. His hand and his arm to his elbow were swollen. Incongruously, compared to the rest of him, all skin and bones.

"It's here," he said, exposing a tiny black speck, surrounded by raised inflammation just inside his wrist.

"You should have bathed it in vinegar straight away," Bazylka chided him.

He slapped his forehead.

"How stupid of me not to have thought of it in the middle of the cornfield," he grinned.

Bazylka indulged him with a thin smile.

"All right, smarty pants. Let's see what can be done." She turned to Stefan. "Any chance of a drop of antiseptic?"

Stefan led them away towards his lodgings in the loft of the barn, where his first aid box had become our pharmacy, all its supplies acquired through Lilli's relentless and secret efforts.

The rest of us, Franek, Ludwik, Michal and myself, sat down to wait on the bench built around the chestnut tree. Michal lifted his feet and knocked his clogs together.

"Invincible, aren't they? What's Holtzmann trying to tell us?"

I told him. I repeated old Frau Holtzmann's words.

Michal raised a dismissive hand as if to brush her words aside.

"That's nonsense, Anna. They can plan what they like, but it'll never happen. What, taking on the whole of Europe?" He tapped his head and rolled his eyes to indicate how crazy such notion was. "Mark my words. They've bitten much, much more than they'll ever be able to chew. Come on, cheer up! Come for a walk with me. You'll never guess what I found today!"

His cheerfulness was just the remedy I craved to lighten my black mood.

"What?" I asked, my curiosity already excited.

"Wait and see," he teased. His eyes smiled and I knew he was bursting to tell me.

As we got up, Franek and Ludwik stopped talking.

"I need a bit of practice," Michal explained pointing to his clogs. "Do you want to come with us?"

"Later," Franek said. "We'll wait for the others."

"Head for the maize field, we'll meet you there."

His gait was springy, despite the awkwardness of the clogs. I had a job keeping up with him.

"Hey, what's the hurry?" I stopped, out of breath, when we reached the meadow. I stepped out of my clogs, glad of the soft ground beneath my feet. Michal did the same.

"Habit, Anna. Everything's done in such a rush. Second nature now."

We walked barefoot from then on, carrying our clogs with us. I was aware of his frequent glances, of the silence between us and racked my brain for something to say. The sky was dusky lavender; we had perhaps an hour of daylight left.

"I hate to see the summer go," I said at last, "shorter days, longer nights…"

"Yes, the pressure's really on to get the harvest done on time," Michal replied. "We've cleared the whole maize field today. Just us four boys. Holtzmann was out, so Elise poached Max and Johann, to do jobs for her."

"I know," I said, "we helped them on the vegetable plot in the afternoon. Beans and peas. Bags of them. That'll keep Elise busy for weeks."

Michal looked at me and with an exaggerated sigh declared, "I can't stand the woman. What did Holtzmann ever see in her?"

His comical expression made me giggle.

"Come on, Michal. Be fair. The woman never stops working. Where would Holtzmann find a more supportive wife?"

"She's cold and cruel," Michal insisted.

"She's very pretty," I reminded him.

"Not my type at all. I'd never choose anyone like her!"

"What's your type then?" I had no idea what emboldened me to ask him this and to carry on. "Who have you left at home?"

I felt his hand touch my shoulder and we both stopped. He looked serious, but not cross. Above us, swallows chased each other in wide, deep swoops.

"There's no one at home. But if there were I'd like her to be like you."

For a split second all I could see were his eyes, looking straight into mine. Brown eyes, speckled with amber flecks. Then the meaning of his words hit me. Like an electric shock. I felt my face turning red. My mind's reaction was to pretend. To pretend this was just a joke.

"Come on, Michal. Enough of this fooling around." I forced a laugh and walked on.

He caught up with me.

"Listen Anna, I'm serious. I promise. Just tell me one thing. Could you like me a little?"

This time my laughter was real. I assured him.

"Of course I could like you a little. You're my brother's friend."

"Only a little?" he asked with a grin.

How could I tell him that I had never considered my brother's friends with anything more than barely contained endurance, when they left old bikes and radios lying around in everyone's way, with screwdrivers and spanners waiting to trip you over. Not to mention their irritating noisy outbursts at some feeble jokes.

But now, as I viewed Michal with discreet, sideways glances, I discovered it was like seeing him for the first time. It surprised me, how his bare, bronzed arms drew my attention, and how much I liked the shine on his sun-lightened hair, and the way it fell freely around his face, no longer greasy with brilliantine. Not bad. Even attractive. I could admit that to myself, for no one was going to read my thoughts.

"Michal," I said, "promise, you'll never tease me."

"As if I would!" His expression was so indignant, it made me laugh again.

"Come," he said, "there's something, you must see!"

We stepped into our clogs at the end of the meadow, then Michal led me along the edge of the field where the maize had been harvested. The short stumps would be set alight and burnt to ashes before being ploughed back into the soil. We stopped about a metre from the old oak tree with its widespread branches. Michal placed a finger on his lips.

"Slowly and quietly now," he whispered, crouching down. I crouched beside him. The smell of the dry earth, of the tall white grass springing up in clumps along the hedge, was intensified in the evening air. I heard the chirping before Michal parted the feather-like leaves of the ferns. Sitting on the ground was a mother partridge, her beige-speckled form camouflaged perfectly in her surroundings. Her wings were spread out to shelter her young brood, which, like fluffy grey balls, rolled in and out, picked themselves up, stretched, ran in a circle before hiding, then to repeat the whole process again, like some life-saving ritual.

The sight of them – so tender, so vulnerable – overwhelmed me with a rush of emotion. I wanted to hold them, to feel their lightness, to feel their downy bodies.

"Lovely, aren't they?" Michal whispered, his lips parted in awe.

"Magical," I whispered back.

There would be other times to tell him more.

"What's taking her so long?" Bazylka was not expecting me to answer. She was just voicing her disquiet.

"Be reasonable," I said, "she's only been gone five minutes. And it's not as if she'd get lost on this farm."

We were in our beds in our dark, cramped alcove. Maryla had stayed in the yard with Staszek.

"It's not easy being the older sister, you know," Bazylka sounded prickly.

"I do know. I've got two younger sisters myself. But Maryla's not a child. Give her some credit. And stop fussing!"

There was a short pause before Bazylka fretted again.

"What have they got to talk about? So long?"

I laughed.

"Bazylka, you sound like an old, disapproving aunt. Calm down, for goodness sake!"

I heard Bazylka's bed creak and sensed her sitting up.

"You think I am a spoilsport, don't you?" she said.

"Aha, that's right."

"Well, you're wrong. I'm not. I just can't help worrying."

"Why?"

She shifted on her bed.

"It's not just about Maryla. It's about Staszek too. He's a good lad. Not fair to lead him on."

"But she's not!" I contradicted hotly, propping myself on my elbow. "Maryla likes him a lot. It's obvious to anyone how those two are with each other."

There was another pause, then Bazylka pondered out loud. "And where's all this leading?"

I could not resist a tiny jab of sarcasm.

"They might just decide to marry one day!"

I only meant to tease, not to hit a raw nerve, not to provoke an explosion.

"Father would never allow that!"

So that was it! Class distinction!

"You know," I said, my indignation compelling me to defend Staszek, "his family is well respected in our village. His father is the gamekeeper on the estate. Has been for years. And his mother cooks for the landlord's family. No one else in the village has a house like theirs. Girls fall over each other to be noticed by him."

"And you too?" Bazylka asked with a deliberate barb.

I snorted to show how silly I thought her suggestion was.

"Me? I don't have to, nor do I care. Staszek comes to our house all the time."

Bazylka went quiet then she sighed.

"Try telling my father all this. He dreams of princes and earls for his daughters."

Suddenly my anger was gone. Would my father, if he were still alive, have wanted a prince for me too? And if so, how could I have been cross about that?

I spoke in a gentler tone, "Let him dream. He's not here to see how little there is to be happy about. Don't begrudge Maryla a little bit of innocent fun."

She thought for a moment.

"But what if…"

"Bazylka, sshh…stop worrying! And promise you won't nag your sister."

I lay back on my striped ticking pillow, its lumpy insides hard against my head.

"This is the best time of the day for me," I said, "I close my eyes and I go home."

"Me too," Bazylka replied. "Imagine the day when this really happens."

I had imagined it countless times, countless different scenes, in sunshine and in snow, in a shower of falling leaves, at dusk and at dawn, running to my mother's open arms, holding her close, free at last of the constant ache in my chest.

But that night when I closed my eyes, another pair of eyes was looking into mine. Brown with honey-coloured flecks, thoughtful, kind.

I felt the ache inside me shrink back. I felt something like a leap of hope, like a quiver of expectancy, and I found myself wishing for the next day to come.

I heard the kitchen door open, shut, the key in the lock being turned, Maryla tip-toeing to our alcove, and then the rustling of her skirt as she undressed.

Bazylka moved on her bed.

"Save your breath," Maryla said, "I don't want to quarrel."

"Neither do I," Bazylka replied. "Thank your supporter for that."

Maryla slipped in beside me. Her thin arms hugged me as she whispered in my ear, "He's kissed me goodnight. And I can't believe it!"

"I can," I whispered back and returned her hug.

CHAPTER 10

We finished our patchwork blouses in time for our next visit to the Neumans' shop in Treibach. To call them blouses was optimistically pretentious. The blouses I used to make at home had collars, sleeves, buttons, and ornate lace or tucks. Ours were made up of two identical T-shapes, for the front and the back, with a neckline left wide enough to slip over one's head. And yet, there was something cheerful about the bright colours, that reminded me of my mother's garden at home. We could not stop chattering with excitement as we put them on. Bazylka's auburn hair, tied back with a strip of emerald material, was rich in copper glints, as it hung loosely against the patchwork of greens. Maryla's shades of blue intensified the colour of her wide-set eyes, and I simply loved my reds and pinks.

"You can hardly spot the 'P's among all the patterns," Maryla said with satisfaction, yet fingering hers, on her left shoulder, to be certain it was there. The obligatory bright yellow "P".

Automatically I did the same, though I knew I had sewn it on.

Franek whistled when we came out into the yard where the boys were waiting, inciting them to do the same.

"Hey, look at this fashion parade!" he cried. "Will you still want to walk with us, now that you're so grand!"

"We'll force ourselves!" Bazylka replied, posturing a haughty stance that made us all laugh.

As we began to stroll towards the path out of the farm, Michal walked beside me, his face animated, happy.

"Red suits you," he said. "You've made a good job of it. Spot-on!"

He made me chuckle.

"Michal, come off it. It's only a rag made up of small bits of rag. You don't have to pretend you like it."

"But I do, I do like it," he assured with his customary earnestness, "I'd never have the patience to produce anything like this. Ten out of ten!"

"Really?" I felt myself turning pink with pleasure.

"Yes. Really."

I wanted to walk with him all afternoon.

The big obvious problem with our blouses was that they made us dangerously conspicuous. We marched at great speed round the back alleys of Treibach, I praying all the time to be saved from coming face to face with the order-keeping patrol. The heart-stopping moment was when we checked the main street, empty on Sunday, shimmering in the sun with its long red banners. The black swastikas, printed bold and high on them, made me think of vultures waiting to swoop down upon us. We craned our necks from behind the corner building, then almost ran the last hundred metres to the Neumans' shop. It was at times like this that I wished I had possessed a magical hat that would make me invisible. We could have all done with one.

Frau Neuman was so impressed with our sewing skills that she brought out another sack of off-cuts specially saved for us.

"Curtain fabric," she said with the air of a proud magician performing the impossible. "Large pieces, sturdy material, will last a long time."

We also bought between us an aluminium bowl, so we would not have to use old Frau Holtzmann's chipped and rust-stained one, when the cold weather came and we could no longer bathe in our pool in the woods.

The boys' requirements were simpler altogether: toiletries, washing powder, antiseptic cream, aspirins; in fact, Herr Neuman joked, that with big spenders like them, he'd soon become a millionaire and be able to retire.

"Perhaps we too should get a washing bowl between us?" Michal suggested. The boys pondered for a minute the joys of washing in icy water in the snow-covered yard, and they all chipped in.

"You should get some wool too," I prompted. "It's time we started knitting hats, gloves and socks for the winter."

"Knitting!" Franek exclaimed. "That's for old grannies! I couldn't knit to save my life!"

"We'll teach you," Bazylka promised with severe affirmation. Franek winced.

"Good thinking, Aneczka." Stefan's praise caught me unawares. I looked at him, and as always, liked very much what I saw. Striking blue eyes, tanned face, wavy blond hair, the grace and the beauty that made you catch your breath that left you needy and aching for more. This had been so at the beginning. Now I was able to bask in his friendship without the pain.

I shrugged, "Just common sense, Stefan. Best to be prepared. Unless you know something that we don't."

His smile was sad.

"I'd do anything to be the messenger of good news."

Frau Neuman asked me, "How many pairs of knitting needles?"

"Depends on the price," I said.

We had enough pfennigs between us to buy four pairs.

Happily equipped with our purchases, we checked the street again, rushed to reach the corner unnoticed, then carried on along the shadowy back streets, eager to distance ourselves from the red deserted town and its hidden menace. We walked fast to reach the spot on the main road from which there ran a path across the grassy plain to the woods. All-concealing woods, where one felt almost safe. But we did not make it on time.

Marching towards us from the opposite direction was a unit of the Hitler Youth, about twenty of them, in their brown uniforms, boys of fourteen and fifteen, too young to be conscripted, but too old to be left idle on Sundays.

We waited at the side of the road to let them pass. As they came level with us, their leader, a slightly older boy, shouted a command. In a flash, they all bent down, picked up stones and dry sods of soil and started pelting us. The attack was so sudden, our first reaction was to turn away and protect our heads with our bags, our hands, our arms. This moment of shock gained them time. We started to run, but they were already encircling us with a chant of *"Polishe Sweine"* and forcing us to cower beneath the rain of stones. I felt their impact all over my body. I felt trapped in this vast open field, with the distant forest hopelessly out of reach.

"Michal!" I cried out in despair.

He crouched right beside me, his arm protective across my back.

"Just watch this," he said, then shouted, "Franek, the leader!"

He left me with a lightening jump, but the falling stones prevented me from turning around to see more. I heard struggling sounds, groaning, then Franek's bellowing order, "Tell them to stop!"

A strangled cry, "Let me go!"

Franek's shout, "Only if they stop!"

Another strangled cry, "Stop, everyone stop!"

The chanting died down. When the last stone fell, we all got up and turned around. The leader of the brown shirts was lying flat on the ground, face down, with Franek and Michal sitting on him.

"Go home, all of you, or I shall twist his neck!" Franek shouted.

The youngsters, deprived of their leader, looked uncertain.

"Tell them!" Franek hissed, tightening his grip on the youth's wrists.

"All right…but let me breathe…" The youth managed a hoarse whisper, his face crumpled in humiliation and pain.

Franek and Michal released enough of their hold to enable him to sit up. In a voice shaking with anger, the youth called to his underlings, "You heard what he says…"

The boys began to walk away, reluctantly at first, then gathering speed. We waited in silence till they were out of sight.

Their leader showed no emotion when we made a tight circle round him.

"Stand up!" Stefan ordered with a firmness I had not heard before.

Michal and Franek pulled the youth to his feet.

"Are you proud of yourself?" Stefan asked.

The youth did not reply. He raised his head high, his prescriptive Aryan features set in arrogance.

"Look what your boys have done!" Stefan spoke with open disgust.

The youth looked skywards, avoiding eye contact with any of us. Stefan stepped closer. He was taller than the youth, his muscular arms fashioned by months of hard labour, were strong, intimidating. He sandwiched the youth's face between his palms and forced him to look at us girls.

We all had cuts and grazes on our arms. Bazylka's chin was oozing blood, Maryla had a raw three-pronged scratch on the side of her face, and I felt riddled with tingling pain where the stones had hit me.

"Look at them, look!" Stefan was angry.

The boy screwed his eyes tight shut.

"He needs a good hiding," Franek said in German for the boy's benefit, tightening his grip on the boy's arm. "He's a bully, and there's only one lesson for a bully like him. Give him a taste of his own medicine."

The boys came so close they formed a cage around the youth. I hardly dared to breathe.

"Right boys," Ludwik said in Polish so only we could understand, Ludwik with the gypsy-black curly hair, "when I give the sign, we do it all together. Punch him, kick him, beat him to pulp. Then, when we've finished, we can stand back and feel pleased. Really pleased with ourselves. Because, we'll be just like them!"

No one moved. I could hear the feint rustle of a breeze across the grass and distant bird calls in the forest.

Then Franek spoke. "You're crazy Ludwik. We can't let him go unpunished."

I felt the same. Pain and anger made me desire instant revenge.

"All right, then," Ludwik nodded, "who's going to start first?"

I wanted to hit out. I wanted to punch that hateful face. I wanted to return all the misery he had brought upon us. But even as my fury raged inside me, my clenched hands remained by my sides.

Franek and Michal released him. He opened his eyes and looked straight ahead as if we did not exist.

"Listen to me, boy," Stefan sounded stern. "What you do is wrong. It is criminal. Don't cross our path again. Ever. You'll be sorry if you do. I promise. Now go! And be a man, not some madman's lackey!"

We broke the ring and watched the boy walk away. At some twenty metres from us, he picked up a stone and threw it in our direction.

"Polish pigs!" he shouted. "You'll pay for this!"

Franek sauntered off kicking the ground.

"I don't believe it!" He was bitter. "How could we! How could we, just let him go?"

In the forest, in the illusory safety of its cover, we stopped to examine our injuries. They were superficial, but clearly visible cuts, raw patches, stinging, red, some bleeding.

"What's Holtzmann going to say about this?" Michal wondered aloud.

"Nothing much, I guess," Franek replied, blowing onto his scratched forearm. "He'll blame us, no doubt."

"Don't say that!" I protested hotly. I wanted justice. I wanted reassurance that this would not happen again.

Franek sent me a pitiful glance.

"He knows which side his bread is buttered on. And who could blame him? He's got a young family to worry about. Surely, you know we don't come first on his list?"

Of course I knew. But it was not a question of wanting special treatment, I just wanted him to be fair to us.

"Let's wait and see," I said, hoping with all my might, that for once Holtzmann would take our side.

As we approached the farm, we could see from the distance the black car, the curved side of its roof glinting like a blade in the afternoon sun. I sensed a current of anxiety pass through our group, then as if to negate it, Stefan said, "Perhaps it's just as well they're here. They can see for themselves."

They were waiting for us. Spitz and Blitz and Holtzmann. Between them stood another policeman, a hunk of a man and the leader of the Hitler Youth, the boy we had encountered barely half an hour before.

Herr Holtzmann stepped forward to meet us.

"What's this I hear about your behaviour? Intimidating a young boy?" I had never heard him so angry before. My stomach turned over. My insides felt watery.

Stefan held out his arms: cut, grazed, bruised. There was a raw, red patch on his left cheekbone.

"Just look at us, Sir, we were attacked with stones."

Herr Holtzmann examined each one of us with a slow, searching glance. He said to the Gestapo man, "See for yourself. This is not the way to treat the workers. We all need them."

The Gestapo man straightened himself to his full height. His eye-level came up to Herr Holtzmann's chin.

"That is correct," he enunciated each word precisely. "They are workers. You must not forget, and neither must they, that, that is all they are. Workers. Slaves. Expendable."

He turned to the boy, "Which ones?" he asked.

The boy, emboldened by his protector, walked up to our group and pointed his finger at Franek and Michal. The Gestapo man nodded to the big policeman.

My legs began to shake.

The policeman strode over to Franek, pulled him out of the line and punched him on the mouth. Franek's bag dropped scattering all its meagre contents, and before he could lift his arm for self-protection, another blow to his stomach sent him reeling to the ground. He doubled up and lay curled in a ball, as Blitz joined his colleague and together they began to kick Franek from all sides.

Everything inside me screamed and I hugged myself tight to suppress my screams. Franek, Oh Franek! And Michal! He'd be next! I felt myself balance on the edge of madness with the pain of it all.

"That's enough!" The command was as sharp as a cracking whip. Merciful. Severing my nightmare. It took me a moment to realise it came from Herr Holtzmann. The policemen stopped, like puppets pulled by string. They looked perplexed, uncertain.

Herr Holtzmann towered over the Gestapo man, his folded arms almost touching the other one's chest. He raised his hand and I caught my breath. He pointed to the long, deep scar that disfigured his face. His anger was barely contained, when he spoke.

"I received this fighting for our motherland. I fought for our people. I did not fight for this!" He thrust his arm in Franek's direction.

Herr Holtzmann was awesome. Blitz was terrifying. I feared them both in this state.

Blitz remained silent for a long time, just staring at Holtzmann. And all the time Franek lay on the ground curled, motionless.

Blitz made a strange move, pretending to push Holtzmann out of the way, when, in fact, he stepped out of Holtzmann's shadow and took central position between them and us.

"Herr Holtzmann," he said, "I could get very angry with you, for interfering with my command. But I'm a reasonable man. I can see that your thinking is temporarily muddled. I shall let this pass. But let me remind you, your workers have no status, except that of slaves. Don't give them ideas. And keep them in check. That is my order!"

He remained in the centre, like an actor on the stage expecting ovation, a small, thin man, with a cruel face, and a cold stare keeping us frozen to the spot.

Suddenly he raised his arm in a *"Heil Hitler!"* salute. His companions responded with mechanical promptness. We watched them clamber inside the car and drive off at great speed, as if in a hurry for their next assignment. All tension left me turning me limp and ready to fall in a heap beside Franek. A voice inside my head kept repeating "Michal's been spared" and I was pulled apart by relief for Michal and by anguish for Franek.

Herr Holtzmann shouted as if telling us off, "I've had enough dramas for today. Sort yourselves out and get back to your jobs!"

He turned his back on us and walked away inside the house.

Michal and Stefan helped Franek to his feet, holding him up while he made tentative steps. He was dazed, his movements were stiff and slow. His mouth was cut, bleeding down his chin onto his shirt. Staszek and Ludwik picked up all their bags.

Bazylka gave hers to Maryla saying, "I'd better go with the boys. Franek will need a compress on his mouth."

We went inside, Maryla and I, into our dark alcove, to tuck away our purchases under our beds. The house was quiet. Elise and her children often spent Sundays at her mother's in Treibach. Old Frau Holtzmann had been fetched earlier by her brother from Kappel. Yet out of habit we moved about furtively like mice.

As we emerged into the light in the kitchen I took a good look at Maryla. The long scratch on the side of her face stood out in swollen wheals. There were other smaller cuts and dark smudges from the soil. I must have presented a similar sight, for I saw her lips tremble and tears well up in her eyes. We clung to each other shuddering with grief.

"Why? Why?" Maryla repeated, her voice choked.

Hot tears stung my eyes then my raw cheek as they rolled down and seeped into the blue fabric on Maryla's shoulder. I needed them to flow and to take with them the unbearable ache.

After a while I released Maryla saying, "We'd better wash our faces. We can't let them see us in this state."

The cold water made us wince but we splashed it generously over our reddened eyes.

"That's better," I said, drying my face carefully with a towel, and checking my eyes in the cracked mirror above the sink, "they won't notice a thing."

Nobody did, when we climbed the wooden steps in the barn to the loft. They were too busy looking after Franek. He was lying down on his mattress undressed to his underpants, with a compress over his mouth. Stefan and Bazylka, crouching beside him, were applying ointment to his cuts and bruises. Michal, Staszek and Ludwik were discussing heatedly all possibilities of dealing with the leader of the Hitler Youth and regretting their missed chance.

Michal turned to me, his face dark with misery. "What rotten luck!" he said.

I knew instinctively he was racked with guilt over Franek's beating, when he had been spared.

"Michal," I said, "do you really think Franek would be hurting less if you'd got beaten too?"

His eyes looked tortured.

"We should have listened to Franek," he said. "We should have taught the little bastard a lesson. At least some of this would not have been in vain."

"Or it would have been worse," Ludwik said. "They don't play by the rules."

Stefan got up and held out the jar with ointment.

"All right everyone," he said, "just one dab on your finger. Apply it where you need it most. That's all we've got left."

As I stood deciding what to do with my meagre ration of cream, Michal said to me, "Can you have a look at the back of my right shoulder?"

We sat down on his striped mattress and he undid the top buttons of his shirt. I pulled the collar back, below where his skin was badly grazed.

As gently as I could I skimmed over the injury with my tiny blob of cream. He did not recoil as I had expected but remained still. I saw his skin come up in goose pimples.

"Don't stop," he begged, "it's so soothing. A moment of heaven in this hell."

CHAPTER 11

The days that followed were hard. Our flesh was tender to the slightest touch, our skin was covered in patches of dark purple and deep blue with shades of yellowing greens in between. The colours made me wonder. So pretty in nature, drawn out by the gentle coaxing of the sun, so ugly on our bodies, the shocking aftermath of a violent act.

Franek could barely move. Each mealtime became an ordeal as he balanced a shaking spoon between his swollen lips, tense with avoiding direct contact, that made his eyes water.

The boys did their best to cushion him against the worst of the jobs, and for the first few mornings presented Herr Holtzmann with suddenly discovered repair works on the various parts of the farm machinery, and in advance, praised Franek's outstanding skills as a mechanic. I did not think that Herr Holtzmann was fooled for a moment, but surprisingly he voiced no objections.

"As long as you hurry up and come up to help the others in the field," he would say to Franek.

Repairing machinery or grooming the two horses (another of Franek's jobs), though less demanding physically than the back breaking work in the fields, still required effort, so I checked on him between my own chores, as he hobbled around hunched in pain.

I saw him one morning, leaning over a metal bar in the open shed by the outbuildings. He had his face hidden in his folded arms. I put down the bucket of chicken feed and ran up to him as there was no one else about.

"Feeling faint?" I asked, tapping him on the shoulder.

He took a moment to lift his face, and when he did I saw wet streaks on it.

"It's not what you think," he said, "I'm not crying. It just all gets too much at times."

Poor Franek. He did not have to explain.

"I understand," I said. "It gets to us all."

"I'm not crying!" he insisted, "I'm just resting for a second."

A movement behind us made us jump. Our heads jerked. Another shock. A beautiful apparition in white and blue. Lilli. She had come round the back, unseen.

"I heard your voices," she whispered. "Here, take this, Franek. I know about the beating. Two tablets in the morning and two at night. It'll help. You'll see."

Franek's battered face lifted and his thick lips parted to formulate a reply, but she pressed a small round metal box into his palm and was gone.

He looked at me, dazed.

"Did this really just happen, or am I dreaming? Did I just see an angel?"

"Yes," I said and meant it.

Her kindness had won me over in our first encounter. Since then, though her errands to the farm had been infrequent, each time she came she smuggled things for us: real soap, real shampoo, real toothpaste. Once, as she passed by me, she dropped a bar of chocolate.

We made a feast of it that night. Hidden in the woods, sitting in a circle, five boys and three girls, we each broke a piece as we passed it round, as if we were sharing communion. With unbearable restraint I let this piece of chocolate melt slowly in my mouth. After months of sugar-deprived, insipid, repetitive diet of cabbage and potatoes, this was the best thing I had ever savoured in my whole life.

Lilli had access to things. She and a few other young girls, picked like objects for their decorative attributes by the Gestapo, had been assigned to serve them in the town's central hotel, which was now the military headquarters and a home for their families. They had their own excellent facilities, considering the shortages all round. Good food in their kitchen, an exclusive well-stocked shop, private tuition for their children and entertainment every night. What Lilli did was risky, but not impossible for someone as determined as she was.

Franek opened the small box. It contained enough pills for a few days.

"You'd better take two straight away," I said, anxious to go.

It was not safe to hang around. We were reminded daily that idleness was punishable.

Before limping off towards the tap in the yard Franek whispered to me, "Who can blame Stefan? She's quite a find. If only I could be so lucky!"

His words made me smile. I felt no jealousy, no resentment. I hoped, that one day, when the war was over and we were all free, Lilli could become the visible member of our group.

We had started to knit. Hats first. The least complicated shapes. Late every night for about an hour before bedtime, we would sit round the kitchen table, unwinding moth-eaten wool, tying together broken ends, saving the short, unusable strands, watch our knobbly knitting grow, comparing the lengths we produced each night. There was a spare pair of knitting needles, but none of the boys showed interest in attempting a skill that they considered womanly.

"They'll be begging to knit before long," Bazylka pronounced with conviction, clicking her needles furiously.

One evening Stefan joined us, after we had tidied up and were about to go to bed. The gentle coded knocking on the window, tap, tap, tap, long pause, several times in succession, signalled that it was one of our boys.

I let him in, he sat at the table and we huddled around him.

"Is there any news?" Bazylka asked, eager for all of us.

"No," he said simply, his eyes reflecting the dim light. "There's no change. All they ever broadcast are glorified versions of the German victories. They're determined to invade Britain. They are bombing London right now, as we sit here."

We were awed into silence. After a while Bazylka asked, "Do they say anything at all about the British?"

"Only what they want us to hear. Incredible numbers of casualties, destroyed buildings, shot-down aircraft, and so on, and so on…"

"Can this really be true?" Maryla clasped her hands, as if in prayer.

"God knows." Stefan raised his eyebrows, "Now, if we had a radio of our own, perhaps, and only maybe, we'd learn the truth."

"And Poland?" I wanted to know. "Any news from home?"

Stefan shook his head,

"The same old garbage about order and discipline and keeping everyone under control. There's talk of segregation and temporary camps."

"What does that mean?" I asked feeling my stomach harden with familiar anxiety. Images of my mother and my little sisters flashed through my mind. So far away. So unreachable.

"I can only imagine," Stefan said, "it's to simplify their own task of surveillance." Then as if reading my fear, he added, "Mainly in the cities and in towns. The countryside is simply too vast to be controlled all the time. But hey, listen," his tone lightened, "this is the reason I came tonight."

He pushed his hand into his trouser pocket and brought out a brown bundle that fell apart on the table.

"Stockings!" we exclaimed together in stage whisper, eager to feel the softness of the thick leg wear.

"A pair for each of you." He sounded pleased. "Hide them well. Find them again when the weather gets cold."

We stuffed them with haste inside our blouses. Ever watchful, ever wary, from habit.

"I feel sick with fear at times," Maryla whispered to Stefan. "Tell Lilli to save her help for emergencies."

"It's one big emergency all the time," Stefan replied. "She assures me she knows what she's doing."

"How can we ever repay her?" Maryla sighed.

Stefan shook his head. His smile was wistful.

"No need. One day, when we're out of here…there'll be time for everything."

CHAPTER 12

Thursday 29th August 1940. That day started for us, farm workers, like any other day, at dawn, with all the demands of the farm pressing us to hurry the moment we dragged ourselves off our mattresses.

It was later – days, weeks later – that isolated, seemingly insignificant moments began to emerge in my mind with ever-stronger clarity, as I went over the sequence of incidents that day, with obsessive repetition. It was as if I needed to look for clues that could have warned us, and not being able to find them, it was as if I needed to reassure myself, that nothing I did that day could have averted the course of events that changed our lives.

I remember the mist over the ground when Maryla and I lugged our churns, heavy with milk, to the crossroads. I remember thinking over the breakfast table, that Stefan's long and tangled hair needed cutting. I remember the comfort of Michal's shoulder against mine and Johann's deep voice on the other table, separate from ours, as he kept repeating one particular word a lot, that made Max laugh.

Later that morning, Maryla and I helped Johann and Max to harvest the plums, after our own jobs were done, shovelling the chicken and the pig muck onto the wheelbarrow and disposing of it in the cesspit behind the farm buildings, then washing all the tools clean for the next time.

I remember the stomach-cramping hunger at the sight of ripe plums. Masses of them, hanging in heavy clusters, pulling the branches down. I remember finally giving into temptation, picking one off the ground and popping it whole in my mouth. Then, the shock of Herr Holtzmann's words, as if magicked from thin air. "That'll be five marks off your pay."

I can still taste the bitterness of my hidden tears at his cruel words.

When he was gone, and Max and Johann were high up their ladders lost among the branches, Maryla crouched down beside me and together we segregated the fallen fruit: the undamaged for bottling into my basket, and the bruised plums for the pigs' feed into Maryla's sack.

"Anna," Maryla whispered, "tomorrow, when I mix the pigs' feed,

I promise you a feast of plums. And don't worry, they won't be the rotten ones."

Saying this, she grinned, her eyes as smug as a cat's, and opened her sack a fraction. Separated from the bad ones, and nestling inside a rag, were large, succulent plums.

Her childlike, mischievous act of defiance cheered me up immediately. I gave her a hug.

"Thanks, Maryla, but please, don't do it. It's too risky, and for what?"

"But we've got to get our own back on him," Maryla protested, her eyes huge, her look determined. She made me smile.

"Not this way," I said.

"What way then?"

I tapped my forehead.

"One place he can never get in. Inside my head. I can call him all the worst names under the sun and he can't touch me." I closed my eyes for a second feigning concentration. "There, I've done it! His ears must be burning like red-hot coals by now!"

Maryla gave me a mystified look.

"Is that it? Your revenge?"

I nodded.

"But what does it actually do?"

"It makes me feel better."

She shook her head, "No! I want more! I want his plums! And we shall have them!"

For lunch that day we had water, bread and cheese. I was glad it was not ham. There was never enough pink flesh on the slices to cut out between the green mould. I ate as much as I could, then saved some for later, pressing a lump of cheese inside a chunk of bread and stuffing this inside my pocket when old Frau Holtzmann was busy with Johann and Max. We all did that, in staggered moments. Constant activity produced constant hunger, yet times between meals were long.

The afternoon turned out exceptionally hot after the cool, misty start at dawn. Bazylka, Maryla and I were sent out to the cornfield, having been hurried first through our routine tasks around the animals, under Herr Holtzmann's frequent and impatient spot checks. He gave us a sack each with instructions to glean the field for any remaining corn between the stubble.

"And don't waste time!" he shouted after us, "I want this finished today!"

All harvest work was being done in a rush before the weather changed, but there was no fear of that happening that day. The scorching sun was ideal for drying the sheaves, grouped in stacks of six, dotted around the field.

We set about our work with nervous zeal, keeping close, three abreast, mindful of every strip as we plodded up and down across the field. All the stooping made my back ache, my head was dizzy in the heat and the unstoppable sweat felt like glue underneath my clothes. The rigid stubble dug into my flesh, leaving a criss-cross of cuts on my ankles and calves. I yearned for the cooling water of our bathing pool.

We finished well before five with a little time to spare before our evening jobs around the animals.

"We deserve a treat," Bazylka decided, wiping sweat off her face with the back of her hand. "Let's pick some blackberries."

The blackberry bushes were plainly visible among the trees on the edge of the wood, a few metres away. We looked around to make sure no one was coming to check up on us, then we ran across the clumps of grass as if this was a race.

The blackberries were the size of small plums, swollen with juice, irresistible.

We picked them in handfuls and gorged ourselves with exaggerated sighs of contentment, as if we were drunk.

"We'd better pick some for the boys," Maryla said after a while, her lips and her fingers stained blue.

She must have read my mind. I had thought of them, sweating it out on another field, and I had pulled out my rag, my ubiquitous rag, and shaped it into a kind of a basket, by tying knots on the four corners. We filled it up in seconds.

"Right, we'd better go," Bazylka said, always the boss, "before we're missed."

"Not so fast!" a male voice shouted. It was like a bolt out of nowhere. We glanced at each other in alarm then slowly turned around. Visible above the ferns were just a face and shoulders of a man. He held up a revolver pointing it at us.

Fear blanked out my mind, then after a moment a strange little thought began to jump up and down, like a small child demanding attention. He had only said three words, but they were familiar. Of course! He had spoken in Polish!

"Who are you?" I blurted out, astonished at my own boldness.

"You tell me first!" he ordered, still pointing the revolver at us. He was dark, dishevelled, with a few days' stubble covering his face. His mouth appeared toothless when he spoke.

"If you've been eavesdropping," Bazylka took over, "then you know we are Polish." She pointed to the yellow "P" on her shoulder. "You'll also know why we are here."

They stared at each other, neither giving way. I did not dare to breathe.

"Listen," Bazylka said first, "just let us go. And we've never seen you, all right?"

"No!" he shouted, "you've got to help me!"

He raised his revolver higher. We stood very still.

"Well?" he demanded.

"Well what?" Bazylka shouted back and crossed her arms. "One shot from your gun and everyone from the neighbourhood will come running. Is that what you want?"

I saw his hand waver.

"If you're a Pole, like us," she continued, "then you only have to ask."

Still holding up his revolver with one hand, he pulled at his open collar with the other. I noticed then that he was wearing his shirt inside out. The yellow "P" was facing his shoulder.

"For goodness sake!" Bazylka said, "put that thing away and tell us what you want!"

He dropped the revolver inside his shirt and I felt limp with relief.

"Please, come closer," he said, his voice suddenly, unexpectedly polite, almost begging.

We moved towards him, parting the ferns.

He was sitting on the ground with his legs splayed. His right thigh had a rag wrapped round it, over the trousers that were stained with blood, dry and brown.

"So what's your story?" Bazylka asked, kneeling down beside him, the nurse in her ready to act.

He caught her hand and moved it away before she touched his leg.

"Just bring me a sharp knife," he said, "I know what to do. And some food. I've lived on berries for the past few days."

I realised now he was not toothless at all. His teeth had been stained black.

"What's your name?" Bazylka asked.

"You can call me Tomasz. I'm from a farm near Rastenfeld. I was attacked. There was a fight. I won. That's all you need to know. And who are you?"

He studied each one of us in turn. With his dark, intense eyes. He was younger than I had thought at first.

Bazylka replied, "You can call us Beata, Magda and Aniela." She reeled off our new names with astonishing quick thinking. "We are from a nearby farm. Now let us go before we're missed."

He grabbed her hand with both his.

"Promise, you'll come back." There was real anguish in his plea.

"Of course, we'll come back," she answered sharply, yet her rough assertiveness was strangely comforting. "But not straight away. We've got jobs to do. It'll be after seven. Stay hidden in the bracken. Have these blackberries while you wait."

She gestured towards me and I placed my rag basket beside him. We emptied our pockets, leaving him our chunks of bread and cheese, saved from the lunch.

The look in his eyes haunted me as we ran back to the field, to our sacks filled with loose ears of corn. We lifted them over our shoulders and made our way down the field in great haste to make up for lost time.

"Not a word to anyone!" Bazylka admonished severely. "Not to Staszek, Maryla. And you, Anna, not even a squeak to Michal!"

"As if I would!" I was indignant. "What do you take me for? Aren't we in enough trouble already, the three of us?"

"I'm sorry," Bazylka's voice was unexpectedly softer. "Can you imagine the fuss if the boys found out?" Her breathing laboured under the weight of her sack. "It's just so scary! I can't bear even thinking about it, about tonight."

"We'll do it," Maryla said quietly, "we'll do it. We've just got to act normal and stay calm."

"Normal? Calm?" Bazylka repeated with undisguised derision.

"What other choice have we got?" Maryla asked, making it sound the most natural thing to do.

I remember that late afternoon going through the motions of all our regular jobs: milking the cows, settling the pigs in their huts for the night, rounding up the hens and locking them safely in their coops, sweeping up the dirt into heaps, ready for the wheelbarrow in the morning, while all the time my secret burned inside me.

It was only when we were away from the others, Maryla and I carrying the evening yield of milk to the crossroads, that I dared speak to her.

"I'm terrified, Maryla."

"So am I."

"We should never have gone to pick those blackberries. This is our punishment! We shouldn't have been so greedy!" I was serious, but Maryla laughed.

"Listen to yourself, Anna! That's nonsense! The blackberries were there. It was providence. Of course we should have picked them! What other treats do you get in this place?" Maryla stopped to change hands. Her fingers were stiff and swollen.

"What about *him*?" I insisted. "That was no providence. That's just one big headache for us!"

"His need is greater than ours," Maryla said. "Perhaps we were the answer to his prayers?"

Put like this it sounded so reasonable.

"I just wish," I said truthfully, "it had been someone else."

Bazylka had instructed me to, somehow, save some food for Tomasz, while I assisted old Frau Holtzmann with the evening meal. I felt sick with panic thinking about it. How could I force myself to remain calm, to be inventive, when Frau Holtzmann's eyes followed my every step, my every move? The only factor in my favour was Frau Holtzmann's limited mobility.

Indeed, when I came into the kitchen straight from my outdoor jobs, she was already settled in her big chair, at her table, where she shared her meals with Johann and Max.

"Hurry, Anna, hurry!" She was impatient. "They'll all be here soon!"

As if I did not know!

"One minute," I promised appeasingly, rubbing my filthy hands under running water, then splashing my sweaty face.

I dashed inside our dark alcove to find my towel. I took this chance to pull out a small piece of material from our sewing sack and stuffed it in my pocket. Rags were useful things to have at hand.

"What's taking you so long?" Her voice was tetchy.

"Coming!" I rushed back, opened the cupboard and took out our aluminium bowls and spoons.

"Your stew is ready," she said, when I looked inside our pot on the range. The stew was made up of cabbage and scraps of black bacon, that looked as if it had been smoked into bits of coal. Next to it was another pot, with the meal that Elise had cooked for her family and Frau Holtzmann's table. It was thick with vegetables and large pieces of chicken. I could have eaten the whole lot myself. I had not tasted chicken since I left home.

"Hurry Anna! Go! Time to slice the bread! And bring the rolls out for my table!" Frau Holtzmann rapped her knuckles on the hard surface making the cutlery rattle.

I rushed towards her to pick up the key, then I unlocked the pantry door and took refuge in the narrow space between the shelves, where she could not see me from her position. I filled her basket with rolls – soft, fresh-smelling, tempting-beyond-endurance rolls – then I began to slice the bread for our table; two dark, heavy, rye loaves. I forced myself to think, but from the jumble in my mind I was not able to pull out one clear, sensible thought. I looked up. Perhaps the small window high up could resolve my problem? Perhaps, if I unlocked it now, I could climb in later, after everyone had gone, and steal some food for Tomasz? Without further consideration I raised myself onto the stool and reached out towards the latch.

A sudden movement behind me made me look back. Elise was standing in the narrow doorway.

"What are you doing, girl!" Her anger was instant. My stomach felt watery.

"There's a fly…" I said, the first thing that sprang to my mind, "I'm just trying to let it out…"

"And let more flies in? Get down this minute! And get out of my way!"

I did as she ordered and waited at the door, calming the turmoil in my mind. I watched her fill her tray with food for her family meal in the parlour. Bread rolls, butter, cheese and sausage. All this in addition to the chicken broth in the pot.

I watched her delicate profile, her crimped neat hair, her slim figure, her small feet inside the dainty, high-heeled shoes, and I was baffled that someone so pretty could be so unkind.

As soon as Elise was gone, Frau Holtzmann shouted at me from her chair. "For goodness sake, Anna, get on with your work! And will you hurry up!"

I went back into the pantry, my frantic gaze darting around, noting, memorising. Elise had cut a quarter from the round flat cheese. If I cut a fraction more, would she really notice the next time she came back for more? There was no time to waver. I cut two thick slices, wrapped them in my piece of rag and hid the bundle inside my blouse, in the space below my chest.

I could hear Frau Holtzmann drumming her fingers to the rhythm of a waltz and humming a love song.

Now for the ham. It lay in a large cylindrical lump. It had not been cut. That was a problem, but the mouldy patches on it decided for me. I did not touch it. Above me hung a bunch of long, dry sausages. If I cut off a piece, that would be noticed straight away. I had no choice, but to cut off a whole one.

"Anna, what's taking you so long!" The love song turned into a shout of annoyance.

"Coming, coming!" I called back lightly, breaking the sausage into smaller pieces and pushing them inside the elasticated leg of my knickers, just above my knee.

I picked up the basket with the bread rolls and took it to Frau Holtzmann, placing it right in front of her. Her dull expression twitched, but her tone remained terse. "Now lock up the pantry and give me back the key!"

"Straight away," I answered obediently.

I went back for the bread for our table. I pushed two slices deep inside my side pocket and invoked the protection of all our guardian angels put together. I prayed for this ghastly evening to be over.

But the meal dragged. I felt sick with apprehension as I ladled the smelly cabbage into our bowls. I feared I might unwittingly give our secret away. I scanned each face as if seeing each of my friends for the first time, and at moments I even wondered if their friendly banter across the table was a cunning cover-up for what they already knew about us girls. The small bundle with cheese pressed against my ribcage and the rough dryness of the broken sausage scratched my thigh.

Michal sat next to me and described his day of hard labour as some kind of an adventure, his eyes sparkling, his smile eager every time I looked at him. All the while my face was stiff with the pretence of lively interest, while the only image dominating my mind was that of a man, who called himself Tomasz, alone in the forest, injured and desperate, helplessly dependent on the goodwill of three girls he did not know.

From time to time I glanced at Bazylka and Maryla and marvelled at how naturally they behaved. Had they forgotten, or had I dreamed the whole episode in the woods?

They had not forgotten. The moment the boys were out of the way and old Frau Holtzmann, who in theory was in charge of the kitchen, but had gladly retired to her room, Bazylka whispered, "Right! Not a moment to waste. Maryla, wash up quickly and dry. Anna, have you got food for him?"

"Yes, I have," I looked furtively at the parlour door, "just give me two minutes."

I dashed inside our dark alcove, pulled out my towel and my clean underwear from my bag under the bed, transferred all the provisions for Tomasz onto the towel, and rolled it all up, together with my underwear to make it look like my usual bathing kit.

I returned to the kitchen and helped Maryla finish tidying up. She filled a bottle with drinking water, and like me, wrapped it up in her towel.

We waited for Bazylka now, who was boiling a knife, with a sharp long blade and some long-nosed pliers, blackened with age, that she had found in the shed. At home my mother used to sterilise the needle with a naked flame for lancing blisters or boils.

Bazylka drained the water and picked up her tools with a clean cheese cloth, wrapping the whole lot in a strip of curtain fabric from our sewing bag. She fetched her towel and we followed her outside.

"Carry on walking," she instructed, "as if you were heading for the bathing pool. I'll just get iodine from Stefan."

Maryla looked scared.

"What will you say? How will you explain?"

"Trust me," Bazylka said, "I'll deal with it."

We reached the meadow and I sensed that Maryla's instinct, like mine, was to run, to get out of sight, to get this nightmare over and done with, but we forced our legs to a steady pace, giving Bazylka time to catch up with us.

When she did, Maryla almost cried, "Bazylka, tell me everything's all right!"

"Calm down," Bazylka gave her sister a reassuring hug, "Everything's fine."

"But didn't he ask?"

"No. He didn't actually." Bazylka raised her eyebrows as if suddenly puzzled. "He seemed distant. Pre-occupied. But if he had, I'd just show him my legs."

Our calves looked as if they had been scoured with a grater.

Perhaps at this point we should have involved Stefan, perhaps involving him would have changed the course of events. I shall never know. Our only concern at the time was to protect the boys from knowing things that could bring them harm.

In the gathering dusk the forest was already casting dark shadows. We had to move fast. We headed straight for the thick growth of bracken where we had left Tomasz. Bazylka called out his name softly. The tops of the ferns shivered and his head appeared above them.

"Thank God you're back!" His sigh of relief sounded like a sob, and suddenly, I was glad to be here with him.

We knelt down around him.

"Right," Bazylka took charge, "we've got to get it done fast, while there's still light."

He stopped her hand in mid air.

"We?" he asked. "No, leave this to me. I study medicine. I know what I'm doing."

"So do I," Bazylka said, "I'm a nurse."

There was a brief pause. I thought I saw interest in his eyes, a kind of recognition.

"All right," he gave in. "It seems you're the boss."

The boss? I thought wryly and my heavy mood leapt for the briefest moment at his unwitting remark.

"You do the iodine bit," Bazylka conceded, "and I'll do the rest. But I'll gag you if you scream!"

I watched with a turbulent mixture of concern and fascination as Bazylka untied the bloodstained rag from around his thigh and helped him to pull his trousers down. The wound in his thigh was surprisingly neat, a small black hole in a swollen, reddened, protesting flesh.

Bazylka examined it closely in the pencil-beam of her torch.

"I can see the bullet," she said. "Here Maryla, hold the torch for me."

She poured a little iodine onto a pad of gauze and handed it to Tomasz.

"On the count of three, right?" she said. "Now: one, two, three!"

He pressed it onto his wound, his face twisting in pain, his deep breathing suppressing his natural reaction to cry out.

"Close your eyes," Bazylka ordered. "Bite on this rag. I'll be as quick as I can."

Maryla shone the torch and I held back his shoulders against me with all my might. I felt his rigid tension, his heat. I could smell the sweat in his hair. I prayed, I begged for this to be over soon.

I held my breath when Bazylka raised the sharp blade, but then, with incredible swiftness she made a small incision in the tight skin around the wound and exposed the top of the bullet.

A strangled cry came from Tomasz and his shoulders pressed harder against my chest.

"Two more seconds," Bazylka whispered. She inserted the long narrow pincers into the wound, gripped the top of the bullet and pulled it out. I was expecting a torrent of blood to spurt out, but there was only a slow jelly-like trickle.

"You can open your eyes now," Bazylka said, showing Tomasz her trophy. She dropped both the bullet and the pliers inside her pocket. "Better not to leave anything behind. You could do with a jab and a stitch or two, but it's no use dreaming. I'll bandage it tight for you and the antiseptic will do the rest."

She used a long strip of the curtain fabric for bandage while Maryla opened the water for him.

"Have a drink. And some tablets. For the pain."

He followed Maryla's instructions in silence, his face glistening with streaks of sweat.

I tied his provisions inside the rag that was now empty of the blackberries, leaving him also some tablets for later.

"Show us you can walk," Bazylka said. "We don't want you collapsing now. After all the effort."

We helped him up to his feet and watched as he straightened himself and attempted a few unsteady paces. We stretched out our arms ready to catch him, if he fell.

"I'll manage," he said, turning round. "It won't be a sprint, but I'll manage."

He looked at us intently, as if memorising our faces. "What can I say? I can only pray that we meet again. In better circumstances. A million thanks!"

"Go!" Bazylka urged. "Go! And good luck, Tomasz!"

I felt a tightness in my throat as we watched him make his way into the depths of the forest, dragging his leg, holding onto the trees for support.

We could do nothing more. We had to go.

It was the briefest dip ever, in our little pool of cooling, invigorating water. We heard the boys coming up, even as we dressed hurriedly and wrapped our wet hair in towels, turban-like.

We met them half way down the hill.

Franek and Michal came up first, followed by Ludwik and Stefan. Staszek walked behind them all humming a song, which his constant singing had made familiar to us all. It was about a girl called Violetta, who died of consumption.

Franek whistled at us.

"Hi beauties! Our three graces!" he called out. "Wise girls always shower to be ready any hour!"

"We've got a poet!" Bazylka exclaimed in mock admiration. "If your poetry is anything to go by, then dream on, Franek, dream on!"

The boys laughed and Michal turned to me. "Are you knitting tonight? Shall we see you later?"

All I wanted to do was to hide in my bed and to sleep for a year. I wanted this evening and Tomasz to go away from my life, far and forever.

"Not tonight, Michal," I replied, and seeing his smile wane, I added quickly, "tomorrow, all right? I'm so tired, I'll drop dead if I don't get to bed soon."

"All right…" he agreed amiably, his brow puckering with concern. "You're not ill or anything like that?"

"No, no," I assured him, "just really tired."

He raised his arm as if to hug me, then, aware of the others, brushed his hair back off his forehead instead.

"Poor Anna. Go and get your beauty sleep."

His tone was like my mother's. My eyes began to sting.

All the heat from the kitchen seemed to be trapped in our alcove. I yearned for a gust of cool air, yet the absolute blackness made me feel secure and safe after this long and harrowing day.

"God help him," Bazylka whispered from her bed. "We did everything that we possibly could."

"Yes, we did," Maryla next to me, whispered back. "I can't stop thinking about him all alone in the forest. Where will he go? What will he do?"

"I'm sure he's got it all worked out," I whispered, desperate to comfort myself and my friends. "He just needs to find some good people on the way. Like the Neumans. Then he'll be all right."

"Yes!" Maryla agreed readily.

I pushed all other thoughts out of my mind.

The loud banging on the kitchen door woke us up. I thought I had been asleep for hours, but when I shone the torch at my watch it said twenty past midnight.

"God almighty!" Bazylka cried. "They've found him! Already! I don't believe it!"

Maryla and I jumped out of our bed and followed her in the dark to the door.

I heard her fiddle with the bolt then the door was pushed back and a large figure filled the door frame. A blinding light was flashed in our faces.

"Get out! All of you! Into the yard!"

Things were happening so fast I felt as if I was in a trance, inside some bad dream. We ran outside as ordered, stopping when ordered and huddled together, acutely aware of our state of undress. Just knickers and vests. After a minute or so my eyes began to pick out shapes in the blackness. To my surprise the boys were already there with Herr Holtzmann standing next to them. They, like us, must have been risen from their sleep unexpectedly, with no time to dress. Their naked limbs looked like pale streaks in the dark.

Surrounding them were six ink-black shapes, I guessed Gestapo men. A man on the side held onto two Alsatians that strained and panted and growled baring their fangs in readiness to attack.

My sickness returned. I felt trembly and weak.

"Right Holtzmann," the man in charge spoke, "I need to check that all your workers are present." He rustled a paper in his hand. "I'm not going to shine the torch. You know your workers. You call them out. I expect all eight to be here."

I experienced the lightest, most fleeting touch of relief. This was not about Tomasz.

He turned to us.

"Step out and form a straight line when your name is called out."

Herr Holtzmann began with Franek. Alphabetically.

"Dobosz Franek. Kolkiewicz Ludwik. Laski Staszek. Majerski Michal. Myszkovska Anna. Prodo Bazylka. Prodo Maryla."

We all stepped out one by one and formed a line.

"Sokolski Stefan."

There was no movement, no sound.

"Sokolski Stefan," Herr Holtzmann repeated.

Silence.

Herr Holtzmann came close to us.

"Where is he?" he asked. His voice was tense, sharp.

None of us replied.

"Franek, where is he?" He sounded very angry. I clenched my teeth to stop them chattering.

"Sir, believe me, I really don't know. We were all fast asleep."

The big bulk of the Gestapo leader stood next to Herr Holtzmann.

"This is bad news, Holtzmann. We come to search your farm for escaped workers from Durnfeld, and what do we find? One of your own workers missing. Bad management, Holtzmann. Not at all pleasing. Not at all."

Even in the dark I sensed Herr Holtzmann pull himself up to his full height.

"He's an excellent worker," he spoke up for Stefan. "There must be a good explanation for this."

"Yes, yes, Holtzmann. An explanation. He's done a runner. That's your explanation!"

He turned to his men and commanded, "Search the farm!"

For about a quarter of an hour we stood in silence, the rough cobbled surface beneath our bare feet, listening to the shouts of men and the vicious barking of the dogs, as they went through every single building on the farm. Lastly, they invaded the living quarters of the Holtzmann family. We heard the cries of the children, woken from their sleep, little Gaby and Bernard, and muffled protests from Elise. Herr Holtzmann swore out loud, and leaving us ran towards his house.

There followed a clamour of more swearing, yelling and screams, then I saw black shapes spilling out of the building and running towards us like fiends from hell. They surrounded us, their heavy breathing drowned by the shrill barking of the dogs.

The leader raised his hand and the dog trainer pulled back the two beasts, hitting them and shouting at them to be quiet.

The leader spoke to us.

"You need to be taught a lesson. For your lack of discipline. For your carelessness. For allowing a friend to be lost."

He raised his hand again.

The attack from his men came so suddenly, so ferociously, our boys had no chance to defend themselves. They were pushed to the ground and stifling their cries, they covered their heads with their bare arms, while the kicks and punches rained on them with uncontrolled fury.

We three huddled together helpless and petrified. The few moments seemed to go on for ever.

At last the leader called out for them to stop. The men straightened themselves and brushed down their uniforms.

"Let's go," he said. "Let's save our strength for the stupid bastards who imagine they can outwit us. They'll soon find out. When we catch them." His words were intended to terrify us more. They made my flesh creep.

They marched towards their black van, almost invisible in the dark, climbed in and drove off. Only then the boys began to move and get up slowly, stiffly to their feet, their groans like needles piercing something deep inside me.

Herr Holtzmann ran up to us from his house and shouted, "You stupid, bloody fools! All fools! Why did you let this happen! Now do you understand? I'll break his fucking bones when I see Stefan in the morning! Get out of my sight! All of you!"

My teeth chattered and my whole body trembled, making me ache all over, when I climbed into bed with Maryla. I clamped my hand over my mouth to stop myself crying. I could only imagine how badly beaten and bruised the boys were. Michal, dear Michal. I had not been able to do anything to protect him. Nor any of them.

"What rotten luck!" Bazylka whispered from her bed. "Everything happening at the same time! We should have warned Stefan. Told him to stay in tonight."

"You know we couldn't," Maryla whispered back, "we'd have had to tell him about Tomasz. He was safer not knowing."

"He's not very safe now, is he?" Bazylka agonised. This was torture for me. I raised myself on my unsteady elbow.

"Bazylka, we did what we thought was right. They don't know about Tomasz. They're not looking for him. And Stefan knows what he's doing. He'll wait for a safe moment. He'll be back before dawn." I lay down, hugging myself to calm down the agitation within me, and felt Maryla move up so that our sides touched. Strangely I found comfort in the closeness of her frail, thin body.

After a moment Bazylka whispered, "We'd better pray hard for Tomasz. I hope he's far away!"

I closed my eyes, willing my body to be still, and prayed for Stefan. I prayed for his safe return from Lilli and for his explanation to be convincing enough to diffuse Herr Holtzmann's wrath in the morning.

CHAPTER 13

There was a narrow ribbon of pale light above the horizon in the valley. The rest of the sky was menacing black with billowing clouds skimming the peaks of the hills, fragmenting and swirling up in contorted formations.

"God! That's all we need right now! A storm on top of everything else!" Bazylka complained.

We were at the tap in the yard, splashing away sleep from our faces, taking gulps of cold, refreshing water.

"The boys will have their work cut out today, for sure," she added, rubbing her wet hands up and down her skirt. Maryla and I did the same. There was no time for a good wash and towels.

We ran to the barn, eager for news of Stefan, and stopped at the half-open door.

"Anybody there?" Maryla called out. There was no reply. "Sweet Jesus," she said, "don't they ever sleep? Can you believe it? They've already gone!"

We dispersed, Bazylka to start milking the cows, Maryla to her pigs and I to my chickens. The wind rose. It whined in all the sheds and outbuildings and rattled loose slats and doors. The chickens screeched and ran around wildly in zig-zags, bumping into each other and fighting over the feed in their bowls. I pulled back the mesh-covered gate to let them out, to give them space in the orchard. There, the wind seemed to disturb them even more, whistling through the long stalks of grass and shaking fruit off the trees.

A distant rumble echoed down the valley. I ran inside the cowshed to help Bazylka milk the cows, glad to be out of the storm's way. Miraculously, the storm passed us by, but the low-hanging clouds remained, and the hot oppressive air.

Later, around seven, when the boys returned from the fields for breakfast, the kitchen was still cast in murky duskiness that blurred the edges of objects, blending them with shadows. The bruises on the boys' bare arms looked like stains. I stared hard into their solemn faces, desperate for news of Stefan. He was missing.

There was a hush in the kitchen, even on Frau Holtzmann's table. Johann and Max, usually robust, ate their breakfast in silence.

"Where is he?" I whispered to Michal, as soon as we sat down to our bowl of buckwheat.

"He never came back last night," Michal answered in whisper. My brain took a moment to absorb this information. Could it be true, then, that he and Lilli had indeed ran away?

"What, not at all?" I asked stupidly.

"No. Not a trace. Not a whisper." Michal kept his eyes down.

"Didn't he tell anyone where he was going?"

"He didn't have to. We assumed it was the usual."

I had a strange sensation. As if my heart dropped. Really dropped. I wished Stefan luck. And Lilli. But the thought of not seeing him again, for a long time, perhaps never, was like a sharp pang of loss.

I looked sideways at Michal. His sunken cheeks made him look vulnerable, like an orphan. The cuts on his knuckles were raw.

"You can have some of my cream later," I whispered, overwhelmed with sudden gladness to have him so close.

The quiet was unnatural, weighing down on us with the heavy, stuffy air. We all heard it at the same time, a car engine, distant at first, then the sound growing louder as it approached. We all exchanged questioning, alarmed looks. Johann and Max on the other table, and Frau Holtzmann too, stopped eating and listened, very still.

The car stopped in the yard. There was a pause then we heard footsteps clicking sharply against the cobbles before Spitz and Blitz walked through the open kitchen door.

"Tell Holtzmann we are here." Spitz spoke to Ludwik who was sitting nearest to the entrance. His big bulk, as usual, and his deep voice made the simplest instruction sound like a threat. But before Ludwik got up to his feet, Herr Holtzmann came through, closing the parlour door behind him, shutting off, protectively, his family.

"What now?" he asked, making no secret of his weariness. The scar across his face looked deeper than ever.

Blitz of the sleek, shiny hair and the bony, angular face, stepped forward.

"We demand your workers to present themselves at the police station in Kappel, at nine this morning. Promptly!"

Herr Holtzmann shook his head making a point of showing his disbelief.

"I can't let them go. There's work in the fields to be finished. Urgent work. Real urgent. It can't wait. Or the rain will ruin it all!"

Blitz allowed for a moment a theatrical pause, then, like an actor, he enunciated precisely, "This is an order. To be obeyed. There's nothing more to discuss!"

He turned abruptly with a swing of his coat, and left the room, followed by Spitz.

No one moved. Our eyes were fixed on Herr Holtzmann. He raised his clenched fists then dropped them.

"God! Good God! You watch and do nothing! I can't believe what's happening to this country!"

His voice was filled with so much anger, I shrank back instinctively against Michal. Herr Holtzmann looked round, at all of us. He did not shout. He said, "Let's finish breakfast quickly, and let's all go to the fields. We've got almost two hours. We'll gather in as much as we can. Just give yourselves enough time to walk to Kappel and I'll hold fort with Johann and Max till you get back."

We walked fast, all seven of us, along the country road, with wide, open fields on both sides. Above us, the clouds followed, agitated, grumbling, while the air around us crackled with pent-up electricity.

Freed at long last from the fear of being overheard, we wondered aloud and tried to guess what all this was about. We were further puzzled when we reached the first houses of the little town. Groups of people, some the inhabitants, some workers like us from other farms, were all walking in the same direction. We spotted our friends from Steinfeld's farm and quickened our pace to join them.

"Do you think this is the end of the war?" Bruno, the mouth-organ player asked Michal and me.

"If only," Michal replied, with a sudden lift in his voice, then pulled down by dejection he added, "more like new rules and regulations!"

Magda, Dorota and Voytek mingled with our group and exchanged news in hushed voices as we all hurried along.

The silence in the small square overlooked by the police quarters caught us unawares. It did not prepare us for the size of the crowd already gathered there; hundreds of workers like us, with the yellow "P"s glowing on hundreds of shoulders like buttercups in a meadow.

Against a blank wall on the other side of the square, a small wooden podium had been erected. On one of the jutting corners, on a solid wrought-iron stand, a brazier was burning, with a long iron rod stuck in the red-hot coals, visible to all.

The square was surrounded by armed police.

"Move over there!" one of them shouted, directing us into a space between the edge of the crowd and a wall.

"Sir," Ludwik made an attempt to explain, "we've been ordered to report at the police station!"

For his trouble he was butted in the chest, pushed and barked at,. "You'll go where I tell you!"

We were herded together and hemmed in by another group similarly shoved and pressed.

"I'm suffocating!" Maryla panicked, her bird-like shoulder squashed against mine.

"I'm right behind you," Michal said, his breath like a feather on the back of my neck.

Gradually the pressure loosened as people wriggled into their own tight spots. I felt prickly sweat in my armpits and on my head, underneath my hair. A pungent, sickly smell of unwashed bodies, bad breath, oozing sores and neglected illnesses rose and hung above the crowd, making every gust of wind a welcome, saving relief.

We did not dare move. We did not dare speak as we waited for the unknown. It could have been five minutes, or five hours, it seemed as if time had stopped. Overhead the sky thundered and intermittent flashes split the clouds.

Suddenly a shout ripped through the silence in the square. Then two shouts, then more, then the noise became a rhythmic, raucous refrain.

"*Polishe Sweine Hure!* Polish pig's whore!"

Maryla gripped my arm. We craned our necks to see more. Only then I noticed a large group of about sixty Hitler Youth surrounding the base of the platform. Their faces were red from the effort of yelling.

"*Polishe Sweine Hure! Polishe Sweine Hure!*"

For a second or two there appeared to be a disturbance at the foot of the dais, then two Gestapo men climbed up, dragging a prisoner between them. The man was naked to his waist. His back, his front, his arms were covered in long, bleeding wheals. His head had been shaved and his face was grotesquely distorted with enormous bruises and swelling.

Maryla whimpered into my shoulder. I felt her body shudder.

They pulled the man's arms behind him. They tied his wrists to the iron hooks in the wall.

The Hitler Youth's yelling rose to a frenzied crescendo, "Whore! Whore! Polish pig's whore!"

Another person was being dragged onto the platform. It was hard to tell at first that this was a woman. Dressed in a soiled coal sack, with holes cut out for her shaved head and for her arms, with her white legs exposed right up to her buttocks, she made a pitiful and disturbing sight. Recognition hit me. Suddenly. Like a hundred glass marbles smashing on my head. I closed my eyes. I felt weak. I prayed, I begged for this not to be true. I opened my eyes. There was no mistake. The prisoner in the sack cloth was Lilli. Then… the man next to her…the man with the mutilated face…

I held back my scream. I felt Maryla cling to me. My mind was doing strange things. Flashing images, hundreds of them. Moments with Stefan. With Lilli. Beautiful Lilli. A fair-haired princess. Stefan. The perfect Aryan boy. An angel.

A wave of movement rippled through the crowd. There was one more person on the podium now, a big, muscular man, possibly the village smith. He got hold of the cool end of the metal rod and pulled it out of the burning brazier. He held it up for us all to see, the metal "P" at the other end, glowing red.

The shouting of the Hitler Youth increased. I could not bear to watch, nor could I bear to look away. One of the guards held Lilli fast against him. Her flailing arms were no match for his strength. The other caught her shaved head between his powerful hands and forced her face up. The end of the hot branding metal hovered above her, centimetres above her left cheek, then the smith's arm came down.

If Lilli screamed, I did not hear her screams. The clamour of the mob drowned all other sounds in the square. The clap of thunder incensed them to yell even harder.

The guards let go of Lilli. She flopped down to the floor, and lay crumpled, lifeless.

Stefan strained from the wall, his taut muscles sharply outlined, his racked arms stretched to breaking point. His battered face became my pain and the cry from his lips my cry, as I stood helplessly watching.

A sudden blast shook the square. Mightier than the yelling of the mob, more deafening than the thunder above us. It tore through my body, shaking every nerve, every bone. Then all went quiet. I watched stunned, as Stefan slumped forward and hung by his outstretched arms. His chest was one massive open wound and the wall behind him was spattered with his blood. No one rushed to untie him, to lay his body down in peace and dignity. They left him half suspended, half supported by his bent, lifeless legs, as a lesson to us all.

Fearfully, I looked up behind us. On the flat roof of some official building were the men of the firing squad, six black shapes etched against the stormy sky, with their guns pointing at the square. I cowered into my tight space. I felt people pressing around me. I felt large heavy drops fall on my head, on my shoulders, saturate my clothes, and I willed heaven to open and I willed a flood to wash everything away, like a chalk image off the pavement.

PART 2

MARCH-OCTOBER 1941

CHAPTER 14

I knew the precise moment when the boil on my left calf burst open. I felt the sticky wetness ooze beneath the blanched cabbage leaf, used as poultice. The immediate relief from all the throbbing that had tormented me all night, was like a dizzying, overwhelming weakness. I grabbed the bedpost for support, panicking I'd drop Elise's cup of hot milk and honey. She lay propped against a stack of white pillows, her face grey, her crimped hair flat and oily. I could not help thinking, with a twinge of guilty satisfaction, that in adversity, the haughty, elegant Elise looked no better than the rest of us.

She had the influenza, and having packed off her children to her mother's in Althoven, she was fighting the illness with all possible home cures.

"Don't faint on me, girl!" her feverish eyes flashed. "We can't all be ill at the same time. I need you to do my work. *Mein Gott!* You can't depend on anyone these days!"

It was a wonder she spoke to me at all.

"Don't worry, I'll do all your work for you," I assured her, watching her sip her drink. "It's only my leg giving me pain. It's never recovered from the frostbite. Third boil this winter."

I waited till she'd drained the cup. She lay back on her pillows, then turning away from me, she spoke over her shoulder, "Don't talk to me about your boils. I've got enough worries of my own. Now go away! Start getting lunch ready!"

I let go of the bedpost, allowing my bad leg to take some of the weight. A spasm gripped where it hurt most, but I carried on patting and pulling the eiderdown around Elise, envious of her surroundings, of the comfortable pine bed with its carved head-board, of the crisp curtains catching the brief winter sun, of the warm glow across the cream walls, across the polished pine floor. So different from our cupboard-size room, a perpetual dark hole, never reached by the sun.

I willed myself to move fast down the stairs, every step sending a sharp pain to my calf. I could hardly wait to take off my stocking, to unravel the rag, to examine my boil-eaten flesh, but Frau Holtzmann was already seated at the table, preparing vegetables for the Holtzmanns' pot.

"Hurry up, Anna!" she scowled at me, her bulbous fingers clumsy with the knife. "Don't expect me to do your work for you!"

"I'm just coming," I said with feigned eagerness, "but I've got to see to my leg. The boil's just burst!"

She did not look up, all her frowning concentration fixed on the potato in her hand.

"Your leg won't drop off," she scolded. "It'll wait, but this needs doing now!"

So I scrubbed my hands with carbolic soap and set about scraping the carrots and the parsnips, all the while thinking about my leg. As if the chilblains on my fingers and toes were not enough, chilblains that drove me mad with itching. Or the frostbite on my calf. I could never have imagined that one unfortunate slip, one fall on the only wet patch by the tap would be the start of so much misery. The burning sensation, the redness, the swelling, the skin flaking that went on for weeks. Then the plague of boils.

"It's your system fighting back," had been Bazylka's verdict, as she prepared poultice after poultice, blanching cabbage leaves in boiling water.

Frau Holtzmann's terse reminder tore into my thoughts.

"And don't forget the washing! There's also a pile of ironing you should have done yesterday!"

I should have done many more things yesterday, but the days were never long enough and my strength totally used up every night.

"I'll be ready in a tick," I promised, dicing all vegetables and placing them with pieces of chicken in a pot to simmer on the range.

I pulled on an extra cardigan that I had knitted with the moth-eaten wool. I wound extra rags around my feet, before leaving the warmth of the kitchen. The laundry room was next door, accessible only from outside. Its bare brick walls and the concrete floor kept the temperatures below zero. There were icicles hanging from the top of the window.

I brought with me a kettle of boiling water to make the washing bearable to my chilblained hands. The pre-soaked whites did not need much rubbing on the washing board; they were mainly bed linens and Elise's nightgowns. Underneath her things, I had hidden our underwear to soak; Bazylka's, Maryla's and mine. The pain in my hands penetrated to the marrow in my bones as I rinsed and squeezed. I wrapped them in rags before lifting the tub and taking the washing out to one of the open sheds, where the wind could blow freely at the washing line.

Afterwards, the warmth in the kitchen, the thawing in my fingers made my eyes water, but I looked the other way when I walked past Frau Holtzmann to the utility cupboard. I fetched out a thick blanket and covered our large table with it. I placed the iron on the range and while it heated I spread out flat the garments to be ironed. Frau Holtzmann dozed off watching me ironing, but the moment I folded the last pillowcase she opened her eyes.

"Time to get lunch." Her tone implied that I was already late.

I prepared lunch for our table, the usual: dark rye bread, cheese, mouldy ham and water. I longed to taste food that tasted like my mother's food. I had vivid dreams about boiled new potatoes with butter and dill. I could recall the fresh smell of cucumber salad, with lashings of cream, as if it had only just been made. And the crunchiness of roast pork. And the tea. Just a glass of sweet tea with a slice of lemon. The very thought of these things made me want to howl with longing.

I heard them outside, stamping their feet by the kitchen door to shake off the snow, men coming in from their work in the forest, with Bazylka and Maryla preceding them, wrapped up in layers of knitted shawls, looking like old babushkas.

There was an extra person on Frau Holtzmann's table. His name was Horst. He had been appointed by the Gestapo to keep an eye on us. All neighbouring farms had a man like him, and all contact with our friends had been forbidden. No one knew what had happened to Lilli after that fateful day.

Horst was in his middle thirties with pale blond cropped hair, pale eyes, protruding like a frog's. I hated the way he would observe us from beneath his heavy eyelids. All conversation stopped when he was around. Even Johann and Max ate their meals in silence and responded to Horst with just a nod. Only Frau Holtzmann appeared unaware of the tension around her and prattled to Horst about some minor incidents in the village and all recent gossip. Surprisingly, Horst listened and asked her to repeat particular names, which she did eagerly, pleased with her suddenly discovered self-importance.

We listened at our table and communicated with meaningful stares and raised eyebrows.

Michal sat next to me on one side, with Maryla and Staszek on the other. Then Bazylka, Franek and Ludwik. There was no gap where Stefan used to sit, yet we all felt his absence. I caught myself often looking up at the slightest sound in the yard, thinking it was him. Seven months after that dreadful day. I looked for him in the barns, in the sheds, around the outhouses, expecting him to come out, to walk towards me with that easy smile of his, with news from the world beyond our farm.

"How's your leg?" Michal nudged me.

"Not a pretty sight," I whispered, instinctively tucking it underneath the bench. "I've been assured it won't drop off." I looked sideways at Frau Holtzmann.

Michal smiled to show he understood. His nose and his cheeks were red and flaky, there were sores around his mouth. We all had skin ailments, we all looked like scarecrows in our rags. I longed for the summer, for a good soak in the forest pool.

Bazylka, Maryla and I had knitted hats and mittens for us all out of the moth-eaten wool.

"Do you wear your mittens?" I asked, looking at his chafed, swollen fingers.

"All the time," he said, spreading his hands to demonstrate their agility. "The mittens you've knitted for me are my favourite things."

This made me smile. I knew he said this to please me. And it did. I was always pleased when he was around. I could not stop wondering what was going to happen to us after the war. There were questions, so many questions I wanted to ask, but it was not easy to find the time or the place for intimate talk in our perpetual group existence. The boys had been moved to the storeroom above the kitchen during the winter months. None of us were ever alone at night time, and during the working hours we were constantly supervised.

I was aware of his warmth against my arm, and I was curious to know if he had feelings for me, the way I had grown to feel for him. I was surprised at myself, at the shift in my expectations, at how the handsome stranger of my dreams, destined to fall in love with me, had been replaced by Michal; Michal with the brown eyes, cracked lips and red hands. Strange how these very things had endeared him to me, had made him special, non-exchangeable.

We heard the sound of the car engine as we got up to return to our set tasks. We stood still and listened. Spitz and Blitz' visits, though frequent and familiar, had lost none of their inherent threat. My stomach churned as we waited for them to come inside.

Herr Holtzmann, who had been eating alone in the parlour, must have heard them too. He strode in at the same time as they entered through the kitchen door.

"Heil Hitler!" Spitz saluted. Horst jumped up from his table and returned the salute with great fervour. Herr Holtzmann acknowledged them with a nod.

"What is it this time?" He made no secret of his irritation. This amused me and terrified me at the same time.

Blitz came forward and took off his hat. Then slowly, he pulled off his gloves, one finger at a time, making us wait. He examined them, flicked off some imaginary fluff on his sleeve, then walking past Herr Holtzmann, he stood on the step in the parlour doorway, thus making himself taller than any of us.

"Holtzmann, I need two of your workers," he announced, and before Herr Holtzmann had a chance to utter one word, Blitz glared past him at us, and at random pointed at Ludwik and me.

"You and you. Pack your bags. You're coming with us!"

His words did not sink in straight away. I remained still, not understanding.

"Did you not hear me, you two?" Blitz spoke sharply. "Get a move on! Now! I'm not used to being kept waiting. *Schnell! Schnell!*"

My stomach contracted, dropped.

Herr Holtzmann moved towards Blitz, his face threateningly close, his folded arms rigid across his chest.

"Just one moment, what's the meaning of all this? I can't spare any workers. Surely you can see that yourself."

Blitz raised his polished face higher.

"You're lucky, Holtzmann, to have so many. Some farmers have no help at all. I want these two to be packed in five minutes!"

The two men stared at each other, as if this was a contest of the longest, unblinking stare. Holtzmann spoke first.

"Where will you take them?"

"Kestner's farm. In Walburgen near Eberstein. Does that meet your approval?"

Blitz' thin lips formed into a sneer, but Herr Holtzmann ignored this with a terse question, "So, what's Kestner done with his workers?"

Blitz stepped down and walked past Herr Holtzmann close to us. His eyes glinted malevolently as he stared at each one of us in turn.

"They are on the run," he said, "but when they are caught…" he looked at us, "you'll be thanking God on your knees, you're not one of them! Now! No more time wasting!"

I was aware of a movement beside me, then Michal spoke out, "Herr Holtzmann, please, let me go in Ludwik's place. I've promised Anna's family, I'd look after her."

I held my breath. I kept my eyes down. I heard Herr Holtzmann's reply, "I don't want any of you to go. Herr Commandant, is there no other way of dealing with this matter?"

125

"We already have," Blitz said. "It's been decided. The workers I've picked are coming with us. That's the end of the matter. We'll wait in the car. Five minutes. Sharp!"

He and Spitz went out.

I felt numb. This was happening to someone else, not me. Michal put his arms around me, and for the briefest moment held me close. His clothes were rancid. Maryla hugged me, her eyes moist, her nose sniffly. I felt Bazylka's hand on my shoulder, I saw the boys' faces, bewildered, angry.

"Come on, Anna," Ludwik said, "We've not got much time. Let's go, collect our things."

I followed him like someone in a trance.

There was nothing for me to pack. All my possessions were permanently kept in my canvas bag under my iron bed. I picked them up and returned to the kitchen.

Horst was already ordering everyone outside, except for Maryla, who had been assigned to take my place in the kitchen. There were red patches around her eyes.

Michal stopped in the doorway and called over Horst's shoulder, "Anna, I won't leave you… I'll find a way…" He was not allowed to finish. Horst shoved him outside and I looked away, unable to bear the torment in Michal's eyes.

"Herr Holtzmann, I'll go upstairs to tell your wife," I said to my master, who had not moved from his spot. He was lost in his own thoughts and took a moment to realise I was speaking to him.

"I'll come with you," he said.

Elise must have heard the commotion downstairs. She lay propped against the stack of pillows, her wide-eyed alarm turning to a whinge as she spoke. "What's going on?"

"Anna and Ludwik have got to go," Herr Holtzmann said flatly. "Gestapo orders. They're short of workers on another farm."

Elise's mouth began to tremble.

"But we can't let this girl go! We can't! What'll I do without her? What's going to happen to me?"

Herr Holtzmann looked weary, his scar darker, deeper than ever.

"There are others," he said, "I don't like this any more than you do."

"But I want this girl to stay, this girl!" Her voice rose hysterically. "Don't you understand? Do something! Now!"

He turned away from her, pulled out a drawer and took out some documents.

Arbeitz Buch and *Karten*. Yours and Ludwik's," he said to me, handing me our papers.

Elise hid her face in the pillows and sobbed, her shoulders shaking. Wonders never cease! Elise who had treated me like dirt, crying for me to stay! I slipped out, leaving them together.

Downstairs, I picked up my bag, and as I hugged Maryla, I whispered the first thing that came to my mind, "Nothing is forever… Perhaps in the summer…"

She shook her head, "I think God has forgotten us…"

Frau Holtzmann cleared her throat. She was still sitting at her table, escaped long streaks of grey hair hanging down one side of her face.

"Auf Wiedersehen, Frau Holtzmann," was all I could force myself to say. I could not say I'd miss her. I could not say it had been a pleasure working for her. But she surprised me.

She held out the pantry keys, saying, "Cut some bread and sausage for yourself and Ludwik. It may be hours yet, before you eat."

I followed her instructions eagerly, and when I returned the keys I meant what I said. "Thank you, Frau Holtzmann. I hope I can return your kindness one day."

She kept her gaze down on her chubby hands, entwined and resting on her enormous lap.

The car sped bumpily along the dirt track taking us away from the farm. Ludwik, his arms cradling his bag on his knees, looked ahead over the shoulders of Spitz and Blitz, two black figures, their silence hard like a prison wall around us, but I twisted in the back seat, desperate to catch the last glimpse of anyone who was my friend, my substitute family. Michal or Maryla. Bazylka, Franek, Staszek. The numbing shock of what had just occurred had rapidly changed into an overwhelming grief. And anxiety. Pressing, crushing me like a boulder inside my chest. I gritted my teeth to stop myself crying out. I stared hard, till my eyes were dry, till they began to sting, till I needed to blink. But if I blinked I could have missed a farewell wave of a hand, a shake of a rag in the air. There was no sign of life back at the farm. The drab buildings stood solid against the greyness of thick snow clouds.

Spitz stopped the car at the small local station in Althoven, then turning round to face us, he gave us two train tickets.

"These will get you to Walburgen and no further. You'll travel south as far as Launsdorf. There you've got to change trains for Bruckel. You'll stay on the train till it gets to Walburgen. There you get off and ask for directions to Kestner's farm in Winkler."

I relied on Ludwik to remember all this.

"Is it very far, Sir?" he asked.

Spitz' orange eyes fixed him with a suspicious stare, and for a moment I did not think he was going to reply.

"Not far at all," he said. "Only about six kilometres as the crow flies. But the train can't go over hills and mountains. It takes a couple of hours on the circular line."

Strangely his words gave me comfort in knowing that our friends whom we were leaving behind would not be very far.

As we made a move to get out of the back seat Blitz shifted his position and raised his leather-clad arm, his finger pointing accusingly at us.

"A warning," he said, his eyes like black glass in his deep eye-sockets, "no clever ideas, do you understand? We always win in the end. There'll be someone waiting for you in Winkler."

They left us standing on an open platform by the railway line, two scarecrows in soiled and tatty overcoats, in pull-on hats made of knotted wool, with rags wound round our legs against the cold. The few people there, waiting for the train with us, stood well away, and though I did not look at them directly, I sensed their curious, furtive glances.

The cold descending upon us from the slate-coloured clouds was unbearably raw, penetrating to my fingers and toes. My calf was sore, every movement reminding me things were not pretty underneath the cabbage leaf, tied over the boil. I could only imagine the bloody mess seeping out into my stocking, making it scratchy where it dried. Now, I'd have to wait till the evening, before I could throw it all off and bathe my leg clean.

"Let's run away," Ludwik whispered in my ear.

This made me jump, but his smile was mischievous.

"Don't joke, Ludwik," I hissed, "I feel quite sick enough already."

His smile faded, his dark eyes became serious again.

"I'm sorry, Anna, it's just…all this… It's enough to make you want to slash your wrists. We've got to fight back. Any way we can. Don't you agree?"

His eyes burned into mine, begging to agree with him, but I was tired, so tired of the constant pretence of being strong, of taking in my stride each new blow meted out to us.

"What do you suggest we do?" I asked, not caring what we did. Everything was such an effort. Thinking. Feeling. Simply existing. If I could change into one of the clouds above us, I could come down in thousands of fragments, melt, vanish, never feel pain again.

"Anna! Listen!" Ludwik's voice was urgent. "We mustn't let them win. Think of anything but them. Anything that will make you feel better!"

"Like what?"

"Like your home, your family, your friends... Anna, do I really have to prompt you? Tell me for a start all the things you're going to do when we're out of this hell!" He sounded exasperated. Why was he asking so much of me! I was hardly able to formulate one coherent thought, let alone play silly games with him.

"What's the point, Ludwik?"

"The point is," he persisted, "that any thoughts we have of the future are better than what we have now. Agreed?"

"Agreed," I muttered, to be left in peace.

We stood close, needing to huddle for warmth, but afraid to appear over-familiar.

The train chugged slowly into the station amidst puffs of smoke and wafts of sulphur. We climbed on expecting to stand unobtrusively away from other passengers, but the train was half empty. We settled down by a window, facing each other, our bags nestling between us and the window frame. Ludwik wiped the mist off the pane with his sleeve.

"This is bliss," he said, though the train was not heated. "Now Anna, you start first, and it better be a long story. We've got lots of time to kill." His worn face lit up with interest.

I was suddenly shy. Exchanging intimate thoughts with Maryla had been natural, spontaneous, but this was different, though I knew Ludwik well. Ten months of enforced group living had made us all very much aware of each other's habits, mannerisms, sayings, needs, preoccupations. Nevertheless I was not prepared to bare my thoughts to him.

"There's not much to tell, and anyway it's all so very ordinary," I said.

"I don't mind. I'm listening. Tell me about your family," he leaned forward, encouraging.

So I told him of my mother, of my two younger sisters and of my three brothers, of my father's sudden death of a heart attack, when the youngest, Marysia was only a few months old. Ludwik listened intently, his eyes never leaving my face.

"How did your mother cope?" he asked.

"Grandma Alice and Granddad Adam," I said, "we'd have been lost without them."

He nodded, adding, "And now this... Crazy isn't it?"

It started snowing and for a while we watched large snowflakes flying in their hundreds against the window pane and disappear instantly as they melted. There was something soothing about the movement of the white weightless swirls as well as in the rhythmic movement of the train. I felt calmness returning to my tense aching shoulders as I let myself relax against the wooden back rest.

"And what about your future?" Ludwik was persistent. "What are your plans?"

"Plans?" I shook my head. "I may just as well dream of growing wings. Wouldn't that be great, Ludwik, if we could change into geese and fly away…"

He smiled wagging his finger comically, as if to say, I told you so.

"Who knows what's possible if you really put your mind to it. Go on, Anna, tell me about your dreams."

It was hard to resist his tenacity, so I told him.

"I don't want much. Jut a peaceful life. And a good job. And enough money to buy my mother things… And things for my sisters…" I trailed off. "But how possible is that?"

"It's all possible, Anna, once we're out of here!" he stated with fervour. "Tell me, what work would you like to do?"

I did not have to think about this one.

"Work for a fashion house. Make beautiful clothes."

"What's the most beautiful dress you'd like to make?"

I looked at him twice to check he was serious.

"Do you really want to know?"

"Of course I do," he smiled. "Julia, my girl, is never happier than when she drags me around all the dress shops."

"Ludwik…" My mind was suddenly flooded with images of muslin and chiffon and silk, and long flowing skirts as alive as butterflies chasing each other. Something stirred in my chest like a shiver of anticipation. "Ludwik, there are so many dresses, so many styles I want to make. Greta Garbo. Pola Negri. Have you seen what they wear? I've made sketches of evening gowns I'd seen on films. I collect fashion pages from our newspaper. Suits, blouses, skirts. I could copy any of them!"

"We'll have to visit you then, Julia and I," he laughed softly.

"I'm serious, Ludwik, I can really do it!" I said.

"I know," he answered, and suddenly, all my previous resentment at his irritating doggedness vanished in an instant. And suddenly, I felt strong, warm empathy with him, noting the dry skin around his nostrils, dry skin like dandruff around his black eyebrows, the white flakes like dots sitting on his eyelashes, his teeth, strangely perfect between his cracked lips. Gone was the swarthy look that had earned him the nickname of "Gypsy" last summer.

"Ludwik," I said, "I won't whinge again. Now, you tell me about your family, your plans."

His father, as I already knew, was an engineer in bridge construction, his mother a maths teacher. He had two younger brothers, Marek and

Dariusz. His girl, Julia, studied law at the same university as him in Katowice.

"That's to keep me on the straight and narrow," he added with a twinkle, "and I want to go back to finish my studies. In engineering. I want to follow my father. Design bridges and travel around the world…"

The conductor came at this point. I guessed it was the sight of us and the stink from our rags that hurried him along after just a cursory glance at our papers.

We changed trains at Launsdorf, after half an hour's wait on the draughty, open platform, and arrived in Walburgen late afternoon. It had stopped snowing but the clouds remained dark in the early dusk. We asked one of the passengers, alighting with us, for directions to the Kestner's farm. The way was straightforward, about a kilometre along the main road to Eberstein.

All around us lay snow-covered fields, rising from the valley in naturally fashioned terraces. There were dwellings dotted above one side of the road, their blacked-out windows, like sinister eyes watching us. On the other side, the fields undulated upwards towards dense forests, beyond which, I imagined our friends going about their jobs on Holtzmann's farm. The frozen snow crunched under our feet, where it had been shovelled back from the road to form a rough ridge.

"A hot, sweet, lemon tea…" I sighed with longing.

"One day soon," Ludwik, ahead of me, spoke over his shoulder. "One day soon, Anna, you'll have pots of tea. Buckets. Barrels. Vats…" He was doing it again, humouring a disgruntled child.

"Just one glass is all I want," I said.

The man, a policeman, was waiting for us by the roadside, at the start of the dirt track that led to the Kestners' farm.

"You two from Holtzmann's farm?" he asked. He was tall, well built, with angular features.

"That's right," Ludwik said.

"Then follow me."

We followed in silence, only our clogs making rasping noises against the hard surface of the compacted ice and frozen mud. The track led us down into the valley, across a railway line and along a wooden bridge over a stream, frozen now, before sloping upwards towards the Kestners' farm. The farm buildings sprawled along a wide ledge on the side of the hill, just below the forest. The middle yard was smaller than the Holtzmanns', with a pond beneath the bare, wide-spread branches of a chestnut tree. The family home had yellow stucco walls, blackened with age at the base, the windows were set back and additionally protected by wooden shutters. The deep roof over the attic rooms had wide eaves that extended to form a two-foot cover right around the building. The house looked solid, secure, but it was not my home.

The policeman led us straight to one of the barns and pushing back the door, beckoned to us to go inside. The strong smell of the cow dung filled my mouth and stung my eyes. A herd of oxen and bulls, lined in individual pens, was sheltering indoors through the bad weather. Three men were scraping the ground around the animals with rakes.

"Jozef! Jozef!" the policeman called out.

A man of about sixty, tall and wiry, with thick white hair, propped his rake against the metal barrier and came over to us.

"We've been expecting you," he said, his eyes wandering curiously over Ludwik and me. "I'm Herr Kestner, what are your names?"

We introduced ourselves. Ludwik Kolkievicz. Anna Myszkovska.

"Right Ludwik," Herr Kestner said, "drop your bag in the corner over there and help Anton and Gerhart. We've got enough work for an army."

He looked at me. "And you, Anna, you come with me."

The familiar, sinking feeling returned in an instant. I latched my gaze on Ludwik, but he was already walking away towards the other two men. I followed Herr Kestner and the policeman outside. They shook hands.

"I'll be off then," the policeman said, "I'll be back tomorrow." I noticed his motorbike parked under the tree.

Herr Kestner led me to the black-painted wooden building next door. It was the cowshed, with about twenty cows standing in a row. I could not see the two milking women at first, only when they got up to milk the next cow. They were muffled in layers of thick clothing, their faces hidden except for their eyes.

"Umtraut!" Herr Kestner called out.

The taller one left her stool and the milk bucket, and uncovered her face. At close quarters, I saw with a shock, how bony she was. Her eyes were sunk so deep, that her brow was like a canopy above them.

"You can take over from me now," were her first words to me, "I've got to go now. Someone's got to prepare the supper. What's your name?"

"Anna. Anna Myszkovska."

"I'm Frau Kestner. And when you finish milking, Frieda," she pointed at the other woman, "Frieda will show you to the pigs' huts and the sheep barn."

I desired a hot drink more than anything, but I dropped my bag by the door and looked around for the bucket with the disinfecting wash. I pulled off my mittens, washed my hands and took Frau Kestner's place by the flank of the next cow to be milked. She stood over me and watched as I pressed and pulled the cow's udder, the chilblains on my fingers swollen and threatening to burst.

"You'll do," she said after a while, "good to see someone with a bit of sense."

When the Kestners were gone, Frieda stood up and spoke to me over the backs of the cows.

"Too much work and not enough people."

"What's happened to them all? I mean, the workers?"

She started on the next cow, and soon the sounds of milking and snorting accompanied her reply.

"There's been a string of them. Some were sent back, God knows where to. Some ran off. Could not stand the pace, the hardship. Those that were caught got punished. We never saw them again. It's a real problem, keeping them." She paused then added like an afterthought, "You must be hungry and tired."

"Just dying for a drink," I said.

I heard the scraping of her stool against the concrete floor and watched her feet, beneath the cows' bellies, walk towards me.

"Here, have this," she said, stopping beside me. She held out an aluminium mug with fresh milk. I drained the cup without stopping. It was warm, creamy, filling.

"A million thanks!" I said, wiping my mouth on my sleeve, and thinking of Ludwik with a twinge of guilt.

"Nothing to it," Frieda said. "That's one thing, at least, we're not short of."

"Don't the Kestners mind?"

"No, it's not as if there's an army of us workers."

I was astonished. I told Frieda of the strict regulations on the Holtzmanns' farm.

"The Kestners can be hard masters too," she gave me a warning smile, "but not about the food."

She had a round, likeable face and looked about forty. When she resumed the milking, I asked her, "So, who else is on this farm?"

"Only the people you saw," she said. "Herr and Frau Kestner run this farm. Then there's old Anton who's been a farm hand since time began, and there's my husband Gerhart and myself. We live in the little hut beyond the farm house, at present, during the winter months. When the warm weather comes, we take out the herd of oxen to the higher ground, on the other side of the valley, and we spend the summer months there."

"Have you any children?" I asked, more out of politeness than curiosity.

Frieda's voice brightened,

"Yes, we have. His name is Leopold, but we call him Poldi. He's fifteen. Lives with my mother in Eberstein. We see them on Sundays. Clever at school and praised for his zeal in the Hitler Junge."

These last two words were like dropping glass on a concrete floor, like spilling ink on a page of finished handwriting, like discovering a hole in a newly bought Sunday-best jacket. My first, spontaneous reaction to like Frieda would now have to be tempered with caution.

CHAPTER 15

When the time came to stop for the day, my tiredness and my hunger were matched by an overwhelming need to be with Ludwik again, to have respite from the anxiety that tormented me like chronic disease. Frieda checked the bolts and the locks on all doors round those farm buildings that she was responsible for, and led me through the snow-brightened night to the main building.

The first impression of the kitchen was that of its similarity to the one in the Holtzmanns' house. A curtain hung over a doorway that would have been our sleeping alcove, but here, I later discovered, was a small, indoor washroom. On a high pine dresser, among the jugs, the vases and the serving bowls, stood a wooden bust of Hitler, painted black. His hollow eyes were levelled above us and would have stared, if there had been any eyeballs, at an elaborately carved cross on the opposite wall.

Herr Kestner and his two companions were already seated at the big table, while Ludwik raised his hand to draw my attention, from a small table tucked in the corner. The sight of him gave me such a jolt of happiness; I would have hugged him, had we been alone.

Frieda went to wash her hands behind the curtain, while I waited for Umtraut Kestner to give me her instructions. She stirred the contents of the pot on the range for a rather long moment before turning round. She was the proverbial, alarming, skin and bones. Her long grey dress appeared to elongate her thinness and her hair, scraped back and tightly plaited, exposed the sharpness of her features.

"I suppose I'd better show you to your room," she said with a sigh, as if I were a nuisance. Even her discoloured teeth were long and sharp.

She led me up the wooden stairs at the side of the washroom. The attic above the kitchen was warmed by the rising heat from below. When she opened my door, one of three in the narrow passage, the air was dry and pleasant, but the timber floor was bare, except for a mattress and a slop bucket in the corner.

"Leave your bag here. Take off your coat and come downstairs to eat." There was no warmth, no welcome in her voice.

"I'll be right down," I said. "Is there anywhere I can have a wash?"

She scrutinised me with her sunken eyes.

"You need a good scrub, girl. That can wait till after supper. For now, just wash your hands."

Her long skirt swished behind her and I got a whiff of a strange smell. Like fish, or stale blood, or something going bad. It made me think of the burst boil on my calf. It still had to wait. Till later.

I threw off my knotty scarf, my knotty hat, and my coat with holes eaten through by dirt, and rolled them quickly at the foot of my mattress. I shook my head to loosen my hair, that fell in wiry curls around my face. I wore it short now, after that lice infestation last autumn.

Downstairs, I washed my hands behind the curtain, then gratefully slipped in beside Ludwik on the bench. There was a small loaf and butter on our table. I could not believe my eyes.

"Anna!" Umtraut Kestner shouted from the other table, "do you think I'm your servant? Get off that lazy arse of yours and serve your table from the pot!"

Her words were like drops of scalding water. I jumped up and picked up our two aluminium bowls. They were deep, made for generous helpings. I ladled the stew. It was thick with vegetables and cubed meat. Its aroma did strange things to me. I felt myself trembling as I sat down and took the first bite into the buttered bread, then the first spoonful of the wholesome stuff. We ate in silence, at first, Ludwik and I, totally overwhelmed by our stroke of luck. We communicated with our eyes only, as we listened to the talk on the other table. It consisted mainly of gossip about people they knew; Umtraut Kestner's terse remarks moderated by her husband's. Frieda and Gerhart's contribution was sociable and bland. They agreed with everything that was being said. Old Anton gave sporadic outbursts of laughter that had no connection with any of the talk. His face looked like creased leather, and his thick white hair was cropped close to his scalp, and looked like a brush. He kept sending glances our way, full of curiosity, then, halfway through the meal, he scrambled out of his seat and came over to stand at our table.

"Are you my sister?" he asked, lowering his face centimetres away from mine. He had bits of food stuck to the stubble on his chin.

"I don't think so," I answered slowly, with what I had intended to be a gentle smile.

He smiled back. Revealing gaps between his teeth.

"Is he my brother?" His head did not turn, only his finger with the bitten nail pointed at Ludwik.

"No," I shook my head.

Anton straightened up, his face creasing with puzzlement.

"You will tell me, won't you, when you find them?" he asked.

"Of course," we both said at once.

From the other table, Herr Kestner called, "Come on, Anton. Finish your meal. And you two, there's more in the pot, if you're still hungry."

We looked at each other in disbelief.

We ate our second helpings with less hurry.

"This is pure heaven," Ludwik spoke softly.

"And I can't stop thinking about the others," I added, my voice hushed by guilt. "The rubbish they're forced to eat…"

"I know…" Ludwik smiled wryly "God, this is so hard… You send us torment even in our rare moments of bliss…"

After supper, everyone left to retire to their dwellings except for Umtraut Kestner, who lingered behind to give us her instructions.

"I'm going too," she said, "I've had enough for today. Make sure everything's washed up, dried and put away. There's enough hot water on the range for you both to have a wash. You'll find everything you need behind that curtain. And no stupid pranks! My brother's a policeman. Remember him? He'll be here again in the morning."

Despite the threat she had left hanging over us, it was great relief when she went away, and we were at last alone.

"She sounds a lot of fun," Ludwik whispered, gathering things from the table. "Imagine having her for a mother."

"I'd hang myself," I said, thinking of my own mother, whose very presence was joy.

"And that ugly name of hers!" Ludwik rolled his eyes, "Umtraut! What had possessed her parents to call her that? With a name like that she couldn't be pretty even if she tried!"

"And what's with Anton?" I wondered, filling the washing-up bowl with warm water.

"Poor chap," Ludwik said, "obviously not all there."

"I'll ask Frieda tomorrow," I said.

We did everything Umtraut Kestner had ordered us to do, leaving all the surfaces clean and shiny. Even Hitler's wooden head. Ludwik spat on it with great zeal and spread the saliva all over, before wiping the sculpture clean and buffing it to a sheen.

I had to laugh.

"What?" Ludwik asked with wide-eyed innocence, his tone smug.

We found a galvanised bath tub behind the curtain, big enough to sit in. I couldn't wait to get in it.

"Ludwik, you will mind the curtain for me, won't you, while I take a bath? I'll do the same for you."

"Goes without saying…" He was already sitting down at our small table, getting his tatty notebook out, ready to sketch.

I fetched my towel and my soap and filled the tub with warm water. I sat on the bench and began to unravel the rags on my bad calf, bracing myself for what I was about to uncover. Ludwik came over to my side of the table, and stood over me, waiting to assist.

"I'd rather you didn't." I looked up, embarrassed. "It's a mess. Smelly. Horrid. I'd rather do it myself."

He sat down beside me and lifting my foot off the floor, rested it on the bench in the space between us.

"What do you take me for? A namby-pamby? C'mon, let's have a look." He spoke like my big brother. With deft fingers he took off the rags, then finally the limp cabbage leaf, covered in dark blood and thick pus. The exposed flesh was red and swollen with a crater-like hole, in the place of the burst boil.

"I warned you," I said, cringing.

"I've seen worse," he said, gathering up all the stained rags together and disposing of them in the fire.

"You mustn't soak that bit," he advised. "Not till it's closed up and healed. I've got some zinc and oil ointment."

He washed his hands and disappeared up the wooden stairs, while I dampened a clean cloth and washed around the oozing hole in my flesh, that was prickly to the slightest touch.

"I'll do the rest now," I said, when Ludwik came back.

"As you wish, but I'm a dab hand with bandages and creams," he smiled. "Had to be. My two young brothers! And their high jinks! Never a day without trouble!"

He watched me spreading some ointment and then bandage my calf in neat overlaying layers to form a belt just below my knee.

"Don't get it wet now," he warned me, even as I sat in the tub, hidden behind the curtain, my knees under my chin, the bandage just above the water, the longed-for soak sending shivers of delight throughout my body.

"I want to stay here all night," I said, feeling my chilblained fingers and toes pulsating, the itchiness gently soothed.

"There's no hurry." His mind was on other things. I could hear his pencil scratching like a mouse. He was sketching in the tatty notebook he had made of scraps of paper, trimmed and folded to resemble a pocket-sized book.

"I'm expecting a grand design," I teased, heady with the vapour rising from the tub.

"The grandest," his voice came back.

I heard a door open and shut. I heard Kestner's voice.

"You shtill here, Ludwik?"

"Just waiting my turn to wash."

"Ish that sho?" Kestner's voice came closer and I saw his shadow fall across the curtain. Ludwik's shadow rose.

"You can't go in there, Sir, Anna's having a bath."

There was a pause as both shadows remained still.

"And who'sh going to shtop me?"

I did not like Kestner's tone. I did not like the thick consonants. I shot up from the tub splashing water around me. I grabbed the towel and wrapped it round my breasts and hips. I grabbed my bundle of clothes and clutched them to my chest.

"Sir, please… Anna's not well… Her leg's covered in boils…"

There was a pause, then, "What ish it with women! Bad head! Bad back! Bad time of the month! Now thish! A bad leg! What a shtory! Get out of my way!"

I watched the shadow of his arm come up, then the curtain pulled back with such force I heard it rip. Ludwik was standing in the doorway, his arms outstretched, forming a desperate barrier.

"Get out of my way!" Kestner repeated, his fist shooting out towards Ludwik's face. Ludwik ducked and sprang inside the washroom, stopping firm like a screen before me, his arms and fists raised and ready. Kestner's fist landed against the door frame. A flat smack sound. He cursed. His face contorted with pain. He rolled his eyes. His knees buckled. His back hit the wall and he slid down it to the floor, falling in a half-moon position, his head missing the tub by a few centimetres.

He lay still like a corpse. Fear made my legs rigid. Ludwik knelt down beside him and slapped his face. I wished Kestner dead, but his eyes twitched.

"Stinking sloshed, the bastard!" Ludwik muttered. "Now, I suppose, it's up to us to help him up to his feet."

At that moment we were startled by a sound. Like a ghostly apparition, with her sunken eyes, with her long grey plait hanging down one side of her long night-gown, Umtraut was moving towards us.

"What's going on?" Her gaze swept over me in my semi-nakedness, over Kestner prone on the floor, at my nervous feet squelching in the wet patch, over Ludwik kneeling, bending over with concern.

"Well, don't just stare!" she rasped, "help me get him to his feet!"

I dropped my clothes back on the stool and tied a secure knot in the towel over my chest. Together with Ludwik we helped Umtraut to pull Kestner up to a sitting position. As soon as his consciousness returned his belligerent mood burst out of him.

"Leave me alone! *Polishe sweine!* Leave me alone!" He pushed out his elbows to shake us off.

"No! You listen to me!" Umtraut shouted back, "or do I have to call Rudi?"

The sound of that name had a lightening effect. His rage calmed down. Instantly. The fact that Umtraut was in no position to call anyone at that time of night did not penetrate Kestner's alcohol-sodden brain. He stopped resisting us, and shakily, stiffly allowed us to help him stand up.

Umtraut draped his left arm over her shoulder saying to Ludwik, "You take the other side."

There was again a whiff of her peculiar smell as they shuffled together towards the parlour door, with Kestner between them, his head slumped forward. I pulled the curtain back and dressed with trembling hands and fingers that were clumsy and slow. I began to empty the tub with a jug and when Ludwik returned we picked it up together and poured away the remaining water into the deep concrete-cast sink.

"What have you done with him?" I asked, wiping the tub clean for Ludwik's bath.

"Don't worry," Ludwik said, pushing back his tangled curls behind his ears, "he's out like a light. In his own bed. He won't bother us again. You can sleep safe and sound. You don't have to wait for me."

I was tired, I ached all over, but I did not trust anything, or anyone in this house, except Ludwik.

"I'll stay here with you," I said.

I sat at the kitchen table, with my head resting on my folded arms, my eyes wide open, as I listened to the splashing, reassuring sounds behind the curtain.

"Where does he get the stuff from?" I asked.

"Makes his own, no doubt," Ludwik answered.

"Must be like turps." I remembered the revolting stuff, the men back home used to extract from distilled potato juice.

"Must be desperate. Old Kestner. Strange, but I almost pity his ugly wife," Ludwik said from behind the screen.

The house was quiet when we crept upstairs to the attic above the kitchen. Ludwik's room was opposite to mine across the narrow passage. There was a third door, firmly locked when Ludwik tried it.

"His supplies of booze no doubt," Ludwik winked.

There were no keys in our locks, no bolts on our doors.

"Don't be afraid, Anna. I'm only a few feet away from you. You only have to shout…"

"That goes for you too, Ludwik. I may not be your Goliath, but I've got two hard clogs. Like mallets. Sleep tight. And dream happy dreams. You'll need all your strength tomorrow."

Inside my room, I wedged my sandal underneath the closed door, my once-white sandal, that was now just a sole, with a piece of string for tying round my foot. Fully clothed, I lay down on the bare mattress and pulled the rough, army-green blanket up to my chin, then over my head. To shut everything out. An ache pressed heavily inside my chest where my heart was supposed to be. I felt like a pebble, buried deep and forgotten in the ground.

CHAPTER 16

There was no sight of Kestner or Umtraut when I started work with Frieda at dawn. It was therefore with trepidation that I went indoors when time for breakfast arrived. But breakfast turned out to be a startling surprise, a mind-boggling abundance of food, throwing us – Ludwik and me – off guard one second and doubling our suspicions the next.

Kestner and Umtraut acted naturally as if nothing had happened the previous night. I noticed a red-blue mark at the side of her mouth that stood out bright on her sallow skin. They talked and laughed with old Anton, Gerhart and Frieda joining in dutifully.

Though Ludwik and I, to our great relief, sat separately on our small table by the back door, our breakfast was the same as theirs; porridge cooked in creamy milk with a blob of plum jam in each bowl, followed by slices of whole-meal bread, cheese and fresh ham. We tucked into our food without delay, sending discreet, disbelieving glances in Kestner's direction.

"Is this a trap?" I whispered, feeling my toes curl with pleasure, like a baby's suckling its mother's milk. "Is this the last meal of a condemned man?"

"We'll soon find out," Ludwik replied, his jaws chewing overtime, his bites large and greedy, his dark curls shaking with each intense movement.

"Here's trouble coming," I whispered.

Umtraut got up and approached our table. She leaned over so close, her smell made me shrink back.

"You two," she screwed her eyes and sniffed. "You two stink to high heaven!"

"But..." I hurried to explain, "we've both had a bath last night."

"It's your clothes, stupid! You've got to get them off. Stay behind after breakfast."

We did, as ordered, stopped behind, cleared away, washed and dried, while Umtraut disappeared for a while. She returned with an armful of clothes and threw them on our table.

"Here, get changed and wash your stinking clothes, tonight, after work. Go on! Don't waste time gawping! I'm going to the cowshed, Anna. I expect you both to be out in five minutes."

She pulled on her outdoor boots, fur-lined and wrapped in a wide strip of felt, her working overcoat, made of thick blanket weave, and covered her head and shoulders with a woollen shawl. She reminded me of our old women in my village, back home.

Alone, Ludwik and I rummaged feverishly through the pile. The clothes were worn but clean. Thick jumpers, trousers, a skirt and two felt over-coats, like Umtraut's.

"Scary! Isn't it?" Ludwik said. "I can't work them out. Angels one minute, devils the next! We'd better hurry before she changes her mind."

We got into our clean clothes with great speed, and left our dirty ones in a corner of the washroom. Then, with our knotty hats, scarves and mittens on, we went outside to face the cold, the dirt, the stench, the never-ending labour around the animals.

"What's the matter with Herr and Frau Kestner," I asked Frieda later, when we were alone in the pigsty, raking and scraping the ground.

She straightened up and looked around. We were well away from the main house.

"Why do you ask?" She lowered her head.

I told her about the previous night.

Frieda came closer and spoke quietly.

"Umtraut is ill, and he gets very angry. Looks to drink for comfort. It's a vicious circle. Story as old as the hills."

"What's wrong with her?" I asked.

Frieda looked over her shoulder, and then lowered her tone to a whisper.

"Some say it's cancer. Down below, you know. Private parts."

"God, that's awful!" I was shocked. Truly.

I had no idea what cancer looked like. Old people in our village would frighten us with stories of a live lump eating away one's flesh. There was no cure to stop it. I had known a woman who had died of breast cancer and a man who had been reduced to skin and bones before his death. Bronek, our childhood friend, had a growth on his chin. It got knocked in a mock fight, and he had died too. I shivered and made a resolution to be nice to Umtraut.

A figure approached us. It was Herr Schwartz, Umtraut's policeman brother. I recognised him from the previous day. There was a strong resemblance in his facial features to those of his sister's, even though hers had been accentuated sharply, by her wasting illness.

I resumed shovelling muck into the wheelbarrow, taking great care not to splash my clean over-coat.

"No slacking girl!" Schwartz spoke sharply, leaning on the metal rail. "Don't expect your keep for nothing! One word from my sister and you'll have me to answer to! *Ferstehein sie?"*

I understood perfectly. Experience had taught me that feigned subservience was better than punishment.

"Yes, Sir!" I replied, not looking at him, too preoccupied with my all-important job.

This seemed to satisfy him and he walked away.

I caught up with Umtraut later, in the sheep barn, after I had fed the pigs, washed them down with a hose and lined the ground with fresh hay. I liked the very young piglets, their floppy ears, their white long eyelashes, their briefly thoughtful look, when they appeared to consider you. I liked the feel of their warm round bodies, quaking in my arms with excitement. Five mature pigs were ready to be slaughtered. I was glad that aspect of farming was entirely the men's domain.

I set about helping Umtraut clean around the sheep. I longed for the thaw, for the freshness of spring days, for the warmth to return to the fields, for the sheep and the cows to be released into the open. Umtraut stopped frequently to take a rest from bending and shovelling the dirt. Beads of sweat gathered over her eyebrows and dripped down the side of her face.

"Frau Kestner," I wanted to be true to my resolution, "take a break. I'll finish this job by myself."

"Take a break!" she snorted, leaning on her rake. "Take a break! You stupid girl! I'd need ten of you first, before I could sit down!"

I said nothing more. When we finished the work and walked over to the cowshed, I made another attempt as we squatted, dipping our hands in the disinfectant.

"Frau Kestner... My new clothes... It was so good of you. I'm really grateful. And Ludwik too."

Her expression did not flicker. She got up and rubbed her hands dry with a towel, as if her life depended on it.

"Don't flatter yourself," she said, "I didn't do it for you. We need our workers to be well and strong. That means keeping you lot dressed and fed. I don't do favours. You can thank Sylvia for wearing her clothes."

"Who's Sylvia?"

"My daughter-in-law." Umtraut made a face, "Now, that'll be a surprise for her, seeing you in her clothes!"

"Will she mind?" I was suddenly nervous.

"Maybe. Who cares? She doesn't give a shit about us. Too busy on her brother's farm."

I could only guess some family complications, but I did not dare ask any more questions. Umtraut was silent for a moment then words burst out of her.

"It's this war! This bloody war! We wouldn't have to slave like this if Dieter was here. And what's he doing now? Ruining his health! Losing the best years of his life! In some God-forsaken Russian backwater!"

I was in full agreement with her, but I remained quiet, lest her wrath turned on me.

That evening, Ludwik was not his usual play-acting optimistic self, when he stopped by in my room, before turning in. We sat down on the mattress and rested our aching backs against the warm panelled wall.

"It's not like you, Ludwik," I chided him. "Yesterday was far worse and we survived. Today we ate like kings!"

"I wish," he said, rubbing his eyes, pushing back his hair, "we could take the food and go back to our friends. I hate it here. Kestner's snapping at me all the time. No respite from his evil temper all day. And Anton's completely mad. Needs watching like a kid. Has this thing about teasing the bulls. He'll get gored one of these days."

"Why do they keep him?" I asked.

"He's some distant relative, so Gerhart tells me. Hasn't anyone else to live with."

I sighed, thinking of my family, my friends. Michal. Every thought of him deepened the void I was feeling.

"Ludwik," I forced myself to sound resolute, "look on the bright side. Our first day here is over."

He shook his head then looked up at the skylight.

"You're right, Anna, it doesn't do you any good feeling sorry for yourself. Look, I can see the stars. Strange, how these tiny dots millions of miles away in the universe make you feel close to your family."

I looked at him, a spark inside me suddenly igniting.

"Ludwik! That's exactly how I feel! Every night I stare at the stars and every night I see our house in the moonlight."

"Great minds, eh?" He winked, a pained smile touching his lips. "I wish though… I wish there was just a note… Just a short message from home… It's been such a long time…"

"Just imagine," I said, willing him to lighten up, "imagine one day all the letters arriving all at once! It'll be like a library! Talking of which, tell me one of your travel stories."

He flopped his shoulders and his head in a show of exhaustion.

"C'mon Ludwik… Please… I love listening. When I close my eyes it's like going to the cinema."

"Really?" He perked up and thought for a minute. "Which one do you want? The time we went to Egypt?"

"I don't care. It's all out of this world for me, anyway."

He interspersed his descriptions with amusing tales of his accident-prone brothers. I closed my eyes and basked in the warm sunshine on the green banks by the blue Nile, in a place free of ugliness, free of dirt and stench, free of grief and pain.

That night I woke up in the grip of influenza.

It was like a bad dream lingering on after waking. Chattering teeth, shivering body, head like a hot stone weighing me down. I opened my eyes. Searing white pain. I closed my eyes and blindly dragged myself off the mattress to rummage through my bag for the jar of aspirins. My swollen throat rejected them making me heave in a wave of sweat. I ground the tablets between my teeth and pushed them down with a gulp of water.

"Please God, make me feel well. I cannot be ill," I prayed, lowering myself down onto the mattress. I curled into a ball and covered myself totally, trapping my hot breath for warmth. Slowly the shaking calmed down and I drifted into sleep.

The next thing I was aware of was someone shouting above me. Through the screen of my eyelashes I could see daylight and a long dark shape looming up.

"Get up you lazy swine!" I recognised Umtraut's voice, "*Raus! Raus!*"

Someone grasped my hand and with a jerk hauled me off the mattress. An acute pain shot up my arm, up my back, up my neck, to the top of my head. I tried to talk, but my parched throat made no sound.

"Get up!" a man's voice ordered. I was grabbed by my shoulders and forced to sit up. As soon as he let go I fell back onto the floor.

"What's the matter with you girl!" Umtraut gave me a kick. "This isn't a holiday! Who's going to do your work for you?"

It's the end, I thought, I'm dying; yet strangely, a tiny, remaining spark of defiance prised open my eyes. I saw her foot coming towards me. Something surged inside me and exploded in anger.

"Stop it! Stop it!" My hoarse yell sounded frightening.

I grabbed Umtraut's foot within the circle of my arms and squeezed it tight. Caught off balance she landed beside me with a thud, her mouth gaping open in utter amazement.

"I've got the flu!" I cried, hot tears flooding my eyes.

She scrambled up to her feet. My action sharpened her rage.

"Get up you bitch! This work doesn't wait for anyone!"

She and her brother Schwartz stood over me as I dragged myself up to all fours. They watched me like prison guards when I took two more tablets from my bag. They followed me down the stairs as I staggered with a feeling of having to hold onto something solid on a fast-revolving carousel. They waited outside the washroom while I splashed my face, rinsed my mouth, and swallowed the crushed tablets. I was desperate for Ludwik just to be near me, but he was already outside doing his shift before breakfast.

"I'll leave you to it now," I heard Schwartz say.

"Thanks Rudi. Come back soon. She's not the only one needing to be shown who's the boss here."

Umtraut supervised my every move as I pulled on my outdoor clothing, then she escorted me to the cowshed.

I stumbled, somehow, from one job to another in a haze of dulled pain, with only a vague awareness of my surroundings. Frieda, at the far end, seemed miles away. I wanted to call out to her, but Umtraut's diligent omnipresence made it impossible. Besides, my throat felt like a tube made of sandpaper.

When the cows had been milked, Umtraut sent me out to deal with the pigs. My legs were wobbly, rubbery, and my hair stuck to my head like a saturated sponge. I brought out the buckets, one by one, heavy with the feed, and filled the troughs with the pigs squealing and pushing around me. I left them to it and started on the never-ending work of keeping their huts scraped and cleaned out of their own muck.

I remember pulling out the wheelbarrow and bending down to pick up the rake. I remember seeing the ground coming up towards me, then darkness descending, then nothing.

I remember returning to dim consciousness, faint light, fuzzy shapes, muffled sounds, someone shouting. I recognised Kestner's voice.

"You stupid woman! What were you thinking! Dead workers are no good to us!"

A large shape loomed above me. Umtraut. She yelled at Kestner.

"You sort it out, then, if you're so clever! Perhaps you'll do her work as well!"

"Get out of my way! All of you!" Kestner shouted. The shapes began to recede from my circle of vision. "Not you, Ludwik, I need you!"

Together, they pulled me up to my feet. My coat was soiled with pig's dirt and mud. Ludwik began to brush it off with his bare hand, but Kestner stopped him.

"Finish Anna's work, then come to find me."

Ludwik looked concerned.

"I'll be all right," I assured him, "I just need some sleep. I'll be back later."

Kestner walked me to the kitchen door. The effort of keeping up with his long strides brought me out in sweat again.

"Go to bed," he said, "and get yourself better."

I picked up a mug, filled it with water, staggered upstairs, took another couple of aspirins, dropped my soiled coat on the floor, then fully clothed I lay down on the mattress and pulled the blanket over my head. All these little actions sapped all of my strength. I felt like a limp, soggy piece of paper. I wondered what it was like to be dead, to be at peace, free of all pain. I missed my mother, I missed Michal with a deep, gnawing ache. Tears of self-pity seeped into my hair, into the mattress underneath my cheek.

I slept, my sleep a jumble of dreams, interrupted at intervals by a distant dim light.

Then there was a sound like rustling. I opened my eyes. Ludwik was crouching beside me, his curly hair outlined against the light from the bare electric bulb.

"God, what time is it?" I clutched my head to hold down the reawakened pain.

"It's nearly eight," he said. "We've had our evening meal. I've brought you some broth."

"Ludwik," I whimpered, "I can barely move. I feel as if I'm dying."

"You're not dying." He was my big brother again. "Come on, I'll help you sit up. The broth will do you good."

Slowly, with Ludwik's support, I raised myself and leaned my head against the wooden wall. It was warm and, in a strange way, soothing. I was suddenly aware of a strong stink of sweat and dirt released from underneath my blanket.

"God, how I pong," I said, feeling my cheeks burning.

"Nothing to worry about." Ludwik was matter-of-fact. "Eat your soup first, then I'll help you down to the washroom."

He held the bowl close to my chest and I began to feed myself, careful not to move my head, careful not to aggravate the pain. The first few mouthfuls loosened my parched throat, filled my stomach with warmth. I found my appetite returning and continued till the bowl was empty.

"There! What did I say?" Ludwik's worn face came alive. "You're looking better already!"

"Thanks Ludwik, thanks for being so good to me." Speaking was an effort. I felt as if I had just climbed to the top of a hill.

"I've got to, haven't I? Who's going to look after me if you're not up to scratch?" he teased.

"Umtraut," I attempted to joke in a fit of coughing.

He chuckled as if I were the funniest comic on earth.

"C'mon," he said, "let's get you up and washed."

I spent another day curled up on my mattress with only Ludwik visiting me in the evening. Umtraut and her brother Schwartz left me alone, but when I returned to all my chores, my bones and muscles still riddled with aches and a dry cough tearing at my chest, she scowled at me, barking orders and finishing each directive with *"Du Polishe Schweine!"*

Frieda tried to comfort me when we were alone.

"Don't take any notice! She'll pick on someone else before long. We live in hope of getting a few more workers."

"Lucky workers!" I replied, my thoughts like a swarm of crows shutting out the light.

Umtraut's insults lasted a few more days, then something happened that took her attention away from me, and forced her and all of us to double our work.

It was the thaw.

On the first day the valley filled with warmth, the melting snow formed rivulets that flowed down the slopes into the swirling, swelling river. There was something exhilarating in the sounds of rushing water, sounds that heralded spring, that ended the misery of the long, cold months. With anticipation we watched every day swathes of grassy slopes appear and spread ever further as the day wore on. It was blissful, liberating, to discard the cumbersome overcoats, to open wide all doors to sheds and stables.

At the end of the month, on a particularly warm day, Kestner called us together underneath the chestnut tree. The hanging branches had the fresh covering of the first burst of buds. Here the air rose fragrant above the stale farm smells.

"Time to get the animals out," he said, scratching his forehead below the rim of his cap. "Anton, Gerhart and Ludwik, you lead the oxen to their usual field, and you two," he turned to Frieda and me, "you take the sheep out."

Umtraut was not well that day and had stayed indoors to do the housework.

The bells tied round the oxen's necks made a joyous sound as the herd passed by and was led over the river bridge to the fields on higher ground on the other side of the valley. There was a hut, Frieda had told me, where she and Gerhart would spend the summer looking after the oxen and the sheep, wash and dry the wool for weaving, make cheese, for which purpose, she had pointed out to me, there was a specially designed cable for hauling up churns of milk from the farm.

When the oxen were out of the way, she and I shepherded the sheep towards the fields closer to the farm, with open shelters dotted around them. The sight of the lambs – some only one, some two months old – jumping sideways, in their uncoordinated way, falling clumsily, looking up with those trusting black faces of theirs, filled me with unexpected joy. The sun was warm on my skin, I felt a stirring in my chest, like expectancy, and hope.

Later, came the onslaught – relentless, punishing all day – of the thorough cleaning, emptying and scrubbing of all sheds and stables, that had been inhabited by the animals through seven long months. That evening, all I could think of, longed for, at suppertime, was to have a quick wash and to lie down. All my bones and muscles had multiplied and conspired to give me pain. Ludwik too, looked like a run-down clockwork toy moving around stiffly, when everyone had gone and had left us to tidy and clean the kitchen.

"I'll be out in a flash," I said to Ludwik, going to wash behind the curtain. Face, hands, armpits and feet. A quick splash, every movement a big strain.

He was asleep, when I pulled back the curtain, his head resting heavily on his folded arms on the table, his fingers, blistered and grazed, jerking spasmodically in his dream. I touched his shoulder making him sit up with wide-eyed alacrity.

"It's only me," I said, "I'll wait for you. Go now. There won't be time in the morning."

A little later, when my head touched the mattress, sleep came instantly, obliterating all my habitual thoughts of my mother, Michal and my friends on the other farm.

I was bent over the rake, scraping the ground in the chicken enclosure, when a hand crawled up my thigh. I jumped up as if catapulted. Kestner was standing beside me, his leering face peering into mine.

"What are you doing!" Shock and anger made me raise my voice. I could smell his stale breath and old dirt and sweat in his clothes.

"Come now, come Anna, one good turn deserves another!"

His breath made me heave. I stepped back, digging the rake firmly between us.

"I don't know what you mean, sir!"

"What! Forgotten already? Who was it who helped you when you were ill? Took your side? Walked you back to the house?" His slow leer exposed his long, chipped, nicotine-stained teeth.

"Sir, I've not forgotten your kindness. I'm grateful. Truly grateful." I forced my voice to be calm as I shuddered with repulsion and fear.

"Then it's time you showed me some of your gratitude." He grabbed the rake, pulled it out of my hands and threw it to the ground. I turned to run, but he caught me by my hair.

"Stop it! Stop it!" I shouted, thrusting out my clenched fists.

"You stop it, you bitch!" He turned me round, and hooking his arm around my waist, he held me tight against him. He looked insane, possessed as he dragged me out of the chicken pen towards the nearest shed.

I screamed. A high, piercing scream that surprised me, that shocked him. He let go of me, and for a split second I was free. Then his punch came, furious and strong, right in the centre of my chest. Like a leaf blown by the wind, I fell to the ground, my hands slipping on chicken excretions.

"You bitch! You stupid bitch! You'll be sorry!"

He stood over me, his face red with rage. I was bracing myself for his next violent move, when I saw Ludwik running towards us. He was followed by Anton and Gerhart. They stopped at the fence, taking in the scene, but Ludwik came forward and helped me to my feet.

"You get back to work, you son of a bitch. This is none of your business!" Kestner yelled at him.

"You've made it my business, sir. You're molesting my friend." Ludwik stood between us, shielding me.

Kestner raised his fist, but suddenly his whole stance looked less certain, less menacing.

"You bastard!" he swore, and seeing Umtraut coming our way he directed his wrath towards her. "And what do you want here!"

She was out of breath, drops of sweat glistening on her brow, on her upper lip.

"What's going on?" she scowled at me, making it clear she had already decided that I was the culprit.

"Disobeying my orders," Kestner barked.

"You should be ashamed of yourself." She chose to go along with his charade, though I had no doubt that she knew well what had been going on. She scolded me, "In this country young girls respect people older than themselves. Don't they teach you anything where you come from?"

Sudden, overwhelming anger took away my caution. I stepped forward from behind Ludwik.

"And in my country, Frau Kestner, old men don't molest young girls. Look at me! I'm not even eighteen! I could be his grand daughter!"

She struck me across my face. My eyes watered, but the indignation boiling within me strengthened my resolve to remain defiant.

"Why are you hitting me, Frau Kestner? You know I've not done anything wrong."

I was expecting her to strike me again, but to my astonishment, she recoiled, her face crumbling as if she were about to cry.

"Come on, old girl," Kestner said gruffly, "let's all get back to work."

After this incident Umtraut gave me instructions only through Frieda. Kestner went about his jobs unobtrusively, keeping well away from us. Most evenings I saw him cycle away from the farm. To Eberstein.

"He's got a woman in town. Gerhart's word," Ludwik informed me.

I could not imagine any woman wanting him. I wondered if Umtraut knew. If she did, she did not show it. She appeared contented in his absence, glad to be the head of the table, to preside over Frieda, Gerhart and Anton, to indulge in gossip, unrestrained by Kestner's cutting remarks.

Ludwik and I sat quietly at our separate table, thankful for our well-cooked meals, talking to each other only after everyone had gone.

The first month on Kestner's farm appeared interminable, but I eased the dragging time by taking pleasure in small, everyday things. Daily tub baths. Frequently washing my clothes. Having them dried in the fresh breeze. Regularly, now that the weather had turned warm.

And then, our first shopping Sunday arrived.

CHAPTER 17

I was careful not to betray my excitement by any word or by the slightest expression, in case Umtraut changed her mind and postponed our two hours of freedom to another day. Her mood-swings were sudden, her bad temper not easily appeased.

However, she appeared agreeable, when she and Kestner called Ludwik and me into the kitchen, just before setting out for the eleven o'clock service in Sankt Walburgen. The church bell could be heard tolling across the valley. She wore a navy felt hat with a brim over her sunken eyes, and a long navy coat that gave substance to her thin frame. Kestner was dressed in a grey suit, its shabbiness lifted by the white shirt.

"Tell Anna and Ludwik," Umtraut instructed Kestner, making a point of not addressing me directly, "to spruce themselves up before they go to town. To Drucker's."

"And no messing about, you two," Kestner said sternly. "Anton will hold fort for a while, but not all day. A couple of hours, do you understand?"

He dug his hand inside his pocket and took out some coins.

"Twelve marks each. And hurry!"

They went off on their horse and cart, and we ran to scrub ourselves clean.

I was glad of my fresh-laundered, fresh-smelling blouse and skirt. I wore the socks that I had knitted the previous autumn. Their knobbly thickness enabled a snug fit inside my clogs. My calf was healed and clean where the boil had been, its site marked only by a patch of dark, puckered skin.

We walked down the track towards the bridge over the stream, spruced up, looking almost normal again. Ludwik's skin, like mine, had improved over the month, turned a healthy, wind-tanned colour. His dark eyes had lost that haunted look, his washed black hair shone with glints of plum and rust. I thought of his girl Julia. I thought of Michal, of his free afternoon, of the wasted time in our separation.

It was two kilometres to Eberstein along the main road, on the high ground. We chose to walk along the parallel rail track in the valley to avoid attracting attention. We passed below the mighty foundations of the Schloss. It was like a fairy-tale castle with turrets, towers, decorative rooftops and carved stonework around the gateway. It overlooked the town and the valley, and with its long red banners and gigantic swastikas, could be seen for miles around.

We came off the rail track at the level crossing in town and went down a side street into the centre. The town was deserted on Sunday, only our clogs carried an eerie echo along the pavement. I felt exposed, I sensed danger even in the slow movement of the red banners brushing against walls.

We walked fast, found the centre and looked around for Drucker's. In my heightened state of apprehension I could hardly take in the prettiness of the place. The pastel coloured houses, the wide façade of the town hall, the lawn cut diagonally across by a narrow stream with an ornate bridge were worth a second glance, but time and fear were rushing us on.

"There! There it is!" Ludwik cried, grabbing my hand, anxious that I kept up with him.

Drucker's was just off the square, first shop in a side street. Descending the two steps into the shop's dark interior was like a blessed escape. The shelves were bare except for empty cigarette boxes stacked in pyramids and empty jars bearing labels of absent contents. It was a while before Frau Drucker appeared from within the depths of her house. She looked about forty. Her two long plaits were crossed over and pinned on the top of her head, forming a crown. She wore a navy pinafore dress and a white, incredibly white blouse. She listened solemnly to our list of requirements: soap, toothpaste, shampoo, aspirins, Vaseline, washing powder, Ludwik's shaving soap, and then she disappeared again.

"Nothing here to nick. What a pity!" Ludwik looked around drumming his fingers on the counter. "Although, I could, I suppose, unscrew the light bulb, or take one of the empty jars."

"You'd need at least twenty!" I played up to his mischievous mood.

"What for?"

"They'd make excellent cupping glasses."

Ludwik grinned.

"Who'd we start with? Kestner or Umtraut?"

At home old women used cupping glasses to cure bad backs, rheumatism, muscle pains and a variety of aches. The spirit-filled and lit jars were placed neck down on the bare flesh, which was then sucked inside the glass as the flame died down. The round brown marks left on the skin took days to fade away.

"Would this be a cure for his brain?" I asked, imagining Kestner with jars sticking out all over his head.

Ludwik laughed softly.

"It's what's inside his trousers that needs drastic treatment," he whispered.

Frau Drucker returned with our order and after we'd paid her, I had three marks left and six saved over the previous months. I had enough to buy a pair of socks, or a pair of knickers, or half a petticoat, or a quarter of a blouse. I needed everything.

"Frau Drucker," I plucked up courage, "have you any fabric for sale?" I showed her the frayed cuffs and the elbow holes in my blouse. Her expression remained solemn.

"The cheapest I have is five marks a metre. With coupons."

That was the end of that. Neither Ludwik nor I had ever been given any coupons.

"What about old curtains? Or old sheets?" I tried again, making my voice polite, genteel.

"No, I've got nothing like that, but," her eyes became speculative, "just wait one moment."

She turned round to the door behind her and pulling it ajar she called out, "Liesel! I need you!"

Sounds of heavy thudding down the stairs preceded the entrance of a girl. She could not have been more than fourteen, but she was bigger than me, bigger than her mother. Her gaze skimmed our faces then she looked down, stooping self-consciously.

"Liesel," Frau Drucker said, "you know that dress you hate so much, I can sell it for you."

Liesel did not look up. She muttered, "My friend at school can have it."

"Don't be silly, Liesel," her mother chided, "you know very well your friend doesn't want your old dress."

Liesel shrugged.

"I'll ask her."

"No, Liesel," Frau Drucker decided. "Bring it down now. You'll be glad of the money."

Liesel turned round stiffly, her face reddening, and clomped away.

"Frau Drucker," I said, "I've only got nine marks. That's all."

"That'll do," she said.

Liesel's dress was made of fabric with a white and black dog-tooth print that gave it an overall grey appearance.

"Why does she hate it so much?" I asked, after she had thrown it on the counter and stomped off.

"It's the colour," Frau Drucker said, a glimmer of a smile crossing her features. "She likes bright colours, flowery patterns, and besides…" Frau Drucker pointed out a brown burn mark at the hemline, "she assures me this was just an accident, but I know my daughter well."

That did not worry me at all. The dress was so big it needed turning up any way and taking in at the shoulders. A white collar and white cuffs would transform it beautifully. If I could scrounge a piece of white cloth. That was my next assignment. For now, my heart beat fast with pleasure, as I thanked Frau Drucker.

That evening I forced myself to speak to Umtraut. What gave me the courage was her affable mood, possibly brought on by her visit to church, possibly reinforced by the convivial atmosphere around the evening meal. Her brother Schwartz and his wife Helga were visiting, and Frieda and Gerhart were already back from their day out with the family. Anton laughed the most at all the jokes, a loud belly laugh, that made even us giggle at our separate table.

I waited for the moment when Umtraut got up, and still in the company of others, I approached her.

"Leave all the clearing up to me, Frau Kestner," I said. "May I ask you something?"

"And what's that?" she asked, with a nod to the others as if to indicate my impertinence.

"Have you got a bag of off-cuts? Bits of material?" I blurted out. "Bits you don't need for yourself. All I want is a small white piece to make a collar and cuffs for my new dress."

"New dress?" her eyes narrowed like a cat's, "what new dress?"

I was aware of everyone listening now.

"It's not really new…" I stammered. "It's new to me, because I've only just got it today. Part of it is damaged. I need to alter it to fit me."

She looked me up and down with her suspicious eyes, and I saw how she noted my worn blouse, my shrunken skirt, and then her expression changed.

"All right. I'll see what I can do." This show of kindness was like a smile from heaven, though I knew it was only for the benefit of her company.

They all retired: Umtraut, Kestner, Schwarz and Helga to the parlour,

Gerhart, Frieda and Anton to their dwellings, while Ludwik and I were left behind to clear away and wash up.

"I wonder if she'll remember," I fretted, collecting the dirty plates.

"You'll just have to remind her," Ludwik was matter-of-fact.

"But how?" I already imagined her wrath.

She surprised me. She opened the parlour door and beckoned to me. "Come Anna. I'll give you the things now."

She led me through the parlour, which was comfortably furnished, but even I, inexperienced as I was, could tell the furniture had been collected randomly over the years, unlike the Holtzmanns', that was good quality and bought as a set. Kestner and Schwartz were smoking pipes, Helga was sitting back in an arm chair, her elbow propped up, a drink in her hand. Kestner's own brew, I guessed.

Umtraut led me up the wooden staircase to the rooms upstairs. There was a passage with two doors facing each other. And another two doors, one at each end. She opened one, revealing a good-sized bedroom, with a double bed, a wardrobe, a dressing table and a flowery bedspread with curtains to match.

"This is Dieter and Sylvia's room. When they are at home," Umtraut sighed and made a face showing disapproval of their absence. "See that sewing machine in the corner? It's hers. Use it if you must."

I knew Dieter was her son, but if Sylvia was anything like Elise, I did not think it was wise to use her sewing machine. Desperate as I was.

"Won't she mind?" I asked.

"Tough, if she does. She should be here anyway looking after her own things and ours. A good daughter-in-law does not abandon her husband's house, his family. It's hardly his fault he's been made to fight in this bloody war!" I watched her ravaged face, fearful of a sudden mood-swing, and I did not blame Sylvia at all for staying well away.

"There's a bag of bits and pieces. Take out what you need," she added.

I hated rummaging through someone else's things, but with Umtraut watching me from the door, I felt trapped, I did not wish to appear ungrateful. Especially that I could hardly contain my joy. I pulled out two long strips of white cotton, possibly cut-offs from sheets, then I tied the draw-strings of the bag, to leave it exactly as before. I picked up the sewing machine by the handle of its wooden casing, and stopped on my way out.

"You're very kind, Frau Kestner. I'm just worried Sylvia will be cross."

A thin smile appeared on Umtraut's lips.

"She'll be livid. If she finds out. But if you don't tell her, I certainly won't."

157

A tiny shiver ran down my back. I did not want sharing secrets with her, not of the kind that gave her a hold over me.

Anxious, imagining angry scenes when Sylvia returned to the farm, I hurried with the sewing and finished altering my dress in two evenings after work. I also repaired Ludwik's two shirts, cutting off the frayed collars and cuffs and machine-stitching the edges to stop them fraying further. I dusted and covered the sewing machine and took it back to Sylvia's room, sneaking in stealthily, like a thief.

Only when I was back in the kitchen, I felt free, at last, and weightless and delighted with my new dress. I rushed upstairs to my room to try it on. It felt right. I had cut ten centimetres off the hemline, got rid of the burn mark, taken it in at the shoulders and down the sides, I had attached a white collar and a wide white edge on the short sleeves.

Ludwik's door across the passage was ajar. I knocked and went in.

"Go on, tell me, it's the best you've ever seen!" my voice squeaked with excitement.

He looked bemused. He was sitting on his mattress cross-legged, his notebook and pencil in his lap.

I pinched the sides of the skirt and spread it out. I knew this was girl's stuff, but I had no one else to share it with.

He came out of his trance and smiled.

"Yes, sure, it's the best in the world!"

"The collar's made a difference, don't you think?" I was determined to squeeze out an honest compliment.

"The collar?" Now he scrutinised my handiwork with interest. "Yes... I see what you mean...and the sleeves..."

"And I've got rid of the burn mark. It's like new, don't you think? Pity it's not a flower print. I love colours. Lots of colours!"

"No, Anna, no!" he protested, suddenly livening up. "It's the simplicity, that's what gives it style."

Now I knew his praise was genuine and I was pleased. I fetched his shirts.

"Something for you too," I said, sitting down beside him.

He picked one up against the light.

"You're a genius!" he declared.

I giggled self-consciously.

"Nothing to it. Boys can do it too, you know. All the best tailors are men. Show me what you've been doing."

His notebook was a wad made up of bits of paper held together in one corner with thin wire.

"It's an imaginary bridge." He showed me his sketch of a long structure with a row of slim towers holding it up and vertical lines that looked like harp strings.

"The middle section," he explained, his face animated, "would be for the rail track. The two sections on the sides would be for the cars. And on the edges there would be a pedestrian walk with benches, ornamental lamps and viewing bays at regular intervals…"

"How do you think of such things?" I asked, mesmerised.

He leaned his head against the wall.

"My mind keeps buzzing all the while. Sometimes I think my brain's going to explode."

I took the notebook from him and turned the pages. They were covered in sketches and explanatory notes. He should have been out, apprenticed to an engineering firm.

"Ludwik, when you go home you'll have all your construction plans worked out and ready. They'll be all fighting over you." My tone may have been light-hearted but my admiration was true.

"They'd better hurry up and finish this war," Ludwik grinned, "or I shall end up designing chicken coops and cowsheds…"

I stood up and smoothed down my dress.

"Now all we need is a grand occasion. Where shall I wear this exquisite gown of mine?"

I did not know it then, but before long I would be wearing it for a special, unexpected event.

CHAPTER 18

It was Palm Sunday, three days before my eighteenth birthday. At home my mother and my sisters would have each tied a few stems of catkins together, with colourful ribbons, substitutes for palm branches. These would be blessed in church by the priest to start the Holy Week. After the service, tradition required that we tapped each other on the shoulder with our "palms", as a reminder that Easter was only six nights away.

Here, life was routine: every day, every Sunday, on Palm Sunday. It was six in the morning. Ludwik and I came down before the Kestners, Ludwik to let out the pigs and the chickens, and I to start milking the cows. It was already light. I flung the doors of the cowshed wide open to let in the cool fresh air. I never quite got used to the acrid odour of the cow dung, its sharpness that bit the back of my throat. I filled the buckets with cold water from the tap, added disinfectant to one of them, washed my hands, dried them and pulled out a stool up to the first cow. She stirred and snorted, starting a wave of sounds across the shed.

I began to milk. Press, pull, press, pull. The milk squirted into the container. My hands tired easily, despite this twice-daily exercise. I stopped now and again enjoying the peace before Umtraut's arrival.

A sudden awareness of muffled footsteps made me look over my shoulder. I was expecting to see Ludwik, but even as realisation dawned on me, with a shock, he spoke softly first.

"Anna... I didn't want to startle you..."

I shot up from the stool and rushed towards his open arms and pressed myself against him and held him tight, feeling the shudder of his and my emotions.

"Michal... Michal," was all I could say.

He whispered against my cheek,

"Anna... I've dreamed of this a thousand times!"

"So did I!" I exclaimed in wonder.

We clung to each other, afraid to let go, afraid this precious reality would burst like a bubble the moment we separated. The scent of the woods, of the clean outdoors trapped in his clothes was like a heady perfume in the staleness of the cowshed.

"How did you get here?" I spoke into his shoulder.

"Walked all night. Through the forest," he spoke into my hair.

I moved my head back to look at him.

"And did Holtzmann let you?"

"I didn't ask. I left when it got dark."

I felt the cold grip of anxiety.

"Michal, what are we going to do?"

He loosened his embrace enough to face me. The same brown eyes, the amber flecks, the smooth, shiny hair, falling over his forehead.

"We've got to persuade them to let us stay together," he said.

"Oh, Michal…" my joy was changing rapidly to fear.

"Anna, if we don't try, there will never be any change!" He held me close, but the snorting and the stomping behind us, reminded us that my job could not wait.

"I'd better go," he released me, "to find Ludwik and to see your boss. There's one more thing. It's sad news."

"What?" My stomach lurched.

"It's Staszek… He'd got the 'flu, but Horst wouldn't allow him even half a day off. Worked him to death…"

"What are you saying?"

"Staszek died of pneumonia…two weeks ago…"

I stifled a cry, but I could not stop the tears. Hundreds of memories of Staszek flooded my mind: his dimply smile, his clear-blue eyes, his songs, his sayings, and his transparent, well-meaning nature.

"Maryla…" I asked, "How's Maryla?"

"Terrible. Can't sleep. Can't eat. Like a shadow going about her work."

"And Bazylka?"

"Frantic with worry."

Dear God! What was it all for?

"I'll come back," Michal said, "I'll let you get on with your job."

I milked the cows automatically, one by one, my mind a tangle of thoughts, my heart torn between joy and grief. I was halfway down the row of cows, when Umtraut appeared. My emotional weariness made me almost indifferent to the expected bad temper of hers.

She stood over me.

"That man of yours; Michal," she said, "he's a good worker. I've just watched him helping Ludwik. Knows his stuff without having to be told."

Her tone was as much of a surprise, as if she had given me gold. I looked up at her in disbelief.

"Yes, he is," I confirmed, "the best."

She considered me for a moment with those sunken eyes of hers.

"Schwartz is coming to lunch," she said. Strange how she called her brother by his surname. "He knows all the right people, in all the right places. We'll see what can be done…"

The impact of her words left me breathless.

"Stop staring like a stud at a mare," she snapped. "We need workers, don't we? Ten more of your boyfriends wouldn't be enough!"

She could be as insulting as she wished, I thought, as long as Michal was allowed to stay.

Schwartz and Helga had cycled from Eberstein to join the Kestners for lunch, after their Sunday visit to church. My nerves were taut as I listened for the dreaded sound of Spitz and Blitz' car, while concentrating hard to catch Michal's name in the rowdy exchange on the Kestners' table. Michal's attention was focused entirely, for the moment, on the food and its taste, as he tucked in with unabashed greed. We spoke in low tones, keeping our talk discreet. We reminisced about our times on Holtzmann's farm, and we each had suddenly so many memories of our dear friend Staszek.

"Shall we go to the woods after lunch?" Ludwik suggested. "Find a nice spot. Hold our own service for him?" His eyes shone like dark liquid.

After lunch, Schwartz came over to our table. We became quiet and looked up expectantly at his tall, gaunt frame.

"Majerski," he said to Michal, "I'll talk to my boss later, when I get home. But my advice to you now is this: go back to your farm tonight. If we can arrange a transfer for you, you'll be told about it."

So that was that. Just a couple of hours. Then he'd have to go. And God only knew when we'd see each other again!

But later, as I changed into my new grey dress, the one with the white collar and the white cuffs, my mood lifted. I persuaded myself that perhaps I worried too much in advance, perhaps Holtzmann would relent and let Michal go, perhaps, at least, allow him to visit me now and again, perhaps I would be freed from the dreadful, suffocating fear.

The boys were ready in Ludwik's room. They had nothing else to change into, but they had scrubbed their hands, arms and faces, and had brushed their hair.

Michal turned around. His face beamed.

"Anna! You've grown!"

"It's the long dress!" I laughed, "makes me look taller."

His eyes scanned me from head to toe and for no reason at all I felt instantly, insanely happy.

We set off across the yard, by the pond, under the chestnut tree towards the footpath that led up to the forest on higher ground. Here, the fragrance of April was all around us, in the freshness of pines, emanating from the catkins and pink-flowering shrubs, from the blue carpet of forget-me-nots, from the clumps of grass, newly resurrected and shining bright green in the passing beams of sunlight.

Michal and Ludwik could not stop talking. There was so much catching up to do. I interrupted after a long while in one of those rare unguarded pauses.

"Hey, listen you two, Easter's only a week away. Do you think Umtraut will let us colour the eggs?" I joked.

They stopped and looked at me.

"Easter? Eggs? So it is!" Michal exclaimed, then added with less enthusiasm, "Can you imagine Elise allowing such things?"

"Then stay with us and make soft eyes at Umtraut," Ludwik laughed.

The very notion made me laugh too.

We found a lovely spot on the top of the hill in the forest. Above us the sky spread like silk of the clearest colour. Through a gap in the trees we could see peaks of distant mountains. At our feet white edelweiss peered through the green ground.

"I think this is the right spot," Ludwik said, "Staszek would have loved it here."

"He'd think of a song straight away," Michal said.

"About the 'Goral' leaving his home in the mountains," I added.

We stood in silence for a long while, with our own thoughts and prayers. Michal spoke first. "Let's pray for Stefan too. Perhaps one day we'll find out where they've buried him."

I felt a pang. Deep in my chest. Grief took so long to heal.

Ludwik began to hum. A song that was about the sadness of parting but also about the joy of being reunited one day. Michal and I joined in.

"Right," Ludwik said when our song came to an end, "time for me to go."

"You don't have to." Michal placed his hand on Ludwik's shoulder.

Ludwik smiled.

"C'mon Michal," he said. "You've not crossed rivers and forests and mountains to be with me. There's not much time, so don't waste it. I'll see you later." His long legs made big strides as he walked away.

Now that we were alone, Michal and I, a strange shyness came over me. I was suddenly very much aware of Michal's closeness, of him looking at me, of something about to be said, and I racked my brain to say something first.

"Anna, it's your birthday soon," he said simply, "on Wednesday, isn't it?"

This took me by surprise. I relaxed and laughed.

"How did you know?" A wide grin lifted his cheeks.

"I know more than you think." He dug his fingers inside his breast pocket. "I've made you something," he said.

"What?" I felt like an excited child.

"See for yourself."

He held out his fist, and let me playfully prise open his fingers, rough and cut, one by one. There, in his palm was a little wooden heart, with a thin leather string pulled through the hole at the top.

"It's beautiful," I said, stroking its polished, pebble-like surface.

"Will you wear it for me?" he asked.

I felt his warm breath as he tied the string at the back of my neck, I felt his fingers touch my skin, I felt his lips, surprisingly soft and warm, rest on my partly exposed shoulder. I shivered, I felt myself melting. He turned me round and covered my mouth with his. It was electric. A blinding flash behind my closed eyelids. Currents racing through my limbs. An explosion of heat at the pit of my stomach, rising, rendering me weak. With remnants of strength I pulled away.

"Michal…" I was confused. I was out of breath.

He cupped my face in his hands and kissed me again. Briefly. On my lips.

"Anna," he said, "I love you. I want to be with you. Always. That's why I'm here. Is that not clear?"

He loved me! Of all the girls in the world he loved me! Me! I was giddy with happiness.

I returned his kiss.

"Michal, it's very clear."

I remember every detail of that brief afternoon: every kiss, every embrace; our entwined, tingling fingers; our arms touching as we lay side by side on the soft moss; the crowns of the trees high above us, looking down from a pure blue sky. So many memories to share of our separate yet familiar lives at home, so many plans to make and discuss, yet so little time, running out rapidly on us.

Later, when we came out of the forest and descended the sloping footpath down to the farm, Spitz and Blitz were waiting for us, their black Volkswagen, like a creepy beast, sprawled across the lane.

They stood very still under the chestnut tree and watched as we walked towards them. Kestner was pacing up and down by the pond, his visibly nervous state making my heart pound harder, my mouth go dry.

Michal gripped my hand.

"Don't worry, Anna. I'll speak to them."

When we came close, Spitz stretched himself to his full height, seemingly inflating himself to intimidate us.

"You're coming with us, Majerski. You stupid oaf! How did you imagine, you'd get away with it?"

My stomach suffered another painful spasm.

"Sir, let me explain," Michal spoke in a carefully polite manner. "I'm just visiting. I've done nothing wrong. I've been helping Herr Kestner. If it's time for me to go back, then I will."

Spitz struck Michal across his face. I held back a scream.

"You fool! You arrogant fool! You don't make decisions here! It's not up to you to choose who you're going to work for. Now get inside the car and don't waste any more of our time!"

There was no chance for fond farewells. I watched, helpless, as Spitz pushed Michal roughly onto the back seat. Blitz performed his usual twirl with the long black coat before climbing into the passenger seat. They drove off in a cloud of dust. I glimpsed Michal's face pressed against the pane, his lips forming words. What words? What was he trying to say?

I did not want Kestner to see me cry, but his hand on my shoulder arrested my hurried retreat. I could only wait with my head bowed, mortified, miserable. His gruff voice was surprisingly steady.

"Don't cry Anna. We may get him back yet. Schwartz has already gone ahead of them to the police station in Eberstein. Now go and help Frau Kestner with the cows."

These were the kindest words he had ever spoken to me.

I rushed indoors to get changed, also to look for Ludwik. He was already gone to start his work in the stables. My mind was in turmoil, my fingers clumsy with the buttons, clumsy with the apron strings. I hurried to the cowshed, though my official free time was not over yet. Umtraut was already milking at the far end, usually Frieda's pitch. I dipped my hands in disinfectant, dried them and began my work.

"Good, is he? Your Michal?" Umtraut shouted over the backs of the cows.

"You'd have an excellent worker!" I replied, though I did not feel like talking.

"In bed, you silly goose!" A forced guffaw followed her words. I did not reply.

She walked over and stood beside me.

"Tell me, what's he like, your Michal. Does he please you? Or just himself? Get what you can from him. Believe me, they're all the same in the end. A whiff of another skirt, and they're off!"

I carried on milking. I did not look up at her. I hated what she was saying. Michal and I loved each other. We were never going to be like the Kestners.

"And let me tell you…" she bent over me, too close, "don't let him put you in the pudding club. You won't see him for the dust!"

Her nastiness had no limits. I wanted to scream at her, to hit out. I got up, picked up my stool and the bucket and moved them to the next cow.

"Frau Kestner," I forced myself to speak quietly, "Michal and I don't do such things. There'll be time for all that when we marry."

She threw her head back and let out a shriek, as if I had just told her the funniest joke ever. Then, still chortling, she said, "Just as well then, for there's no room for your bastard here!"

She walked away, her long, thin back stooping, her skirt brushing the dirty ground, leaving me consumed with helpless indignation at her final insult.

It was later, when alone at last, lugging the heavy churn to the main road, that I gave in to tears of frustration and grief. I could not stop thinking about Michal, longing with an ache to be with him, back on Holtzmann's farm. Even if again, I had to put up with Elise's malice, with old Frau Holtzmann's demands, with their revolting food, with all the harsh conditions. So wrapped up I was in my misery, it took a sudden screeching of birds by the roadside to make me aware of the pink evening sky, the early transparent moon rising, the distant croaking of frogs. Reassuring normality carried on around me but I needed more than that, I needed certainty and someone to comfort me.

I went looking for Ludwik after running all the way from the main road. He was in the stables tending to the horses. Anton was clearing the ground around Hannibal the bull, who was kept in control with thick restraining ropes and a big basket of hay set before him.

I stood next to Ludwik and began to wash down and wipe Blackie's flank.

"Ludwik, I can't bear it. The waiting's killing me. They'll never let Michal come to work here. I'd just like to know for certain, one way or the other!"

Ludwik spoke calmly, like my big brother.

"Be patient, Anna. We'll know soon enough. Schwartz may still have his uses. Who knows?"

"Do you think so?" I was clutching at straws.

"Let's just wait and see." It was not so much a smile, as warmth in his voice that gave me hope.

We heard Schwartz's motorbike, half way through our evening meal. It was pork and vegetable stew. Much as I disliked Umtraut, I could not fault her cooking. At times, begrudgingly, I even allowed feelings of gratitude to penetrate my distrust.

Schwartz walked in and went straight to the Kestners' table. He was wearing his black policeman's uniform.

"I've just come from the station," he said. "They're keeping him here, overnight, for punishment."

"Who? Majerski?" Kestner stopped eating. We all did. My heart stood still. Only Anton slurped his stew and smacked his lips with relish.

"Herman, my friend, is on duty tonight," Schwartz said. "Good time to negotiate. Are you coming?"

Kestner rubbed his forehead. Umtraut indicated a seat for her brother to sit down, but he declined with a wave of his hand.

"I'm on duty too. I've got to get back."

"So…" Kestner was thoughtful, "what are the chances?"

I could hardly breathe. Ludwik's eyes were fixed on the table as he listened intently.

"I don't know. That's the honest truth," Schwartz shrugged. "Officially, Majerski's Holtzmann's property. He's got all Majerski's papers. But…" Schwartz spread his hands and looked at us over his shoulder. We resumed our eating, straining to hear his every word. "You know Jozef, what the best currency is these days."

We all knew. Kestner rubbed his forehead again.

"Yes, but how do I know how much is enough? A chunk of ham? A side of bacon? A whole pig? Holtzmann's much bigger than us. I'm no match for him. I bet he's already got the whole county in his pocket."

They all fell silent and I chewed slowly staring at Ludwik.

It was Umtraut who spoke first.

"It's worth a try, Jozef. We need workers badly. God knows how much longer I can carry on like this. Some days I can barely stand."

They exchanged glances.

"All right, I'll go," Kestner said. "Give me five minutes."

"I'll go ahead and wait for you there." Schwartz gave them a perfunctory salute and left in a hurry.

Impulsively, rashly, I got up and approached Kestner. I saw alarm in Ludwik's eyes.

"Herr Kestner, please let me come with you," I begged, "I've got to see Michal."

Both he and Umtraut looked taken aback.

"Are you mad?" Umtraut recovered first. "What sort of a whim is this? I forbid it! You're not going anywhere!"

"Please, Frau Kestner, please..." I was close to tears.

"No!" she got up and started clearing away her own bowl, her mug and cutlery.

"Shut up, woman!" Kestner was still eating. "I give orders here! If I say she can go, then she will!" He banged his fist on the table, startling Anton, then making him laugh.

Umtraut scowled.

"You won't be so cocky when Dieter comes back!"

She dumped her things with a clatter on the draining board, and stomped off towards the parlour, slamming the door behind her. Kestner did not comment. He finished eating, wiped the bowl with the last piece of bread and then stuffed it in his mouth.

"Right," he said with his mouth full, "let's go. You can take Umtraut's bike."

Hurriedly I pulled on my outdoor clothing, my long cardigan, my coat, against the evening chill.

"Good luck!" Ludwik whispered, starting to tidy up.

The earlier pale moon was now a bright globe in the vast starry sky. The landscape around us had a calm diffused luminosity, with each tree and shrub clearly outlined. No lights or torches, strictly forbidden, were necessary. I cycled behind Kestner down the path to the valley, then, on the other side, we walked up the hill pushing our bikes to the main road. To my relief he kept quiet, saving me from the additional strain of having to talk to him.

The road to Eberstein was silvery, deserted. Kestner's hunched back and his long legs, working the pedals with nervous speed, somehow intensified for me the urgency of our mission. The closeness of the first few houses assailed me with anticipation and anxiety in equal measures. The police station was situated in a side street near the *Rathaus*. Its lime stucco walls took on a greenish tint at night, and the decorative brickwork around the windows cast the recesses in black shadows. There was no sound, no light, not a person in sight.

We tied our bikes to the metal hooks fixed in a row to the side wall, and stealthily, like shadows, made our way to the front door. It was double width, thick oak, seemingly impenetrable, but a push from

Kestner yielded a gap wide enough for us both to slip through. Inside there was another double, glass-panelled door, beyond which I could see a massive semi-circular counter, with a dim light hanging over it. The official behind it, I guessed was Herman, mentioned earlier.

Schwartz was talking to him over the counter. He looked openly displeased when he saw me coming in with Kestner.

"What's she doing here?"

Kestner shrugged. "Wants to see her boyfriend."

I did not expect him to explain that it was his spite against Umtraut that had brought me here.

The man behind the counter, stocky with ginger hair cropped short, nodded to Schwartz.

"Take her to him. Five minutes. No more!" I knew this was not kindness. They wanted me out of the way.

Schwartz opened a door and led me down a corridor lined with numerous doors and port holes between them. As I passed by I realised they were cells. Some were empty, some had solitary men in them. He stopped by number nine.

"I'll come back in five minutes," he said and left.

I peered through the small window. It was a narrow room, lit by a miniature bare bulb, with a bench at the far wall and a bucket in the corner. Michal was lying down on his side with his face to the wall.

I tapped on the glass pane. He did not stir. I tapped again, this time making the coded, familiar sound; long, short, short, several times. He rolled over and slowly sat up. I waved, mouthing through the glass, "It's me!"

He got up and stiffly came up to the window. It was then that I saw with a shock the cuts and abrasions on his face, his swollen mouth, his closed, bruised eye. His hands too, when he lifted them to open a section of the window, bore marks of heavy blows.

"What have they done to you?" I could barely speak.

With his good eye he looked at me for a long time, all his pain, his longing, his love contained in one glance.

"Anna…just seeing you…how's this possible?"

I told him. He shook his head.

"No chance. Holtzmann's coming to fetch me in the morning. But there had to be punishment first."

I slipped my hand through the porthole and touched the side of his battered face. He turned his head and kissed my fingers. I could not hold back my tears.

"Don't cry Anna, please don't cry. You've made me so happy!"

He clasped my hand in his and we remained silent just holding onto each other. Stefan's words came back to me. It now seemed such a long time ago. "There are things in life worth risking everything for." Dearest Michal! He had risked so much just for a day with me.

"Michal," I said, "if it takes ten years, a lifetime, I'll be waiting for you."

"I know…"

I thought I saw a sparkle of amber in his good eye. I heard the door at the far end swing open and saw Schwartz coming towards me.

"Michal," I placed my fingers over the wooden heart at my neck, "every morning and every night I'll touch this heart and it'll be like touching you."

He kissed my hand once more and then I had to follow Schwartz.

Outside in the black shadows between the buildings, as Kestner and I untied our bicycles, I asked, "So, what's going to happen now?"

"Nothing." Kestner bent down to clip his trouser legs. "Holtzmann's beaten me to it. I can't compete against him. He's already oiled all the cogs that matter."

So that was that! I had prepared myself for disappointment, yet when it came, so irreversibly certain, I had a feeling as if all the while I had been falling through the darkness into an abyss, and now I had hit the bottom with a thud.

"You know the way home, Anna," Kestner said. "Off you go! I've got some business to attend to."

I knew well what business that was, but, in my own grief, I had no capacity left for anyone else's concerns.

I cycled alone down the deserted road, my habitual anxiety drowned in my sorrow. The silver beauty of the night around me, seemed only to intensify my despair, my loss. I worked my legs hard, pushing the bicycle to its limits, longing to reach the safety of my room, to find solace from this unbearable pain in Ludwik's comforting words. "As long as we're alive, Anna, and well, each new day is a promise." I wished I had the power to look into the future, to see the day that would bring Michal back to me.

CHAPTER 19

The toothache was relentless. I could not get to sleep despite my exhaustion. I lay still, afraid to aggravate the pain and watched the full moon linger inside the frame of the skylight above me. Could Michal see it too? Did he think about me the way I thought about him? All the time? It was the same moon that shone back at home. On our village. On my mother. I longed for her hand to soothe my hot forehead, for her camomile tea to deaden my pain.

The dentist, Doktor Adler had been specific. If I wanted the second tooth filling, I had to pay. His dental supplies were limited, he had told me, his first obligation was to the military. The civilians came next, then lastly, imported workers like myself.

I was desperate. I offered him everything I had.

"Two marks and ten pfennigs."

His expression had been thoughtful, speculative.

"I don't want your money. But I've got a family to feed. Do you understand?"

I understood perfectly. And now, what had to be done, could not be put off any longer.

Mercifully I drifted into sleep, and for a while out of pain. When I opened my eyes, it was dawn and time to stir myself off the mattress. There were jobs to be done first before breakfast, before I dared myself to approach Kestner with my request. I helped Umtraut and Frieda milk the cows, I carried the churn full of milk to the main road for collection, I let out the pigs and the chickens and brought them their feed, all the while worn down by the ache, that stuck like a leach.

At breakfast, the warm porridge made my eyes water.

"Are you all right?" Ludwik asked, his eyes wide with concern.

"I shall be when I get this awful tooth done."

I made myself get up and walk over to the Kestners' table.

"Herr Kestner, I've got to see the dentist. My tooth's killing me!"

They stopped eating, only old Anton continued to slurp and smack his lips.

"But you've only just been!" Umtraut protested, a vertical crease forming on her brow. "I won't allow it! You skiving off again!"

I pointed at my cheek. I knew it was reddened and puffy.

"He ran out of the filling stuff. He told me to come back."

She sucked in her lips making me think of my cat's bottom.

"I'll pull it out for you, and be done with it," she said.

"Don't be daft, woman!" Kestner raised his voice. "Can't you see the girl's in pain? Go and get it sorted Anna, but get your jobs done first!"

His kindness did not fool me. He was scoring points against his wife. I found it strangely satisfying for a brief moment, that for once, the differences between them turned out to my advantage.

"In that case," Umtraut said, "you can do all the outdoor jobs yourself. I'm stopping in. I suffer pain too, you know!"

I knew. I would have given her much more than distant sympathy if only her tongue had not been so hateful.

"I wish there was some way I could help you," Ludwik said apologetically, when I sat down beside him, "but I've already been relegated to whitewash the walls and creosote all the timber around the farm."

Now that the fields had been ploughed and covering rapidly with a fresh green stubble of wheat, barley, rye and sweet corn, the men were catching up with all the jobs around the buildings, best done and finished in dry weather.

"I'll cope," I reassured Ludwik.

My big worry now, was not the number of tasks awaiting me, but how to distract Umtraut's attention long enough, to take the pantry key, go up to the attic and steal enough food to satisfy Doctor Adler's needs.

It was mid-morning before I finished the basic jobs, all the while racking my brains for inspiration. I stank of sweat and pigs which I had been hosing down. I needed a good scrub myself. But first things first. I had an idea. It was not much, but anything was worth a try.

I ran up the path to the higher ground in the woods. Had this been a summer month, I would have gone looking for bilberries. Now, in mid-May, the ground was covered in lush greens of ferns, nettles and weeds of all kinds.

To my delight, I saw what I was looking for. Separating the patches of bluebells, were random pathways overgrown with dandelions, their bright yellow heads like stars scattered against the blue. I squatted and picked the tender young leaves beneath them. I remembered my mother's green salads, and the sweet, milky taste of dandelion leaves. I picked enough to make a generous salad for the five of us, now that

Frieda and Gerhart spent most of their days on the other side of the valley, looking after the herds of oxen and sheep. Holding my find gently inside my rag bag, I picked a bunch of bluebells for Umtraut. I prayed for the smooth running of my plan.

I found her in the kitchen. She had just finished kneading the bread dough on the big table and was clearing things away. She greeted me with the usual scowl and was just about to call me the expected names of tramp and lazy bones and bitch and swine, but I intercepted her from the door.

"Frau Kestner, Look what I've found!" I came towards her, forcing a smile over my toothache, holding out the bluebells. "The flowers are for you, and this," I uncovered the dandelion leaves, "is lunch for all of us."

She stopped wiping the table. Her scowl hesitated, giving way to surprise.

"What's the meaning of all this?" She rubbed her sticky hands on her apron and pulled back the edge of my rag to see better the fresh, firm, glistening young leaves.

"Frau Kestner," I rushed to explain in an amiable, appeasing tone, "we used to pick dandelion leaves at home. My mother made delicious salads. A little natural dressing, oil, vinegar, honey, salt and pepper…and it was no worse than the real lettuce…"

She snorted.

"Do you think I don't know all this? I've been picking things in the woods long before you were born! Mushrooms, bilberries, blackberries, elderberries, rose hips… I don't think you could teach me anything new, that we've not already discovered!"

I guessed she was pleased. Any additional free food was welcome. But then she looked at the bunch in my hand and the inevitable scowl returned.

"And what are these for?"

"I picked these for you."

Her eyes narrowed with suspicion.

"No one gives me things. Why would you?"

I shrugged.

"The ground is covered with them in the woods. I thought they'd look nice on the windowsill."

I went behind her back and got a jug down from the shelf, and a salad bowl. Holding my breath, I lifted the pantry key off its hook and hid it in my pocket. The first part of my plan was accomplished.

I took the jug to the washroom, where I filled it with water. I brought it back, arranged the flowers in it and left my offering for Umtraut in a spot of sunlight on the windowsill.

"I'll wash the leaves later," I said.

She had her back turned to me, as she placed the bowl with the bread dough on the high stool near the range, leaving it there to rise. She answered with her usual irritation.

"Stop messing about! Now scram! And don't take all day!" But I felt there was the tiniest touch of thaw in her harsh manner.

I ran up the wooden stairs and took off the clogs before tiptoeing barefoot to the pantry. With my heart beating fast, my toothache pulsating, I unlocked the door and went in. It was like walking into a forest of hanging sausages, chunks of smoked bacon and ham. My immediate instinct was to grab the nearest thing by the door and to run off with it, but I forced myself to make my way to the far end, where theft would be less likely discovered amidst the dense clusters of processed meats. I picked up a knife from the cutting bench, cut off a sausage, a chunk of bacon and a chunk of ham and hid them inside my rag bag.

The thudding in my ears was like a raging storm. I feared that Umtraut, downstairs, could hear it. I stepped outside and listened. All was quiet. I turned the key in the lock and rushed to my room. The second part of my plan was complete. Now for the third part. Replacing the key without being seen.

I threw my grey dress over the rag bag with the spoils in it, rolled the lot into a bundle and carried it under my arm downstairs into the kitchen. Umtraut was in the washroom doing the daily laundry in a large bowl placed on a tall bench.

"Not gone yet?" She spoke over her shoulder, bent over, so no one would see the bloodstained knickers and vests. I had seen them drying in places she had thought were hidden from the rest of us.

"I need a quick wash," I said, fixing my gaze on her back, while replacing the key on its hook. It was done!

She hunched even more, flexing her bony shoulders, intent on forming a screen.

"Can't you see I'm busy here? Go and wash in the yard. And for goodness sake girl, hurry up!"

I did not need telling twice. There was no one about in the yard. I undressed to my knickers and brassiere and washed under the running tap, scrubbing my face, my arm-pits, my elbows, my bare legs. Then I picked up my two bundles, the soiled clothes and the fresh, and ran inside the barn to dry myself and dress unseen. I had a dozen eggs hidden in a hole in one of the bales. I placed those carefully, one by one, on top of the stolen meats in my bag, and padded the whole lot with hay.

As fast as my legs could carry me, I crossed the yard and ran up the footpath into the woods. Here I could continue my journey unseen, along a track, parallel to the railway line in the valley, parallel to the main road to Eberstein. As I passed by the Schloss I could see inside its many levels from my high vantage point. Armed guards standing on towers, patrolling the walkways along the thick walls, an enclosed courtyard, black cars, long red banners, swastikas. Everywhere.

I hurried on and kept up the fast pace to the end of the woodland path, where it descended to meet the level crossing near the town. From there, it was just a short distance to Doktor Adler's street, but that did not lessen my fear of being noticed, the yellow "P" like a torch shining on my shoulder. Anyone had the right to stop me and demand to examine the contents of my bag. It was every citizen's duty to be vigilant at all times.

Dizzy with anxiety, I reached Doktor Adler's door and pulled the string. The door was faded oak with peeling streaks of old varnish and set in crumbling stucco walls with patches of mildew rising from the pavement. To my overwhelming relief, the door opened almost immediately. I was ushered in by the dentist's assistant, a middle-aged woman, with grey, crimped hair, and a thinness disguised by the white overall.

"I am Anna Myszkovska," I reminded her, "I was here last week. This is for Herr Doktor."

She nodded, and without a word, took the bag from me. She led me down a dark corridor with brown painted walls, to a small waiting room.

"Wait here, *bitte*."

I was left alone, with four dark-wood chairs, a faded print of a landscape on one wall, and a photograph of the *Fuhrer* facing me. I could not stand the sight of his mad staring eyes. I changed places and sat underneath his portrait. The blue sky beyond the window was beautiful, normal, calming.

I longed for calm and normality, but before long dark thoughts of suspicion crept into my mind. What if Doktor Adler did not keep his promise? What if this was a trap? What if the Gestapo were waiting for me in the other room? I heard the footsteps coming. Light, woman's footsteps. The door opened. It was the dentist's assistant, her spectacles reflecting the light from the window.

"He's ready now."

I was sat down in a worn leather armchair and my head tilted back against the adjustable head-rest. The ceiling above me had been white once. The whole room, though scrubbed clean, had the colour and texture of old parchment. Doktor Adler peered down my mouth, a breath of garlic preceding him. He was balding, and though clean shaven, had a shadow on his face, that dark-haired men often do. He poked around my mouth, giving me a jolt when touching the source of my pain.

"It's your wisdom tooth coming through," he said. "I'll give you something for that. The two small cavities shouldn't be a problem, I'll do them in no time."

He rubbed some ointment around the base of my teeth.

"Numbing ointment," he said, "I've got no anaesthetic."

I braced myself. I just wanted him to get on with it. I wanted it to be over.

The drilling began. I resisted the pain with my rigid body, with my gripping fingers, with my screwed eyes, and only when it stopped I felt the sweat trickling down my face and neck.

He completed his work in silence, scraping and filling, that felt like nails being driven into my gums. I held onto the armchair when I got up to go, feeling light-headed, my tongue feeling thick as I thanked him.

He slid off the high chair and pulled out a drawer from one of the flat cupboards that lined one whole wall. He took out a jar, and shook out a few pills into a small brown paper bag.

"Take these for your wisdom tooth. Against inflammation. You must take them all. One in the morning and one at night. If you need me again," his gaze was unblinking, "you know what to do."

"You're very kind," I said, limp with relief, now the ordeal was over.

My empty rag bag lay on the floor by the entrance door. I picked it up and stepped outside into the sunshine.

The moment I entered the hallway by the kitchen, Umtraut called out to me, "What's taken you so long! I've been waiting with jobs for you this past half hour, you lazy trollop! What do you think this is? A holiday camp?"

Her grumpiness was of the usual sort. She had not discovered my theft. I let go of my fear in a slow deep sigh.

"Two seconds, Frau Kestner!" I called back amiably.

She was standing at the kitchen table rummaging through two large card boxes. They were open and heaped with winter clothing.

"Take these to Sylvia's room. And afterwards..." she stretched over to the key rack and removed the pantry key, "bring me down a chunk of bacon. About a kilo piece. I can't stand all those stairs. You think you've got pain! You've no idea what real pain is!" Her face went into a scowl.

I picked up one of the boxes, but she stopped me. She pulled out a dress, navy cotton with a pattern of white roses.

"Take this," she said, "alter it for yourself. I've no more use for it. You can patch the holes under the arm pits with the bit you cut off from the bottom."

I was too stunned to reply.

"Stop gawping, girl! What are you? Deaf as well as stupid? Now scram! The cows will be bursting their udders!"

I picked up the box and she stuffed the dress on top, right under my chin. It smelled of her, of stale fish, of stale blood. I could put up with that. There was plenty of clean water in the tap.

"You're very kind, Frau Kestner," I said, "I'm really grateful."

She gave me a push.

"Get on with it, girl! Enough of your silly talk!"

Umtraut's condition deteriorated suddenly one night at the end of May. In the daytime she was her usual self, bad-tempered, shouting orders, scowling. She noticed the purple-blue patch on my calf as we swept the yard with the large broomsticks for outdoors.

"What's that beauty spot doing on your leg?" her tone was reprimanding as if I had committed a crime.

"It's the frostbite. It's where I've had the boils," I explained the obvious.

"Want to get rid of that?" It was a strange question. I stared at her.

"Don't just gawp at me, girl! Come on, come with me, and do as I tell you!"

She threw her broomstick down, grabbed my hand and dragged me along the orchard to where the grass was fresh with nettles growing in abundance round the edges.

"There! Take a run through them. Young nettles are the best!"

I thought she was mad. I feared the sting of the nettles but I feared her rage more.

Screwing my eyes and bracing myself, I lifted my skirt high and walked into the nettles. It was like thousands of tiny insects biting all at once.

"Go on, swing your leg a few times." She stood over me till she was satisfied I carried out her instruction to the last.

When I was released from this ordeal, she examined my calf. It was covered in a rapidly spreading rash of raised spots, stinging and itching unbearably.

"This'll get your circulation going. You'll see!" Even when she displayed a rare hint of friendliness, she creased her face ferociously. I could not bring myself to thank her.

The nettle rash bothered me all day. I showed my leg to Ludwik, when we sat under the chestnut tree after supper. The lighter, longer evenings were our favourite time after each day's work.

"That's awful!" Ludwik ran his finger over my bumpy skin, "but, though you won't believe me, in fact I can hardly believe it myself, I think Umtraut, for once was trying to be kind."

"How come?" I could never associate Umtraut with kindness.

"Well, you'd be surprised how nettles can be used to cure all kinds of things. Nettle tea for indigestion. Or liver, or bladder. Stronger infusions for treating bruises and cuts. Good for washing your hair too. Makes it stronger and thicker, so they say. And even the nettle fibre can be used for weaving sail cloth and twisting into thick ropes."

"Much good is all that to me!" I cried, "I need a cure for this nettle rash before it drives me insane!"

I was shaken awake at dawn. It was already light. My mind came alive in an instant when I saw Kestner leaning over me.

"Get up, Anna, quick! My wife's in a bad way. I've got to fetch Schwartz, to take her to hospital. Go! Stay with her!"

I sat up, pulling my cover, a tatty old sheet around me.

"You go, Herr Kestner. I'll be right down with her."

I waited for him to leave, before getting up and pulling on my skirt and my blouse. Ludwik's door across the passage was ajar and I could hear he was getting up too. We came out at the same time, he brushing back his curls with his fingers.

"Did I just hear Kestner's voice?" he asked.

"It's Umtraut." I told him Kestner's instructions. "Ludwik, you'll have to get the cows in for milking. I'll be down as soon as I can."

I rushed to the washroom, splashed my face and brushed my teeth, then I made my way up the other staircase to the Kestners' bedroom. Kestner had left the door wide open. I stopped there taking in the scene.

Umtraut was in bed, her long grey plait stretched down beside her, her eyes closed and sunken, her skin like a thin film over the bones of her face. I thought she was dead. Her voice startled me.

"Don't just stand there, girl, gawping! Come here, or go to milk the cows!"

I came in and pulled a stool to sit down beside her.

"Herr Kestner has ordered me to stay with you till he comes back with Herr Schwartz," I said. "Is there anything I can do to help?"

She snorted.

"How could you possibly help? No one can help me now. It's too late! I'm leaking to death."

"Don't say that!" I protested, unable to think of anything else to say.

"Look for yourself then!" She made a movement, a slight movement as if to pull back the cover, but her hand fell limp by her side. I lifted a corner of her eiderdown and folded it back. What I saw shocked me. Her nightgown was covered in large, dark blood stains, the towels across her pelvis and underneath her were soaked.

"Good God! What's happened to you!" I cried.

"It's the cancer," she said, "it's got to me at last."

I was frightened. I started to gabble, as much to comfort her as myself.

"They'll be here soon. They'll take you to hospital. You'll be in good hands, Frau Kestner. Everything will be all right…"

She lay silent, with her eyes closed. I was desperate for the sound of Schwartz' car. Nervously I brushed down my skirt and noticed that the prickliness had gone from my leg. The skin was smoother and was losing its patchiness.

"It's all such a waste," I heard her speak in a low, tired voice. "Such a waste, this bloody war! Our lives… Dieter's life… What's it all for? Now, I'll never see him again…"

I watched a tear shine in the corner of her eye and trickle down her temple.

"Frau Kestner" I said gently so as not to irritate her, "the war may be over soon. Who knows? Your son may be home any day now…"

"Only if he's wounded. God forbid that! The war's not over. Hitler's invaded Russia now."

This was indeed bad news. Was this war never going to end? My thoughts flew to my mother, to my sisters and brothers. I felt a sudden strong pang of yearning to see them. And Michal. When would I see him again?

I waited in silence for the sound of Schwartz' car and wove fantasies of the times when the war was over, when Hitler and Stalin killed each other off, when their armies retreated back to their own countries, leaving the rest of us free to return to our normal lives.

My heart leapt with relief at the sound of a car engine. I moved to the window and looked out. Kestner was getting his bicycle out of the black Volkswagen, and Schwartz was running towards the house.

"They're here," I said.

"Anna," Umtraut was breathing hard, "open the linen chest. You'll need sheets and towels. Also, a blanket from the wardrobe."

The moment the men were up in the room, I spread a sheet on the other side of the bed. Kestner and Schwartz lifted Umtraut onto it and padded her all round her hips with towels. I helped to wrap her in a blanket, and like a long parcel, the men carried her downstairs. I followed and watched as they lay her down on the back seat of the car. Her face had the colour and the stillness of death.

"I don't know how long I'm going to be," Kestner said, jumping into the passenger seat while Schwartz started the engine. "See to all the animals, Anna. Call Ludwik and Anton. And fetch Frieda. To do the meals."

They drove off in a cloud of dust and I went inside to remove Umtraut's blood-stained sheets from the bed. I immersed them in cold water to soak in the washroom and reflected on Umtraut's illness. It had robbed her of her privacy, it had forced her to share her intimate secrets with me; me, just a lowly slave worker, the butt of her constant ill-temper.

I felt no resentment, just relief to be freed of her. I pitied her. I felt gratitude for my good fortune. I had my mother at home. I had Michael who loved me. I had hope. She had none of those things.

We worked hard, the four of us, to finish the most important jobs in time. While Frieda and I milked the cows, Ludwik and Anton saw to the pigs and the chickens. They took the horses out into the field, then the cows, when we had finished milking. Ludwik helped Frieda to prepare the food supplies, ham, bacon, eggs and cheeses, for the weekly collection by the army truck, while I carried the milk churn to the main road for the regular daily collection.

Breakfast was later that morning, but once we sat down, there was none of the usual tension, the urgency to eat fast, to rush back to our work. Frieda and I put out identical things on our two separate tables. We all had a bowl of porridge. There was bread, butter and cheese, and rye coffee.

"This is silly!" Ludwik called out across the room. "Frieda, Anton, I invite you to sit at our table!" He got up, turned Hitler's bust to face the wall, walked over to the other table and picked up the bread and butter. Anton carried on eating, his small round eyes looking up at Ludwik, vague, unaware. Frieda was worried.

"What if anyone finds out?"

"Who? There's no one else on the farm," Ludwik smiled persuasively. "For once we can sit together, eat together, like civilised people."

She nodded in agreement.

"You're right, Ludwik, but I don't make rules here. It's too risky. For me, for my family. Do you understand?" Her wan smile was apologetic, and Ludwik's faded away. He shrugged and put down the bread and the butter back on the table. He returned to sit down beside me. Forming his hands into a shape of a trumpet he placed them against his mouth and called out, "We'll just have to carry on shouting across the kitchen, won't we?"

This made Anton burst out laughing.

I liked working with Frieda. Whatever we did she shared the tasks equally, fairly with me. There was something motherly about her. I liked her rosy cheeks, the crinkles round her eyes when she smiled. She never tired of telling me about her family. She amused me with stories of her two younger sisters and their complicated love lives. When she mentioned her fifteen-year-old Poldi, her eyes sparkled, and her voice rose with pride. Unbeknown to her, Poldi was the only black mark in our relationship. Knowing of his association with the Hitler Yunge was what made me wary of saying too much about my own family in Poland. I never discussed Michal with her.

Kestner returned in the afternoon and came looking for us as we hoed the soil around the potato plants. His knitted eyebrows and deep grooves on each side of his mouth made him look old and worn.

"What's the news?" Frieda asked, leaning on her hoe, wiping her forehead, smudging her cheek.

"No change," Kestner replied, his voice heavy. "She's comfortable. She's in good hands. She was sleeping when I left." He paused, thinking, then his face livened up. "There's some good news though. I've been to the Arbeitz Bureau in Sankt Veit. They'll be sending us two workers tomorrow."

"Where will they get them from?" I wondered.

"Who cares? I'll be glad of anyone. Anyone at all. Even the Jews!" Kestner replied with an ugly smile.

When he left, Frieda muttered to me, "Even the Jews! Did you hear that? They should have thought about that before getting rid of them."

That night when I washed before bedtime, I noticed the red patches on my calf had disappeared. So did the purple, bruise-like stains around the dents left by the boils. The skin was white again, making the three pale blemishes almost invisible. Umtraut's remedy had been genuine. I could not get her out of my mind, as later, in bed, I prayed for the safety of all the people I loved.

CHAPTER 20

Miracles happen. I heard their voices and Kestner's gruff vowels as he led them towards the kitchen across the yard. The newcomers. I had been looking out for them all day, dashing from one job to the other, like a juggler out of control. I stirred the stew in the pot watching the door as they walked in. A girl and a lad. Maryla and Bruno. Bruno, the Sunday musician from Steinfeld's farm.

My heart flipped over, then we were in each other's arms, Maryla and I, hugging, laughing, starved of each other's company for so long. She was very thin. It was like pressing frail twigs against me. I loosened my hold and turned to Bruno.

"Welcome." I shook his hand. "God knows, we need you here so badly!"

His brown hair was a dense thatch, his grey eyes alert, his smile perfunctory.

"I had no say in this," he said.

"Anna," Kestner interrupted, "show them to their rooms. And no messing about. Supper in half an hour."

I led them up the wooden stairs to our rooms. Earlier, Kestner had brought up two extra mattresses.

"Not bad," Bruno said, surveying Ludwik's bare room. He dropped his bag beside his mattress and followed us.

"Tell me, tell me everything," the words rushed out of me, my mind bursting with questions. "How's Michal? Bazylka? Everyone? Did Spitz and Blitz send you here?"

Maryla dropped her bag on the floor. We lingered by the open door before going back downstairs.

"One answer at a time," she said with a wan smile. "Michal. He's fine." Just hearing his name made me glow inside. "Never stops talking about visiting you again."

"God no!" I protested with fear. "He mustn't do anything so rash again!"

"He won't Anna, believe me. He's biding his time. Waiting for the right moment. Bazylka… She doesn't change… Works hard and bosses people around…"

I laughed.

"Everyone?"

"Everyone. Poor Franek, of course. And two Ukrainian girls. Holtzmann's got them some time ago. Twice my size. Both of them. Holtzmann shed no tears seeing me go."

"Maryla," I chuckled, "I'm twice your size. But don't worry, we'll soon fatten you up. Food here is pretty decent, even if nothing else is."

I spoke to Bruno. "We'll look after you too."

"They've split me up from Dorota," he said. I knew she was his girl. I made an attempt to cheer him.

"At least she's in good hands, with the Steinfelds," I said. "Any news of Lilli?"

He shook his head.

"No one has seen her since that awful day. The Steinfelds never mention her. But a farmhand from Treibach told one of ours, that the nuns in Sankt Veit have taken her in."

We pondered his words for a moment.

"And Stefan?" I asked. "Does anyone know where they buried him?"

Bruno shrugged. "The same farm hand told us, the last time he was in Kappel, that there's not a trace of what happened there."

Suppertime had the atmosphere of a morgue. Kestner had only Anton for company and made no effort to speak to him. His dark expression and deliberate silence stopped all conversation on our table. Ludwik and I struggled to contain our impatience, our need to barrage Maryla and Bruno with more questions. They ate greedily, their eyes watering, their noses pink with pleasure.

Kestner rushed his meal. "I've got to go to town," he said, passing by our table on his way out. "Make sure everywhere's locked up, in case I don't get back before the curfew."

That woman in town had a real grip on him. To leave us entirely alone on the farm was incredible! It felt like being let out of prison.

Old Anton finished his bowl of stew then licked it clean before getting up to go. He had crumbs stuck to the spills down his front.

"Anton, your shirt needs wiping," I said. I led him to the washroom and with a wet cloth removed the fresh dirt off his chest. Old crusty stains were too embedded in the fabric to be budged. He stank of horse manure.

"Who washes your shirts, Anton?" I asked.

He considered me for a moment with his dot-like eyes.

"Umtraut."

"She's ill. You know that?"

He nodded vigorously.

"Listen now, scrub well at the tap. Your hands, your elbows, your feet. Change into clean clothes and bring these back to me. I'll soak them for you. Will you remember all that?"

He nodded, screwing his eyes in concentration. He spread his fingers and enumerated,

"Scrub hands… Elbows…" he hesitated.

"And?" I prompted.

"Can I wash all over?"

"Good thinking!" I praised.

We cleared things together, washed up, dried, wiped all surfaces around the kitchen, while listening to Bruno. In the world outside our farm, things were changing, but the forecast was not good for us. No country in Europe appeared strong enough to block the Wehrmacht invasion. The Germans had Norway in the north, Yugoslavia in the south, also the Balkans and Greece. Rommel's tanks were already patrolling the coast of North Africa. British cities were being consistently bombed. Even Ireland, a neutral zone, had bombs dropped on Dublin.

"How do you know all this?" Ludwik was bewildered.

"From Steinfeld," Bruno's gaze was hard. "He lets me listen to the radio sometimes. A lot of it is propaganda, to be sure. Hitler's speech for instance. How he's going to conquer the whole world. How his Reich will last for a thousand years!"

"He's well on his way to achieving that!" Ludwik's voice had an angry edge to it.

"I just want to go home," I said.

"Home?" Bruno sighed. "There may be no homes left to return to."

"Don't say that, Bruno." I covered my ears. "I'm not going to listen to you!"

He came over and lifted my hands.

"Anna, we've got to face facts. Can you imagine what's going to happen to our people, their homes, when the Germans start fighting the Russians on our soil?"

I did not want to imagine, I could not bear to think of my family being caught up right in the middle of that bloody conflict.

"Let them kill each other off," I cried, "and leave our people alone!"

We sat down at our table by the open door, our spirits low at this grim prospect. It was Maryla who spoke first.

"Listen everyone!" Her light tone was forced. "We won't solve anything sitting here worrying. Let's just take one day at a time. Right? Tonight, for example. Hey, we're on our own. Isn't that a treat? Bruno, play something cheerful for us!"

Bruno took out his mouth organ and began to play old sentimental tunes. We drummed our fingers on the table, we hummed, but then the familiar words of the songs took over. I felt my spirit lift.

Later, in the dark, as we lay on our mattresses side by side, Maryla and I, I sought her hand to give it a comforting pat.

"It's good to have you back," I said.

She gave my fingers a gentle squeeze.

"I was upset at first when they picked me," she said, "but now I'm really glad. Perhaps the change will do me good...Take the pain away..."

Her deep sigh went through me.

"Maryla, we all loved Staszek too..."

I sensed she was crying. I raised myself on my elbow and stroked her head, as I used to, to comfort my younger sisters when they were upset. She blew her nose and after a while she said, "If only they'd allowed him a day or two in bed. It's that awful Horst. He's got no heart. I can't forgive him. Ever! The pain, Anna... The pain inside me... Sometimes I wish I was dead too."

I moved up to her and hugged her to me.

"Don't ever wish that, Maryla. I need you. We all need you. Tonight. It just wouldn't have been the same without you."

Despite Umtraut's absence, life continued on the farm with strict adherence to routine, to a pattern, that I felt was beneficial to Maryla's state of mind. There were moments when she gave in to intense grief, but most days all feelings were numbed by sheer exhaustion. We got up together every morning at dawn, milked the cows, took them out to pasture, fed the chickens, fed the pigs, cleaned, raked, scraped, hosed down all dirt and brought in the fresh hay for lining the ground in enclosures.

The afternoons were spent on the vegetable plot. We grew carrots, parsnips, turnips, beets, peas, beans, some of which were ready to pick, together with early new potatoes and greens from the lettuce and herb garden.

Maryla's skin had improved. The scabbiness around her mouth and eyebrows had disappeared. Her small, thin face had regained its freshness and her thick plait shone gold against her browned neck.

Kestner had noticed the change in her too. I did not like the way he came up close to us and stood watching as we worked, his bushy eyebrows throwing a shadow over his scheming, predatory eyes.

"Short-sighted sod," Maryla muttered the first time he came.

"A pervert," I warned and told her of his pass at me.

His woman from Eberstein cycled to the farm some nights before the curfew. Some nights he had only his bottle for company. He visited Umtraut infrequently, only when Schwartz could procure extra petrol for a chunk of bacon or ham. I pitied Umtraut, alone and suffering on a hospital bed, her days and nights stretching out before her, empty, devoid of the warmth of a familiar face, of the touch of a loving hand.

Frieda had been appointed to take Umtraut's place. She was now our cook, our baker, our dairy maid. Every Tuesday afternoon she prepared carton boxes, filling them with butter and cheese, eggs and sausages, ham and bacon for collection by the army truck. Her chubby, welcoming face never failed to charm the driver. He eagerly exchanged pleasantries with her, sometimes leaving a mint sweet for each one of us.

Maryla and I crushed ours and left some for the boys. Ludwik and Bruno worked in the forest, felling trees, cutting them to manageable lengths, which then were pulled in truckloads by the two horses to a place near the farm, where all the finer sawing and chopping took place. The firewood was neatly stacked and covered, ready for winter. At the end of each day, the horses were brought inside the stables and groomed; big, gentle beasts. Ludwik and Bruno washed down their backs and sides, brushed their flamboyant manes and the frills of long hair around their hoofs. The horses snorted with pleasure.

Old Anton's bull, the herd stud, in a separate enclosure, snorted with unrest. I never went near it. Its massive size, its inflated flanks, its stamping hoofs ensured a well kept distance from everyone. Except Anton. He showed no fear and controlled the beast with peculiar cries of command and jerky pulls of the rope attached to the animal's nose-ring. Pity, I thought, Anton had no such control over his master. Kestner was a thorn in our existence.

"Already sloshed," Ludwik whispered across the table, one morning.

Maryla sidled up to me and we ate in silence, listening to the commotion on the other table. I felt sorry for Frieda and Anton who were subjected to Kestner's drunken rantings. Anton carried on eating, his puzzled round eyes following Kestner's every expression, every movement. Frieda sent helpless glances in our direction, while Kestner grilled her with stubborn, repetitive questioning.

"He's missing his woman," Bruno whispered with a comically knowing expression.

"She's come to her senses, at last," Ludwik whispered back.

Kestner suddenly got up, scraping the chair against the floor with a piercing sound and staggered to our table.

"What's that you were saying just now?" He towered over us.

Ludwik replied with an engaging smile, "Only that the weather's excellent for harvesting the early fodder." His face caught the light reflecting from the polished surface of the table.

Kestner blinked then remained standing and staring at Maryla. It was weird. We stopped eating, anticipating his next move, fearing his aggression. He turned around and walked out of the kitchen.

Maryla heaved a sigh of relief.

"I thought he would never go!"

Ludwik leaned across the table, his expression serious, "Stick together, you two. Don't get in his way. We'll be working on a field nearby."

Later in the day it was a treat to escape to the vegetable plot. The stench of the morning's cleansing work around the cowsheds and pigsties clung to our clothes, but all we could do was to air them in the fresh open space, and the warm June sunshine. The continuous droning of the tractor reassured us the boys' presence nearby. They were harvesting the specially grown grass that had been cut and left to dry, and was now gathered to be tied in bales. The cattle fodder for the winter.

"It's like old times," Maryla said, kneeling beside me, as we picked the plump pods of beans. "I just wish Bazylka was here with us."

"I miss her too," I said, "even her bossiness."

Maryla laughed. It was good to hear her laugh.

"No, really," I protested, "I never minded her being the boss. It felt as if someone was always looking out for us." I touched the pebble-smooth heart at my throat. "I miss the others too."

"It'll never be the same again, will it?" she said. I knew she had Staszek in mind. She sat back on her heels, rubbed the sweat off her forehead and looked skywards. "That's how it's going to be from now on…"

I wanted to comfort her, to lift her sadness. I remembered my teacher's words after my father's funeral. "There's a reason for everything in this life, even for the bad things." But this was not the time to be reasoning with Maryla.

"You've still got us, all of us," I reminded her gently.

He came upon us unexpectedly, his long shadow falling across the bean plants. I looked up in alarm.

"Maryla, *komm mit mir*," Kestner ordered, "I need you to help me with a job."

She got up to her feet and I stood up with her.

"I'll help too, Herr Kestner," I offered.

"I don't need a crowd. Maryla will do." He ordered her to walk ahead of him to the farm house.

I waited only long enough for his back to be hidden behind a thick screen of sunflower stalks, then I ran. This was the longer, semi-circular path back to the farm but I sped along it with trebled energy, with everything on the way flying by – fruit trees, the pigs, the chickens, the outbuildings – till I reached the barn. Here Ludwik and Anton were pressing and tying the dried grass into bales.

"Ludwik!" I was out of breath, "Kestner's got Maryla!"

Ludwik let the pliers and the wire fall out of his hands.

"Where?"

I told him, as fast as I could. We rushed out of the barn leaving Anton slowly gathering the hay together with a long rake.

I did my best to keep up with Ludwik sprinting across the courtyard, past the pond towards the house. As we reached the kitchen windows we heard Maryla's screams. We turned the corner and stopped, shocked by the sight before us.

Kestner was pulling Maryla by the hair, his other hand over her mouth to silence her. She had jammed her feet against the doorstep and was resisting his force by holding onto the door frame, her knuckles white with the strain.

Ludwik leapt forward with a shout.

"Let go of her! Let go of her!" He brought down his rigid hand, like a sword over Kestner's wrist. Kestner roared and loosened his grip on Maryla's hair. She ran to me, dishevelled, terror in her face. Kestner lurched forward as if to chase her, but Ludwik jumped in his way. Kestner swung his arm at him, but Ludwik ducked. Kestner lost his balance and fell to the ground, sprawled over the doorstep.

Ludwik shouted to us, "Run you two, run!"

We stayed put, holding onto each other fearing for Ludwik now. Slowly, Kestner struggled to his feet, his face purple with fury.

"You'll pay for this, you son of a bitch! You'll be sorry!" He waved his fist at Ludwik, who by now, was standing well back.

"You'll be sorry too, Herr Kestner," Ludwik spoke quietly, "when Herr Schwartz hears about this."

Kestner scowled with hatred.

"Get out of my sight!" he yelled, "Get out!" He stepped inside the kitchen and slammed the door.

We scurried across the courtyard, back to the barn, where Bruno had just arrived on the tractor with another load of hay.

"What's up?" he asked, jumping down.

"What's going to happen now?" Maryla asked. Her mouth was trembling.

"Can someone tell me what's going on?" Bruno looked around.

Ludwik put both his hands on Maryla's shoulders, calming her, soothing.

"He won't be pestering you again, old Kestner. We too have given him a shock. It'll make him think, the disgusting old pervert!" He dropped his hands and looked at Bruno. "There's two of us. Against one."

"Four," I said.

Bruno scratched his head, his face expressing a sudden dawning of what had just occurred.

"The filthy old fart! What baffles me is how that woman of his in Eberstein puts up with him? She needs her brain testing!"

It was later, when we were back on the vegetable plot, squatting between rows of beans, that Maryla wept. Quietly, large drops rolling down her cheeks and falling to the ground. I sighed, inwardly so she would not hear.

"Shall I plait your hair?" I asked.

She shrugged. I smoothed her hair with my fingers, gathered all the escaped strands around her face and plaited them as neatly as it was possible without a comb.

"There!" I said. I could not think of anything else to say that would lighten her mood.

She wiped her face leaving long sooty smudges across her cheeks. She looked like a chimney sweep, and I wished she could see herself. Perhaps that would make her smile.

"I'll be all right," she sighed, "but tell me, Anna, why is it, that every time I get to the end of my tether, and can't take any more, something else is dropped on me? When will it all stop?"

It pained me that I had no answers, and with a rush of gladness I saw Ludwik coming our way, his long strides making his head bob up and down above the greens surrounding us. We stood up, glad to stretch our aching backs and legs.

"You're my hero," she stated simply, when he stopped before us, his cheeks pink with exertion.

"And you need a good scrub," he laughed, pulling a rag from his pocket. "Your spit or mine?"

This amused her.

"Clean water will do," she said, allowing him to lift her chin and wipe the soil off her face.

"There, that's better," he said.

She opened her screwed eyes and for a moment I was struck by the expression in them, by the image of his dark head bending over her upturned face.

"I've just come to check," he smiled, "but I can see you're doing fine without me. I'll be off, then. Don't worry about Kestner. He's not likely to be back for ages. I think he's got the message now…" Ludwik gave us a mischievous grin. "There's too many of us…"

We watched him walk away then Maryla turned round and hugged me.

"What's this for?" I asked.

She was thoughtful for a moment. "I hate Kestner," she said, "I want to kill him. Stab him. Shoot him. Trample all over him. And then I think what a miserable old man he is. He's got no one to really love him. And I think how lucky I am. I've got you. And Ludwik, and Bruno."

The next day, Dieter Kestner returned from the war.

CHAPTER 21

It was the last day of June. The heat was oppressive, the air laden with pollen, with floating dandelion seeds, with the incessant buzzing of insects. I longed to escape into the shadows around the buildings as I toiled with Maryla in an open chicken pen, scraping the ground and loading the dirt onto the wheelbarrow.

We heard the sound of the lorry the moment it turned off the main road to come down the farm track in a cloud of dust. Anxiety gripped my stomach. This was habit now, the unexpected, the uncertain filling me with dread.

For a few seconds the lorry was lost from view in the dip of the valley, before emerging again, like a shimmering phantom from the hot ground. It swept in a semi-circle around the pond and came to a halt, its tall, army-green tarpaulin roof pushing up the ends of the branches of the chestnut tree.

The driver and his assistant, two uniformed soldiers, jumped down, came round the back, unbolted the wide, upright bar and pulled down the three metal steps to the ground. Maryla and I walked right up to the fence, wiping our sweaty faces. We could see right inside the deep, dark recess of the lorry. There were men sitting on benches facing each other on both sides. It was clear they were the wounded being sent home from the front. Bandaged hands, arms in slings, legs in plaster stood out white from the shadows. A man sitting near the edge had his head so heavily bandaged, only one side of his face and one eye were visible.

The two able bodied soldiers helped a man make his slow, careful descent down the three steps on his good leg and crutches. His other leg was encased in plaster up to the knee. He held it off the ground with the utmost effort and concentration. He looked between thirty and forty, but it was hard to tell his exact age. His features were pronounced with emaciation and his skin was the colour of his grey, close-cropped hair. We guessed this was Dieter, Kestner and Umtraut's son.

We watched Kestner emerge from the stables and make long, hurried strides towards the newly arrived. His bushy eyebrows were knitted as ever, but there was a lift in the hard lines around his mouth, there was a bounce in his step. He took over from the two soldiers and helped the injured man turn around to face his friends on the lorry.

"*Alles Besten! Viel Gluck!*" they shouted and waved. The lorry began to pull away, but he waited till it disappeared from view.

"Come, Dieter," Kestner said, his arm protective on his son's shoulder. "Come and rest. It's high time you were home."

Dieter let his crutches fall to the ground and with his freed arms clasped his father to his chest. For a moment, Kestner's face looked human, like the face of a father, who had lost and found his son.

"Can you believe this?" Maryla whispered next to me.

We resumed our work, discreetly watching them make slow progress towards the kitchen door. Then Kestner spotted us. I was expecting a barrage of angry words, but his voice, though gruff, had none of the usual threat in it when he called out, "Anna! Run to the woods! Fetch Ludwik this minute! Maryla! You come here, and make coffee!"

Maryla looked at me with alarm.

"Don't worry," I said, "Ludwik and I will be back in minutes. And there's Dieter."

When I returned with Ludwik, Maryla was in the kitchen brewing coffee from roasted barley seeds. We could see and hear Kestner and his son in the parlour.

"Come here!" Kestner ordered us, and when we did, he introduced us formally. "Anna, Maryla, Ludwik, this is my son Dieter." I thought I detected the tiniest touch of softness in his hard features, in his rough voice.

Dieter was sitting in an armchair, resting his injured leg on a stool. Up close, I could see his grey face was mottled with faded red and purple patches, just as my frost-bitten calf had been before Umtraut's cure of nettles. I noticed his hands with a shock, the tips of his fingers missing, fourth and fifth on both hands.

He followed my gaze.

"Frost bite," he said. "Hands and feet. Two toes amputated to stop the gangrene spreading up my foot. And a shattered calf. Russian shrapnel." He tapped the hard plaster on his leg. There was a small hole in it. "For fresh air," he explained. "Helps to speed recovery, so they tell me. God knows, how much longer this is going to take. Great reward, hey? Fighting for the Reich."

"You're home now, Dieter," Kestner intercepted. "That's all that matters now." He sat down on the edge of a chair next to his son. "We need you here. This place is like a hungry beast. Twice as many workers would still not satisfy its greed."

"Am I allowed to get better first?" Dieter winked in our direction. Kestner's eyebrows bristled.

"What do you take me for, son? A heartless, cruel monster?"

Dieter placed his hand on Kestner's arm, gave it a tender pat, peering into his father's face,

"*Liebe Vater*, I'm just happy to be home."

Kestner cleared his throat and looked at Ludwik. "On your bike. To Lorenz farm in Walburgen. Find Sylvia and tell her to come home. Her place is here, with her husband, on this farm. And you girls, bring us the coffee!"

We left them with coffee and milk, with left-over bread crusts and jam, and hurried outside, eager to get away from Kestner.

"What did you make of that?" I asked Maryla as we ran across the yard.

"I think…" Maryla paused by the cowshed to catch breath, "I think there will be changes soon."

There were changes that very evening. We trooped into the kitchen, Ludwik, Bruno, Maryla and I, having scrubbed our hands and elbows at the tap in the yard. Two women were busy preparing the evening meal; Frieda, and I guessed the other one was Sylvia. She looked up and smiled, her plain, round face amiable at first sight. She was younger than Dieter, comfortably plump, her dark hair plaited and pinned across the crown of her head. She wore a long, grey, practical dress, a long, practical, patterned apron, as if she were ready to tackle any kind of work.

"My name's Sylvia," she said, wiping her hands on her apron as she came towards us, "now tell me yours."

We introduced ourselves. She looked with sharp interest at each one of us, as she repeated our names. Then she pointed at the table.

"Sit where you like. The meal's ready."

The two tables, the master's and the slaves' table, had been pushed together. Dieter was already seated at the far end. We remained standing, uncertain of our place.

"Come on. Sit down. I don't bite," Dieter spread his hands to indicate both sides. I could not keep my eyes off his mutilated fingers, then suddenly, aware of his gaze on me, I looked away as we sat down at the end that was our table, the boys facing Maryla and me.

I looked around and noticed something else. Hitler's mahogany bust had been turned round to face the wall. I nudged Maryla. A mischievous smile curled Dieter's lips.

"He's been watching this room for far too long," he said.

Kestner came in followed by Anton. He stopped by the door and surveyed the changes, deep creases forming on his brow.

"What's all this?" he asked, a hint of aggression in his tone.

Dieter sent him a welcome glance.

"A little common sense, Father, don't you think? We work together, we eat from the same pot. It's plain stupid having to sit in two separate groups. Come, Father, sit beside me, and Anton, sit on my other side."

Anton did not need telling twice. Like a happy child, singled out by his teacher, he walked up to Dieter and slid onto the bench, next to his new master.

Kestner remained at the door, a deep flush colouring his face. "If you think I'm going to play second fiddle to you, son, then you're greatly mistaken!"

All went quiet in the room. Sylvia and Frieda stood still at the range, their eyes fixed on Kestner.

"Father, please," Dieter's tone was appeasing, "I'm too tired for fights. Come… Sit down beside me… It's a long time since we've been together like this…as a family…"

"Family!" Kestner snorted, catching sight at the same time of the back of Hitler's bust. "And that! Have you gone mad? Schwartz will go berserk!"

Dieter's smile was easy.

"What's he going to do? Shoot his own nephew? Haven't I done enough for the Reich?"

Kestner straightened himself, raising his voice. "You're pushing your luck, you fool! I won't be party to any of this. I'm going! And don't expect to see me before the morning!"

He went out and Dieter shrugged as if to say, judge for yourselves. Strange sadness overwhelmed me. I could not imagine falling out like that with my mother.

"Let's start and enjoy our meal," Dieter said to us.

All the activity resumed as we tucked into a thick, nourishing stew, bulked out with freshly baked and buttered bread, dismissively aware of a distant clanging of Kestner's bicycle on the cobbles.

We listened at our end to Dieter's questions about people he had not seen for the last couple of years, and to Sylvia and Frieda's answers as they brought him up to date with all the latest news. The conversation was lively, creating a feeling of normality. Even Anton's excitement rose above his usual preoccupation with food. When the meal was finished, I got up to collect the bowls.

"Don't go yet," Sylvia stopped me, herself getting up. We watched as she opened the lower part of the dresser, and brought out a thick round cheesecake. I held my breath in surprise and anticipation. She placed it on the table, and began to cut slices and send them down to us on little cork mats. Dieter studied his like some treasure find, his thin face creasing with pleasure. Sylvia kissed him on the top of his head before sitting down beside him.

"Good job you're here," she said, "otherwise you'd have missed it!"

We all giggled.

The cake was heaven in my mouth.

"This is magic!" Ludwik exclaimed. "How did you do it, Frau Kestner?"

Sylvia laughed, exposing her large teeth that looked as if they could grind stones.

"Don't call me Frau. It makes me feel old. I'm not that much older than you lot, you know…" Her round face shone pink like an apple. "The cheesecake is no magic. We've got all the things we need already, our own cheese and butter and flour. I brought some honey with me to substitute the sugar. Of course, in the good old days, there were lemons as well. Lemons? What are they? You may well ask."

For the first time since leaving home I felt that these enemy people were like us, that I would have been glad to have them as neighbours back at home. I felt a sudden, strong surge of hope, of better things to come. There was just one thorn left in our existence. Kestner.

I asked Frieda about him the next morning, when we were milking cows together, now that Sylvia was in charge of the house. Frieda looked over the backs of the cows to check no one was listening. There was only Maryla at the far end.

"It's like this," Frieda spoke in a hushed voice. "This farm belonged to Umtraut's parents. Nothing here is Kestner's. They never liked him. They never wanted Umtraut to marry him."

"Why?"

Frieda made a disapproving face.

"He was always a womaniser. Shameless in his younger days. Even when he started courting Umtraut. There was always trouble, between him and her father. They hated each other. But when Umtraut became pregnant, old Schwartz could not stop the marriage. But he could stop Kestner inheriting the farm. He left it all in his will to young Dieter."

This was a surprising revelation. This explained everything: Umtraut's dedication, Kestner's cavalier attitude, Dieter's natural command of his farm. The more I thought about it the more I liked it.

"What about Schwartz?" I asked, "Umtraut's brother? Didn't he want a cut out of it for himself?"

"Oh, I'm sure he did," Frieda said with a knowing smile, "but old Schwartz was unbending. It was like this: either you stay, work hard and get your share, or if you go, there's no handout for you to expect. Young Schwartz hated life on the farm. He chose to join the police."

As I digested this information, I felt another surge of hope, I felt that Dieter's arrival could be a new, brighter dawn for us, slaves, whereas for Kestner, with Umtraut gone, there was nothing left to hold him on the farm.

It was therefore, with some curiosity and not without irrepressible excitement, that a few days later, in the middle of a hot afternoon, when all workers were far from the house, Maryla and I, hidden in the greenery on the vegetable garden, watched Schwartz' black Volkswagen arrive and stop under the chestnut tree. Schwartz got out but before he made a move towards the house, Kestner came out of the kitchen door. He was dressed in his old grey suit and lugged a suitcase with him. Schwartz helped him lift up his one piece of baggage onto the back seat. Kestner stood and looked around, but there was no one about to send him off with fond farewells. He bent down his long frame into the passenger seat, and the car drove off.

"Good riddance," Maryla said, "I never want to see him again."

Later in the day, when I came to the dairy to collect the milk for the army truck, I said to Sylvia, simply, "I saw Herr Kestner going away this afternoon. Is he going to be away long?"

"Father," she answered, squeezing the whey out of the cheese through a muslin cloth (she called him "Father"!), "Father's gone to spend some time with Eva, his daughter, near Sankt Veit. It'll do him good. He's been through a lot lately." She looked perfectly serious when she added, "He can stay away as long as he wishes. Now that there's the two of us to worry about the farm, he doesn't have to any longer."

Her words made something inside me leap with joy.

Incredible things happen! On the 4th of July, a year and a month after I had been plucked out of my home, our first post arrived. Our local postman was a familiar figure, on his black bicycle with the wire baskets, one on the handle bar and one behind his seat, but the sight of him never stirred any excitement for us. This particular morning, as Maryla and I washed the rakes, the spades and the wheelbarrow at the tap, he stopped in the yard and spoke to us.

"*Gruss Gott!*"

We looked up in astonishment.

"Some of this post is for you," he said, holding a thick pack of letters. We followed him to the kitchen door, where Sylvia came out wiping her hands on her apron.

"*Gutten morgen, Herr Schmitt. Danke shone.*" She took the letters from him and looked through the pile.

"Anna Myszkovska. Anna Myszkovska. Anna Myszkovska," she read out, handing me three letters. Two had my mother's handwriting on them, one was from my brother. All three envelopes had been cut open. I was dying to look inside, but I waited for Maryla to get hers. There were none for her, none for Bruno, but five for Ludwik.

"Yours must be with Bazylka," I said, seeing her disappointment.

"I guess so!" she said with a sigh and walked off towards the vegetable garden.

"I'll catch up with you in a minute!" I called after her, but she gave no indication of having heard me.

With a twinge of discomfort at my own joy, I rushed upstairs with Ludwik's letters, all of them, like mine, cut open, and having placed them at his bedside, I went to my room to read my post. Since Sylvia's arrival we had sheets on our mattresses, pillows and a chair each.

I sat down and pulled out my mother's letter dated 30th July 1940, one whole year ago, in reply to my very first letter sent from Holtzmann's farm. The letter had been censored, with black ink obliterating some lines altogether. A quick glance at the other two made it clear that all post had received the same treatment. My mother wrote that she was greatly relieved that I had reached my destination safely and she advised me to use my earned money wisely and to save for the time when I returned home. A new start, she wrote, is a far better start with a full pot of gold. At home, she wrote, Alina and Marysia had been helping her on the allotment all summer, as everything was in short supply and many things were unavailable altogether. In case I was wondering, she suggested, what to send them for winter, thick stockings and fur-lined boots for the girls would be received with great pleasure.

Her second letter was dated end of November. She expressed concern at my long silence and reminded me to remember my family when I made a better life for myself in Austria.

I smoothed open my brother Jan's letter anticipating words of concern, apology, grief, for having unwittingly banished me from home, by his timely escape from recruitment to work for the Germans, when I had been forced to take his place.

Jan wrote:

"*Dear Anna,*

Paper's scarce. So I'll be brief. I need your help. I'm getting married. Her name is Yagoda. The sooner, the better, if you get my meaning. Before there's talk. I need a suit. Friends tell me that Austrian cloth is the best. No doubt, by now you're well settled in and earning a decent wage. You've no idea how bad things are over here. I regret now that I've been such a fool to run away. Weren't you lucky to be sent in my place! You owe me one."

I did not carry on. I stopped myself from crushing his letter into a ball of litter. Holding the three sheets in my hand I ran downstairs and out of the house to the vegetable garden. The previous evening's downpour had done wonders for the peas and the beans, but also for the weeds surrounding them. I found Maryla pulling out the fresh growth of nettles and dandelions. It was obvious from her reddened eyes that she had been crying.

"Here's something to cheer you up," I said, pushing the crumpled sheets of paper into her palm.

She stepped back, retracting her hand, as if burnt.

"Don't be silly! What are you doing?" She sounded annoyed.

"Read them! Read them!" I insisted. "This will really make you laugh."

Her annoyance turned to worry.

"Anna, what's happened? I don't like you in this mood."

"Maryla…" I forced calm into my voice, "just read them."

I set about the weeds with ferocious zeal, unable to stop the tears that ran down my nose, down to my chin and dripped onto my chest. All those months of longing…all those dreams…all the heartache, the sweat and the tears… And now this! From my own family!

Maryla put her arm around my shoulders and made me stop. We sat among the weeds on the raw soil, facing each other like two survivors from a shipwreck.

"Anna…" Her eyes were huge in her small heart-shaped face, "how could they possibly know otherwise? They think we are doing normal work. Getting normal pay. Don't be too hard on them."

I felt suddenly very tired, drained.

"And even if we could write them the truth," Maryla continued, "could anyone really imagine, really understand all this?" She patted down her dusty rag of a skirt then looked towards the farm buildings, beyond which the pigs were rooting about in the muddy ground in their enclosure.

At lunchtime, Ludwik was very quiet. His eyes were fixed on the table as he chewed slowly, seemingly lost in thought.

"Ludwik," Maryla nudged him, "you had the most letters. Tell us all the good news."

He raised his eyes at her with a blank stare.

"Ludwik?" She peered into his eyes. "Ludwik!" She clicked her fingers.

He stared as if he had never seen her before.

It was eerie, disconcerting. Dieter caught my eye. The conversation at the other end died down.

"What's wrong, Ludwik?" Dieter asked across the length of the table.

Ludwik appeared to struggle with his thoughts.

"My girl… Julia…is dead. They've killed her. And my father… They've taken him away…"

We fell silent. I looked away, unable to watch Ludwik's pain.

"They shot her in the street. At random. In a round-up. My father… Nobody knows what they've done with him."

Our silence turned to something solid, oppressive. I could hardly breathe. Maryla hid her face in her hands. I noticed a beam of sunlight on Sylvia's face, a patch of soft fine dawn, like white velvet.

Dieter cleared his throat and rested his clenched fists on the table, his mutilated fingers tucked under, out of sight.

"This is shocking news, Ludwik," he said in a gruff voice. "Appalling! What can I say? What can anyone say? We are all victims of this mad war. Good God! Give us all strength!" he invoked. In anger, not in prayer.

I did not feel strong at all that day. Waves of tearfulness attacked me, but I fought them off by tackling all my jobs with determined zeal, such that leaves you exhausted, such that suffocates all other sensations.

After the evening meal, when all the jobs were done, Bruno sat down with Maryla and me under the chestnut tree. Ludwik had walked off by himself. We could see him crouching on the bank of the stream, his head hung forward, his shoulders hunched, a motionless, solitary figure.

"I can't bear to watch him like this," Maryla said, her eyes pained, her hands clasped tight in her lap.

"Go to him," Bruno said. "He may think he wants to be alone, but I'm not so sure…"

"I'm afraid, I'll make things worse…" Indecision was tormenting her.

"Play us something cheerful, Bruno," I said.

He took out his mouth organ and wiped it with his handkerchief, a dirty old rag.

"Something cheerful," I prompted him.

He played the cuckoo song with its lively rhythm, the swaying tune of the Daisy by the Stream, the dance of the Tatra Mountains people and many others, yet as we hummed along, Maryla and I, the sadness inside me would not shift away. I fingered my little wooden heart at my throat and thought of Michal and felt the emptiness beside me.

"I'll go to him," Maryla stood up. "I've got to see if he's all right."

I watched her walk down the stony dirt track, her feet avoiding rough ground, her head bobbing up and down, her thin, long neck and her narrow shoulders, cut out sharply against the peachy evening sky.

Bruno played an old love song. I hummed and sang the words in my mind.

"For you I gather stars
Scattered on midnight blue
Collect silver moonshine
As I wait for you."

I watched Maryla stoop down to Ludwik, her hands gesticulating gently as if to support her words. Ludwik lifted his head and appeared to listen to her.

"For you I weave garlands
Of rubies, violets blue
Jasmine pearls and emeralds
As I wait for you."

Ludwik and Maryla formed dark silhouettes against the bright surface of the stream. I watched her lower herself to sit down beside him and her arm stretch out to embrace his shoulders.

"The night's soft fragrant breath
A bird's sweet melody
Touch me, bewitch me, promise
Your homecoming to me."

I saw Ludwik's shoulders drop as he submitted to Maryla's embrace and rested his head in the crook of her arm.

CHAPTER 22

Umtraut Kestner died in Sankt Veit hospital in the second week of July. Dieter had visited her as often as Schwartz' time and petrol supplies allowed, but her final hours had been spent alone, with no member of her family close to her. Her body was brought home in a black van.

Maryla and I stood at the side of the dirt track, resting our milk churns on the grass, and watched the black van come to a slow halt under the chestnut tree. Two men got out, followed by Kestner and a young woman, whom we guessed to be his daughter, Eva. Dieter had been notified earlier of their expected arrival and came out on crutches, flanked by Sylvia, Ludwik and Bruno. All men, except Dieter, picked up the coffin and carried it through the main door into the parlour. We returned to our chores. Work did not stop for the dead.

The mood that evening was sombre, depressing. Sylvia had cooked a thick vegetable soup with barley, delicious as always, but Dieter did not touch his. When Anton asked for a second helping, he passed him his bowl.

Kestner, forced by circumstances to sit next to his son, spoke now and again, exclusively to his daughter, while she in turn, made every effort to include everyone in the conversation. But it did not gel. We four ate in silence at our end of the table, listening to the clinking of spoons against the bowls. I could barely wait for the meal to be over, so we could get away from the stifling atmosphere of the feuding father and son.

At long last, Dieter spoke to us, studiously avoiding to look at his father.

"The coffin with my mother will be left overnight in the parlour. Feel free to visit her for the last time. The coffin's closed. She's too ravaged by illness, to be seen. She wouldn't have wanted people to stare at her."

Later, when everything had been cleared away, wiped and dusted and polished, the four of us went together to pay our last respects to the woman who had been treating us like rubbish.

The parlour, with the curtains drawn, was cast in semi-darkness. The coffin was laid on the table and adorned with bunches of field flowers, poppies, cornflowers and large white daisies, I guessed, picked and arranged by Sylvia and Eva.

Eva sat with her father on one side of the room, and Dieter, obscured by the raised coffin from their view, sat on the other side with his bad foot resting on a stool. Kestner appeared to be asleep in his armchair, his way of cutting himself off from everyone else.

"Come closer," Dieter beckoned to us.

We walked right up to the table. The metal plaque on the coffin bore just the inscription of her name and dates. Umtraut Magdalena Kestner. 1883-1941. Magdalena. Such a melodic sound to it. Perhaps if she had been called that, she would have been a different person.

For the sake of her family, I made the sign of the cross, but I did not pray for her. Instead, I pondered over what had made her so cruel, so hateful, so hard. At the same time, mindful of my mother's rule never to speak ill of the dead, I wondered if this also applied to unkind thoughts. I made myself recall the two acts of kindness she had shown me; her advice on the nettle remedy for my frost-bitten calf, and the old dress she had given me. I had altered it to my size, and planned to wear it the next day, if we were allowed to go to the funeral.

We went outside into the balmy, warm, pink evening and made our way up to the higher ground, from which we could observe people from neighbouring farms and houses, scattered on the slopes, come up to our farm, to pay Umtraut their last respects.

Bruno played softly on his mouth organ some old sentimental tunes. Ludwik, lost in thought, listened, his shiny eyes fixed on distant hills. I had not seen him cry since those letters from home, nor had I seen the lines on his constantly pre-occupied face relax for long, except when he was with Maryla. Most evenings, they would stroll together down to the stream and talk, while I stayed with Bruno under the chestnut tree. Bruno talked about his girl Dorota, and I talked about Michal. It felt as if we were all pawns scattered all over a chess board, pining, reaching, yet unable to touch the ones we loved.

"Do you mind, Anna?" Maryla would ask afterwards, needing to be assured. "Do you mind me going off like that with Ludwik? It's good for him to talk, to get things off his chest. It's good for me too, he understands me."

"Maryla, why would I mind?" I spoke the words she wanted to hear. "Who will support us, if we don't support each other?"

Now, as we sat together, unseen by the procession of visitors to our farm, Maryla rested her head against my shoulder.

"Strange, isn't it?" she said, "It all feels so awful. I thought I'd be glad of Kestner's misfortune. He deserves to be punished, doesn't he? For all the horrible things he's done. But all I feel now, is pity for him."

Ludwik turned to her.

"I feel sorry for his family. He's just feeling sorry for himself. I hope his conscience torments him."

Bruno stopped playing.

"That's if he's got one," he said. "I don't feel sorry for him at all. When has he shown her any affection, any respect? He's a swine! And if there's a hell, it's the perfect place for him!"

His exaggerated passion felt suddenly comical in the solemn mood.

"Come now, Bruno," I remonstrated gently, "where's your Christian spirit? Where's the forgiving bit?"

"Forgiving?" he snorted. "It's easy to forgive, when you've not been hurt. We've all been hurt one way or another. Ask Ludwik about forgiving… Ask Maryla…"

Maryla lifted her head off my shoulder. Her eyes filled up, but her voice was steady.

"How can I ever forgive Horst for what he did to Staszek? I'd be letting Staszek down if I did. I hate Horst. I loathe him. I wish him dead every time he comes to my mind!"

I understood perfectly what she was saying. I hated Spitz and Blitz with all my might for what they had done to Michal. I hated the prison guards who had inflicted such merciless pain on him. I prayed for justice every night, for the punishment they all deserved.

"Just now and again… Just once…" Ludwik mused, "I wish I could become that avenging angel!"

"It's too late for Stefan and Staszek," Bruno said. "We don't even know where they're buried, and here is Umtraut, the wicked old witch, having a send-off like a queen!"

"No justice, is there?" Ludwik agreed. "But the funeral's not just for her. It's for her family too. Dieter and Sylvia are decent people. She was his mother, after all."

Umtraut's funeral took place the next morning at ten, at a time when most of the morning's work around the animals had been done. We four, the Polish workers, were not allowed to attend, not on account of Dieter's whim, but on account of the numerous decrees that took away our rights as human beings. Nevertheless, we stood by the pond underneath the chestnut tree and watched the funeral cortege slowly make its way down into the valley and up the other side to the main road.

A black-painted cart drawn by a black horse carried Umtraut in her coffin, decked with bunches of home grown flowers brought by the neighbours the night before. Kestner and his daughter Eva, both dressed in black, led the procession, with Anton close behind. He had been ordered to clean himself up. His freshly washed hair stood out stiff, just as it had dried, giving him a somewhat petrified appearance. Sylvia was pushing Dieter on a wheelchair, which Schwartz had managed to acquire just for the day. I knew his wife Helga, but the other twenty, or so, family members were strangers to us.

We were left alone on the farm, just the four of us, and suddenly I felt as if all weight had been lifted off my shoulders.

"We could do anything we like now, or nothing at all! No one would ever know," Bruno said, echoing my very thoughts.

"And there's not even Anton to keep an eye on us," Maryla laughed.

"Strange, isn't it?" Ludwik said. "This is such a big change in their lives, and yet, here we are, in the same old routine, and the same uncertainty that anything will ever change for us."

"It already has," I said. "It's so different now, with Dieter and Sylvia in charge."

"It is," Ludwik agreed, "and I don't resent them. But as our days stretch into months, into years, I feel as if time has forgotten us. What a waste! I had dreams, I had plans, once, when I was young. I'm twenty-two and I feel like an old man. I feel as if my life has finished!"

He spoke in earnest, but Maryla smiled, stretched her arm around his shoulders and gave him a hug.

"Stop it, Grandpa! Our lives are not finished yet. Not by a long run! Just think of all the unexpected twists and turns in the last few months! Who's to know what's around the corner? The war could be over even as we speak!"

He did not disagree with her but his expression showed he was not convinced.

"And another thing," he added, "people die and life goes on as if nothing's happened... It's so heartless! Cruel!"

"How else would we survive?" Bruno reasoned. "There's nothing shameful in that. And besides, we've got to go on living for the sake of the ones we've lost. Don't you see Ludwik, for as long as we're alive, their memory lives on with us."

I held my breath, my nerves pricking up. This was sensitive territory. Ludwik took a moment to reply. "You're right, but how do you deal with a boundless void that your life has become?" He got up. "I'll see to the horses," and he walked away.

Bruno was about to follow, but Maryla held him back. "You did your best. Leave him. He needs time. Play something cheerful for us."

He lifted the mouth organ to his lips and played a polka tune, a children's nonsense song, about an old woman who kept her cockerel in a shoe. For some reason this made me cry.

The first few mornings of October rose misty with a touch of autumn chill, then blossomed into golden sun-filled days. Harvest was now all done, the pressure to finish on time all off, only the regular work around the animals remained and the felling of trees in the forest.

I did not look forward to winter, to the sharp air like needles in my lungs, to the chilblains on my fingers, to the pain and the itching in my toes. I wondered how many more winters were we to endure before we were free to return home. I missed my family, despite their silly letters, but most of all I missed Michal. I felt him close to me, every night when I closed my eyes. I pictured his every expression, the shape of his mouth, his earnest brown eyes, the straight line of his eyebrows, giving width to his face. His gift, the smooth, pebble-like heart at my throat, was a constant reminder of his love for me.

This particular Sunday morning, like all other mornings, Maryla and I rose at dawn to milk the cows. It was Frieda's day off, and Sylvia would rise later to prepare meals for us. For this work we threw on our oldest, most worn, most patched clothes, such that had withstood the endless washing off of the cow dung and the pigs and the chicken dirt. I had hoped once that Sylvia would give us some of Umtraut's clothes, but she had gathered them in a bundle and took them to Eberstein to sell. It seemed that Maryla and I were sentenced to look like tramps for the rest of our lives.

We splashed our faces and brushed our teeth in the washroom. We fetched sterile buckets from the dairy and went inside the cowshed to start another working day. I switched on the dim light.

A figure came out of the shadows towards us. My bucket fell out of my hand and rolled to and fro with a metallic sound.

"Michal!" I was overwhelmed with fear and images of his beaten face, still vividly fresh in my mind.

But he strode forward, his arms outstretched, his face beaming.

"Anna! Anna! Come here!" He held me to his chest and kissed me all over my face. He let me go only long enough to give Maryla a hug, then his arms were around me again.

"Michal! What have you done!" My joy was stifled by dread, by a foreboding of disaster.

He stood back, withdrew a piece of paper from his breast pocket and waved it at us.

"Official permission! From Holtzmann himself! We've got nothing to fear, Anna, as long as I'm back for work tomorrow morning!"

I rubbed my forehead. I could not take in his words.

"But why? Why would he suddenly change his mind?"

Michal shrugged, a big grin lifting his cheeks.

"I have no idea! Mind you, I did pester him all summer to let me see you. Just once. Now he says I am allowed to visit you every Sunday. I'm baffled! I can only guess things are changing at the front. Perhaps not so good for them. But maybe better for us!"

I clung to him, feeling his warmth, inhaling the scent of woodland, fresh in his clothes, in his hair.

"I've got so much to tell you," he said, his eyes shining.

"Me too," I pressed my lips to his face.

"I'll leave you two lovebirds," Maryla said, walking away with a teasing smile.

"I'll come in a minute," I called after her, then I said to Michal, "I can spend all afternoon with you. Just with you."

Happiness animated his face.

"I've got a plan. For us both. But only if you say yes."

"What is it?" My fear was gone. I was caught up in his excitement.

"Wait and see!" He kissed me again. "I'll go to the stables now, to look for Ludwik."

"And Bruno," I said.

"Bruno? From Steinfeld's farm? The musician? With the mouth organ?" His surprise was mixed with joy.

At breakfast, Michal was called inside to sit at the table with us.

"I expect a good morning's work from you." Dieter made his conditions clear.

"Sir, no one has ever complained about my work," Michal replied solemnly. "You can rely on me."

Dieter and Sylvia were in a hurry. They were going out. They stopped at the kitchen door, dressed in their Sunday best, Dieter requiring now only a walking stick for support. He turned round. "Now, you've all got your jobs to do. I expect them to be done, when we get back for lunch."

Breakfast passed as if in a dream for me, my happiness inflated by Michal's closeness, his arm resting against mine, his own excitement contained with controlled calm with which he gave replies to all the questions thrown at him. About Bazylka: she was well and got on fine with the Ukrainian girls. About Franek: he was on loan two days a week at Steinfeld's farm. Any news of Lilli? None. Franek would have said if anything was known. And the others? What about Horst? And Spitz and Blitz? The bastards! Did nothing ever happen to them? Like a bomb, for instance, blowing them up to smithereens!

"Ludwik, Bruno, steady on…" Michal laughed, "Franek's got it all planned out. When the right time comes. We've made a pact, he and I." His smile faded, his tone became unambiguous. I felt a shiver down my spine.

"Good! Count me in to help you!" Ludwik cried with fervour.

"And count on the fourth musketeer," Bruno joined in. Their light-hearted banter did not fool anyone. I had that need too, strong and deep-rooted, for a justified retribution. But just then I did not want to mar my happiness with thoughts of revenge in some distant future. All I could think of was that afternoon.

"Where are we going?" I asked, skipping like a child at Michal's side, as he held my hand and walked towards the stream. I had changed into my grey dress with the white collar and thrown my old coat loosely over my shoulders. It was yet another of those golden days, with all the tones of saffron and ochre around us, with floating gossamer threads filling the air.

Michal smiled mysteriously and did not reply till we reached the wooden bridge over the stream.

"Before we go any further," he said, "I've got to be absolutely sure that you want the same as me."

"What's that?" I was mystified.

"Do you still love me, Anna?" he asked.

"Still love you?" I was dizzy with happiness. "Michal, how can you even ask? I love you now, and I'll always love you."

He put his arms around me and kissed me on the lips.

"Anna, that's exactly how I feel too. I love you forever. I want to marry you," he said. He said it just like that.

Marry me? I was astonished. I had never imagined it like this in my dreams of white weddings, elegant receptions and horse-drawn carriages.

"Marry me?" I repeated, looking into his expectant eyes. "When?"

"As soon as we can! Anna…" He could hardly contain his eagerness. "As a married couple we've got more of a chance, maybe, of being allowed to stay together… On one farm…"

His enthusiasm swept me up. I wanted nothing more than to be with him, every day of my life!

"Michal, if only! Of course I'll marry you! But how? How can we persuade the priest when we're not permitted to enter the church?"

"We'll go to him now, to the presbytery… There's no law against that!"

He grabbed my hand and we ran together up the track to the main road till we were out of breath.

Sankt Walburgen was just a kilometre away, its scattered houses set on the slopes of surrounding hills. There was a cluster of houses close to the church, a whitewashed building with a tall, slender spire and a row of arched windows set into the walls like a cut-out shiny ribbon. We took the quiet path across the cemetery and followed it to the door of the priest's living quarters, tucked behind the church. There was no one about to stop us, our yellow "P"s well hidden underneath our outdoor clothing, yet the priest knew who we were, as soon as he opened the door.

"Come in, come in, you poor war orphans." He invited us inside, closing the door quickly. "Come into my study."

It was a small, dark room, with shelves full of books lining the walls. There was a sturdy old desk, a worn leather chair and four wooden chairs in a row by the window.

The priest was a small man, with a thick growth of grey hair around his wide tonsure. Strangely, the network of creases around his eyes gave him a kindly appearance, that encouraged trust.

"Sit down, sit down," he indicated the chairs by the window. "No one will disturb us now. They value their Sunday afternoons."

He sat down at the desk and resting his elbows on the top, joined his hands together, as if in prayer. He asked us about our families, about the work on the farm, before getting to the point.

"So what have you come to see me about?"

Michal leaned forward, and out of habit lowered his voice.

"We've come with a request. It's simple. Anna and I want to get married."

An indulgent smile spread across the priest's lips.

"We are serious!" Michal explained hurriedly. "We want to be together. To live and work on one farm. It's hard being constantly apart."

The priest studied us for a moment with that benign expression of his.

"I know you're serious," he said, "and it fills me with gladness to see young people wanting to do things the proper way. There's too much looseness these days. The war is such a convenient excuse for all kinds of goings on. However, as you know, I'm not permitted to marry foreigners, such as yourselves. The only way around this restriction is for you both to take on Austrian citizenship."

Michal and I looked at each other. God no! We were born Poles, we would remain Poles.

"This would be on paper only," the priest said, reading our minds.

We stared hard into each other's eyes. This was an impossible dilemma.

"But…" the priest continued, "if you become an Austrian citizen, Michal, you'll be immediately conscripted to fight. You're just of the right age."

My mind was made up. We were not going to become Austrians. Michal was not going to fight.

"So what are we to do?" I asked.

The priest rested his chin on the tips of his fingers and thought for a minute. Then he said, "All I can do is pray with you now, and give you my blessing. Come, follow me to the church."

He led us down a short passage at the back of the church into a room, which turned out to be the sacristy, at the side of the altar. The church was empty, with that hushed, semi-darkness that by its nature surrounds you with calm.

Michal and I knelt down at the altar, while he remained standing to recite a prayer over us. With his thumb he made the sign of the cross on Michal's forehead then on mine.

"Go with my blessing," he said.

We stood up.

"So what's to happen now?" Michal asked, "Are we to live in sin?"

I felt a blush burning my face. The priest placed his hand on Michal's shoulder.

"I think," he said, "that right now, God has greater worries than two young people in love. Your intentions are noble. I have not the slightest doubt that you'll get married as soon as you're free to do so. Now, go my children, go! Go with my blessing."

We came out into the golden afternoon, into the peace of the cemetery around us. Michal held me close and I hugged him with all the bubbling joy inside me.

"Shall we go to tell the others?" I asked.

"Later," he said, his solemn look suddenly giving way to a wide smile that touched every part of his face.

We held hands and walked briskly, lightly, as if on air, down the track to the main road. Here, another country lane, like the one near our farm, led down to the railway line, across the stream towards the forest on higher ground. There seemed no need for communication between us. I sensed a feeling of unity, an unspoken understanding, that we both wanted, craved the same things.

We found a secluded spot, covered in thick, soft moss, surrounded by bracken and ferns, with filtered light and the afternoon warmth coming down gently, as if all nature had conspired to assist us.

I slid off my coat and spread it on the ground. Then we lay down and held each other and kissed avidly, aware of each other's desire even through the layers of clothes, and I wished heaven to be like this for me after death.

"I've never done anything like this before," I whispered.

"We'll learn together," Michal whispered back.

He unbuttoned my dress and helped me take it off. It did not seem to matter that my brassiere and my knickers were grey and frayed. I discarded them too. He threw off his shirt and his vest, revealing his summer-browned skin, his muscular shoulders and his clearly defined ribcage, starved of all fat. He began to kiss me again and to touch me in a way no one had ever touched me before, and I wanted more, I wanted all the things that good girls are not supposed to want and enjoy, things that only the married women have to endure, out of duty.

His skin was surprisingly soft and smooth, his nakedness not at all unappealing. He looked vulnerable and strong at the same time, and I loved him all the more for his trust in revealing all of himself before me.

Afterwards, when our needs had been fulfilled, when we lay hot and exhausted in each other's arms, I understood why this ultimate intimacy could become an addiction, an obsession that drove those under its spell to risk everything.

I remembered suddenly, with a chortle of amusement, all the stories handed down, like Chinese whispers, of how awful it was supposed to be the first time.

"What's so funny?" Michal asked, seriousness creeping into his face.

I told him, adding, "Well, we've proved them wrong, haven't we?"

He kissed me, a thousandth kiss, then it was time to get dressed and return to the farm.

As we strolled, hand in hand, along the woodland path, there was one thought that niggled me, even in my dazed state of euphoria.

"Michal," I had to say it aloud, "you know my mother would disown me, if I had a baby."

He stopped and took me in his arms.

"Dearest Anna, you've got me to protect you. She'd have to disown us both. And her grandchild. But it's not going to happen. Not till the right time. There are ways of playing safe."

I did not tell him my monthly cycle had stopped being regular a long time ago, that months of hard labour had taken their toll on my body. Instead I said, "I shall miss you, Michal, terribly!"

"I'll come back next week, and every Sunday after that." He squeezed my hand. "God, how I've dreamed of this! Of us being together. And we will be together, won't we? The days in between don't count. Every Sunday will be our day, a day to look forward to all week. And now," he glanced at his watch, "there's just time to go back and tell the others."

"Which part shall we tell them?" I teased.

He laughed out loud.

"That we're married, of course!"

PART 3

MARCH-AUGUST 1942

CHAPTER 23

I had a secret. It was torture holding it back from Maryla, my best friend, but I had to wait till I told Michal first. I kept glancing at her now and again, across the kitchen table, wondering what her reaction would be when she knew. My nerves were taut as I listened for the sounds of Michal's clogs at the kitchen door.

It was Saturday night, and with all the work done for the day, the four of us – Ludwik, Bruno, Maryla and I – enjoyed a couple of hours' rest before bedtime. The boys were playing pontoon, with cards so yellowed, stained and tatty round the edges it was hard to distinguish the kings from the queens. Maryla and I were finishing off hemlines on our newly made skirts, that we had put together from pieces cut off from some old garments that Sylvia had brought from her mother's. Maryla's was grey and white fine dog-tooth, and mine was plain brown. A good, unobtrusive colour.

Sylvia and Dieter had retired to their part of the house for the night, Frieda and Gerhart had gone to their family in Eberstein till the following evening, and old Anton was most probably asleep in his den of rags and straw near his beloved bull. It was quiet, except for the sporadic shouts from the boys whenever one or the other was winning the game.

I looked up at the kitchen clock. The hands had not moved. It was eight minutes to nine. For a hundredth time. If only Michal could make it out of the station before curfew time, the rest of the short journey on foot could be finished unseen through the woods.

He had visited me every week over the winter months, except for three Sundays when additional snowfalls and drifts as high as the pyramids had made his journeys impossible. He had befriended a train driver in Treibach who had allowed him to stoke up the locomotive and thus travel on the last train on Saturday nights, for a chunk of ham or bacon or sausages. Michal did not have to steal from Holtzmann. By a stroke of luck he had been sent regularly to Elise's relative, an aunt of eighty-five, who lived on her own and needed a pair of young hands to do the heavy jobs around the house. She had taken a liking to Michal and allowed him provisions required to bribe the train driver.

"Ace!" Ludwik shouted, making me jump. His curls bounced around his face when he laughed. He picked a card from the top of the deck, face down.

"Not so fast!" Bruno looked self-assured as he considered his hand with studied calm.

Please God, I prayed, please let him be here! Maryla's hand touched mine.

"Any minute now, Anna. Stop worrying." She knew the torment I went through each time, until the moment he arrived.

And when he did, this time, I had to tell him. I would wait till he had eaten, rested, joked with the boys. I would wait and tell him when we were on our own.

"My win!" Bruno cried, his cheeks pink with pleasure. "Only three cards! Clever or not?" He displayed a king, six spades and five hearts, adding up to twenty-one winning points.

"That's because I've made it easy for you," Ludwik teased with a cheeky grin, dealing the cards for the next game, "but this time you'd better watch out!"

Bruno was just about to voice his indignation when I heard the familiar, coded tapping on the door. I rushed to pull back the bolts, to turn the key, to let him in.

Michal walked in muffled in layers of clothing. He could have been anyone, but for me the sight of him was the sudden lightness, the overwhelming joy. I closed the door with haste, mindful of the blackout regulations, and took from him his woollen hat, mittens, scarf, coat, felt tubes that he had worn over his legs and clogs, and folded them in a pile on the stool by the door, while he joined the others.

He had brought with him his own cheese sandwich and just asked for a glass of water, but I had kept back half a teaspoon of tea and made him a hot drink. The surprise in his expression was all the thanks I needed.

The evening passed in light-hearted banter and exchanges of news, all the more interesting now, that Bruno had been allowed to visit his girl Dorota on Steinfeld's farm. He had not had Michal's luck of knowing a friendly train driver. His journeys on foot through snowdrifts had to be reduced, reluctantly, to just monthly visits, till the winter was over. There had been no news of Lilli. No one had seen her since that dreadful day.

We were alone, at last, but still I would not speak of what lay heavy on my chest. I waited for Michal while he had a wash behind the curtain and practised in my mind the words I would use to break the news. He came out, smiling, clutching his shirt and the towel to his chest.

"I can't wait to rest my weary bones," he said, following me up the wooden stairs.

Maryla had been an angel, moving out on Saturday nights, so Michal and I had the room to ourselves. She slept in the boys' room. This would have been unthinkable at home, but unusual conditions created unusual needs that pushed aside accepted conventions. Besides, Ludwik had been like a brother to her, and Bruno had thoughts only for his girl Dorota.

We lay down on my mattress with just the square of silver light from the pane in the roof above us, shining on the wooden floor.

"I've got something to tell you," I said.

"So have I, hundreds of things!" Michal held me close, his face buried in my hair.

I drew away from him, lay flat on my back, took his hand and placed it on my stomach.

"Mmm... I like the feel of this," he said. "You look so much better, now your appetite's come back. You worried me sick Anna, when your weight dropped off."

These days I could eat a horse. My skirt was so tight I had to leave my three top buttons undone. My girlish flat chest had filled and rounded in recent weeks and pushed against my brassiere with tingling sensations.

Michal moved his hand to touch me elsewhere but I pushed it back and held it in place at the base of my stomach.

"What am I supposed to do?" he asked.

"Nothing. Just wait and see."

We lay still and I waited for that little kick that had been such a shock a few days back. A distinctive movement, so unlike the familiar workings of my digestive system, a fact, real, unmistakable, confirming my suspicions that had plagued me for so long.

The kicking came, gentle, like the swimming tadpoles I used to catch in a jar, again and again.

"What is it?" Michal asked, raising himself on his elbow, yet leaving his hand on the surface of this strange activity. I could just about make the contours of his shadowed face.

"It's our baby," I said.

The quiet was absolute while he considered my words. Then he sat up, ruffled his hair with his fingers, rested his elbows on his knees and nodded, as if suddenly everything made sense. I sat up beside him and placed my arm over his bare shoulders.

"What are we going to do?" I asked.

I could imagine hundreds of fears crowding his mind. Telling Dieter and Sylvia. Telling Holtzmann. My deportation, so long desired, so untimely now. Our separation. Yet again. My mother's horror. Her shame. My misery.

But he turned towards me and took me in his arms.

"Anna, my dearest Anna, you're not alone in this. We'll deal with this together. Now let me think! Such a shock! So sudden! When? When is our baby due?"

"I've no idea!" I said truthfully, I knew so little about such things, "but, if it's begun to move, I guess we're half-way through."

He spread his fingers and counted on four months.

"July?" he asked.

"I can only guess."

He became quiet, rubbing his forehead, pushing back his hair, clasping his hands, squeezing his fingers, then suddenly he turned to me, as if his mind was made up.

"We'll tell the Kestners after breakfast tomorrow. We've got no choice. Anna. I'll beg them not to send you away. I'll suggest to them, that Holtzmann may relent now in this situation, and let me go. They'd be gaining an extra pair of hands." He made it sound so simple.

"They'd like that, Michal, I'm quite sure, but Holtzmann will never let you go, and here, they'll not want to keep a pregnant worker. I can't go home, Michal, my mother will kill me!"

"Then she'll have to kill me as well. If they send you away, Anna, I shall run off with you too. We'll go to my uncle's, where nobody knows us, and we shall get married there."

He hugged me and we lay back on the mattress, holding hands, comforting each other.

"How long have you known?" he asked. "Why haven't you said anything before?"

"Oh Michal, why do you think?" I said wearily, "I had hoped I was just imagining things… I prayed it would just all go away. Then, three days ago… I felt the baby move…"

"And you knew? Just like that?" He was quiet for a moment as if going over events in his mind. "So…that sickness in December…your lack of appetite…then your recovery… I was so relieved when you started looking well again…" He slapped his forehead, "God, what a fool I've been!"

I had to smile.

"Did it never occur to you that this could happen to us?"

He thought for a moment, kissing the top of my head.

"Frankly, no. I thought these things happened only to other people." I sensed his grin. "Anna, we should have used that rubber after all!"

I shuddered at the memory of that disgusting thing. Michal had brought it one Saturday night, a gift from Franek. Impossible to acquire, Franek had bragged, but somehow, he had got it through a friend of a friend on Steinfeld's farm. Reusable. Long life, Franek had guaranteed. Reusable? My suspicions shot up like mercury. There were some things one did not share with others. I threw it in the fire together with the rag it was wrapped in.

"You can't be serious," I said. "Have you any idea where that thing had travelled before it got to us?"

Michal chuckled, adding, "And Maryla's advice on contraception, that didn't help at all, did it?"

I smiled, glad for the few crumbs of humour in our predicament.

"It's a little difficult," I said, "to get up in the middle of the night, after you-know-what, for a soak in a hot tub. In a house full of people."

"Sleeping people," Michal reminded.

"Even worse if anyone woke up. How would you explain a midnight bath?"

We both laughed at the very thought of such a scene, stifling our laughter against each other.

I sobered up first.

"Michal, we must be going mad. There's nothing much to laugh about."

The hot baths were a myth. My safe period was non-existent. We had nothing left that we could have safely relied on. Nothing but abstinence. That was for the saints.

Michal stroked my belly.

"This little one here is not all bad news," he said. "Soon there'll be three of us. That's no reason for grief. Let's sleep on it, Anna. Let's wait and see what tomorrow brings."

I told Maryla as soon as we entered the cowshed at dawn.

"Good God! Anna! What are you going to do? Whatever you do, please don't leave me!" Her face was pale in the dim yellowish light. She threw herself at me, then immediately stepped back, pulling aside the flap of my long cardigan.

"Mustn't squash the little one. Let me see, is it showing yet? I'd never have guessed under all those baggy layers! Anna, why didn't you tell me?

Why did you make it so hard on yourself?" I saw hurt and reproach in her eyes.

"Maryla, I wanted to, believe me, so many times! But I was afraid to admit it, even to myself."

"Poor Anna!" Her thin arms embraced me amidst the sounds of impatient snorting, and the air heavy with the stench of the cow dung. She released me and raised her hands, all fingers crossed.

"For you," she said, "so they don't send you away. Anna, your child will have two mothers. You need never worry about anything on your own, again."

At breakfast, in the company of Dieter, Sylvia and old Anton, our boys carried on in their usual fashion of easy banter, betraying nothing of what I knew Michal had told them. Our life as slaves of the Reich had taught us to be on our guard, even with people who appeared kinder and more compassionate than most. Their life too had been blighted by inhuman regulations, and if they were to be forced to choose between their good and ours, it did not require a genius to predict their choice.

Every time Ludwik or Bruno spoke to me across the table, I could not help wondering what real thoughts they hid behind their pretended normal behaviour. Were they shocked? Disgusted with me? At home, I would have been shunned by every lad in the village, pointed out lewdly with fingers.

When we got up to clear away the breakfast things, Ludwik moved up close to me and whispered, "Don't be afraid. You've got us."

He was gone before I could reply, but at the same time Michal was already moving towards the parlour door to catch Dieter and Sylvia before they left for the Sunday service. I stood behind.

"Herr Kestner," Michal said, "I've got something to tell you."

They turned around, waiting to hear more. They were already dressed in their Sunday best: dark suit, dark dress and hats in their hands, ready to put on. They had never made a fuss over Michal's frequent overnight stays, accepting us as a couple from the beginning of Michal's regular visits. Their only condition was that he returned their favour with seven hours' work on Sunday mornings. But this was something entirely different. My stomach churned with nerves.

"Herr Kestner," Michal said, "there's no easy way of saying this. Anna's pregnant. It's my baby."

Sylvia's bag dropped on the floor. Like lightning I bent down and picked it up for her. Our eyes met. Hers looked bewildered, pained.

"Why, Anna, why? A slip of a girl like you! It doesn't make sense!"

I did not understand her reaction. I did not know what to say. I looked up at Dieter, who was talking to Michal.

"When?" Dieter asked. "When is it due?"

"J…July, I th…think," I stammered.

He nodded slowly.

"We've got a bit of time. It's a problem. No getting away from it. Real problem, for all of us. I've got to report this, you know. Regulations. They'll want to send you back, Anna. That's what they normally do. Too many mouths to feed. Not enough food for our own people." He paused and thought for a moment. "I'll speak to my Uncle Schwartz later. See what he says. *Gut Gott*, we need workers! We don't want to lose any of you."

They left, Sylvia icily quiet, and I cried. Dieter's words had sounded like a death sentence.

Michal put his arms around me.

"Anna, listen! Crying won't solve anything. Let's just take one day at a time, right? There's nothing more we can do right now. Save your worrying for another day. Now, let's get on with the morning's work, and spend the afternoon together."

My neck and shoulders were aching with tension as I waited for Dieter on Monday afternoon to return from the Arbeitz Bureau in Sankt Veit. I listened for the sound of his little grey truck that he had acquired through family connections, as soon as his leg had healed enough for him to be able to drive. I could not imagine how he was going to persuade the officials to allow me to stay. In my mind I lived through all kinds of fearful consequences of my condition, all the while wishing just for one thing: that I could marry Michal. At least then if I were to be sent home, I would arrive as a respectable, married woman.

Sylvia had called me after lunch to help her with the washing. She had said nothing more about my pregnancy since her strange reaction the day before. I wondered if I were in for a reprimand or some words of wisdom. I had no defence. I braced myself for a meek acceptance of her confrontation.

There were piles of white linen waiting to be washed after the winter months: sheets, eiderdown covers, pillow cases, table cloths. Now that the weather had turned sunny, with fresh, drying winds, the opportunity was perfect to get rid of the backlog. Sylvia had soaked a load overnight. Thoroughly rinsed, it now required two people to wring out the water. We picked up the tub by the metal handles and carried it to the washing line, stretched underneath the cover of an open shed.

"I envy you, Anna," Sylvia said suddenly, "I wish your baby was mine."

I was taken aback. With my mind clouded by chronic anxiety, I was unprepared for a reaction like hers.

"Sylvia, what are you saying? How could you possibly envy me? Me, with all my worries? Do you know how they treat a girl like me in my village at home?"

She pulled a sheet out of the tub and rested a moment, her big red hands clamped around the wet cloth.

"That's exactly what I mean," she said. "It's all wrong! You don't need a child right now, whereas I do! I'd give anything to have one. It's so unfair!"

She began to twist the sheet at one end and I picked up the other. When all the water was squeezed out we shook it out and pegged it on the line.

"Dieter's been back since last June," she continued, "that's nine months. Nine long months! And nothing! Every month it's the curse!" Her large features looked suddenly childlike, as if she were about to cry. I had no idea what to say.

"Sylvia," I leaned over the tub and began to pull another piece of laundry, "he's still recovering. Give him time. He's been through a lot. It'll all happen when you least expect it. You'll see!"

Small words intended to soothe, yet she clutched at them as if they were true hope.

"You're right, Anna, you're right," she agreed eagerly, "I just wish it would happen soon!"

We worked quietly for a few moments, then Sylvia spoke again. Her openness surprised me.

"Life's never quite how you imagine it's going to be," she paused, struggling to hold up a large eiderdown cover. I helped her to throw it over the washing line. "I was only sixteen when I had Lotte. You can well imagine no one was jumping for joy then."

I knew about Lotte, Sylvia's illegitimate daughter, who was fourteen now, and had been adopted by her grandparents. I knew this from Frieda, ever the eager source of information.

"And now," Sylvia continued, "when I want a child for Dieter it's not happening. He's a good man. He deserves a child of his own."

I counted on his goodness when I waited for him to return home that afternoon, as I worked in the shed with Maryla, removing the cow dung from around the cows, lining the ground with hay. I longed for the spring to settle, for the air to warm up, for the fields to be clear of snow, so we could release the cows from their winter confinement and take them out to pasture. I heard his truck and I could not wait a moment longer.

"I'm sorry, Maryla, I've got to go. I've got to know. God, how I'm dreading it!"

"You go and find out. I want to know too." She waved me off and continued to scrape the ground.

I walked briskly out of the shed, my protective hand over my belly, and waited for him under the chestnut tree, shielding myself behind its thick trunk, from the splashes of slush and mud, as his old truck pulled up nearby in a clash of rumbling, screeching and blasts from the exhaust pipe. Slowly he opened the door and carefully slid off the seats, his good leg taking his weight, then supporting himself on his walking stick, he beckoned to me to follow him.

Sylvia was preparing the evening meal, chopping the vegetables for the stew. She stopped as we came inside, wiped her hands on the apron and pulled out a chair for Dieter to rest on. She helped him take his jacket off, worn at the collar and the cuffs, and hung it over the backrest of the chair. Then she stood, waiting, her strong arms folded on her ample bust.

"Well then, don't keep us waiting. Did it help having Uncle Schwartz with you?"

Dieter shrugged, his eyes giving away nothing inside their deep sockets. His gaunt face had the perpetual undernourished look.

"Maybe. Maybe not," he said. "They were officious enough, even with Schwartz by my side. Asked me endless, stupid questions, till my brain felt dizzy. But perhaps this was friendly compared to how they treat others, only a simple man like myself is unable to appreciate their kindness."

"So what did they say?" Sylvia took the words out of my mouth. The suspense was killing me.

Dieter slid his hand inside his jacket pocket and took out a brown paper bag.

"What's this?" I asked.

"This, Anna," Dieter said, "is a bag that contains medication for you. You are to take it with water. This will make you so ill, so sick, that you'll lose the baby."

His words were like a blow out of nowhere. My legs wobbled. I gripped the edge of the table for support, and watched, petrified, as he pushed himself up to a standing position, leaned on his walking stick, limped to the range, removed an iron ring and threw the bag with its contents into the fire.

"That's their first good advice disposed of," he said returning to his seat.

I felt weak with relief. I could have kissed his hand, both hands, with all the fingers missing.

He folded his arms and hid his mutilated fingers underneath his armpits. Sylvia brushed back a lock of hair from his forehead.

"The second advice was," he said, "that you be allowed to give birth, but then, that your baby should be taken away and placed in an orphanage so it can be brought up and trained for slave labour. They have grand plans for the Reich."

I could not control my trembling mouth nor the tears blinding my vision.

"Anna, listen!" Dieter's voice was firm, "I'm telling you first what they said to me. Now hear what I said to them. I said your child does not need to go to an orphanage to be trained. I said your child will get all the training it needs, right here on the farm!"

I wiped my eyes with the sleeve and swallowed hard to loosen my throat. Sylvia stroked his head as if he were a pet.

"And did they listen to you?" she asked.

"They did, when I told them I would take all responsibility for Anna and her child. They made me sign some papers, of course, but now," his face loosened in a vague smile as he looked at me, "now Anna, now you and your child are my property."

His words meant well, or perhaps as a jest, were like another blow, denting my gratitude. I had nothing to offer in return except my work.

"I won't let you down," I said.

"I know you won't. That's why I did it. There will be no slowing down when the baby arrives."

"You did the right thing," Sylvia said, going back to her cooking.

I walked across the yard to tell Maryla. I felt great relief but no joy. Life was to go on. Rise at dawn, slave all day, crawl to bed exhausted, grab snippets of time with Michal once a week. This was the existence in plan for our baby.

Maryla chided me for my dark thoughts.

"Anna, be happy for now. At least you've been saved from what you've been dreading the most."

She was right of course, and I was not angry with her, but suddenly I was seized by a rage, by a startling, uncontrolled rage. I threw down the rake and began to shout.

"I've had enough, Maryla! Enough of everything! I'm tired of always having to be patient. Uncomplaining! I'm tired of always having to pretend that everything's all right, when it bloody well isn't! Of having to show gratitude. For what? For scraps of what should naturally be ours! Don't make me feel bad for wanting normal, ordinary things! Is it too much to want to be with Michal, to be like a family when our baby arrives? Am I really asking too much?" I picked up the rake and began to hit the ground with it. I stopped, suddenly aware of how still Maryla was. I looked up and saw concern in her eyes, and pity and hurt. I was overcome with misery at my behaviour causing her pain.

"Forgive me, Maryla. God knows, you don't deserve this on top of everything else!"

She stretched her arm around my shoulders, comforting as ever.

"Anna, shush…things will be fine, I promise. I'm no substitute for Michal, I know, but not many babies can boast of having two mums! I think we'll manage quite well between us."

My rage, like a fever, was suddenly gone. I felt tired, limp. My eyes started to prickle.

"Don't cry!" Maryla pleaded.

"I'm not crying… I'm just thinking… I've never imagined, never asked for any of this, and yet, if this was not happening, this bloody war and the rest of it, I'd never have met you, Maryla…"

She thought for a moment and smiled.

"Strange, isn't it?" she said. "Now, I couldn't imagine my life without you in it."

"Like a chronic pain," I said wryly.

"Something like that," she replied with a hug.

We picked up the rakes and began to scrape the muck off the ground.

CHAPTER 24

At the beginning of July I was moved to a red-brick little hut, at the side of the farm-house, with stone steps leading up to it, a few metres up to the higher ground. It had a tiny cubby-hole of an entrance, with only enough room for shoes and boots, and two doors leading to the two halves of the hut. I was given one half, a room big enough to accommodate an iron bed, a chair and a chest of drawers, if I had one. In the corner, by the dividing wall, there was a round iron stove, indispensable in the cold winter months.

"It'll be better for you here, and your baby," Sylvia said, the thoughtful landlady, her long white apron tied over her long grey dress. "And when Michal visits you, you'll have a place of your own."

All that was true, and I should have been grateful, but Michal's weekly visits were short, and in my condition I was reluctant to be separated from Maryla.

"A little bit scary here on my own, if anything were to happen," I said.

"Nothing's going to happen," she reassured me, a little briskly, "I've told you everything you need to know. All your things are ready. And besides, you'll have peace here."

She meant her workers would have peace when the baby arrived. I could not blame her for her concerns. We all worked hard, long hours; we all deserved uninterrupted rest.

I thanked her and went to fetch a sweeping brush and rags to dust and clean the room. These days I could not dash from place to place the way I used to. My belly was big, my back constantly uncomfortable, my legs and feet aching.

I had been aware with some unease of Sylvia's watchful, envious eyes on me, and every month, when she informed me "It's the curse again", she made it sound, as if in some way it had been my fault. She had asked me once, how I was coping. Guardedly, I had replied that everything was fine.

"You've got all the luck, haven't you?" she had cried in dismay. "Have you any idea what other women go through? Some get swollen faces and hands, some get patchy skin, or bad teeth, or their hair starts falling out! You look like a plump chicken ready to roast! Thank your lucky stars!"

I thanked my lucky stars and did not tell her about my aches and pains. I only told Maryla, when we lay exhausted on our mattresses every night.

"You shouldn't be working so hard," she worried constantly, but there was no way of halving our work, that doubled and trebled at the height of the summer.

Now, as it was evening time and all work had been done for the day, Maryla came back with me to the hut.

"At home," she said, "you'd be checked over by a doctor, seen by a midwife. Here it's all left to chance."

"And nature," I said. "Believe me, there's nothing that feels natural about pregnancy. It feels as if I shall never be normal again."

"You will, Anna, you will," her mood lightened, "except that it will never be like the old times. Not after the baby arrives. I shall miss you," she said, washing the four panes of glass in the little window.

"You won't," I laughed, trailing the brush slowly around the floor to prevent dust rising. "You'll be relieved to be well away from us when the baby starts screaming."

She stopped, hand and rag poised for a moment.

"So much has changed…" she said, "some days I think I'm dreaming. You know, despite everything that's happened to us, to you, to me… I'm able to feel moments of happiness… Your baby…it's like a sign of hope…"

She had a dreamy, thoughtful look in her eyes. I thought of her and Staszek, and of what might have been. Indeed, I was lucky. I had Michal. Soon there would be three of us. I searched in my mind for adequate words of comfort, but she intercepted with a smile.

"It's all right, Anna, I'm happy for you, and you be happy too. I'm coping well…that's what I meant about things changing… Last year I wanted to die. Now, I can actually think about the future…" She turned to the window and carried on wiping. "I can thank Ludwik. It's helped to talk. We understand each other."

One would have to be blinkered not to notice how they constantly sought each other's company, sat together at mealtimes, their sides touching, how their eyes shone with intensity and their faces came close when they talked about the most ordinary things.

"It's good that you've found a soul-mate," I said with feeling.

She turned from the window, her expression wavering.

"Don't get me wrong, Anna, I've never stopped loving Staszek. I could never forget him!"

"You don't have to make excuses," I rushed to reassure her. "Not to me, Maryla. God knows, you both deserve a little comfort, you and Ludwik."

Her eyes became moist.

"I cannot describe how it hurt. It was so terrible, so terrible!" she said, "and now I feel as if I'm healing."

I put my arm around her thin shoulders and hugged her to me.

"I'm so glad to hear that, Maryla, honestly! It was no fun seeing you wasting away. We've all got a future to think about. Despite this crazy war. Now, do you want to help me bring my things over?"

My things were only the sheet and the pillow case, my canvas bag with my few clothes and a separate bundle I had prepared for my baby. Maryla had helped me in the evenings to sew baby vests, jackets, pantalettes, bootees and bonnets out of old flannelette sheets that Sylvia had given me. We spread them out on my new bed, three changes of each garment, then I folded them into little piles and packed them inside a pillow case in readiness for when my time came. Inside this bundle, I also slipped in my Arbeitz Karten and the train ticket that Sylvia had bought me in advance.

Michal had been planning to make a wooden cot and with each of his visits he brought a few finished and polished sections, to be put together, when all the pieces were in one place. He had also managed to get me a wicker basket, big enough for a carry cot. I lined it with my old cardigan for softness and warmth.

"I wish I could come with you when the time comes," Maryla said, linking her arm through mine, as we came outside and sat down on the old bench in front of the hut.

It was a warm evening with a soft opal sky. The farm buildings below us appeared deserted, so quiet they were, and the only sounds to reach us were the occasional shouts of excitement from underneath the chestnut tree, where Ludwik and Bruno were playing cards.

"Sylvia and Dieter don't want any fuss," I said. "She's made that quite clear. They'd never allow you to waste working time on me. It'll be bad enough with myself out of action for a few days!"

Maryla shook her head.

"How on earth will you be able to cope on your own?"

"I've no idea," I answered truthfully, "I just pray nothing will happen to make them cross and send me away."

A pain in my back, as sharp as a knife, pulled me out of my sleep. It was like a force pushing against my spine, while my belly turned as hard as stone. This is it, I thought, panic rising within me, sweat drenching my scalp. The pain subsided, and with it, my fear.

"It's all natural. It'll come and go. Could go on for hours." I hung onto Sylvia's words, rolling slowly to one side and leaning on one elbow as I pushed myself up. I dropped my legs over the edge of the bed and rested my big lump on my lap. In the pearly light of dawn, my watch indicated twelve minutes past four. I had three quarters of an hour to get myself ready in time for the earliest train at five in the morning. In my heavy, clumsy state things took longer; I did not have a minute to spare.

I slid off the bed and splashed my face in the bowl of water left on the chair the night before. I brushed my teeth, tied back my hair and threw on my long grey dress, the one with the white collar, which mercifully was still loose enough to fit over my pregnant stomach.

I picked up my canvas bag. I had kept it ready for weeks, packed with my few and my baby's belongings. The cool air outside was soothing to my brow, calming to my nerves. It felt strange, the absolute peace suspended over the farm, no one awake, no one aware of this frightening, unavoidable, solitary journey ahead of me.

Carefully I made my descent down the stone steps, till I reached the latrine, a tall, wooden hut next to the stables. The stench inside could never be eliminated, but it was free of flies at dawn, and the wooden bench with the round hole in it had been scrubbed and kept clean, by each of us workers in turn. As I was emptying my bladder, my stomach contracted again, and pain shot across my back.

"Please God, please let it wait," I cried desperately, feeling sweat gather on my forehead and scalp. The pain peaked then subsided after half a minute. In haste, I pulled up my knickers together with the rag padding between my legs. I could think of nothing else except getting myself down to the little stop on the railway line before the next contraction. At least there, I could sit down and brace myself against the next attack of pain.

The small open platform between Eberstein and Sankt Walburgen served as an additional stop on the railway line for people living in houses scattered on the hills. It was a blessing that it was so close to the farm. I waddled down the stony dirt track towards the bridge over the stream, from which I could see a group of people already gathered and waiting for the train. I came up close and greeted them with *"Gruss Gott"* leaning on normality to ward off attention. Their replies were perfunctory, their thoughts elsewhere, and I was glad I did not merit a second glance. The bright yellow "P" on my shoulder was well out of sight underneath my baggy cardigan. The pain came as I had expected. I lowered myself down onto the green verge, hugged my knees and tensed myself against it, till it ebbed away.

Impatiently I strained my eyes for the sight of the train. It was on time, already full, when it arrived, exhaling stale atmosphere, heavy with odours of sweat, oily hair, rancid clothes, bad breath. I stood in the middle passage, hemmed in on all sides. A bag with live chickens was pressed against me, five heads peaking out, five beaks chirping in alarm. A woman's bucket at my feet scratched my calf with its contents: potatoes and onions. Bunches of carrot and beetroot leaves, sticking out of a man's sling bag, brushed against my face every time he moved. All these people, I guessed, were on their way to the market with their humble wares.

I closed my eyes and gave into the rhythmic swaying of the train, but the stops and the starts, and there were so many, pulled painfully on the muscles of my legs, that I had set firmly wide apart for balance and support. The contraction that came was stronger than the one before. My pelvic bones felt as if they were being racked to breaking point, my stomach was gripped by a powerful spasm. I wanted to scream to release the pain as it peaked with acute ferocity. I felt my face crumble, my eyes fill up, I felt a hand on my arm, I heard a woman's voice, "*Kommen Sie, setzen Sie sich hier hin.* There's a seat by the window."

Space was made for me to push between the standing passengers, to stagger over feet and bags, to drop myself onto the end of the bench, cleared especially for me.

"*Danke, danke shone,*" my voice sounded hoarse, not at all like my own. I closed my eyes and prayed for this torment to be over.

The train chugged along, stopping at every village and hamlet. The carriages were packed solid. Every contraction increased my panic that my longed-for deliverance would occur in front of an audience.

Finally, it seemed like after countless hours, Sankt Veit came into view. The train slowed down and stopped. All the doors were flung open, the crowd rushed out and I was left with empty space around me and fresh air blowing through the carriage. Slowly, I followed the others out of the train and out of the station.

The station square was just as I had remembered it. Two years ago. When we had been the wares, herded inside pens like cattle, for the farmers to examine and decide their choices. Now the square was set up with rows of stalls, where the sellers were taking positions and sorting out their goods for display.

The buildings beyond the intersecting roads were alien, massive and imposing, decorated with rows of hanging, long red banners, and black swastikas.

"Is it far to the hospital?" I asked a woman nearby. She took in my shape and frowned with concern.

"Twenty minutes on foot. Take this road straight up and follow it round the bend."

The streets were quiet at this early time of six-thirty. I made my way as fast as my heavy bulk allowed me, past the closed, unlit shops, to the bend where the street changed character. Here big mansions stood well back from the main road, their lush gardens fenced off with brick walls and tall, wrought-iron gates.

I stopped and held onto one such gate as another contraction gripped my stomach and back. I felt violently sick, but on an empty stomach, all I could do was retch. Repeatedly, till my eyes streamed and my mouth oozed with excessive saliva.

A man and a woman passed by. I heard her say, "Disgusting! Already drunk at this time of day!"

I walked on and in the distance, on higher ground I saw the spire of the hospital building. Somehow, this sight spurred me on with renewed strength, even though the gradient of the rising road slowed down my progress and made me come out in sweat.

Then at last, it was within my reach, the wide-open gate, the metal railing, the enormous building painted white like a palace, with rows of tall windows, with wide stone steps leading up to the main entrance. There were ambulances parked in the vast courtyard. There were people going about, people who would help me. I felt safe, I felt as if I had arrived home.

Another contraction. Ferocious, pulling me apart. I gripped the railing, screwed my eyes and moaned to ease the pain. Then something broke inside me, and a warm wetness saturated the padding between my legs.

"Help me please!" I called out to the two nurses coming my way.

Their faces were a blur at first, but when they leaned over me, their capable arms supporting, comforting around me, I believed they were angels. One was dark haired, and the other had a white gauze scarf tied around her head, covering most of her face, so that only her eyes were visible. Her eyes, clear blue, large with surprise, made me look harder.

"Anna, is it really you?" she asked first.

For a split second nothing else existed. Only she, only he, in another time, in another place. With a sob, a shuddering sob, I clung to her.

"Lilli, oh Lilli," was all I could say.

CHAPTER 25

With Lilli in charge, I would have allowed her to take me to the ends of the world, such was my relief, that I had no longer to cope with this ordeal on my own.

She took my bag from me, linked my arm through hers and led me away, up the grand entrance and down a long corridor, the end of which was like a dot in the distance. It gleamed with white walls and polished, sparkling floors.

"This seems like a palace," I said, doing my best to keep up with her pace, "I've never seen anything so clean."

"It's the nuns," she said, her eyes smiling above the gauze wrap. "Cleanliness next to godliness, you know…that kind of thing."

"The nuns?" I could not see any nuns.

"Yes, they run this hospital. You'd hardly tell them from us. They dress all in white, like the rest of the staff."

There were sick bays leading off the main corridor, but the labour ward was situated at the very end. I understood why even before we reached the desk of the ward sister on duty. Shouts of women in labour and baby cries could be heard from behind closed doors.

The nurse who was assigned to me was a nun, Sister Katarina. Her face was calm, her smile welcoming. I trusted her on sight.

"You're in good hands," Lilli said to me, embracing me warmly. "I'd love to stay, but I can't. I'll explain everything later, when I come back tonight."

"Promise?" I was loath to let her go.

"Cross my heart, Anna. There's so much I want to know. And besides, you may have great news of your own by then."

She hugged me again, and before disappearing behind the swing doors, sent me a farewell wave.

Sister Katarina took out a pile of towels from a cupboard behind the reception desk and then beckoned to me with a smile to follow her.

The labour room had ten beds in it, with some curtains drawn round them. There was an atmosphere of hushed sounds, nurses' instructions, sounds of hard breathing, sudden shouts of pain. By one of the open beds, a woman stood leaning her bulky weight on her elbows planted firmly on the bed. Her face was contorted with pain, her hair hanging down in sweaty streaks.

Sister Katarina led me to a bed by the window. She drew the curtains around us, saying, "Take everything off, Anna, put on your night gown and get on the bed."

My nightgown that once was white cotton, had been worn down to a threadbare gauze. It was the colour of an old duster.

"It's been washed," I assured Sister Katarina, "I've kept it clean and packed for a long time."

She smiled and helped me onto the bed. She spread towels beneath me saying, "I need to look at you properly now."

It was a struggle pulling off my knickers, together with their soggy contents. I was so embarrassed I wanted to cry.

"Don't worry, it's all natural," she said gently, guessing my feelings. She dropped all the stuff in a brown paper bag. "You'll get your knickers back all washed and dry. Now let me have a look at you."

The pain gripped me again with such force, I was unable to suppress a moan.

"Don't hold back, scream if it brings you relief. Now, knees bent and apart," she instructed. I was aware of her peering at me, of her firm flat hand pressing against the base of my stomach. "It's going well, you're three fingers dilated."

I found her gentle voice comforting, soothing, and though she was a total stranger, whom I had only met a few minutes before, I was overwhelmed with gratitude to her. She hung a stethoscope on her neck and listened to my chest, then she checked my blood pressure.

"Have you been seen, checked, monitored by anyone during your pregnancy?" she asked.

I had to smile.

"Who would worry about me, Sister? A working girl? Or my baby? No, I've not been seen by anyone. Not once."

"You're lucky, Anna. You've got youth on your side."

I drifted in and out of intensifying pain for what seemed like endless hours, wondering all the while why this natural event had been designed to be such torture. My feet were twisted with intermittent cramps, my elbows were sore from leaning my weight on them as I strained, my back felt as if it was being pulled apart. I needed my mother, I wanted Michal, yet at the same time, I was glad they were not with me to witness my indignity and the whole bloody mess.

Our baby was born at five minutes to three in the afternoon.

"It's a boy!" Sister Katarina announced. Great relief and calm descended on my tired body, like a soft blanket, and I lay back and watched her hold up my baby by his tiny feet and pat his back. There was a faint spluttering noise before a robust scream cut through the air. Her face beamed. She wrapped him up in a square piece of cotton, like a little parcel, and placed him in my right arm against my breast. Almost immediately, his squirming tiny features settled in deep sleep.

"What's his name?" she asked. We had discussed names for our baby, Michal and I, so I replied without hesitation.

"Miroslav, after his grandfather. We shall call him Miro."

"We'll get him christened, right here, in hospital," she whispered, her face animated with promise.

I looked down at the miniature face, at the black down covering his crown, and I was filled with so much love for him, I felt I was going to burst. No one would ever take him away from me.

"Another contraction," Sister Katarina said, peering between my legs, "and it will all be over."

"What contraction?"

"The placenta," she explained, "It's what has kept your baby nourished while he was waiting to be born."

I was amazed at the size of it when it slid out of me. It looked like a giant liver. She took it away in a kidney-shaped dish, then came back and wrapped towels around my hips.

"Stay still and rest," she said. "We'll wheel you down to the maternity ward, and then I shall have to leave you, Anna. Sister Benedicta will take over and look after you for the rest of the day. Get some sleep, if you can."

That was not possible on the maternity ward. It was a long room, with twenty beds, ten on each side, facing each other. The hushed atmosphere was constantly broken by baby cries, and my compulsion to check on Miro, asleep in his cot, robbed me of my sleep, though I tried hard to lay back with my eyes closed. I could not stop looking at him. Pride, joy, awe, and overwhelming tenderness bubbled inside me, despite my utter exhaustion. I wanted Michal, I wanted my mother, I wanted everyone I knew to show off my baby to.

There was an old-looking woman on my right side. Some of her teeth were missing and her colourless skin was creased and worn. I found her looking at me when I opened my eyes. I smiled.

"You may well smile," she spoke through the gaps in her teeth. "It's your first, no doubt. I've got nothing to laugh about. It's my seventh.

That scoundrel husband of mine is a right good for nothing! Can only do one thing right! But you don't need brains to do that!"

I raised myself on my elbow. It was raw, making me wince.

"Boy or girl?" I asked.

"A girl. More trouble. They're always trouble, the girls…" She threw a glance her baby's way.

"She's beautiful," I said.

"Then take her! You can have her with my blessing!" She lay back and stared at the ceiling.

On my other side was a young woman. She looked as if she were truly asleep, with not a care in the world. Her glossy auburn hair was tied back with a velvet ribbon, and her pastel green nightgown was silky and trimmed with lace. She looked like one of those beautiful women who visited the most fashionable ladies' shop in Krakow, the place I had aspired to, dreamed of working in one day, and dazzle everyone with my designs and excellent craftsmanship.

The afternoon and the evening were governed by a strict routine in this order: hot milk for the mothers, then babies' feeding time (I was instructed by Sister Benedicta how to feed Miro), the evening meal for the mothers (this was thick vegetable and lentil broth with bread), a short visit exclusively for husbands, followed by the babies' nightly feed, before they were taken away to the nursery.

Some women, like myself, had no visitors. The bedraggled woman on my right tolerated her husband's presence only long enough to give him instructions on looking after the rest of the children at home.

"Go now, go," she urged. "You're of no use here!"

The groomed young woman, on my other side, sat propped up against her pillow and looked into her husband's eyes as he stroked her hand and whispered endearments. He wore a light linen suit and two-tone beige and white shoes that looked as if they had just been taken out of a box. I could only guess that in these troubled times only someone with connections could still enjoy all the privileges of the rich.

I lay on my pillow and studied patterns on the ceiling made by moving branches of a willow tree outside the tall window behind me. Miro was asleep in his cot at the foot of my bed. Sister Benedicta had been pleased with his first performance and mine. My breasts were already swollen in readiness for his next feed. I could not wait to tell Michal and in my mind I had endless conversations with him.

Then I saw Lilli approaching, her eyes bright above the gauzy wrap around her face. I pulled myself up and patted the space on the bed beside me, but she stopped and leaned over Miro first. She stroked the dark down on his head saying, "A little miracle, isn't he? I'm so happy for you, Anna."

She sat down and I hugged her long and hard.

"I've come early," she said, "before my night duty, so we have time to talk."

I could not take my eyes off her.

"Lilli, where have you been all this time? None of us knew what happened to you. We even wondered if you were still alive. Tell me... tell me everything."

She thought for a moment, looking at me intently, as if discovering my face for the first time, her clear blue eyes, glittery like water.

"The nuns took me in. After what happened. First as a patient. Then I decided to stay. To train as a nurse, to be like them."

"Are you a nun?" I was avidly curious.

She shook her head and gave a short laugh.

"No. I'm not a nun. I couldn't be. Like you, I've got a little boy of my own. Little Stefan."

She watched me for my reaction. I was stunned.

"You mean?..."

"Yes, I was four months pregnant when," she sighed, "when they killed Stefan."

I was quiet, taking it all in, going over the events of that awful day in my mind, calculating.

"So, he must be about eighteen months by now, your little Stefan. Where is he?"

She nodded replying, "With my parents. They look after him when I can't. I've been given a small room here at the convent, but I go home as often as I can, naturally."

I was overwhelmed with all this news, and I just gazed at her, holding her hand in mine.

"And your face, Lilli, how is your face?" I could not help asking.

She bent down her head, slipped off the gauze scarf and shook out her cut hair so it fell around her face like a curtain. Then she lifted her head and pushed back the hair off her left cheek.

I did not recoil, for even in her damaged state she was still beautiful, but I felt my throat tighten at the terrible injustice of her suffering, at the indelible reminder of the tragedy, that would remain with her for the rest of her life.

Her left cheek was badly scarred, the top skin puckered and criss-crossed with a net of tiny white marks around a visible groove in the shape of the letter "P".

Guardedly, I looked over her shoulder. The linen suit man was too absorbed in his wife to notice the likes of us. Lilli slipped on her scarf and tied it so that her cheeks were covered again.

"Not a pretty sight," she smiled wistfully, "but who cares now? The only two men I have ever loved were Stefan and now our little son. Now that's enough about me. Tell me Anna, what's been happening to you and all your friends?"

I did my best to pack as much news as it was possible into the short half-hour visit.

"I've not told you yet everything," I said, when it was time for her to go. "Will you come again, Lilli?"

"Every day, I promise. And when you leave the hospital, I'll bring Stefan for you to see."

Before night time, Sister Benedicta came right up to me and whispered, "Our priest is in the chapel now for the vespers. He can christen your child. Just give me the names of the godparents."

I had discussed that with Michal too. I did not have to think.

"Franek Dobosz and Maryla Prodo."

She wheeled the cot away, as if she were taking it to the nursery for the night.

I was kept in for a week. I had no visitors except Lilli. I missed Michal with an ache that would not go away, not even when I slept. But time did not drag. I had the best rest in two years. I had food prepared for me, I was taught to feed my baby, to bathe him daily, to change his nappies. I knew every centimetre of his tiny body. I recognised his cries, his snorting little noises. I watched him for hours as he made faces in his sleep, while his match-stick fingers curled and stretched as if they had a life of their own.

On Friday night, my last night in hospital, Lilli came to see me before starting her duty.

"Mothers and their babies are normally discharged around eleven," she said, "I'll be waiting for you outside tomorrow morning."

On Saturday, after the doctor's daily visit round the ward, Sister Benedicta brought me Miro's birth certificate. There was no name in the father's section.

"His father is Michal Majerski," I said to her. "We wanted it all to be proper and legal. We wanted it so much, but we were not permitted to marry."

"I know, Anna," she replied, "and God knows it too. He'll make it all right one day. Trust Him."

I fed Miro just before leaving, dressed him in the clothes I had made for him out of the old flannelette sheets, and wrapped him in the fleecy baby blanket that Sylvia had given me. I washed myself down all over, then I padded my knickers with a double folded strip of towelling. I put on my grey dress with the white collar.

I made a sling with my old cardigan by tying the ends of the long sleeves together and hanging the loop over my neck. I placed my sleeping baby inside it, resting him against my chest, picked up my canvas bag, and with a few hushed "*Gruss Gotts*" I left the ward.

It was sunny and hot outside, and I was blinded at first by the glare reflected from the white buildings. I heard my name being called out. I squinted, shielding my eyes. Then I saw Lilli, a dark figure in the deep shadows between the buildings across the yard. She had a pushchair with her and I could just make out a halo-like outline of a small child's head.

Mindful of my load, I descended the wide concrete steps carefully then rushed towards her. She had her gauze scarf tied around her head, covering her face, but even in the shadows her eyes were luminous. She bent down and picked up her son.

"This is my little Stefan. My parents are in town today visiting my uncle. I asked them to bring Stefan along, especially for you."

He had pale blond hair, just like Stefan's, just like hers. I stroked him and he considered me with a serious look before turning away shyly. I tickled his cheek and he looked back at me, his face suddenly taking on Stefan's expression. My heart lurched, my throat tightened, I swallowed hard.

"He's beautiful," I said, "I wish I had something to give him."

With my free hand I rummaged inside my pocket and brought out a ten pfennig coin.

"For good luck," I said, pressing it in his small hand. He turned it round and examined it with curiosity.

"I've got something for you," Lilli said, slipping a little bundle inside my cardigan sling. "A few baby things. It's not as if I need to save them for another baby...who would want me now?" Her eyes shone bright. I stepped closer and kissed her on the cheek through the gauze.

"Lilli, my dearest Lilli, you've still got us, all of us Poles. One day, we won't have to meet like this, hiding in the shadows."

"Promise?"

"Promise."

We clasped hands and held onto each other for an intense long while, before separating and going our own ways.

The route to the station was comfortingly familiar. Miro's warm body against my chest sent waves of protective tenderness through me. No one stopped me, no one took any notice of us. People rushed by, pre-occupied, distant. On the platform, groups huddled together, silent, waiting, carefully avoiding eye contact with the two armed soldiers patrolling the station. I felt a tap on my hip and turned around. An old man behind me had made room for me on the edge of a wooden bench. I pushed back the cardigan sleeve off my shoulder and showed him the yellow "P". He raised his eyebrows, shrugged and tapped the space next to him, as if to say "So what!"

I sat down beside him and he peered inside my cardigan sling. The lines on his wizened face lifted with delight.

"How old is your baby? A boy or a girl?" he asked.

"Just one week old. It's a boy," I replied, each word filling me with pride.

He nodded thoughtfully.

"Make the most of him. Enjoy him. You may not think it now, but this time is so short. The time of his babyhood. Before you know it, he'll grow too big to sit on your lap, too heavy to be picked up, too old to be patted and kissed. You'll be left wishing his growing up hadn't happened so fast."

I smiled. It all sounded so remote.

The old man sat with me on the train. Miro slept inside the sling against my chest, and I too became drowsy in the swaying motion of the carriage and the lulling warm breeze blowing through the open windows.

"Close your eyes," the old man said, "I'll wake you up before your station."

"First stop just past Walburgen," I said, my eyelids as heavy as lead.

It seemed like only a moment before he was shaking me out of my sleep.

"*Danke shone*" and "*Gruss Gott*" were all the thanks I could give him, as I rose, a little dazed. The train stopped and I descended onto the small concrete square of a platform, holding onto my precious bundles, my baby at my chest, and my possessions contained in one canvas bag. I waved to him as the train moved off, wishing now, I had said more, wishing I had told him how he reminded me of my grandfather.

The familiar sights around me – the herds of oxen and sheep dotted on the slopes on one side, and on the opposite side of the valley, the farm with its outbuildings; the orchard, the vegetable plots, the chicken pen and the pig enclosure, the cows grazing in the fields – all these things made me feel as if I were coming home.

Miro stirred inside the sling, his tiny features creasing. I brushed his cheek with my little finger and his head turned and his mouth clamped itself around the tip and sucked. He was asleep within seconds. I started to walk along the rail track towards the familiar bridge over the stream.

It was just after two. The farm looked eerily deserted. They would all have had their lunch by now, and were out again, hard at work; the men harvesting corn in the fields, and Maryla with Frieda digging out potatoes. As I approached the farm, up the beaten track, I wished there had been someone waiting, someone to receive me, to share my joy at my homecoming with my newborn son.

Dieter's truck was missing, that meant he was out in town. I directed my steps to the dairy, the small brick house at the far end of the cowshed, expecting to find Sylvia there. But there was no one about. I guessed she must have gone out with Dieter.

I needed to see Maryla. I had missed her every day and I had imagined countless times the look on her face when I gave her my baby to hold. But first things first. I would grab some lunch, feed Miro, then go looking for her.

It was at the precise moment that my hand turned the handle on the kitchen door, that I became aware of a movement behind it. Something made me hesitate for a split second, but then I thought the obvious. Sylvia was at home after all. I pushed the door, entered and froze.

CHAPTER 26

She was at the kitchen table. Behind her stood a big man holding her rigid against him with one arm, and with the other, pointing the barrel of his rifle up against her throat.

Even before my brain could make sense of the sight before my eyes, a strong hand grabbed my shoulder and the door behind me was banged shut.

"One squeak from you and you're dead!" a rough voice made me recoil. He spoke German with a foreign accent. This man too was wielding a rifle. I dropped my bag and clutched Miro to my chest, my arms forming instinctive protection.

Sylvia cleared her throat to indicate she wanted to speak. The man holding her captive relaxed his grip and lowered his rifle.

"This is one of the Polish workers," Sylvia's voice was hoarse, "she's not your enemy."

I swallowed hard. And prayed. Desperately.

The men could have been twins in their unkempt appearance: matted hair, black beards, torn and smelly clothes, threatening ferocity in their deep-set eyes. They stood still for a moment as if deciding on their next move, then Sylvia's captor barked instructions.

"I want food for six men. And water. Fast. One stupid move and you two can kiss each other goodbye. And the brat!"

I was trembling. My arms tightened over Miro. Don't let him wake. Please God, I prayed.

"The pantry's just there," Sylvia nodded towards the side door, "but the main food store is upstairs, above the kitchen."

"Take me there!" the man commanded, "and you girl, keep my friend good-tempered. His rages are legendary!"

My teeth began to chatter. I watched, helpless, as he pushed Sylvia towards the stairs.

My captor let go of my arm, saying, "Not a move till they get back!"

He remained so close, I could feel his stiff shirt brushing against me, I could smell his rancid presence, hear his heavy breathing.

241

A sudden rush in my breasts, a swelling, made me aware of wet patches spreading rapidly into the fabric of my dress. I closed my eyes. Please God, not now! My nerves were stretched to breaking point. The slightest movement, the tiniest sound were each like another painful pull on the rack.

The clomping on the wooden floor upstairs seemed to go on for unbearably long time, then at last, I heard Sylvia and her captor coming down. She had stuffed an old pillow case with food provisions and was struggling with the weight of it down the stairs.

"And bread and water too," the man ordered gruffly.

She dropped the full sack on the floor, opened the pantry door and stood back.

"Take what you need," she said, sweat glistening on her forehead.

From where I stood, I could see him helping himself to three loves of bread that Sylvia had baked that morning.

"Those empty bottles on the floor," he said, coming out, "fill them with water."

She did as he commanded, while all the time I remained under guard, hot and sticky, with an ache across my shoulders and back and with cramp in the pit of my stomach.

"Let's go," Sylvia's captor said. Then sending us a final narrow-eyed glance, he warned, "You two, one word to anyone and you're dead meat. If anything happens to us, our friends will pay you a visit. There are lots of us. It's the easiest thing to start a fire. In the middle of the night."

They went out and Sylvia and I remained motionless till we saw them pass by the side window.

Sylvia rushed into the parlour, to the windows at the far end of the house. I peered inside the sling at my chest. Miro was asleep. Then I too hurried after Sylvia into the part of the house forbidden to enter, to us workers. I stood beside her and we watched the two men make a hasty retreat up the high ground and disappear into the forest.

"Yugoslav partisans," Sylvia said, turning round, her cheeks burning, her lips parched, "Dieter keeps warning me about them all the time, but you've seen for yourself, what defence have we got against them? Even with all of us here, what would we have done? They'd simply shoot us all!"

She breathed out a long, deep sigh, then her gaze fell upon the bulging sling at my chest. Sudden interest reanimated her face.

"Show me, what have you got there!" She slid her large hands inside the sling, brought out Miro and cradled him in her arms. His little features creased for a moment then he slept on.

"It's a boy," I said, "Miroslav. We'll call him Miro."

"I can see you both in him," she said, "Michael's brow and your mouth."

I gave a nervous laugh.

"Then you're better at it than I am. The only expressions I recognise are squirming to be fed, squirming to be burped, and squirming to fill the nappy."

She pressed her full lips to his forehead and I wondered what her thoughts, what her feelings were, and I wished, I wished with all my might, that she would soon be nursing a baby of her own.

"Enough play," she said briskly, giving Miro back to me. "God, we've wasted so much time! You go and find Maryla, and I'll start baking again."

"What if they come back?" I couldn't help feeling jittery.

"They won't, now that they've got what they wanted. There's some broth in the pot. See to yourself and the child first."

Later, with Miro fed and changed, and myself dressed in old rags for work, I was still nervous of danger lurking in the dark shadows around the buildings, that were normally places of respite from the heat. Carrying Miro asleep in a wicker basket, I walked as briskly as the ache in my back and stomach allowed me, and made my way towards the vegetable garden, to find Maryla.

I saw the top of her sun-bleached head above the rows of peas and beans, which we grew on a long strip of land. I called out to her and she came running, her arms open wide to embrace me.

"I've missed you! How I've missed you!" She clung to me for a moment then released me and knelt down to look at Miro in his basket.

"It's a boy," I told her, anticipating her question, "little Miro."

"He's beautiful! Let me hold him!" Her face beamed as she picked him up and held him close. "I love him already!" She kissed the top of his head, sitting back on her heels. "Tell me Anna, tell me everything!" Her voice was high with excitement.

I sat down beside her on the ground, feeling the cramps in my stomach intensify. I lay down and curled myself into a ball.

"What's wrong, Anna? Are you ill?" Her joy turned to concern.

"I'm all right. Just utterly, utterly exhausted."

"You poor thing." She stroked my head as if I were a child. "You just stay here and rest. No one comes to check on us. They're all too busy."

"What about Frieda?"

"She's with Gerhart today. On the other side. Stay here, Anna, and sleep. I'll look after Miro. Trust me."

So I slept on the dry dusty ground, sheltered from the sun by the tall leafy stalks.

When I woke up, with a start, the hands on my watch had moved an hour. I sat up and brushed the dust and dry leaves off my face and arms. My back felt better and the dragging ache in my stomach had eased off. I stood up and looked around above the rows of beans. There was no one about, except Maryla, her head visible above the lush greenery a little way down the field. When she noticed me approaching, she came out holding up Miro's basket.

"Look, as good as gold. Still sleeping. We'll make a good team, you and me!"

My soul leapt with gratitude as her words filled my heart with courage. With her help, I believed I would manage.

"Maryla…" I wanted to tell her she was a treasure, an angel, the best friend in the world, but words appeared to fail me. I hugged her with all the feeling her kindness had ignited within me. She smiled with pleasure and shrugged.

"Anna, it's no big deal. You two are like family."

While Miro slept in his basket at our feet, we plucked the long pods of the runner beans and caught up with each other's news. Maryla listened with wide-eyed shock to my account of the partisans' visit that afternoon, and her curiosity seemed insatiable when I told her of my chance encounter with Lilli.

Ludwik and Bruno stood over Miro's basket and peered inside, their faces lit with admiration. It was suppertime, and I had placed the basket at the end of our table.

"Definitely his mother's nose," Ludwik decided, studying Miro's miniature features.

"And his father's muscles," Bruno added. "Strong, working arms."

I smiled with pleasure. I had not imagined young men like them to show interest in a newborn baby.

"Lucky man, your Michal," Ludwik said, sitting down.

"Worked for nothing last Sunday," Bruno remarked, "but twice the reward this time, when he comes."

I wished I could hurry time. It could be another two hours before I saw him. I prayed he had chosen the train rather than the long trek on foot through the forest.

Dieter and Anton came together and stopped by Miro's basket. Anton chuckled like a child being shown a new toy. Dieter nodded approval.

"Good work, Anna. We need boys." That was all he said. Then he limped to his seat at the head of the table.

After the meal was over, he raised his voice to draw our attention.

"You've all heard what happened this afternoon. There's not much we can do. It's usually food they want. Any resistance and there could be bloodshed. There's not enough police force to spread around the farms. They know that and they take advantage."

"So…we're just to stand back and let them raid the farm?" Bruno asked.

Dieter shrugged and spread his hands, his hands with mutilated fingers.

"We've got no choice. Even if our food supplies were reduced to just milk and eggs, we'd still survive, but we won't survive riddled with bullets. Just give them what they want. They think they can rise against the Wehrmacht. It's a pie in the sky. This won't last long. They'll be crushed like gnats."

My feelings were very mixed as I listened to Dieter. I was glad there was someone bold enough preparing to rise against the Germans. At the same time Dieter's reservations echoed my very own. What chance did these hotheads have against the power of the mighty Wehrmacht? Instinctively I touched Miro asleep in the basket and I fought hard to shake off thoughts of carnage if we were all caught in the crossfire.

Later, after all the necessary jobs around Miro were done, and he was fast asleep in his basket, I washed and lay down beside him on the bed, intent on keeping awake as I waited for Michal. My tiredness was stronger than my will. I slept.

A tapping on the window woke me up. My first instinct was to check Miro. He was peacefully asleep by my side. I turned my head. Michal's smiling face was peering through the glass pane, his fingers making rhythmic sounds.

I slid off the bed, unlocked the door and fell into his arms, finding everything I had been longing for; his strength, his warmth, his love, my security.

"Anna, how I've missed you! All week I've lived in fear that I'd never see you again! It's been torture! Show me, show me our little son!" He released me from his embrace and looked over my shoulder.

"They've told you already?" I meant our friends, down below by the chestnut tree.

"They couldn't wait!"

We sat down on the bed and I pulled the basket towards us. Even in the descending dusk I saw Michal's eyes sparkle and his face melt with happiness. He picked up Miro, placed him in the crook of his arm and began to rock gently.

"You don't have to do that," I laughed, drunk with joy.

"But I want to. It's the happiest feeling, Anna! You and our baby!" He sat down so that our sides touched and lowered his head as if to hide his face from me. I noticed his mouth trembling.

"What is it, Michal?" I encircled his waist with my arms and held him close, feeling him, feeling a stifled sob in his chest, feeling tears drop on my bare arms.

"Michal…my dearest…sweetest…" I hugged him till he composed himself, till he was able to speak.

"Anna, last week was absolute hell. Now, I feel as if I'm in heaven. God, I never want to leave you again!"

I hugged him harder.

"Neither do I. I don't want to let you go. Ever! Let's put Miro in his basket. Come, lie down beside me."

The narrow bed was not wide enough for the three of us. We pulled the chair right up to the level of our pillow and placed Miro's basket on it, so that we could watch him at all times.

"I've brought you a few things," Michal said, picking up his sack from the floor. "I'm best of friends with Frau Lientz now. Remember, Elise's old aunt that I do odd jobs for? When I told her you were in hospital, she rummaged through her drawers and found some underwear for you. It's old, but it's clean and still in good condition. She's also given me some cream for you and Miro, and a dummy for him."

"Why is she doing all this?" I was overwhelmed with this shower of presents. In the dark I could not examine any of them. Just the feel of the underwear told me it was silk.

"She might just fancy me," he giggled softly, lifting my mood too, "but the truth is Anna, she is a lonely, grumpy old thing. No one visits her. Some days I'm the only visitor to her house. She can be such a pain and it's not easy being patient at all times. I don't argue, I just say '*Jawohl Frau Lientz*' to all her demands."

He stepped out of his clogs and we lay down facing each other, our limbs entwined like ivy shoots, cocooned in our happiness. We had so much to tell each other and so little time.

August was a gruelling month. I existed on the very edge of sanity, aching all over with exhaustion, dizzy with lack of sleep, my brain numbed to virtual inertia, dependent on instinctive reactions. Yet deep down inside me, faint echoes of hope kept me going, hope of a sudden, all-changing event in our lives.

I nursed Miro and slotted his needs in between the regular requirements of the animals and the pressing deadlines of harvest. Maryla did her best to help me any way she could, taking turns to carry Miro round with us, minding him during my snatched moments of sleep, checking on me in my hut every morning at dawn, so I would not oversleep.

Sylvia kept her distance. Her only token display of interest was at mealtimes, when she would glance briefly, as she passed by, inside Miro's basket.

She had created an impression of intense activity around herself and made it clear with her brisk manner that she had no time for idle chat. I dreamed passionately of possessing a magic wand to wave around her, so she too could have a child for Dieter. I imagined, not without a touch of bitterness, that having had Lotte at such a young age, she was not unaware of the awesome task of baby rearing, yet she never displayed towards me the slightest softening in her strict work discipline.

Now and again Dieter would ask me, "How's it going?"

The first time he asked, I answered truthfully. "It's hard work. Harder than I had ever imagined."

His reply had been, "It's hard for all of us. Harvest time is no joy ride."

After that my reply was always the same. Everything was fine.

But it was not fine. Each day I pushed myself with remnants of ebbing strength, worrying about Miro, worrying what would happen to him if I became ill.

One particular morning Maryla tapped on my window as usual, I waved back, she went away to start milking the cows, and I closed my eyes for just one more moment in bed. Miro's nightly feeds starved me of my sleep.

When the knocking on my window resumed, and I sat up with a start, it was not Maryla's face but Sylvia's that was peering through. Nervously I unlocked the door for her. She did not hide her annoyance.

"What are we going to do with you? You're letting us down. It's hardly fair on Maryla, is it?"

God, she did not have to tell me! I was overcome with misery.

"It won't happen again," I said. "It'll get easier when Miro starts sleeping through the night. I feel so tired all the time!"

"We're all tired Anna; if you can't cope, then you're no good to us!"

Her harsh words made me want to cry, but before I could say anything, she continued, "I've been thinking. You'd be better off with someone else looking after Miro, while you work."

Of course I'd be better off. At home, in normal times my mother would have been my support.

"My sister in Walburgen," she said, "has had a baby recently. She could look after yours as well."

I did not understand.

"How would that work? That's quite some distance from our farm."

"It's quite simple. Miro would stay with her, and you could visit him on Sundays."

I thought at first I'd misheard her, but her expression was clear, persuasive as she added, "You'd be free, Anna. You'd get your sleep and your rest. You'd get on with all your jobs unhindered."

I looked down at Miro blissfully asleep in his basket. The only way anyone could force me to part with him, would be if they killed me first.

"I can't do that Sylvia. He'll stay with me and I'll look after him. I promise you I won't let you down again."

Her eyes narrowed and her smile became stiff.

"Suit yourself, Anna, I was just trying to help. This is no place for a nursery. If you can't do what you're here for, then we shall have to send you away." She went away leaving me with a heavy heart.

After this incident I would sit up automatically the very moment Maryla's tapping on the window reached my consciousness, even when my brain was still doped with unfinished sleep. I did my best to ensure that Sylvia would not find fault with my timing and thoroughness with which I milked the cows, prepared feeds for the pigs and chickens, and scraped their pens clean. Afternoons were easier, away from the smells of the farm, away from Sylvia's random checks, out in the open fields, where Maryla and I tied the cut corn into sheaves, while Miro slept in the shadow of poplars that marked the divide between the sweet corn and the rye crops.

Michal came every Saturday night. Waiting for him was torture, my imagination filled with every possible danger awaiting to ambush him on the way, then, the sight of him would melt me with happiness. Sunday lunchtime would trigger anxiety within me that grew as minutes ticked away. Five o'clock and he would have to leave us, and the cycle of waiting would begin again.

Frau Lientz made his train journeys possible for him with cuts of ham and bacon that she put aside each week to bribe the train driver with. I blessed her in my prayers every night. Her unselfish generosity was a mystery to me.

"She says I remind her of her son who died young," Michal explained. "I think she is a decent old soul underneath that bristly manner of hers."

From Michal's descriptions I imagined her as an ugly old dragon, nevertheless I felt eternally grateful to her for saving him from treks through the forest, where dangers multiplied as the war dragged on.

"Give her a hug from me and Miro," I said.

Michal made a face and wiped his mouth as if he had just kissed a frog. Then he was serious.

"I will, I promise. She'll like that. She's got no one else to hug her."

Every time Michal travelled on the train in the guise of the fire stoker, he brought a few things with him. Miro's wooden cot was finished now and slotted into the space between my bed and the wall.

Transporting the pushchair was a complicated matter. Frau Lientz had remembered suddenly one day, that there was an old pushchair abandoned in the attic. Michal brought it down. It was heavy, rusty metal, but the back rest was still workable and could be pushed back to form a cradle whenever needed. Michal rubbed down the rust with a metal scourer, oiled all the metal sections, then dismantled the pushchair so it could be transported in three parts; the chassis with wheels, the long handle bar, and the body itself. To transfer these parts unnoticed, Michal walked an extra mile for the next three Saturdays, to a stop outside Treibach, where the train driver would help him onto the locomotive. At the end of his journey, at our end, there would be a delegation waiting for him, to help him carry his load; Ludwik and Bruno, Maryla and I, with Miro in my arms.

The pushchair proved to be a godsend. Its easy manoeuvrability meant that I could take Miro everywhere with me, outdoors and indoors, and leave him to sleep in his self-contained capsule, raised above the dirty ground, with a muslin cover over the bonnet to protect him from the flies.

One rainy day at the end of August, when the harvest in the fields had been done, when the root vegetables had been dug out, cleaned and stored in the cellar, Maryla and I were helping Ludwik and Bruno to thresh the wheat. This was done inside one of the empty barns and the air was thick with dust and husks flying on the draught created especially by leaving doors open wide at both ends of the building.

I had left Miro just inside the open door where the air appeared less polluted. He was now six weeks old and the times of wakefulness between his feeds were becoming longer. He was a quiet, contented baby and usually his dummy would appease the first sign of any distress, but this particular day he was unsettled and cried a lot, and the only thing that calmed him down was when I picked him up and carried him resting against my chest. Each time he appeared to be asleep I would place him back in his pushchair, and each time he would wake up, whimper and wail. Now, as I helped Maryla to scoop the grain into sacks, Miro's cries echoed around the barn.

"Go to him," Maryla said. "Get him out of this place." Her hair, her shoulders, her clothes were covered in white dust. I stood up, torn between a strong instinct to nurse my child and the relentless pressure to work, exacted on me by my boss.

Bruno and Ludwik stopped too.

"Go on, Anna," Ludwik said, "no one's checking on us at the moment, and when they do, I'll tell them a thing or two."

Anxiety made me hesitate.

"What will you say?"

"Just leave it to me and go!"

It rained heavily when I pushed Miro across the muddy, slippery yard. The rocking of the pushchair stopped his cries. There was no one about and Dieter's truck was missing.

Inside my hut, I dried my hair with a towel and rubbed the wet crumbs of dust off my clothes before picking up Miro, to feed and to change him. Afterwards I rested him against my shoulder, and like a floppy rag doll, he slept, his little arms dangling by his sides.

Thoughts of the future, like black ravens circled inside my head. What would I do if he became ill? What would I do when he needed more of my time and attention, when he became aware of his surroundings and could not be left to sleep all day? I missed Michal, I missed my mother, I wished Dieter and Sylvia showed a little understanding and allowed me more time with my child. But Sylvia insisted all workers were treated the same. In fairness. I could not argue with that.

When I placed Miro back in his pushchair, to my great relief, he was truly settled this time. I pushed him outside. It had stopped raining but the air was dank and heavy with farm smells, through which, like an invisible ribbon, the aroma of cooking wove its way. This meant that Sylvia was back, and so was Dieter's truck, parked under the chestnut tree.

I hurried to the cowshed, where Maryla had already started milking at the far end. She came over to me and peered down at Miro.

"Bless him. He seems all right now."

I expressed my worries that had been festering in my mind all day.

"Anna, let's take each day as it comes. No one's noticed your absence this afternoon."

"There's nothing Ludwik could have said in my defence if I was discovered to be playing truant."

"You weren't playing truant, Anna. Ludwik had a well prepared speech. Can you imagine one of their own forced to cope with what you have to do?"

I was not convinced Ludwik's loyal intervention would have made any difference, but for now, for a short while, my problem was deferred.

Maryla and I finished all our jobs around the cows, the pigs and the chickens, and then we scrubbed and cleaned ourselves before the evening meal. Miro's pushchair followed our every move, with him asleep inside.

There was an extra person at the table that night, an elderly woman. Just like Sylvia, she wore a long dark dress, a white apron, and her grey hair had been plaited and pinned into a crown at the top of her head. Her hands were rough, thickened by hard work.

"This is my aunt Valeria," Sylvia introduced her. "You'll call her Frau Schneider."

We each in turn told her our name, with Anton, like an echo, repeating every word.

"My aunt will be staying with us for a while. There are never enough working hands on this farm." A meaningful look passed between Sylvia and Frau Schneider.

After supper, when all things had been cleared away, all surfaces wiped and polished, and only four of us, women, left behind, Sylvia said to me, "Don't go yet Anna, I've got something to tell you."

Maryla and I stopped by the door, my hands on the handle bar, ready to push Miro outside. She and Frau Schneider leaned over the pushchair, and Sylvia pulled back the muslin cover.

Frau Schneider's face creased in delight.

"He's beautiful," she said. She picked him up and cradled him in her arms. I was anxious that he should not wake and become grizzly again, but he hardly stirred. There was something maternal, comforting in the way she held him, something that made me warm up to her with trust.

"You don't have to drag Miro around the farm with you any longer," Sylvia said. "My auntie's here to stay, to help out with house. Miro can stay with her, indoors."

I looked at Maryla to check if she'd heard the same. Her eyes expressed wonder and delight.

"I...don't understand..." I stammered.

"I'll mind him while you work," Frau Schneider said looking down at Miro and rocking him gently. "My husband died last year, my three sons are in the army, and their wives have gone back to their own families. Here, at least, I can be of some use to Sylvia and Dieter."

"I don't know what to say…" I held back my excitement.

"There's nothing to say," Frau Schneider replied, placing Miro back in his pushchair. "Bring him here every morning, then just pop in to feed him during the day, and I'll do the rest."

I waited till we reached the chestnut tree before I spoke to Maryla.

"Well, what do you think of that? Wonders never cease!"

"I think your prayers have been answered," her eyes were round with disbelief.

"They sure have. I don't get it. Why is Sylvia being so good to me?"

"Search me!" Maryla gave an exaggerated shrug. "It doesn't matter, whatever it is. What really matters is that you'll be getting the support you need. At long last! I can't explain it, but I've got a good feeling about this Frau Schneider. I think she'll be good for Miro."

"So do I, Maryla!" I allowed my excitement to bubble. "I pray to God she does not disappoint us."

She did not. Within days she became to Miro like a loving grandmother. However, what we did not guess at the time, but what became inevitably apparent to us all, was that Frau Schneider had been brought over for Sylvia's sake alone. The truth answered and satisfied my initial questions, and knowing it did not diminish my gratitude for this positive turn in my life. I grew to like Frau Schneider. I trusted her, I knew – I was certain – she would not neglect Miro, even when Sylvia's child was born.

PART 4

APRIL-JUNE 1945

CHAPTER 27

It was the 17th of April, my twenty-second birthday. Miro was two years and nine months old, and I had been in slave labour for almost five years.

It was a sunny day, rather warm for spring. Sylvia and Dieter had gone to their weekly meeting with the authorities in Eberstein, and the rest of us were left to get on with our regular jobs around the farm. Ludwik and Bruno were in the forest with old Anton, cutting the trunks of the trees that had been felled last autumn, into smaller, manageable sections. Gerhart and Frieda were already in residence on the other side of the valley with the herd of oxen in their care. As soon as I finished cleaning out the cowshed, my next job was to help Maryla plant potatoes on the vegetable plot.

I kept an eye on Miro through the wide-open doorway and watched him playing under the chestnut tree, where he was building a tower on the bench, out of the wooden bricks that Michal had planed for him.

Frau Schneider had been like a grandmother to him when he was a baby, but now that little Suzi, Sylvia and Dieter's daughter was two, Frau Schneider often took their child away from the perils of the farm into her clean house in Walburgen.

Miro stayed with me. I could not bear to be parted from him. His first language was German, but he recognised some words of Polish when we talked among ourselves and I believed his mother tongue would come naturally as soon as our circumstances changed. He had Michal's brown, solemn eyes and my dark colouring and curly hair. I never tired of watching him, now chatting to himself as he stretched on tiptoes to reach the top of the growing tower.

I glanced up and through the bare branches of the chestnut tree I saw a figure in the distance, on the other side of the valley. Dieter and Sylvia warned us constantly to be wary of strangers. Stories were rife of partisans roaming the country, of revenge killings, of bodies stuffed under the bales of hay, stuffed under the floorboards of deserted buildings. This stranger's gait was steady, unhurried. He appeared laden with bags and a rucksack. If he were a peddler, he had no chance of any sales here, but he could simply be a town person desperate to trade his possessions for food. In the past two years the town people came in droves to the farm. Dieter and Sylvia's parlour resembled an old curiosity shop with its collection of furniture, the bulk increasing every week. Once, in a surprising moment of openness, when I helped her dust all her newly acquired possessions, Sylvia showed me a box of jewellery. The lid could hardly close on the heap of necklaces, bracelets, brooches and earrings, all made of precious metals and stones.

"Crazy, isn't it?" she had said, a pleased smile animating her large features. "What use are they to me on the farm? I'll sell them, of course, as soon as the war is over. Better the money in my pocket than a chain around my neck."

The stranger disappeared in the dip of the valley. Now was a good moment to remove Miro and myself from the yard, before his reappearance close to the farm. The main house was safely locked. He could wait under the chestnut tree.

I ran to Miro and swept him up in my arms saying persuasively, "Time to feed the chicks," but he wriggled and protested.

"*Nein! Nein*! No! Miro build house!"

I ran with him to the chicken pen, where the newly hatched chicks appeared to roll about like fluffy yellow balls, suddenly forming a one-directional mass, as they ran up to the mesh, sensing the promise of food.

I placed Miro down next to the bucket with seeds. His house-building was instantly forgotten. He dipped his hand into the chicken feed and threw fistfuls of it over the mesh. All the while I kept a watch on the part of the track were I was expecting the stranger to emerge from the valley.

"Now, let's go and help Auntie Maryla to plant potatoes," I suggested, before Miro's enthusiasm emptied the bucket of all the chicken feed. He did not need telling twice. He had accompanied Maryla on the vegetable plot many times and, infinitely mesmerised by the holes in the ground, the earthworms and the slugs, could be relied on to amuse himself.

He ran ahead of me. The potato plot was hidden from the lane by a line of outbuildings and some shrubs at the end. We found Maryla on her hands and knees, digging small holes, a foot apart in a neat row. Miro crouched down beside her and eagerly ran his fingers through the loose soil.

"There's a stranger coming up to the farm," I said.

Maryla sat back on her heels, stretching her stiff shoulders. She kissed Miro on the top of his head, gave him a trowel to dig holes, then followed me to the edge of the shed, that screened us from view. We looked out and waited.

The man's head emerged, round like a ball, underneath his down-pulled beret, then his shoulders, his rucksack, his arms, his bags. Stooping under the weight, he walked over to the bench under the chestnut tree and dropped all his baggage on the ground.

It was only when he straightened up and stretched out his arms, when he slipped off his beret and shook his hair loose, that recognition hit me like lightning.

"Michal!" Maryla and I shouted together. He waved both his arms and began to run in our direction. I picked up Miro, babbling like a child myself.

"It's Daddy, Miro! Daddy! Daddy's here!"

We met in the middle of the field, Miro in my arms wild with excitement, shouting, "*Papi! Papi!*" as we all hugged, all four of us, insane with joy, my brain bursting with questions.

"What's happening, Michal? How come you're here? In the middle of the day? No wonder I didn't recognise you! It never occurred to me that it could be you! With that beret of yours covering half your face!"

Michal got his breath back and laughed out loud.

"Girls! Girls! You'll never believe what news I've got for you!"

Bouncing Miro in his arms to squeals of delight, he began to walk back to the chestnut tree. Maryla and I ran along by his side.

"The war's finished!" I prompted him, not actually believing that myself.

"It's a matter of days," he almost sang, "but there's more! Treibach's been taken over by British troops. Spitz and Blitz are dead. So is Horst!"

Maryla and I stopped, stared at each other, then ran on after him.

"Say that again!" I called out.

"I'll tell you everything! There's so much to tell! Let's sit down first. I'm dying of thirst."

I fetched him a jar of water, then we huddled around him on the bench, while Miro sat on the ground amidst his wooden bricks.

"I can hardly believe it myself!" Michal's usually serious eyes were wide with excitement. "Two days ago Spitz and Blitz were found dead in their car. Under the railway bridge near our farm. It was Bazylka who discovered them. First thing in the morning when she took the milk to the crossroads. She raised the alarm and we all ran there to have a look."

"Poor Bazylka!" Maryla shuddered.

"It was a shock," Michal continued, "for all of us. We all wanted them dead, the bastards, but when we actually saw their bodies, riddled with bullets, their brains spattered all over the seats and windows, it was awful! I can't tell you how horrible it was. I felt sick. Max and Johann had to pull them out of the car onto the side of the lane, so that Holtzmann could move the car out of the way, so that he could drive into town and notify the police."

"Who shot them?" I asked, pushing away the shocking images that crammed my mind.

"The partisans, of course. There's not the slightest doubt about that. No one else has got the guns. A group of them was flushed out of the forest the day before and shot by the SS. This was revenge killing... And do you know what was even worse? Their bodies lay there most of the day, feeding flies and maggots. It was all very strange that no one rushed to come down and to take them away. No one came to interrogate us, no sniffer dogs, nothing! We didn't know it then, but they'd already got wind of the British troops coming and left Treibach in haste to save their own skins."

Maryla and I were quiet, shocked by Michal's news. My thoughts were like bees whizzing around in my head. Blitz and Spitz, the scourge of our lives, gone. Dead. Was this really the end? Would we be leaving soon? I dared not tempt fate with premature joy, but I could not help a surge of hope, thoughts of my mother, my sisters, my brothers. Vladek and little Jozef. Where were they now? Jozef, no longer a boy. I could not imagine him as a young man of nineteen.

Miro scrambled up to his feet and lifted his arms to show he wanted to be picked up. Michal lifted him onto his lap, gave him a cuddle, then unbuttoned his breast pocket and held it open.

"What can you find in there, Miro?"

With serious determination, Miro plunged his little fist inside the pocket and was puzzled by the object that he brought out in his hand. It was a sugar cube.

"Pop it in your mouth," Michal said.

Miro did, and his mouth began to dribble, and his eyes turned pink with pleasure.

"Frau Lientz," Michal explained. "Good Frau Lientz."

"And Horst? What happened to Horst?" Maryla asked.

Michal took a deep breath and resumed his account.

"Yesterday morning he did not turn up for work. The first time ever! It was weird not having him around, shouting and waving his whip. Franek and I got on with sowing the barley in the field nearest to the main road. At about ten we saw the first jeeps and lorries making their way towards the town. They were British. We were astonished.

Gobsmacked! We watched them and waved and suddenly, the reason for Horst's absence became all too clear to me. He had been warned. I looked at Franek. He must have thought the same. 'Horst!' he said. There was no time to waste. We had dreamed of this moment for years. We had stalked him many times!"

I grabbed Michal's arm, my heart pounding fast. "Michal, you didn't! Tell me you didn't kill him!"

There was fire in his eyes and passion in his response.

"We wanted to Anna. He was evil. Ever since Staszek's death. I couldn't count the times he'd whipped us and kicked us to the ground. He deserved what he got."

I held my breath. I hated Horst with all my might, but killing him… the very idea made me shudder.

"We ran to the town," Michal continued, letting Miro slide off his lap. "We ran along the path hidden by the rail track. The town was in chaos. There were people everywhere. Out in the streets to watch the British arrive. There was not one German uniform in sight. No one took any notice of us. We pushed our way through the crowds till we got to Horst's street. We saw a group of people huddling round his doorway, bending over the doorstep. We came close to see what was happening. We were too late. Someone had been there first. Horst was lying sprawled across the doorstep, his arms flung out, his face smashed beyond recognition."

I glanced at Maryla. A large tear formed in the corner of her eye, trembled and slid down her cheek leaving a wet trail. She brushed it away.

"Even if he rots in hell, it won't bring Staszek back," she said.

"I don't suppose you have any idea who did it?" I asked.

Michal shrugged.

"It could have been anyone. He'd upset so many people. Not just on our farm. We did not hang around, Franek and I. The last thing we needed was to be seen near Horst's house. We returned to the farm and I went straight up to Holtzmann. I told him I was leaving. I told him it was time I was with my family."

"And he let you go? Just like that?"

"No. Not just like that. He begged me to stay. Can you imagine it, Anna? Holtzmann begged ME! So I stayed till the end of the day, packed my bags this morning and came on the train."

Disbelief and more disbelief! I was dizzy trying to absorb so much news, so much change in such a short time. I stood up and looked around our farm.

"So what's going to happen now? Are we leaving, or what?"

My words were drowned in a sound that grew by the second, filling the air, the whole countryside around us, making me feel as if every cell in my body was vibrating.

"Quick! Take cover!" Michal shouted, running with Miro in his arms to the nearest shed. Maryla and I ran close behind him, banging the door shut once inside.

"God, not another air-raid! Not now!" Michal's words could hardly be distinguished in the overpowering din. Miro hid his face against Michal's chest and pressed his hands over his ears. The walls of the shed began to shake. We waited. Nothing happened for a long while. Michal gave me Miro to hold, then he pushed back the door a fraction and looked out.

"It's the British planes!" he shouted. "They're not going to bomb their own troops!"

He flung the door open and ran out. The sky was filled with hundreds of bombers. All British. Flying north. There was something awe-inspiring about the sight, yet at the same time overpoweringly exhilarating. Maryla jumped up and down waving her rag. Miro watched her, his fear turning to fascination, to uncontrolled laughter. We laughed with him and waved till the last line of planes disappeared behind the distant mountains.

Ludwik and Bruno came running down the path from the forest leaping up and punching the air.

"Is it Berlin next?" Ludwik shouted. We had all heard by now that Dresden and Cologne were in ruins.

The boys greeted Michal with bear hugs and for their benefit he recounted his news again, with hundreds of questions thrown at him. Ludwik and Bruno were as stunned as we had been.

"So, what happens now? When do we leave?" Ludwik was pacing up and down, rubbing his hands with impatience.

Michal shrugged,

"I suppose the British will decide. We've got no money, anyway, for the train tickets home. I wonder what Dieter and Sylvia will say. Where are they?" he looked around.

"In town," Bruno said. "The regular weekly meeting with the Gestapo."

"Not any more," Michal shook his head, "they'll get such a shock!"

"Even more of a shock," Bruno added, "when I do what you did, Michal. I'll ask Dieter to let me go. Back to Steinfeld's farm. To Dorota."

A smile appeared on Michal's lips. Secretive, yet bursting-to-tell-all smile.

"Go on, Michal, tell us," I coaxed him, "I know you're dying to say something."

Everyone looked at him expectantly. There was excitement lighting up his eyes.

"You'll never guess!" he teased.

"No, we won't, so you'd better tell us. Quick!" I said.

"Very well then," that smile again, "Franek and Lilli have been seeing each other for over a year!"

We were, again, silenced by surprise, then Bruno exclaimed, "I'll be blowed! All the time I've been visiting Dorota, there's never been even the slightest whisper! How did they manage to keep it to themselves?"

"It's not something they could trumpet around," Michal said, "Franek had sworn me to secrecy."

"But when did that happen?" I asked. "When did they have the chance to meet?"

"When Franek was on loan at Steinfeld's farm. Two days a week."

"And you never told me!" I reproached him.

He placed his arm around my shoulders and gathered me to him, his voice appeasing. "Anna, it was to protect them. To protect you, me, each one of us. Who could forget what happened last time?"

"That girl sure knows how to complicate her life," Maryla sighed. "What's going to happen to her now?"

Ludwik gave her an affectionate peck on the cheek. They had been a couple officially for a year now, sharing my hut with me, living together in the tiny room next to mine.

"I don't think you need worry much longer," he said. "It's a matter of just a short time before the war is officially over. They won't have to hide. They won't have to be afraid any more. Franek can take her with him to Poland."

Poland. The name of my country caused another surge of feelings, an explosion of memories. My thoughts ran ahead of me to all the familiar things: to the low, squatting houses in our village, to the long line of poplars along the road, to the undulating fields beyond, the lake and the nightly frogs' chorus. I felt Miro's arms around my legs. I picked him up and gave him the reassuring hug that he had come for and I imagined my mother's happy face at the sight of her grandchild.

Dieter's truck made its presence known; first, with its faulty silencer down in the valley, then with its bumpy appearance as it came into view and halted with a shudder in the yard. No one moved, no one rushed to our allotted jobs. There was an invisible yet tangible change that we all felt.

261

Sylvia and Dieter approached us with slow, heavy steps, facing us, yet not looking at us directly. Dieter's limp appeared more pronounced than usual.

"You know, don't you? You've heard," he said, stepping in front of us. His face was drawn, weary. Sylvia fixed her gaze on the ground. "There's been no meeting with our authorities. The British are in town. The Schloss is now their headquarters. There have been arrests," he cleared his throat, "I've been ordered to carry on as before, until further notice. I can't do that on my own."

It was a strange moment. No one appeared to know what to say. Except Bruno. He stepped forward.

"Dieter, please let me go. Back to my girl. To Steinfeld's farm. You've got Michal in my place."

Sylvia moved quietly and walked away towards the house. Dieter rubbed the crease between his eyebrows.

"I cannot detain you, Bruno," he said, "I cannot detain any of you. But don't all rush off just yet. For your own sakes. There'll be havoc and danger everywhere. Wait, at least till it all dies down. And you, Bruno, take the train. Don't take chances through the forest."

There was something wistful in the manner in which Dieter limped towards the kitchen, his head bowed, his shoulders hunched.

"I'll be off, folks," Bruno said without hesitation. "It won't take me a minute to pack."

We stood together and waved him off, his rucksack flung over his shoulder, as he walked down the lane to the rail track in the valley. Then we returned to our jobs. Dieter had no longer any power over us, but the animals did not know that.

Late afternoon that day, there was an inspection of the farm by the British patrol. There were four of them. The driver stayed in the jeep, while the officer in charge, flanked by his aides, commanded Dieter to show him around all the buildings on the farm.

We were summoned to assemble in the yard. I stood close to Michal, close to Miro in his arms, a shiver of anxiety running down my spine as I watched the armed soldiers walk back to us.

"Are these all your workers?" the officer in charge asked Dieter in German. He was tall, slim, good-looking, with thick wavy hair tucked underneath his cap. His teeth flashed white as he spoke.

"*Jawohl Herr*," Dieter replied, "these are my Polish workers, my wife Sylvia and my relative, Anton. There's also a couple, Gerhart and Frieda. They're on the other side of the valley minding the oxen."

The officer nodded.

"Have you been providing food for the army?"

"Yes. Daily provisions of milk and weekly provisions of all other products."

The officer nodded again.

"I'm afraid our demands will be the same. You'll be paid, of course," he paused. "Any trouble with the partisans?"

Dieter gave a heavy sigh.

"They come for the food. We daren't refuse. They take what they need."

The officer surveyed us with a steady gaze.

"You'll be patrolled and checked daily to ensure order. There will be changes soon, but I urge you to carry on as before until further notice. Does anyone wish to say anything? Ask anything? Lodge a complaint?"

Dieter's expression turned dark. Sylvia stared at the ground. Ludwik spoke out.

"Dieter and Sylvia have been good to us. They are as much victims of this war as we are."

The officer nodded, his eyes thoughtful.

"Have any of you been subjected to deliberate maltreatment?"

We talked all at once, then allowed Ludwik to be our spokesman. Calmly, clearly, he recited the litany of our grievances; Spitz' and Blitz' brutality, the attack with stones from the Hitler Junge, the killing of Stefan, Horst's inhuman treatment of Staszek, Michal's beating in Eberstein by the SS. All three officers listened with serious concentration.

"Here in Eberstein?" the leader asked Michal. Miro hid his face against Michal's chest.

"That's right, Sir."

"Would you be able to identify them?"

Michal replied with a wan smile.

"I couldn't forget them, if I tried. They reduced my face to pulp."

"Come to the police station at ten tomorrow," the officer spoke with a hint of order. "We're inundated with complaints and allegations. We need witnesses if justice is to be done."

I was gripped with fear.

"Michal," I whispered in Polish, "I don't want you to go. I don't trust anyone. I don't want us to be separated again!"

"What's that you're saying?" the officer demanded. I thought I detected an edge to his tone.

"Sir," I clung to Michal's arm, "please don't take him away! We've been forced to live apart for four years. I don't want to lose him again!"

He surveyed us both, unhurriedly, his gaze stopping on Miro for a moment, then his expression softened, as if from a smile within.

"There's no danger of that," he said. "No. This will only take a few minutes. You can come too if you wish."

My fears could not be quashed in an instant, but his calm, polite manner encouraged me to believe that he meant what he said.

It had been a strange day, my twenty-second birthday.

"I've not forgotten it," Michal said, releasing me from his embrace.

We were sitting on the edge of the bed, with Miro asleep in his cot beside us, with dusk falling outside, casting our room in semi-darkness.

"I'd forgive you if you had, honestly," I replied, "so much has happened today."

But he picked up one of his bags, rested it on his lap, rummaged through its contents and brought out a matchbox.

"Open it," he said, his eyes shining in the wan light.

Inside, wrapped up in scrunched paper, was a silver ring. He took it out and slid it on the fourth finger of my right hand. It was thrilling, but I allowed myself a tiny quip.

"Frau Lientz again?"

"Not the way you think," Michal said, and I heard pride in his voice. "I paid for this ring with my earned money."

"How much?"

"Anna, how can you even ask! She was going to give it to me for a day's work, but I said no, I insisted on paying for it."

I hugged him with all my might.

"What other wonders have you got hidden in your rucksack?" I asked, running my hand over the worn canvas. There was a hard object, like a piece of wood, hidden underneath. "Have you been carving more stuff? Let's have a look!"

Michal's hand came down on top of mine and held it still.

"Better for you not to see it."

There was something in his tone that made the hairs on the back of my neck stand on end.

"Michal, come on," I whispered, "no secrets between us, all right?"

"It's for your own safety," he whispered back.

Dusk blurred his expression, but I stared hard into his shadowed eyes. I pushed his hand out of the way and slipped my hand inside the bag. My exploring fingers curled themselves around the barrel of a handgun. I brought it out.

"Michal, what's this? Where did you get it from?" My mouth was suddenly dry as Horst's smashed face flashed through my mind. "Did you and Franek...?"

"No, we didn't, Anna," he protested vehemently and then pressing his finger to my lips, he took the pistol from my hand and pushed it deep inside his rucksack.

I wanted to believe him. I could not bear it otherwise. He embraced me, holding me close to him.

"I found the gun in the forest. It's not even loaded. I thought I'd keep it, as a deterrent. That's all there's to it. Now, have I convinced you?"

I felt light-headed with relief.

"Michal... I'm so glad, so glad you're not like them..."

"That's only by pure chance."

Why did he have to say that!

"Please! Don't torment me!"

He pulled me and we flopped on the bed together, our arms entwined.

"Don't worry about it, Anna." His lips were touching my cheek. "I've not got him on my conscience, but the poor sod who has should be hailed as a hero!"

The next morning we cycled to Eberstein on a tandem, one of Dieter's newest acquisitions traded for food. We left Miro with Maryla digging holes around her where she was planting potatoes.

The little town of Eberstein looked different now, bright and uplifted in colourful pastels, no longer dragged down by the red and black of the Nazi banners. The streets were teeming with sand-green uniforms and flower-printed dresses, the air filled with the sounds of people going about their normal business. Even the police building looked brighter in the sun, but I could not erase the memory of that other night, still so vivid after all the time, when I had cycled with old Kestner to visit Michal in prison.

"I've got butterflies," I said to him, as we got off the tandem and he secured it to the hook in the wall.

"We're together, Anna. Don't be afraid," he said, taking my hand and leading me inside.

Everything was the same, as I had remembered it: the dark panelled interior, the reception desk, built up to the ceiling with a thick glass partition, separating the officials from us. Only they, too, were different now: four young men, in pale green uniforms, absorbed in paperwork, in absolute calm.

Michal explained in German to one of the young men the purpose of our visit. He nodded and in broken German told us to wait. Michal smiled to me reassuringly and squeezed my hand. I wanted it all to be over, to get out of this building, away from the haunting memories.

From the door, which I remembered to lead down the corridor to the cells, an armed soldier came out and walked over to us. He spoke in good German.

"I want you to look carefully at the prisoners in each cell. There have been allegations about a particular group in the SS. The more witnesses we have, the stronger the case for prosecution."

He led and we followed. The same long and drab corridor, the row of portholes, windows into the cells. My feet and my hands felt very cold. There was a cramp in my stomach. The place seemed claustrophobic, lacking fresh air.

"Are you all right with this?" I asked Michal. His features were tense.

"It's got to be done. Not just for myself," he replied.

He stopped at every porthole, giving the occupants of each cell a long, considered look. At the seventh window, he turned to the guard.

"That's one of them. The one on the right."

I forced myself to look inside. The cell was similar to that of Michal's, with just a wooden bench at the far end and a bucket in the corner. The two men sitting there were pointedly deep in conversation. Pointedly avoiding glancing our way. The one identified by Michal looked so ordinary. There was nothing about him to mark him out as a torturer, a killer. But for people like Michal, he would have escaped unpunished.

Michal found and pointed out his other two tormentors, and then we were back in the reception area, glad to get away from a place saturated with evil.

"What will happen now?" Michal asked our escort.

"They'll be put on trial, and sentenced, but these things take time. You'll be gone by then. That's why we need your written and signed statement. Do you agree to that?"

He led us away to a little side room, with just a desk, a typewriter and a few chairs.

"Someone will see you in a moment or two." He left us on our own.

We sat, huddled together, Michal very quiet for a long time. His anger startled me when he spoke. "I'm glad, I'm really glad that they've caught the bastards. They deserve to hang. But no punishment, however just, will bring back the dead."

CHAPTER 28

Dieter did two strange things. The first one on the evening of the day when the first British patrol visited our farm. He got up from the supper table, before the end of the meal, and while we were still eating, he went round the house and removed from the walls and doors all Nazi mementoes; photographs of Hitler, miniature banners, swastikas, slogan posters and finally, the wooden bust of Hitler. He dropped the heavy object into the sack and we heard it hit the floor and crush the glass and the frames inside. We watched him in silence. He took the sack outside, returned after a couple of minutes, sat down and continued to eat.

In the days that followed, he listened daily to the radio in his parlour, the parlour crammed with furniture and still the forbidden territory to us workers. He kept us informed of the progress of the allies and of the retreat of the Wehrmacht, but his reports were short, evasive, even when the boys bombarded him with questions. Nevertheless, even when details remained blurred, a general picture was emerging, a picture sharp with certainty that big changes were about to occur.

On the 1st of May, after we had finished our evening meal, he asked us to remain at the table. I entertained Miro, on Michal's lap, as quietly as it was possible, with miniature chunks of wood, that Michal had shaped to resemble cars and trucks. Dieter appeared to have difficulty voicing his thoughts. He coughed, cleared his throat, opened his lips, pressed them together, thought for a while. Then he spoke.

"The war's coming to an end. Any day now this is going to be made official. Berlin's taken over by the Russians. And Hitler's dead."

This was the news we had been waiting for, desired, prayed for every day. Now that it had become real, it was hard to believe.

"How did they execute him?" Ludwik asked.

"He killed himself. In his bunker. Last night. And all the others who were with him."

We needed a moment's silence to absorb this information. Sylvia began to shift, but Dieter stopped her.

"One more thing. You'll be wanting to pack your things and leave. Don't be in a hurry. There's destruction everywhere. Roads, rail tracks, bridges…demolished. Believe me, you're better off stuck here with us for a while longer, than at the end of a rail track that plunges into a river." He was desperate for us to stay.

"We're not going anywhere yet," Michal assured him, "in any event, the British are in charge. No doubt, they'll be telling us what to do next."

We all stood up to go, but he stopped us again.

"There's one more thing I want you all to do with me. Sylvia and Anton, you come too."

And this was the second strange thing he did.

He led us outside, across the yard, past the chestnut tree, along the wall of the outbuildings to a plot of land, well removed from the rest of the farm. A stack of dry wood had already been prepared there in readiness for a fire. He put a burning match to it and the wood began to rasp amidst the bright leaping flames. Miro watched with rapt fascination, his arm around Michal's neck. Our faces reflected the red, the orange, the gold of the glow as we stood around the fire in a circle.

Then from behind a clump of grass, Dieter dragged out a sack, the one filled with the Nazi ornaments that he had taken off the walls a few days earlier. One by one he threw them into the fire, creating a ribbon of bright sparks snaking upwards into the air. Hitler's wooden bust came out last. Dieter dropped it right into the white-hot centre. It lay there for a brief moment, a black, heavy lump, before being engulfed in flames.

None of us clapped, none of us jumped for joy. Only Dieter shouted out, "May he burn in hell! Where he belongs! For ever!"

The much-awaited directive from the British did not come the next day, or the next, so we continued with all our routine chores as before.

Miro's piercing scream was like a pain shooting through me. I threw down the rake and ran out of the cowshed. Anton was standing with Blackie, the work horse, holding him still by the reins, in the middle of the yard, looking down at Miro, shock contorting his face. Miro was down on the ground, his head covered in blood.

"God, oh God, please help me!" I cried, running up to my child. I picked him up. Amidst the bloody mess a deep cut was visible at the side of his head.

"It was Blackie! Blackie did it!" Anton's cry was turning into a wail.

I did not wait for explanations. I pulled out a rag from my pocket and sitting Miro down on the ground, I wound it around his head. I picked him up and ran down the lane towards the main road to Eberstein. My only thought was to get him to the surgery as fast as possible. There was no time to call anyone. The boys were in the forest, and Maryla some distance away on the vegetable plot.

I became hot, sticky, rapidly running out of breath. Sheer desperation drove me on. It was like reaching an oasis, when my feet hit the tarmac of the main road. I heard a car behind me and instinctively flagged it down. An army jeep overtook me and stopped, half on the verge.

There were four British soldiers in it. One, in the back, jumped down and held the door open for me.

"I need a doctor!" I shouted in German, coming level with him, "*Danke! Danke!*" I climbed onto the back seat, followed by him, and we were off. I was weak with relief, my legs shaking, my tongue scratching dry. Miro, silenced by shock, clung to me like a limpet. The young soldier talked to me, but I did not understand a word. He patted Miro's hand, showing his white smile beneath the trimmed moustache.

We were there within five minutes.

"*Halt, bitte,*" I requested, and the driver stopped the jeep at the green square surrounded by pastel-coloured houses.

"*Danke! Danke! Danke!*" I kept saying, even as I jumped down, and with Miro in my arms I ran to one of the side streets. I had been here once before, when Miro's fever would not relent and had made me sick with worry.

Just like the dentist's surgery, the doctor's surgery was on the ground floor of a large family house. The front door was open. I ran inside, straight to the reception desk, praying we would not have to wait long.

The waiting room was full of people. I felt sweat seeping into my clothes.

"An accident!" I almost cried at the receptionist, my voice begging, desperate.

To my astonishment, she stood up and ushered me down a corridor. There were two chairs outside a door.

"Please wait here," she said, "Herr Doktor will see you next." I was ready to kiss her hands, her feet.

When the door opened and an old woman came out, I saw Doktor Brunnen in his swivel chair at his desk. He beckoned to me to come in. He was a bald man, with a shiny face and half-moon glasses half way down his nose.

"I've got nothing to give you. It all happened so fast!" I blurted out.

He indicated for me to sit down, his eyes fixed on Miro.

"How long have you been in this country?" he asked.

I did not have to think.

"Five years. Why?"

He looked at me, a wry smile softening his features.

"Then I think you've already paid enough."

He began to undo the rag, wound around Miro's head, while I explained what had happened.

He examined the wound, which was already congealing.

"He's lucky, the poor little mite. It's a miracle he's got away with just a scratch. One stitch will do the trick."

I cringed at the thought of it, but he wasted no time. He washed his hands before getting out two sealed brown paper bags out of a drawer. One contained suture, and the other a needle.

"Hold him tight," he said, giving Miro a sugar cube. Solemnly Miro pushed it in his mouth and watched with innocent, unknowing eyes, the doctor's hands descend upon his brow. He cried out when the needle pierced his skin, and I stopped myself from crying out with him, feeling like a traitor to my own child, but Doktor Brunnen was indeed deft and fast. He stuck a plaster over the stitched cut.

"There, it's done. Come back in a week."

I could not thank him enough. I never saw him again.

I walked along the main road from Eberstein to our farm, with Miro asleep in my arms, warm, precious, and blamed myself for this accident. If only I had listened to Frau Schneider and allowed him to be taken with little Suzi to her nice clean house, away from all the dangers, from the dirt of the farm, this would not have happened. The remorse at the thought of Miro's pain brought tears to my eyes. His pain was my pain, yet I knew, even now, that no hardship could have forced me to be parted from him.

Maryla and Anton came down to the bridge to meet me.

"I didn't do it. I didn't do it!" Anton kept reassuring me. "It was Blackie. Miro ran in front of Blackie." His face was puckered like a child's, as if he were about to cry.

"I know, Anton. Look, Miro's all right. Everything going to be fine."

Gently I disengaged Miro from my shoulder and held him out like a sleeping baby.

"See for yourself, Anton. Just a little plaster. It was an accident. Stop worrying."

Anton bent over Miro and kissed him on the cheek.

"I'll go tell Blackie it wasn't his fault. Just an accident."

We followed him up the lane, his head bobbing in his quirky gait.

"You look worn out," Maryla said. "Let me take Miro, and you go and sort yourself out. I'll watch him like a hawk. He'll come to no harm, I promise."

I longed to plunge myself into cold water and come out cleansed and refreshed. And it was strange to think that I had the freedom to do these basic normal things, whenever necessary, without the fear of being punished for wasting working time.

It was the next day, in the afternoon, as I was alone in the kitchen, washing down and polishing all the surfaces, that I had a visitor. It was a cloudy day with a fresh wind blowing, so we had opened all the windows and doors to give the house a good airing. He stood on the doorstep and knocked even though the door was wide open. I looked up from the floor where I was on my hands and knees, scrubbing the flagstones, and recognised the soldier who had been so attentive to Miro in the jeep the previous day. He took me by surprise, for I had not heard any car sounds to warn me of his presence. He greeted me with his white smile.

"*Gutten Tag,*" I said, rising from the floor and wiping my hands down my skirt. "I'll take you to my boss, Frau Kestner, come!" I beckoned to him. "She's in the dairy."

We walked side by side, and though I could not understand what he was saying, it felt good to be escorted by a tall, good-looking man, with a gun slung over his shoulder for my protection.

"*Ihr Son, alles gutt?*" He made an effort to speak in German.

"*Ja, danke. Danke shone!*" I replied gratefully. "He's perfectly all right. Amazing recovery. Helping his father in the woods today."

Sylvia was busy patting bricks of butter into shape on the big marble slab. She gave him a look as if he were a nuisance. He spoke in English, and only from his gestures and the few words that sounded similar in German, we guessed he wanted to check out the farm for partisans. They had nothing to fear from the British, but severed groups, with their own newly-formed agendas, still hid in the forests and around farms.

"Go with him, Anna, and show him what he wants to see. We've got nothing to hide." Sylvia was impatient to get rid of him.

He took his time, and patiently I shadowed him. He looked inside every shed, stable and outbuilding; he looked behind bales, behind farm machinery; he lifted floorboards that were loose; he climbed up to the lofts. He left the living quarters till last. Having checked all the rooms in the main farmhouse, he came outside with me and pointed at my hut.

"Only I live there, with my husband and child. Our friends live in the other half," I tried to explain, making suitable movements with my hands.

He read my lips but his expression remained blank. He started going up the stepping stones. I followed. He pushed the door open and went inside. I stood on the doorstep, waiting. He would discover soon enough that our bare rooms were hardly a hiding place for anyone.

I watched him standing by the window in my room, his profile handsome, clear-cut, as he concentrated on something or someone he had spotted outside.

"Come," he beckoned, and I responded, not thinking.

The moment I stood next to him, he put his arm around my shoulder and turned me, so I was hemmed in between the bed, the cot, and the wall on three sides, with himself cutting off my escape to the door.

"What are you doing!" I cried, my arms shooting out to push him away. His strong embrace was like a clamp.

"Shshsh…" He held me still. "*Warten!* Wait!" Increasing his pressure with one arm, he loosened the other and threw his cap and his gun on the bed. Then from the inside of his jacket he brought out a bar of chocolate. He threw that on the bed. Next came out a packet of cigarettes. Then stockings, transparent; I had not seen such before, like two strips of ribbon cut from a silk veil.

"*Sich lieben, ja?*" he said in German. "Let's make love, yes?" His eyes, demanding, impatient, looked straight into mine.

"No! No! No!" I began to struggle. His smile, so attractive moments before, turned into a leer, his perfect white teeth became the fangs of a predator. "Let me go! Please! Let me go!"

He laughed softly and placed his open mouth on mine. I began to gag. Then pure instinct of self-preservation took over. I bit him hard on the lip, as I brought up my knee against his groin. He let out a yell, let go of me, doubled up and fell sideways on the bed. I fled and ran out of the hut, past the house, past the chestnut tree, along the line of outbuildings, past the pigs and the chicken pens, through the orchard to the other side, where Maryla was digging and planting vegetable seeds.

"Maryla, quick! We've got to hide!" I ran up to her shouting. I grabbed the spade from her, threw it to the ground and pulled her with me into the ditch that ran the length of the field. Lucky for us it was dry.

"Right down!" I cried, pressing flat her back as we crouched. My heart was like a pounding hammer, my legs like rubber sticks.

"What's going on?" she whispered, her eyes round with alarm.

"It's the soldier. He's armed!" I peeped between the blades of grass.

"What soldier?"

"Shshsh… I'll tell you in a minute."

We were as quiet as the earth around us. And soon I saw what I had been waiting for. He appeared in our field of vision, passing under the chestnut tree, tall, erect, with the rifle slung over his shoulder. To my relief he marched straight on down the lane, without a glance sideways.

"But he's British!" Maryla exclaimed, raising her head.

"Wait!" I pulled her down and made her stay still until he disappeared from view.

"So, what was all that about?" she asked, sitting up.

I sat up beside her on the edge of the ditch. What I was about to tell her was so shameful, I wondered whether some things were best left unsaid, but my whole being yearned to throw off my burden, to cast it away like a poisonous thorn.

So I told her.

"But please, Maryla," I begged, "not a word to anyone. Not even to Ludwik. Or Michal."

"But why?" She was puzzled. "You've been wronged, Anna. You must report it."

I could not bear the thought of all the fuss.

"Can you imagine?" I said, "all the interrogations, suspicions, his word against mine? We've all been through enough already." I did not tell her about the handgun at the bottom of Michal's rucksack. Though he had assured me it was not loaded. "Please Maryla, let it be just our own secret, all right? No harm done. It's a good lesson for us. Don't trust anyone!"

She sighed.

"All right. Don't worry. I won't say a thing." She paused. "Will there ever be an end to it all? Will we be ever allowed to go home?"

After the evening meal, when Michal and I returned to our hut to put Miro to bed, it was a shock to find the soldier's gifts still on the bed.

"Hey, what's this?" Michal asked, picking them up one by one and examining them as if they were new inventions; a bar of chocolate in a silver wrapper, a packet of cigarettes with a smiling sailor on the box, and silk-like stockings as thin as gossamer.

I held Miro close. He stretched out his little hands demanding, "Show Miro! Show Miro!"

"It must have been the soldier," I said. "You know, the one who came today and spent ages inspecting the farm."

Michal scratched his head, smiling at the cigarettes.

"Why would he do that?"

I could honestly say I did not know. I was just as puzzled as Michal. The soldier must have been livid with me when he left.

I sat down on the bed and began to undress Miro. Michal sat down beside me. He scratched his head again.

"We are so used to distrusting everyone, we even question kindness." I did not say anything and Michal carried on, "I've had the odd cigarette here and there, but not a whole packet since we left Poland. We shall enjoy this, Ludwik and me."

He broke the chocolate into five equal parts and giving Miro and me a chunk each, he went outside to Maryla and Ludwik.

Miro's eyes went dreamy as the chocolate melted in his mouth. I sucked on mine slowly, saving the final traces on my tongue for as long as possible, and held Miro close, imagining how our normal life would be, perhaps soon, when we returned home.

I wiped Miro's face, hands and feet with a wet cloth, then he settled in my lap for the nightly ritual of a story before bedtime. Ludwik had made him a book out of scraps of paper, with drawings of farm animals and their young ones. He had included dogs and cats, which Miro had never seen in reality, as they were too costly to keep in these difficult times. Cats had been considered at one point to kill rats on the farm, but Sylvia had been adamant, that rat-eating, semi-feral cats should not be anywhere near two small children. Dieter used rat poison instead.

Miro turned slowly the pages of Ludwik's worn scrap-book and commented on each of the animals, tracing their outlines with his finger. The last page depicted Muszka, Grandma's cat at home. He never tired of listening to Muszka's adventures, knew them by heart and pounced on any changes in my recitations, like an over keen examiner.

I tucked him in his cot with his little Ba-ba, a soft toy I had made out of the sheep's wool, with buttons for eyes and black thread for nose and mouth. Then I rolled up the stockings into a tight ball and hid them at the bottom of my bag, before going outside to join Michal, Ludwik and Maryla.

It became routine for Dieter to give us an account of the latest news after the evening meal. On the 8th of May, the atmosphere hanging over our table was heavy with silence. Dieter looked pre-occupied, his jaws tense, even as he ate; Sylvia, usually eager to impart gossip from town, chewed slowly, her mind elsewhere; only Anton enjoyed his meal with his usual, slurpy relish.

At our end we kept up the pretence of normality making small talk, glad of Miro's distracting exclamations as he manoeuvred his little wooden bricks around his bowl, while I spoon-fed him. Just as we were about to get up and start clearing the table, Dieter raised his hand.

"It's official," he said. "The war is over. It was announced this afternoon. In London, by Churchill. You are free to go." His smile was thin, his dark eyes untouched by it.

None of us moved. It was a moment for celebration, for jumping and dancing with joy. We exchanged uncertain smiles with our boss and his wife. They got up and went into the parlour, closing the door behind them. Anton began to extract himself from the narrow space between the bench and the table in his jaunty manner. Crumbs of food were stuck to his chin and his chest.

"Wash that off at the tap, Anton," I reminded him.

The four of us stayed behind and cleared things away, washed up, dried, cleaned and polished, as always.

Later when we gathered under the chestnut tree, it felt like any other evening.

"It'll be hard for them," Ludwik said, running his fingers through his tangled curls. "It's the wrong time of the year. With the whole summer ahead of them, and the harvest."

"Ludwik…" Maryla's tone was reproachful, "don't feel too sorry for them. We've done our bit. I want to go home. They'll find other workers. There'll be men coming back from the war. They've got their Hitler Yunge. Let them discover the joys of slaving away for a few pfennig."

I moved up close to Michal and placed my arm around his waist.

"I shall believe it when I see it," I said.

We watched Miro playing on the dusty ground with chunky wood off-cuts, pebbles and sticks.

"All I want is to be able to make a proper home for him," Michal said.

The next day, 9th of May, was a perfect May day, with a clear blue sky, strong sunlight and deep shadows. The chestnut tree was like a giant pink umbrella covered in fluffy blossom. I remember clearly, where everyone was, when the army lorry arrived at our farm at ten o'clock. Its noisy engine sent out a signal long before it appeared. We abandoned our work and came into the yard. Dieter and Anton stood by the stable door, Sylvia on the kitchen doorstep, Ludwik and Michal came out of the machinery shed, holding their rags and oiling cans, and Maryla and I with Miro between us, stood at the cowshed, watching.

Two armed soldiers jumped down from the high cab, the driver remained behind the wheel. They crossed the yard and walked up to Sylvia.

"Who's in charge of this place?" one of them asked in German.

"My husband and I," she replied, stepping down and indicating Dieter, who by now was approaching from the stables with Anton close on his heels.

The soldiers waited till Dieter joined them.

"We've got orders to collect your Polish workers," one of them said.

Dieter shaded his eyes, rising his hand slowly as if to delay the inevitable.

"I was expecting this," he said, "but not quite so soon. So, when will you be taking them?"

"In half an hour. No longer," the soldier tapped his watch. "That's all the time we've been given. We've got others to collect. Three other farms."

This was astonishing.

"Did you hear that?" Maryla whispered.

Dieter pressed his hand to his forehead.

"But that's impossible!" he cried. "Give me a day or two! Where will I get workers? How will I run this farm?" His desperation had an angry edge.

The soldier listened, his cool unruffled.

"I've got my orders," he said. "These are not my decisions. Tell your workers to pack. We'll wait half an hour."

Dieter turned round and waved his arms about. Like a drowning man.

"Come here, everyone!"

We assembled, fast and nervous. Dieter's face was grim, his voice rasping.

"In case you've not heard clearly, the soldiers have orders to collect you from this farm. Half an hour is all you've got to pack and get ready. A fine farewell party this is!" He turned to Anton, "Go and fetch Gerhart and Frieda. The oxen can stay unattended for one day."

Anton, eager to please, rushed off in his hastened, quirky gait, even before Dieter finished talking. Dieter put his arm on Sylvia's shoulder. "Let's go," he said, "I don't want to watch this!" They went back into the kitchen and shut the door.

"Right," the soldier said to us, "half an hour, on the dot."

We dispersed and ran to put away our things, Maryla and I our rakes, and the boys their oil and rags. I picked up Miro and ran to the tap where I scrubbed him and myself clean.

There was so little time. In the hut I sat Miro on the bed and told him strictly to sit still. I threw off my dirty blouse and skirt and got out my grey dress with the white collar. Michal came in and changed his shirt. The rest was simple. Our belongings had been kept permanently in our three bags. I picked up Miro and my canvas bag and Michal picked up the rest. The cot and the pushchair, now folded under the bed, had to be left behind.

We came down to the lorry, followed by Ludwik and Maryla. The metal steps were down, the soldiers were having a smoke.

"Are you taking us home?" Michal asked.

The one who spoke German shook his head.

"Our orders are to take you to Sankt Veit. After that someone else will take over."

Just then the kitchen door opened and Sylvia ran out. She carried two brown paper bags.

"Provisions for you!" she shouted. She came up to the lorry. "You may be glad of some food later. Dieter won't come out. He's too upset." She hugged each one of us in turn, fast and nervously, pressed Miro to her chest, kissed him on the head, and as we began to climb the metal steps, she turned and walked away without a backward glance.

There were benches on the lorry. We dropped our bags on the floor and sat down. Everything was happening so fast. I felt a little dazed.

We stopped at three farms on the way to Sankt Veit and picked up fourteen people; five girls and nine young men. They were like us, snatched from their families at the start of the war. We could not stop talking; the theme of our common experiences was inexhaustible. We were like old friends by the time we reached Sankt Veit.

The station square was teaming with hundreds of people, among them the British soldiers directing, keeping order. Our lorry stopped at the end of a long queue of lorries parked on the main road. As we climbed down, our German-speaking guard pointed us to the registration tent at the other side of the square. The tent was huge, army-green, pitched on the cattle-market site, where five years before, we had been examined and hand-picked like cattle by the waiting farmers, when we had first arrived.

I carried Miro, Michal held onto our bags, Maryla and Ludwik stayed close behind as we made our way through the crowd.

"Maryla! Anna!" It was Bazylka's voice.

We stopped and looked around. Above the heads of people I saw her jumping up and down waving her hand. Maryla and I let out ecstatic screams and the crowd parted letting us through.

She was with people from Steinfeld's farm, with Bruno and Dorota, and right beside them stood Franek and Lilli. And little, four-year-old Stefan, his white-blond hair shining like a halo in the sun.

I was dizzy with joy, as I went from one to the other, embracing them, holding them close.

"Let me look at your little one," Bazylka said, caressing Miro's cheek, "and what's this on your forehead?" The two loose ends of the suture hanging off his brow looked comical now.

"A long story…" I was able to laugh at it, "the stitch should have come out today, but as you see…"

"Nothing to it." Bazylka put on a knowing expression, "Your auntie will sort it all out for you."

I put Miro down next to little Stefan, black curls and flaxen hair almost touching. They considered each other with solemn curiosity, then Stefan took out of his pocket a miniature wooden horse. Miro hurried to show off the little wooden truck that Michal had chiselled for him. Their spontaneous chatter made us smile.

I could not take my eyes off my friends whom, excepting Lilli, I had not seen for four years. Bazylka and Maryla, kept apart for so long, clung to each other again and again, laughing and talking, cramming the time of their separation into a few moments. Bazylka's face was worn, her body was as thin as a boy's. Gone were the full breasts and the rounded hips I had so admired once. Only her green eyes and her titian hair had remained the same, faithful reminders of her youth.

And there was Franek, daddy-long-legs, lines forming already on his face. And Lilli, dear Lilli, her eyes smiling above the gauze scarf covering her face.

"How is this possible?" I asked.

Franek bent his head conspiratorially. "Everything's possible with the currency that's in demand."

He took some documents out of his bag and showed me an Arbeitz Buch. It was Lilli's with her name changed to Lilla Stanczyk, and a photograph of her taken before her left cheek had been scarred with a branding iron.

"Listen around you," he said, "half of them are still speaking German. Lilli blends in very well." It was true. Five years in a German spoken environment did not change in a day.

Lilli embraced his thin waist and gave him an affectionate squeeze. "He's brave to take us on."

"Nonsense!" he protested laughing. "She bewitched me! The very first time I set eyes on her!"

I remembered that first afternoon on Steinfeld's farm too. Vividly. Like bright cut-outs standing against a black background. Even now, as I cast my eyes down, images of Stefan and Lilli making love secretly, hidden in the ferns, filled my mind. And later, Franek's concern, that the farmer's daughter was not allowed to join us workers in our Sunday one hour's recreation of song and dance. I shook off these memories. They belonged to another time.

Now, everyone was talking all at once. Bazylka, true to character, took charge. Some things never changed.

"Come on, everyone! Let's go! The sooner we register, the sooner we get out of this place!"

We all picked up our bags and pushed our way through the crowd to the registration tent. It was hot and stuffy inside, despite the flaps at both ends being tied back. There was a long line of tables, behind which uniformed officials were checking people's identity papers. The long queues facing each official were off-putting, but the whole procedure was rushed amazingly quickly, and soon our group was sent through to a smaller tent, where packed sandwiches and bottles of water were handed out. We were then guided to the nearest parked lorry on the main street. No one told us where we were going, but we assumed it was the train station in Klagenfurt. Vienna, then home.

Inside the lorry, there were benches set out to seat forty people. There were nine other children apart from Miro and Stefan. We all found a space, dropped our bags and settled for the journey, glad to be with our friends. No one minded being pushed together; our euphoria made us unaware of such insignificant discomforts.

The lorry moved off, and a welcome, soothing breeze freshened the air underneath the tarpaulin roof.

It was lunchtime. The sandwiches were eagerly brought out. They were made up of some pink meat and sliced cheese. The taste was unusual, unforgettable of my first meal, on my first day of freedom.

Miro slept in my lap after lunch. Little Stefan cuddled up to Lilli and watched the trees fly by over the rim of the lorry's tail-gate. We four girls grouped together at one end of our facing benches, and the boys at the other end. Talk was non-stop!

Then suddenly, there was a figure bending over us.

"Beata?" The man asked hesitantly. "Beata?" He was tall, dark, with well-defined features and intense eyes. There was something vaguely familiar about him. I racked my brains trying to remember where and when I had seen him before. I looked to Bazylka for a clue. She was smiling, and a blush was spreading right up to the roots of her titian hair.

CHAPTER 29

"Tomasz!" She made an attempt to move up on the bench, but that was impossible, as we were so packed.

"It's all right," he said, sitting on the floor at her feet. His smile was shy. "I can't believe this is really happening!"

His gaze lingered intently on each one of us.

"I saw your group earlier in the square. I made sure this time I didn't lose sight of you again."

It all came back! The wounded man in the forest! It seemed so long ago now!

"Tomasz...there's something I must explain." Bazylka's blush deepened. Unusual for her. "My name's not Beata. It's Bazylka. And this is my sister Maryla. My friends Anna and Lilli."

He nodded.

"Of course, I remember, only different names!"

"We didn't know who you were!" Bazylka rushed to explain.

"No," he conceded, "and I presented a fearsome sight, didn't I? You were wise to be on your guard." He smiled, showing white even teeth. That time they had been blackened by wild berries, his meagre source of sustenance, during his escape.

"So what happened? How did you survive?" Bazylka asked, looking down into his eyes. His gaze appeared fixed, as if for a moment, they were totally alone.

"Pure luck," he replied, taking his eyes off her slowly, then sweeping his glance around the rest of us. "I came across a farmer who was a decent man. He took me in and I stayed with him to the end. With Radek and Kayetan, over there." He nodded in the direction of two boys further down.

"I've got something of yours." Bazylka's smile was hesitant. She slipped her hand inside her bag and brought out a small rag tied in a knot. She undid the knot and spread out the square piece of material on her lap. In the middle, there was a bullet, smooth and shiny, the bullet she had extracted from Tomasz's thigh. Five years she had kept it! Bossy

Bazylka. No nonsense Bazylka. Who could have suspected her of such sentiment?

Our boys got interested and started pressing from their end of the bench, craning their necks to see what was happening.

Tomasz picked up the bullet and held it between his forefinger and thumb, surprise and wonder lifting his face.

"Why didn't you throw it away?" His eyes appeared to glow.

She looked down, all her attention suddenly focused on folding the rag in her lap, as if her whole life was depending on it.

"It wasn't mine to dispose of." She raised her eyebrows but not her eyes. "Just as well I didn't. Now I can return it to you in person."

He replaced the bullet in her lap. This surprised her, forcing her to look at him again.

"Please keep it a little longer, Bazylka," he said. "Until such time when I can thank you properly. How do you thank someone who has saved your life?"

She smiled and blushed, and in a meek voice, not at all like hers, she replied, "All right. As you wish."

Our boys kept asking what it was all about and we told them in fragmented bits, and then general talk followed and other people joined in, and we discovered that many of them had been liberated from labour camps, some had been forced to work in ammunitions factories, some forced to repair recently bombarded roads or to remove rubble from destroyed buildings, and that our work on the farm appeared like a vacation compared to what they had been through.

We also discovered some disturbing things. A number of our companions had access to the news in the press and on the wireless. There was no clear-cut certainty that we were being sent home. Poland freed from the Germans by the Red Army, was now under Soviet occupation.

"But how's that been allowed?" someone cried in dismay.

"Not only allowed but approved. Yalta agreement. Last February. Churchill, Roosevelt and Stalin are apparently great pals together, now," a young man with a healing cut across his face informed us.

Ludwik stood up wringing his hands.

"It's back to square one, isn't it?" His steady voice camouflaged his anger, "We've had so little time of freedom. Just twenty years. So many people died then. Thousands more have been killed now. And for what? For another invasion? Another partition? Another dictator to oppress our nation? God, how can you watch this and not do anything?" He plunged his fingers into his tangled hair and remained still like a statue of some tragic character, until the swaying of the lorry forced him to sit down.

I leaned over Lilli's lap to Michael.

"What now? What are we going to do?"

Michal gave me a long, thoughtful look.

"Right now, Anna, we are on a lorry, in the middle of a foreign land. We've got no choice but to wait and to be patient."

That was not what I wanted to hear. A heaviness settled on my chest. Thoughts of my mother, of my sisters filled my mind. And Vladek, and little Joe. Where were they now? Was it possible I had not seen them for six years? When would I see them all again?

Just then I became aware of a male voice giving an account of the Warsaw uprising, the previous summer.

"The capital's in ruins. Thousands dead. Thousands sent to concentration camps. It'll take years to rebuild the city, but you can never bring back the dead."

I saw Bazylka grip Maryla's hand.

"I've got to go back," she spoke with fervour, "I've got to go back, no matter what. I've got to find our mother and father."

"I'll come with you," Maryla said, "you won't be alone."

"She wouldn't be alone," Tomasz spoke, "I'm from Warsaw too. We'll go back together."

"Count me in," Ludwik said.

When our lorry passed the signposts for Klagenfurt, it became obvious we were not heading for the grand railway station there. We entered a woodland area and after a few kilometres the lorry stopped in a side road in the forest. A shiver of anxiety ran down my spine. I clutched Miro to my chest who had been asleep most of the journey and opened his eyes now.

"Are we there yet?" he asked.

The back flap was unbolted and let down, together with the folding metal steps.

"Toilets and refreshments," one of the British soldiers announced to us in German.

Their manner was laid back, friendly. I relaxed.

"Just a stop for a wee," I explained to Miro.

We climbed down with everyone else. The men went one way, and the women, some with small children, went in the opposite direction, to hide in the ferns.

Miro and little Stefan performed willingly with competitive arcs of urine, then Lilli and I distracted them in turn, showing them the caterpillar-like curled tips of the ferns, while we tended to our personal needs.

Back by the lorry I looked inside the brown paper bag, given to us by Sylvia. She'd filled them with bread, sausages and apples. The bread and sausages I saved for later, but the apples I gave to Miro and Stefan. Their faces livened up immediately, and soon they were munching and running round in circles, chasing each other.

The armed soldiers stood nearby enjoying a smoke. They were joined by a few of our people who endeavoured with much gesticulation and a mixture of Polish, German and a few English words to engage in some form of conversation. The atmosphere was that of a social gathering.

Our group stood together, stretching arms and legs. Michal produced the box of cigarettes out of his breast pocket. He peeped inside the box then his face took on a sad clown look.

"Disaster!" he said. "There's five of us and only four cigarettes left!"

"I don't smoke," Tomasz said with a hint of self-deprecation.

"I'll cut mine in half," Ludwik offered.

"No, really. Thank you. It's the health thing, you know…and being a medical student…it just wouldn't be right…"

"Health, shmealth!" Franek laughed, "a man's got to have a pleasure or two! I never say no to a ciggy, especially when it's offered free!"

They had a smoke and enjoyed pleasantries and just for a short while our worries were forgotten and it felt like a picnic on a Sunday afternoon.

Then the soldiers called out it was time to go and one counted us as we climbed back inside the lorry.

"*Vierzig Erwachnsene.* Forty adults. *Sieben Kinder.* Seven children. *Ja?*" he said.

"*Jawohl!*" we answered and were off.

The place we were taken to was an ex-prisoner's camp outside Villach. We discovered later that political prisoners – Russians, Poles, Jews, Hungarians, Czechs and other nationalities – had been detained there throughout the war years till the British forces took control of the area. A high percentage of the prisoners were professional people –lawyers, doctors, teachers, engineers, architects, academics – who, when set free, were deployed by the British to help out with the gargantuan task of repatriating vast numbers of people scattered across Europe by the Nazi labour-enforcement machine.

We were driven down a central concrete road to the other end of the camp, which was surrounded by a high metal mesh fence. The barbed wire had been removed from the top and the watch towers stood empty. The gates had been left wide open at both ends. Rows of houses stood by the roadside, houses built of wood and corrugated metal sheets, painted black. Young people like us, with small children, stood by and waved as we passed. Beyond the fence, there were meadows covered in dandelions and daisies, trees fluffy with fresh foliage; a peaceful landscape, stilled by the afternoon heat, marred only by this man-made blot.

The road ended in a large square. Around it stood solid brick buildings with metal window frames and reinforced glass panes. Our newly arrived contingent was sent to one of these administration blocks. Moving along in an orderly queue, we were shown into a spacious white-washed hall, where uniformed officials divided us into further queues behind people already waiting there. The far end had been transformed into a temporary office by a line of tables where papers and identity cards were examined and checked.

Michal took Miro from me and held him in his arms so he could see above the crowd. Some children were too big to be picked up. Trained by the rigours of their recent captivity they stood still and anxious against their mothers, clutching their hands.

Three officials made themselves noticed by jumping onto a stage block at the side of the tables. A hush fell over the crowd. They were joined by a man in civilian clothes. He was about forty, with grey hair, grey skin and a worn grey suit.

It was an electrifying, unexpected shock when he greeted us in Polish.

"Welcome, my fellow countrymen!"

A spontaneous, roof-raising applause broke out. He raised his arms. A shadow of a smile crossed his emaciated face. The noise died down and he spoke.

"My name is Bronislav Czerski. Until recently I was a prisoner here. My crime was my profession. I'm a lawyer. My fortunate knowledge of English has made me useful to our British friends…" he nodded at his companions, "and hopefully, I can be of use to you, my friends. This is just a transit camp for a very short time."

"When are we going to be sent home?" someone called out.

Mr Czerski nodded in sympathy.

"Please be patient. The war has only just finished. There are thousands of displaced persons like us. The problem is simply too vast to be solved overnight. The situation is this: right now we are under British protection. Their orders are to issue each one of us with an UNRRA card. This stands for United Nations Relief and Rehabilitation Administration. Long words. UNRRA is so much easier to remember, isn't it? Anyway, when this is done, you'll be sent further, to one of the refugee camps run by units of General Anders' army. They are stationed along the eastern coast of Italy."

"What!" There were a great number of disappointed voices as people looked at each other in disbelief.

"But that doesn't make any sense!" someone protested. "We'll be sent further away from our country!"

Mr Czerski raised his hand and waited till the noise died down.

"Believe me," he said, "there are good reasons for this. Those of you who've had access to news in the press or on the radio, will know that though the war has ended in Europe, Poland is still not a free country. General Anders has experienced Soviet persecution first hand. He is fearful for those who return home in a hurry. The refugee camps will buy us time to reflect and to make unhurried decisions…" He paused allowing us to digest this information. "First things first," he continued after a while, "when you've registered, you'll have your photograph taken, then you'll be shown to your barracks, then around the camp. There's a communal dining hall, there's a building with toilets and washing facilities, there's also a surgery and a sick bay. To hurry the process of having your papers checked, please have them ready as you move up the queue."

I braced myself for a long wait, but they dealt with us with efficient speed. Michal and I came up to the table together. It was laden with wire baskets, filled with forms, blank sheets and ink bottles. Mr Czerski positioned himself behind the three seated officials, moving from one to the other as the need to interpret arose.

"One at a time," he said to us.

"We are a couple," Michal explained. "This is our child. We were not allowed to marry."

Mr Czerski translated this, the official nodded as he examined our Arbeitz books. He filled in new forms then we were sent outside, where a photographer was already waiting with a camera fixed on a tripod and pointing at a grey blanket hung across a wall.

We waited for everyone in our group. Maryla and Ludwik, Bazylka and Tomasz, Bruno and Dorota came through. I worried for Lilli and Franek. What if her true identity were to be discovered? Would that make any difference? Would she be sent back? Michal was looking out for them too, his gaze tense, his face set. It seemed like a very long time. Then Franek came out of the building holding little Stefan by the hand, and Lilli close behind them.

I ran up to her and gave her a hug.

"Everything all right?" I whispered.

"Everything!" her eyes smiled above the gauze scarf.

We were led by a German-speaking soldier down the concrete track to one of the barracks. He stopped and turned round to face us.

"I'm afraid we have no facilities to accommodate families. Women and children will be housed in this barrack," he pointed to the right, "and the men will be just across the road in this one."

A murmur of dismay threatened to erupt into an outcry, but the soldier raised his hand in a pacifying gesture.

"We've been receiving orders in a hurry," he said. "We've not been given time to set up anything properly yet, but the good news is that you'll only be here for a night or two."

Even as he spoke another lorry packed with people was arriving at the gate. We stepped off the track to let it pass, formed two groups, male and female, and walked towards our assigned accommodation.

As Bazylka pushed the door open we were hit with an overpowering smell of chlorine that stung our throats and eyes. I held Miro back from stepping inside.

The place looked as if it had been hosed down perfunctorily. Whatever dirt had not been flushed out, it was allowed to dry again on the floor, on the walls and on the bare mattresses on twenty iron beds. There were dark smudges like blood, yellow stains, brown patches and bits of excrement attracting madly buzzing flies. Cockroaches and beetles scuttled along the edges of the long floor, and a mass of other strange bugs crawled on the windows and walls. The sight of all this made me shudder.

"We can't stay here!" Bazylka protested, pinching her nose to demonstrate her revulsion to the soldier. "We need scrubbing brushes, soap and buckets of water!"

He nodded.

"Komm mit mir."

While she was gone, we dropped our bags on the grass strip separating the barracks, and I unpacked Miro's bricks to keep him and Stefan occupied and out of the way. Then Lilli and Dorota, Maryla and I began to bring out the mattresses, one by one, for scrubbing and washing outdoors.

The task was repulsive, but I was thankful for the brushes and the soap and the buckets for carrying limitless supplies of water. We drowned all the bugs and insects with dripping brushes and swept them outside into a hole in the ground. We washed down the walls and the windows, we scraped and scrubbed the floor, we left the doors wide open at both ends to give the barrack a good airing. The weather favoured us. Even as we brushed out the stains on the mattresses with soap and water, the sun bleached them pale yellow and white, giving them the appearance of printed patterns on the thick canvas. The boys followed our example in their barrack across the road and scrubbed and cleaned with great zeal.

I was famished by seven and eagerly joined the others, forming groups on the road. We walked down to the dining hall together, dreaming aloud of our favourite dishes, the boys smacking their lips and rubbing their stomachs. They made me giggle with their rapt exclamations of *"platzki"* and *"bigos"*, with their ecstatic heaven-sent glances.

The meal was served in a vast dining area, not vast enough to accommodate all of the hundreds of the inhabitants of the camp at the same time. Groups of around a hundred per sitting were given half-hourly slots to consume their meals.

Our group dined together and marvelled at the bright green colour of the soup. It tasted of boiled water. This was followed by unsalted boiled potatoes and carrots and two slices of anaemic-pink meat. It was hard to tell which animal it had come from. I longed for Sylvia's thick chicken and vegetable broth. The only delicious food on the menu were tinned pears. I could have eaten a barrelful of them, but as Miro could not be coaxed to eat even one morsel of the main course, Michal and I saved our desserts for him.

The sanitation block, where I took Miro to wash him before bed-time, had toilets in two separate sections at opposite ends of the building, for men and for women. The toilets were a row of cubicles, open at the top and bottom, where every sound could be heard and every gesture imagined by its rustle. For the first time in five years I used real toilet paper, shiny and stiff, no softer than newspaper, but white and clean. I made it softer for Miro by scrunching it in my fist.

The middle section of the building had a row of screened showers along one wall, and facing them, there was a row of shallow concrete wash-basins. This section was open to everyone. At this early time in the evening it was being used mainly by mothers with their young children.

Lilli and I undressed our little boys and sat them inside the concrete basins, which we had lined first with small, folded flannelette sheets. Miro and Stefan enjoyed the luxury of warm water and begged for more time with every attempt to get them up and dried.

Back in our barrack, I covered the bare mattress with an old towel, to protect us from direct contact with its surface. It stank as if its stuffing had been made of dirty old socks. The barrack was now full of other women and children, the late afternoon arrivals, unpacking, sorting out their things in a buzz of chit-chat and activity. Miro and Stefan were wide awake with curiosity. It was pointless trying to get them to sleep. We took them outside and joined our group on the grass between the huts.

It had been a long and strange day. Our spirits were low, our expectations dashed, our conversation, forced by over-cheery pretence, was fragmented and continually drawn either to our sentimental past or inevitably, to the uncertainty of the future.

"Listen, folks!" Ludwik said at last, "this is only just the beginning. Nothing of greatness is achieved in a day. Give it a chance!"

I leaned against Michal, I held Miro to my chest and wished for a magic carpet to transport me home.

Later, in the middle of the night, Miro woke me up with cries of, "Tummy hurts! Tummy hurts!"

In my semi-awake state I stroked his head, gradually becoming aware of other children's cries, hushed voices, rustling sounds, doors being opened and shut. I sat up. Miro lay beside me curled up and whimpering. Even by the faint moonlight I could see a dark stain on his white night shirt at the same time as the sickly smell of diarrhoea made the situation clear.

"Oh, my poor darling!" I slid off the bed in search of a towel and a clean shirt for him in my bag under the bed.

"What's up?" Lilli spoke softly from the bed next to mine.

"Miro's got the runs."

I scooped him off the bed together with the sheet and carried him outside onto the grass. I noticed other mothers, like shadows, hurrying to the sanitation block with distressed children in their arms.

I stripped him, wiped his bottom with a rag, made a nappy from another rag and dressed him in a clean shirt. He cried all the time, holding his stomach and drawing up his knees. My hands stank, but I returned him onto our bed first before going to wash.

Maryla, on my other side, was awake.

"I'll watch him," she said. "The poor thing! That's all we need now! A massive epidemic!"

The washroom was dimly lit. There were a number of women washing down their children, who cried and shivered on the concrete floor.

"And can you wonder!" a woman with a squirming baby came to share my washbasin. "Such filth everywhere! Goodness knows what diseases are trapped in all this dirt!"

I had very little sleep that night. Miro cried a lot and I cried with him, utterly helpless to stop his pain. Bazylka, the ever vigilant nurse, woke up too and advised continual drinks of boiled water. Such a simple home remedy! If only we had access to it!

I kept coaxing Miro to drink the remainder of our bottled water, but he kept pushing away my hand and became increasingly distressed with each new wave of stomach cramps and uncontrollable runs. I changed him several more times, adding to the stinking pile of clothes outside. Each such attack required a trek to the sanitation block to wash the stench off my hands. Finally, at dawn, we both fell asleep, Miro curled up against me.

I woke up with a start to see Michal looking down at me.

"I was worried when you didn't come out. Bazylka and Maryla told me what's happened. They've gone to shower. We've got to take Miro to the surgery."

I sat up and looked around. Other mothers were too preoccupied with their own children to notice Michal's presence. Little Stefan on the next bed was crying while Lilli dressed him.

"I think he's got the bug too," she said, her eyes darkened with worry, her scarf slipping, exposing her scarred cheek.

"Then lets go together," Michal said, picking up Miro.

He and Franek joined the queue of mothers and their sick children outside the surgery while Lilli and I made a dash to the wash room for a quick, much-needed shower. They had only moved a few steps when we came back. It was nerve-racking having to listen to the children's cries and whimpers around us, while ashen-faced mothers rocked their babies to hush them. Miro rested limp against Michal's shoulder, his face flushed and his eyes sunken underneath his eyelids. Little Stefan lay motionless in Franek's arms.

Finally, we crossed the threshold and found ourselves in a large waiting room next to the sick bay. It was crowded and stuffy with the smell of soiled clothes. It made me feel nauseous and I swallowed hard to suppress the reaction to retch. My eyes began to water. How did Michal stand it? Or the doctors who were stuck in this nightmare?

There were two of them, one at each end of a long table. Though all the symptoms described by each parent in turn were similar, the doctors examined each child separately. Some children showed symptoms of severe dysentery. Those that were passing blood were detained in a make-shift ward, while the rest of us were told to give our children plenty of boiled, cooled water. This, we were told, would be available in the kitchen at all times. Bazylka would be pleased. We were also given three large tablets, to be crushed and administered at equal intervals throughout the day.

Michal and Franek minded the boys, whom we lay down to sleep on a blanket spread on the grass, while Lilli and I tackled the piles of washing.

Bazylka and Maryla joined us with theirs. Afterwards we laid out the wet garments in rows on the ground, and the strong, bleaching sun did the rest.

Improvement was slow in Miro's condition in the next three days. He slept most of the time and existed on water, but when the fever left him and he asked for fruit, Michal and I were light-headed with relief. Little Stefan was recovering too. I prayed with gratitude for our group, I prayed with desperation for the constantly wailing sick babies in our barrack.

No child in the camp was being spared the illness, which was now spreading to the adults as well. The washroom and the toilets were regularly hosed down, but the staff assigned to this revolting task had a job keeping up with the accelerated frequency of visits to the sanitation block, and with keeping a vigilant check on the washbasins, where stacks of soiled nappies and clothing were continuously brought in by the worn-out mothers. I wished there had been some magic way of halting my body's natural needs just for a few days, so I would not have to go near those places.

Waiting for our Displaced Persons Identity Cards was another form of torment. Each morning I rose with a feeling of expectancy and each night I lay down oppressed with a dread of another disaster lurking to pounce on us before we got away from this dreadful camp. After five years of relentless hard labour, life was empty with nothing to do. We kept each other's spirits up by gathering on the grass outside our barracks, and while watching over our sick children, we talked and dreamed, and the boys played card games or stretched their legs with walks outside the camp compound and each night they made a big show of looking forward to their meal of powdered egg, corned beef and tinned fruit. We girls, too, kept up the pretence of light-hearted fun. We laughed to please them.

On the fifth day of our surreal existence our Displaced Persons Identity Cards were ready. A note on the notice board by the dining hall informed our contingent of a meeting outside after the evening meal.

There were about a hundred and fifty of us. Miro was mercifully well enough to be carried around, his thin arms and limp legs dangling. We sat down on the grass in a wide semi-circle when Mr Czerski and two officers came to speak to us.

"Your new documents are ready," Mr Czerski said. "Tomorrow morning your transport will leave and take you south to the Polish forces in Italy…"

"And then?" someone asked. "What's going to happen after that?"

Mr Czerski shrugged.

"No one really knows. We take each week as it comes. Your new identity cards are very important. Keep them with you at all times. They're everything. Your passport, your food, your clothes, your housing."

We were called inside the same administration block where we had registered on our arrival, and the same officers sat behind the long table, covered in neat piles of typed sheets and printed documents.

Michal held Miro, against his shoulder, and we moved behind Lilli, Franek and little Stefan. The officer compared the photograph in her Arbeitz Buch to the one in her new identity card. He lifted his gaze and gave her a long searching look. He said in German, "Can you remove your scarf?"

My heart began to pound. What now? What if the truth were to be discovered?

Lilli slipped off her scarf and shook her hair loose. Her left cheek was covered by a small square of bandage padding stuck down with plaster.

"Toothache," she explained, "it helps to keep it warm."

He nodded and looked down at Stefan, who was clinging to her thigh.

"Your child?"

"Yes." His mother's inherited fair skin, the pale-blond hair and the clear blue eyes made that plain.

"And father?"

"Killed by the Germans."

The officer's hard stare melted in a blink. He nodded and handed her the new identity card together with her old Arbeitz Buch. She was one of us.

Our spirits were lifted that evening, buoyed by the prospect of an early morning start, that would distance us from this, our very first stop on the way to freedom, so unexpectedly harsh. We walked to the meadow outside the camp and settled down on the ground, amidst the dandelions and the buttercups. Miro rested his head on my lap and fell asleep. Little Stefan settled himself against Franek's chest with the possessiveness of a son towards his father. His eyelids too, began to droop after a while as conversation flowed above him. All talk was inevitably of our immediate future and of the dreams beyond.

Michal had fresh ideas for the furniture workshop, when he returned home. Franek could not wait to get back to his motorbikes and repairing cars. Bruno had worked on the railways. His love had been the railwaymen's band in which he had played the trumpet. He was wondering what had become of all his musician friends. Ludwik and Tomasz were comparing their unfinished studies, exclaiming every now and again at the coincidence of their common acquaintance with so many academics and professors.

"We just want to get back to our parents," Bazylka sighed. "Don't we Maryla?"

"I thought it would be just a matter of days," Maryla replied, chewing on a stem of grass. "First the Nazis, now the communists!"

"Communism, shomunism!" Franek interrupted. "They won't know what's hit them when we show up with Anders!"

"The only problem is," Ludwik reminded him, "that we are allies now. Friends! Bah! Can you imagine that?"

I did not want to imagine what it would mean to have an imposed, repressive regime. I only wanted to think of my mother, smiling and happy with me in her arms, of my sisters and brothers, of our house surrounded by flowers and sheltered by a row of willows.

"What about you, Lilli?" I asked, feeling for her, having to leave her family behind. She was sitting quietly, leaning her shoulder against Franek's, stroking Stefan's limp hand. She straightened up, slipped off her scarf and shook her hair loose.

"A fresh start will do us all good," she said. "Once we're married and settled, my family can visit as often as they like. It's just a day's train journey from Klagenfurt to Krakow." She smiled at Franek and he returned her warmth with a hug from his free arm.

"It won't be long," he promised.

Bruno began to play on his mouth organ. Dorota moved up to him and began to sing. She had a clear, light voice. We all joined in, first in all the well known childhood songs, then the more serious, patriotic ones. However, when Bruno played "Goral, are you not sad to be leaving your mountains?" we begged him to stop before we all drowned in tears.

People began to trickle out of the confines of the camp, and before long we had a crowd sitting around us on the grass. The atmosphere turned to that of a family party, as memories were resurrected and hopes renewed of great changes just within our grasp.

It was later, much later during the night, that I woke up with pains in my stomach, colic sensations like nails pushing against the stomach wall, and my distended bowel threatening to explode.

CHAPTER 30

Running with clenched buttocks and a stomach that was bearing down in an unstoppable urgency to evacuate its contents was torture. I moved as fast as the excruciating cramps allowed me, staggering then quickening my pace, tears of strained endurance streaming down my face.

The thirty or so metres to the sanitation block seemed like an unending mile. I burst into the dimly lit washroom, all my attention focused on finding the nearest free toilet cubicle. The stench was overpowering, the toilet seat, the walls and the floor were spattered, but I was beyond caring. I sat down and gave into the need of my body.

When the wave of pain and relief passed over, and I was left like a husk, fragile, empty, sweat-drenched, I pulled myself up onto my shaky legs and held onto the door. The sticky floor echoed my every step with a smacking sound. It was covered in blood and excrement, left behind by the poor wretches who had not made it in time to the toilet basin. Picking my way along the few remaining patches of dry floor, I plodded to the showers. I stood underneath a jet of soothingly tepid water until all the dirt had been washed off my hands, my legs, my feet, and the clogs.

I had two more such attacks before dawn. I could not understand where all this stuff was coming from, as each time I had been left hollow, with nothing more left to evacuate.

Miro was fast asleep, his breathing peaceful and steady. I lay beside him, bent double, nursing my worn stomach and prayed and begged God to give me strength to be able to leave with the others in the morning.

I did not get up for breakfast. Bazylka and Maryla took Miro with them and within minutes Michal was by my bedside, his face puckered with worry.

"Dear Anna, what are we going to do with you? How will you cope with the journey? Listen, we don't have to leave today."

I knew how much he wanted to. We were all desperate to leave this place behind.

"No. We're leaving with the others," I said, "I'll be all right, as long as I can lie down somewhere in a corner. Even on the floor."

Our friends helped us carry our belongings. Michal carried Miro and I walked bent forward, holding my fragile stomach in my crossed arms.

There were three lorries picking up a hundred and fifty people. We climbed aboard ours and I found a space at the end of a bench in a dark corner. I closed my eyes longing to find sleep in the lulling sway of the lorry, but every bump in the road reminded me with a jerking pain how raw my stomach was.

At the railway station in Villah, we were directed onto a platform where a long train of cattle wagons was waiting for us. Some wagons were already full of people.

"This is really travelling in style!" Ludwik remarked, but there was no time to stand and stare as the crowd behind us was pushing us on. I followed my group on my rubbery legs, my mind dazed and slow.

Michal sat Miro on the floor and pushing our two bags together, the ones filled with clothes, patted them flat and made a cushion for me to lie on. It was bliss to curl myself into a ball, just to lie still. I closed my eyes, glad to blank out all activity around me, checking just now and again, that Michal was standing beside me. He held Miro high up so they could peer through the slats in the top part of the wagon.

I felt the train pull out of the station, and then I slept, for when I opened my eyes again, two hours had passed and the train was again stationary. The sliding doors were pushed back with much clanging, metal hitting metal, sunlight flooding our wagon and I heard voices, English first, which I did not understand, then someone calling out in Polish.

"Listen everyone! That's as far as we can go. The rest of the track is destroyed. Now, we'll be making the rest of the journey on lorries."

I sat up with a sudden wave of nausea and pain shooting up to my brain. I became rigid, willing the sensations to subside as we waited for the wagon to empty, before our group began to move.

Outside we had come to the edge of a forest, with a level crossing nearby. The rail track here had been reduced to rubble, with iron spikes sticking out in all directions. The road moving away at an angle from the bombed area was riddled with pot holes. It was a mystery how the lorries and the ambulance parked on the verge had managed to reach this spot in the first place.

The soldier allocated to the group in our wagon pointed at his watch then spread his ten fingers three times to indicate we had half an hour to see to our personal needs. With a wide sweep of his arm towards the bracken and the bushes deeper in the forest, he made his message understood. He also drew our attention to the makeshift table placed on the ground at the back of the nearest lorry, on which there was bottled water and food wrapped in brown paper bags.

"See to Miro and yourself first," I said to Michal, "I'll sit by our things and rest."

I sat amidst the luggage left by our friends, doubled up, nursing my delicate stomach.

Maryla and Bazylka came back first. Bazylka stretched out her hand.

"Come on, Anna. Hang onto to me. I'll help you to get there."

"And I'll look out for Michal," Maryla assured me.

I clung to Bazylka's arm and wobbled along on my unsteady legs. There were people everywhere. I worried I would not be able to walk far enough, away from prying eyes.

"Here will do," Bazylka decided for me. "This clump would hide an elephant." She stood with her back to me and spread out her skirt in a wide screening fan.

I had no strength to argue or to worry. I squatted and gave in to the pressure within me. A warm flow gushed out and the ground at my feet turned red.

"Bazylka!" My voice was distant, not my own. Things became fuzzy, grey, black. The blackness absorbed everything, even my pain.

Into the blackness came a sound, first distant and faint, then as it got stronger, I recognised the drone of an engine. I was lying flat on my back, on a firm surface, that was not the floor of a lorry. I tried to open my eyes. My eyelids were heavy, like iron lids. Through the pin-prick slits between my eyelashes I glimpsed a ceiling and a face peering down at me. There were muffled voices. There was an ache in my arm as if it had been jabbed. My stomach was still, hollow, shaped inwards like a bowl. I attempted to raise my head. It had turned to stone. Blackness engulfed me.

Later, it could have been seconds or days or weeks later, flashing lights flew past me, like windows in a long corridor. In my semi-conscious state I was faintly aware of activity around me, of long white walls, of countless doors, of a lulling, soothing motion, as if I were being wheeled around. I slept.

It was dark when I opened my eyes, but not dark with the blackness of my unconsciousness. My brain appeared to float when I turned my head.

I was on a bed, between clean crisp sheets. There was a wide entrance across the room from me, and a long corridor, and a soft light, gentle to my aching eyes. It was clear I was on a ward in a hospital.

Slowly, carefully I turned my head. The two beds next to mine were empty, but the two furthest away from me on the other side appeared occupied.

"Michal! Is that you?" I whispered, my tongue like a rattle inside my dry mouth.

There was no movement from the beds, but a white figure materialised and floated towards me from the open doorway. She leaned over me.

"*Anna, bese aqua con compressa,*" she whispered, holding a glass of water for me to see and two large tablets in a small ceramic container. She placed them beside me on the locker and helped me to raise myself a fraction from my lying position. A nauseous sensation curled around my stomach. She held my shoulders as I drank and swallowed the pills.

"What's the name of this place?" I asked in German. "Where's my family? My little boy Miro? My husband?"

"*Shsh...Dormi bene*, Sleep well," she whispered back.

But I needed to know. I pointed my finger at the other beds.

"Is that Michal? Miro?"

"*Donne Inghlese*, English ladies," she replied helping to lower me back onto the pillow.

I closed my eyes against hot, stinging tears.

Bright sunshine woke me up in the morning. I opened my eyes, bracing myself against more pain, but as I moved my gaze about the room, I became aware that it no longer hurt to move my eyes, that my hollow stomach had been stilled, that my body appeared to be free of all sensation. I did not dare move for fear of disturbing this cocoon of comfort.

I noticed that the room was not as big as I had expected a ward to be. It had only six beds. Two women, who did not look at all like patients, were busying themselves around two beds furthest away from me. When they noticed that I was awake, they came over and stood at the foot of my bed. Even in my state of slowed-down reaction, I got the impression that they were tall and slim and very pretty in their floral dresses. My immediate need was to ask them about Michal and Miro. Had they seen them? Did they know where they were?

They exchanged uncertain glances and one of them spoke in a language I did not understand. I guessed it was English. All I could do was to stare back into her clear, well-meaning face, and swallow my disappointment. She smiled, showing pearly teeth, then indicated with hand gestures that she and her companion had to go.

I listened with envy to the fading echo of their heels down the corridor as I lay back, totally on my own, the hospital whiteness around me, almost luminous in the streaming sunlight. Weak as I was, I was nevertheless determined to find out what had happened to Michal and Miro. I knew from bitter experience, I was certain of it, that Michal's absence now, was not of his own choice. I could only imagine his anguish at our separation and my eyes filled with tears of pity for him and for myself.

After a while I noticed that my flat material purse, which I had worn like a necklace on a string around my neck, had been left on the top of my locker. With a shaking hand I pulled it towards me and looked inside. All was well. My new identity card was safe, together with a picture of Michal, Miro and myself, taken on one occasion, when Sylvia's cousin had come to visit her with a camera.

A young nurse came towards me carrying a white enamel bowl. Her dark colouring was not unlike my own. I took instantly to her brown smiling eyes. She placed the bowl on the locker, wet a face cloth, and indicated her intention to give me a bed bath.

"No thank you," I said in Polish, "I'll do it myself."

I took the wet cloth from her and began to wipe my face. A wave of utter tiredness swept over me. My hand fell away from my face, lifeless. She took the wet cloth from me and began to wipe me down, bit by embarrassing bit. When she had finished, she said, *"Returno momentito."*

She took the bowl away and came back a few minutes later with a bed pan. I was weak, but not so weak as to be devoid of self-dignity. I covered my eyes with my hand. She closed the door, came back to me and talked a lot, none of which I could understand. She removed my hand from my face, helped me to sit up, and held me upright, while I performed. I knew that without her support I would have crashed down onto the floor, but that awareness did not diminish my sense of utter humiliation. Afterwards I was shocked to see the bedpan soiled with a bloody mess and wondered how much longer this awful nightmare was going to go on. The saintly nurse cleaned me and covered me right up to my chin with the crisp, pristine white sheet. I shivered underneath it with the effort of it all, despite the warm temperature in the room rising by the minute. She opened the windows wide and took away the covered bed-pan with its foul-smelling contents. The fragrance of the orange blossom from the trees outside filtered into the room. Soon I began to drift into sleep.

Later, a doctor and a senior nurse came to see me. The nurse had a round face and cheeks that looked as if they had been polished. Her greying hair was tightly knotted in a bun at the back, just below her nurse's coif.

The doctor was tall and thin, with a mop of dark hair above his high forehead, giving his face an elongated appearance. He spoke to me in English first. I did not understand him.

"*Parla Italiano*?" he asked. I did not understand that either.

"Sprechen sie Deutch?"

At long last!

"Yes, I do, and Polish too," I answered in German. "Please tell me, where am I? And where's my family?"

The doctor smiled, showing his rather long teeth.

"This is a British military hospital in Udine. I am Dr Goodman, and this is Sister Wilson. There are no wards for women, so we'll keep you here, in this room designated for the patients' wives and their relatives."

"Keep me? For how long?"

"You've got dysentery. It is an infectious disease. We've got to get you better, so you are no longer a threat to yourself or to anyone else."

"How long will that take?" I could not bear the thought of being separated from Michal and Miro for another day.

"With medication, rest and a strict diet, your worst symptoms should disappear within a week."

"A week!" my hope shrunk like a burst balloon.

"That's the minimum. We'll keep you a few days longer to be certain of your absolute recovery."

His voice was gentle, his gaze showing concern.

"But I can't stay here that long!" My lip began to tremble. "Please, have a look at this."

I pulled my cloth purse off the locker and with clumsy shaking fingers loosened the drawstrings. I showed them the photograph of Michal, Miro and myself.

"This is my family," I said, "my little child. I've got to see them. Where are they?"

Dr Goodman took the photograph from me and with Sister Wilson, they studied it for a moment. Then his face lifted in an amiable smile.

"As soon as we get you ready to leave," he said, "one of our officers will advise you on where to look for your husband and child. You were brought in as an emergency case. There wouldn't have been room for your family in the ambulance. We'll give you another injection today, then tablets regularly for the next few days. Your diet will consist only of boiled rice and boiled water, I'm afraid." He handed me back the photograph, adding, with a twinkle in his eye, "But don't worry, it'll only be for the first three days." That was not my biggest worry. I had no appetite anyway.

"I'll come back tomorrow," he said, after talking to Sister Wilson in English for a moment. "Is there anything else you'd like to know?"

"Only where my family is…and what's happened to my clothes?"

"I expect," he said, "the night nurse has taken them away to be disinfected. Ask her tonight."

They left, but despite the doctor's encouraging words, I felt little comfort. Missing Michael and Miro was like an ache. Unable to imagine them in any particular place, I felt bereft, like a sole survivor of a shipwreck, thrown onto a shore of a distant island.

A little later, the young nurse, the helpful, patient angel, the one with the dark hair and the soft brown eyes, came with an injection for me. I did not understand what she said, but her soothing voice and her deft hands made me feel as if I were being looked after by someone who cared. I drifted into sleep.

I slept most of that day and was only half awake when made to drink water with tablets and when propped up to use the bedpan.

In the evening the night nurse woke me up and helped me to sit up against the pillows. She was the person from the night before, big, plump and maternal.

"*Come sta piccola Anna?* How's my little Anna?" she asked. I could only smile back.

She brought a tray with a bowl of rice and a glass of water and placed it on my lap. My head was fuzzy, my stomach hollow, my body pumped out of all energy.

"*Mange, Anna, mange,*" she encouraged me.

I placed a spoonful on my tongue and rolled it about in my mouth. It tasted like wet chalk. I managed to swallow three spoonfuls with gulps of water, then my face came out in sweat. I looked beseechingly at the nurse. She understood, removed the tray, and was gone for a while. She came back with my clothes, the long grey dress with the white collar, and my underwear, all washed and neatly folded.

I grabbed her hand and pressed it to my face.

"*Danke, danke, danke!*" I wished I could say more, in her own language, but her benevolent expression reassured me that she understood.

It was on the fifth day that I began to feel a marked improvement. The best, the most exhilarating thing for me, was to be able to walk to the bathroom and take a shower without assistance. The bathroom was spotless white, with a marble floor, and I felt like a princess each time I stood under the jet of warm water, washing away sweat from my hair and body. I had not felt so well scrubbed and clean for years, and my only regret was that I could not share this joy with Michal and Maryla.

I was also allowed to go outside into the enclosed quadrangle, as long as I stayed away from the convalescing soldiers there. Most of them were young, no older than me, with a number of different injuries; head, shoulders, arms, legs, feet, heavily bandaged, some limbs in plaster casts. Some had visitors who accompanied them on their exercise walks around the quadrangle.

One morning, as I sat on a bench, drying my freshly washed hair in the sun, a young man with a bandaged foot stopped by me and leaned on his crutches for a rest. His arms and his face were spattered with hundreds of healing cuts. His blue eyes picked up the light reflected from the sand stone when he said "Hallo" to me and much more, none of which I could understand. All we could do was shrug and laugh before he hobbled on.

I was no longer limited to a diet of boiled rice, but was served macaroni with cheese, macaroni with tomatoes, or macaroni with powdered scrambled egg. My appetite returned and I looked forward to the meals.

I pestered Dr Goodman every day to let me go. On the tenth day of my hospital stay, Dr Goodman said to me, "In normal circumstances, a fortnight's hospitalisation is the minimum requirement. But these are not ordinary times. I am satisfied that you are fully recovered. You may leave tomorrow morning." He took out a piece of paper from the breast pocket of his white overall. "I've written the address for you of our military headquarters, here in Udine. It's not far from here. There's a section there that deals with Displaced Persons. They'll help you find your family, Anna." He gave me his long-toothed smile, and I was ready to throw my arms around his neck and hug him.

"Thank you, so very much," I said, my chest bursting with anticipation of the next day.

That night, when I was in bed, willing the sleep to come, willing the night to pass away, my room companions arrived. There had been a constant turnover of them, and I guessed that they were, perhaps, allowed to stay for only a limited time. The older of the two ladies came over to my bed and said, "Hallo Anna," which I understood, and then as she carried on talking, she picked up my hand, slipped something inside my palm and closed my fingers over it. I opened my hand. It was a roll made up of lira notes. I was astonished. I sat up, shook my head, and stretched my arm towards her.

"I can't accept this. It's far too much!"

She pushed my hand back to me gently, saying four words in German, "*Fur dich. Fur essen.* For you. For food."

The younger woman came over to me and gave me a bar of fragrant soap and a tube of toothpaste. I could not believe my luck. I wanted to say so much to them, total strangers, whom I would not see again, but whose kindness would set me up on the journey ahead of me.

"*Dank you, dank you, dank you, veri, veri match,*" were all the thanks I could give them, and I was glad that I had learnt a few words of English.

It was busy outside the hospital's main entrance. There seemed a constant flow of ambulances, arriving and departing, orderlies carrying the sick on stretchers, people hobbling on crutches, mingling with the military and the civilians in a two-way pedestrian traffic. I stood still for a moment, to get my bearings, to establish my sense of direction, of left and right, of north and south, in this blinding-white square that was streaked at random with sharp, dark shadows. This was Udine.

It had all sounded so easy, when Dr Goodman explained. Now, faced with a crossroads forking out in several directions, and enormous buildings blocking off views beyond the hospital compound, I had no idea which way to turn first.

With Dr Goodman's note ready in my hand, I was just about to accost the very first person walking towards me, when I was forced to jump back, out of the way of an ambulance, pulling up right beside me. Two orderlies rushed up to the back door, opened it and carried down a man on a stretcher. His head was totally covered in bandages, stained with dark blood. Behind him, leaning on crutches, a man with a leg in hard plaster was helped down by a medic. Then a woman stepped down. She was middle-aged, with a weathered face, unkempt hair and an arm in a sling made of a large square head-scarf. She had a yellow "P" on her left shoulder.

It was electrifying to see that "P".

I rushed towards her and ran alongside, as she was led towards the main entrance.

"Excuse me, please, do you speak Polish?"

She was startled at first but then her pained gaze fell upon me.

"Of course I do!" she lifted her left shoulder.

"Where are you staying?" I asked.

"There's a camp outside Udine. Can't stop now. Broken arm." She looked anxious to keep up with her group.

"Just tell me one thing," I begged, "how do I get there?"

"Jump in the ambulance. They're going back."

I turned and ran out of the building. The woman's ambulance was still there. The orderlies were helping patients climb onto it; convalescing soldiers, released from the hospital.

I ran up to the driver of the ambulance, a British soldier, who was leaning against the bonnet, enjoying a smoke in the break.

"Please sir," my Polish made him look at me. "Please take me with you." Then I added in Italian, "*Sono Polacca.*" With feverish fingers I loosened the string on my rag purse and pulled out the photograph. "*Mia famiglia. In campo Udine.*"

He cast a glance at my photograph through cigarette smoke. I showed him my DP card.

"*Prosze. Bitte. Prego. Pleez,*" I begged with words that came to my mind, my face crumbling in frustration.

He nodded with a slow, polite smile.

"It's OK. Don't worry!" He opened the door and pointed at the middle seat, next to the driver's. "For you," he said.

"Me?" I mimicked his gestures, making sure that I understood him correctly.

"*Si, signorina, si,*" he smiled encouragingly.

I climbed in, my heart beating fast, and prayed he would not change his mind. I heard the back door slam, at the same time as the driver got in and another soldier settled in on my other side. The engine was started and we were off.

Once out of town, we were forced to make constant detours around the main routes that had been eroded by bombs. I marvelled at the colours in the fields, vast expanses of poppy-red, iris-blue and daisy-white, defiant against the bomb attacks, growing out of craters and uneven ridges.

It was a hot day. The humming of the wind through the open windows and the droning of the engine made conversation difficult to sustain. My companions exchanged sporadic remarks, while I was glad to be left alone with my thoughts. I willed the journey to hurry, to end. I imagined a hundred times the moment I found Michal and Miro, I pictured our joy, our great relief, as I held them both in my arms.

With all the additional mileage imposed by alternative routes, it was hard to assess how far south from Udine we drove. It was lunchtime when we arrived at the camp.

Nothing had prepared me for the sight. I had been expecting a setting similar to that of the POW camp that we had left behind in Villah. Barracks, or huts, or even sheds. This camp was a wide open field, with just a mattress for each family to mark their personal space. Hundreds of people, seen from the distance like colourful litter scattered on the landscape, were sitting on the ground. Where in this sea of faces would I find Michal and Miro? There was hardly any noise, just a hushed murmur rising from the crowds. It was strange and eerie.

Our ambulance drove along the dry stony track that cut through the fields and led to a large, square building, with sand-coloured stucco walls, a sloping red-tiled roof and shuttered dark windows. Behind it to one side there were smaller outbuildings, and on the south side, tall cypresses in a dense row, threw the much needed shade over this whole area.

One could imagine that this was once a comfortable family home, now taken over by the army to serve hundreds of displaced people. People of all ages: mothers with babies, children, young people like myself, the elderly and infirm, some of them lying down on their mattresses, as if they were already dead. Further, at the side of the big house, green tents had been put up, one, like a huge roof on stilts, with rows of occupied camp beds, the temporary hospital ward.

My driver pointed me to the entrance of the main building. I thanked him and shook his hand. He looked taken aback, then smiled and said something I did not understand.

Inside the building, my eyes took a moment to adjust to the darkness after the glare outside. The entrance hall was spacious and lofty with a semi-circular staircase leading up to the upper floor. There were closed doors all round, a desk in the middle and an officer sitting behind it sifting through piles of documents.

I went up to him holding my photograph in readiness.

"I'm looking for my family," I said in Polish.

"One moment," he replied in English, getting up. I watched him go away, with a sinking feeling, but then he returned accompanied by another officer.

"I speak Polish," his companion said to me, and for a brief second it felt like coming home.

"Thank God! Thank God!" Relief made me into a jabbering wreck.

There was a clean-cut look about him, and on the shoulder of his khaki shirt, the red half-moon with the white letters POLAND.

Showing him the photograph, I explained my predicament, my illness, my separation, my desperate need to find my family. He listened attentively till I'd finished.

"They should be on our register," he said. "Without registration they wouldn't get any food. I'll check for you. What name was it again?"

"Majerski. Michal Majerski."

"The cabinet in the middle," the English officer prompted from his desk. There was a row of metal cabinets against the wall.

The Polish officer pulled out a drawer and brought out a wad of papers marked with a capital M. He placed them on the table and began to check through, his deft fingers working fast, as if counting bank notes. I held my breath each time his fingers paused, but then he carried on, to the end. He checked again, the full thick wad of printed forms. His tone was apologetic when he looked up at me.

"We've got no one with that name registered here," he said. My heart dropped.

"But where could they be?" I asked. "I'm certain he'd have registered for Miro's sake."

I saw pity in his eyes.

"It's quite possible," he said, "that they've been sent down further south, by-passing this camp altogether."

My lips began to tremble.

"Don't cry," he said gently. "You'll find them. It'll just take a little longer. The best thing you can do is to register here. You'll get food and water and a mattress. Every day there are lorries taking people south, to better conditions than these, in organised Polish army camps. You'll go too, when your turn comes."

"When will that be?"

"In a few days."

Days! Waiting another hour was torment.

"We've got hundreds of people, as you've seen no doubt, waiting like you, to be transported. And not enough lorries."

I stifled my desire to howl. I had no choice but to follow his advice.

I registered, I was given food vouchers and a mattress, which I dragged along the grass to the nearest group of people. There were four of them: an elderly couple, their daughter, I guessed, and her son of about ten. They looked up as I approached.

"May I join you?" I asked, "I'm on my own."

"Sure you can," the mother of the boy said. "The more the merrier!"

I let the mattress drop and I flopped on top of it.

"So where are you from?" the woman asked.

I told them briefly, showing them the photograph of Michal and Miro.

"You've not seen them, by any chance?" I was praying for a miracle. They had not.

I discovered that the woman, like myself, had worked on a farm in Germany. Her elderly parents had been interned in a labour camp, where they made army boots in a factory. All the while we talked, the boy lay quiet on the mattress, his head covered with a light scarf to shade him from the sun.

"He's feverish," his mother explained, "but there's nowhere to take him. The sick bay is full."

For lunch, I queued with them at one of the tables set up along the central track, from which soldiers served meals. It was basic food – macaroni with bits of meat in tomato sauce – but there was enough to satisfy hunger.

Afterwards, I could not sit still. A tiny spark of hope that the information I had been given could be incorrect niggled and niggled inside me. I wandered round the field all afternoon among rows, countless rows of mattresses crammed with people, and I searched, praying at each turn for a glimpse of familiar faces. Not only Michal, but any of my friends.

When evening came, compulsion drove me to do it again. Then darkness came, forcing me to abandon my quest. I lay down on my mattress with hundreds of people settling for the night around me, with the immense, vaulted, starry sky above me, and I felt like the loneliest orphan in the world.

The toilets were a row of holes dug deep in the ground, each one screened off individually by sack-cloth stretched on tall rigid poles. They were set well back from the main building, but it was not possible to control the stench that drifted in all directions, nor the flies that shot about like fragments of a black cloud. I pitied the woman who was paid by the army to sit on a chair nearby and hand out toilet paper, crinkly and grey, one or two squares, depending on the need. This was luxury, after years of using cut, old newspapers or leaves of wild plantain or moss.

I had no choice but to brace myself and endure the necessary visit there, making it as quick as possible, while fighting off my reaction to gag on each intake of breath. Afterwards, at one of the taps fixed to the outside wall of the building, I rinsed my mouth for a long time with a dissolved blob of toothpaste, given to me by the kind English lady. I washed my face and hands and joined the queue for breakfast.

Breakfast was a thick wedge of cheese pizza and an aluminium mug of coffee. I walked over to the area where lorries were waiting in line, and where people designated to leave the camp that day were gathering round them with their belongings. I sat on the grass to watch, as I ate the pizza and drank the coffee. I would have given anything to be one of those lucky ones.

One by one the lorries filled with people and began to leave. The last one was almost ready to go. The two soldiers in charge folded the steps and were just about to lift up the tailgate, when a sudden idea struck me. I jumped up and ran towards them shouting, "Don't leave me! Don't leave me!"

They stopped in mid-action, puzzled.

"I'm sorry! I'm so sorry!" I grovelled. "Forgive me, please, for being late!"

They rolled their eyes in a show of patient endurance.

"There's always one, isn't there!" one of them said. But then, they grabbed me under my arms and hoisted me onto the lorry. The flap went up, the locks clanged, the go-ahead signal was given, and we were off.

It was a long drive, along meandering country roads, with stops every two hours. The air inside the lorry was stuffy, pungent with sweat, ailing, flatulent stomachs, stale menstrual blood and babies' dirty nappies. I was lucky to have a tight spot, right against the tailgate of the lorry, where the breeze, fresh and soothing, blew into my face.

We arrived at the camp near Adria around four in the afternoon. To our surprise and relief it was totally different from the previous place. It was a city of tents, sheltering its population against the blazing heat, or possible violent storms.

While the soldiers busied themselves with sorting our crowd into orderly queues, I was suddenly gripped with panic, with an urge to resume my search, to check each tent before darkness fell. I detached myself from the crowd and ran.

People, hundreds of them, had spread out on the straw-like grass between the tents, mothers with their babies, women washing, hand sewing, knitting, children playing their games, men repacking their few possessions, enjoying a chat and a smoke. I walked among them peering inside each tent, calling out Michal's name, showing his photograph, giving descriptions, explaining our separation, but no one was able to help me. They had come from a great number of different places in Germany and Austria, but had not come across anyone from my group of friends.

All the while, even from a distance, I had kept a vigilant eye on the crowd by the registration block, and when it had diminished to just a few people, I went back to join them.

All officers indoors were Poles; the language was no longer a problem. I explained my plight, when my turn came. The officer checked the list of all names under M. He checked it a second time.

"Don't worry," he said. "Your husband and child are most probably in Forli. That's a camp especially set up for young families."

His words were like first glimmers of clear light on a foggy day. I felt drained, shaky.

"How can I get there? And when?" I asked.

"There's a transport of mothers and children leaving tomorrow morning. You can go with them."

He became fuzzy. I grabbed hold of his desk for support.

"You'd better sit down," he said, getting up and leading me to a chair by the wall. "I'll still be here when you recover."

I recovered and came out with food vouchers in my hand and a rolled rubber mat underneath my arm and I looked for a patch of grass where I could bed down for the night. I felt dizzy with renewed hope. I felt anxious too, imagining all kinds of things going wrong the next day, creating obstacles in my search for Michal and Miro.

But nothing did. After breakfast the next morning a transport of four lorries left the camp. Mothers, their children and me.

The camp in Forli was another city of tents. The moment I jumped off the lorry, I ran towards the nearest ones. I did not want to take place in the queue, to register, to look for Michal on the list of names. I wanted to find him in person, to see him, to touch him, to hold him, to finish my search. Just as the day before, I walked between the tents, among people and their children, showing Michal's photograph, explaining my situation.

"There's so many like him," one man said. "Men with children, separated from their wives, women on their own separated from their husbands, children alone, without their parents. I wish you luck!"

Please God, please let me find them, I prayed, despair driving me to tears. A woman came out of the tent with a small child in her arms.

"I heard you calling," she said. "Is it Michal you're looking for?"

"Yes! Michal! And our little son Miro!" I almost shouted.

"That tree over there…" she pointed towards the centre of the field. "It's one of those tents."

"Thank you! Thank you!" I wanted to hug her, but my legs were already carrying me forward.

CHAPTER 31

I found Michal and Miro outside their tent in the dappled shadow of a large olive tree. There were a number of them scattered singly or in clumps around the field, towering over the tents.

Miro was sitting back on his heels, his thin shoulders stiff with held-in excitement, one hand poised in the air, his whole attention concentrated on the tower he had made of wooden bricks, his other hand attempting to balance the final brick on the very top.

Michal, sitting next to him on the grass, had bits and pieces spread around him, and something resembling a shoe sole held rigid between his knees. He appeared to be stitching parts of a sandal together.

I took all of this in, in a blink of an eye, and rushed to them crying out, "Michal! Miro!" The rest became a blur of sensations: Michal's arms around me, his kisses, Miro's laughter, his moist mouth on my cheeks, my face in his hair that smelled like fresh hay.

Then I sat down beside them on the grass and I cried. I hid my face in my hands, but I could not hold back the sobs that were like pain itself. I felt Michal's arm across my shoulders, Miro's soft hands on my face, Michal's lips on the back of my neck. Slowly, the grief ebbed out of me, and peace and stillness took its place.

"People will think I've made you cry," Michal smiled, brushing back a wisp of hair from my face.

There was no privacy in this place, with hundreds of tents surrounding us and hundreds of people going about their business outdoors. Next to our tent, a young woman stood rocking her baby and watched us with interest. She did not avert her gaze when I caught her eye, but nodded, as if to say, she knew what I had been through.

I blew my nose and dried my eyes.

"Not knowing where you were…all this time…" I turned to Michal.

"I know, Anna." He held me close. "It's been a nightmare these past two weeks. They wouldn't let me come with you. And there was Miro…"

I pulled Miro onto my lap, cuddled him, kissed him, drank in his smell of everything he had been in contact with that day: the sun, the dust, the grass, the orange on his sweet breath. Satisfied quickly with my attention, he climbed down and with one swipe of his hand destroyed the structure that he had built with so much care.

"I bet you can't build a bigger one," Michal teased him.

"Yes I can!" Miro protested. His lips pursed with determination, he began to stack bricks one on top of another.

Michal and I talked. I told him everything he wanted to know; about the doctor, the nurses, the English ladies, my encounters with all kinds of people, all of them willing to help.

"I've not done too badly myself," he said. "Maryla's been like a mother to Miro, and Lilli and Bazylka like doting aunts."

"Where are they all?" I asked, looking around.

"They've gone ahead of us to Riccione. To join the army."

"They've gone to join the army? And you Michal…what will you do?"

"I'll join too, of course," Michal replied, his eyes sparkling, "but I had to wait for you first, didn't I? They nearly took Miro off me."

"Who?" I was incredulous.

"The people in charge of this place. It was meant well. They wanted to give me a chance to join before it's too late. They'll stop recruiting soon; and here, they run a home for orphans."

"Miro? In an orphanage?" I could not bear to contemplate such a thought. "Michal, thank God you waited."

He hugged me and pressed his face to mine.

"Anna, I'd never, ever abandon him." We watched Miro stack the bricks with the utmost concentration. "I can't tell you how glad I am to have you back. We can go to Riccione together. I'll enlist and you'll see how different our life will become when I'm a regular soldier with a regular pay. And extra jobs besides…"

I felt the excitement ripple through his body, lift his voice. I leaned away from him to look into his face.

"But when will we go home?"

He shook his head, his happy expression undimmed.

"We will go home, Anna. In time. But while our army is needed here to help out the local people, I want to stay and be part of that and rebuild our lives at the same time."

He lowered himself onto the grass and lay flat on his back. He stretched out his hand to me.

"Come!"

I did not need persuading. I rested against him, feeling his warmth, his enthusiasm. I watched the sky shimmering between the dusty-green leaves on the branches hanging over us.

"Michal," I sighed, "I'm so happy, it's frightening."

He turned his head and kissed me.

"Don't be frightened. This is just the beginning, my love."

We lived at the camp near Forli for two days. Each family occupied a small tent, and though the tent cloth was not soundproof, it offered a semblance of privacy and marked out an area of personal space.

The administration block was a large brick building, with a kitchen next to it, where meals were given out at regular intervals to be taken away. There was a separate spacious hall for the use of the army, which was open to us, civilians, for special meetings and announcements. On Sundays, I was told, the hall became a chapel for the duration of the Holy Mass, conducted by the army chaplain for the congregation and the crowds gathered outside. To my regret, my two-day stay did not extend to Sunday.

The sanitation block was sheer delight. It had a row of shower cubicles on one side, and facing them, a row of large, flat ceramic basins. The whole area was kept clean with regular hosing down, brushing and mopping by women from the auxiliary services. I showered and washed my hair daily. I could wash Miro as often as it was necessary. I washed all our clothes and draped them over our tent to dry. It felt good to sort out all our little personal things before our next journey.

There was a shop that sold all the basic requirements for our simple existence. With the liras given to me by the English ladies, I could buy soap, toothpaste, washing powder, shampoo, needles and thread. I also treated myself to a pair of scissors. I felt like a lottery winner.

Next to the shop, there was a room with clothing run by the Red Cross. We were entitled to one garment per person and one pair of shoes. All the best things had gone. The damaged clothes that had been left behind made my choice a difficult one. The two uniformed women helped me to rummage through the carton boxes, marked separately Men, Women, Children. They too were disappointed with the leftovers and promised to keep something back for me when the new consignment of clothing arrived in the next few days.

"I won't be here that long," I said, sitting Miro down on the floor, to try a pair of sandals on his feet. They were girl's, a little loose, shiny blue with pearly buttons on the sides. I took them anyway.

One of the ladies pulled out a dress from underneath the jumbled pile.

"How about this?" she asked, willing to help.

The dress was dark brown with a print of tiny beige flowers. Rather dull, I thought, but would have been snapped up, I imagined, if it had not been for the holes underneath the armpits. I held it against me. It was long. I saw its potential straight away.

"I'll take it," I said, "I just need a piece of white fabric."

"Help yourself. Keep whatever you find." She left me to it.

Miro held onto the edge of the box, almost as tall as him, and looked inside as I moved the rags about. Something white caught my eye. I pulled it up. It was an old lace petticoat. It was torn and riddled with holes.

"May I keep this as well as the dress?" I asked.

The women smiled, and one of them replied, "Just make sure no one sees you taking off with these crown jewels."

Inside the men's box, the only attractive garment was a pair of corduroy trousers, deep blue, dotted at random with tiny white spots. There were gaping holes on the knees. Michal would laugh them off, but I took them anyway, my mind already buzzing with ideas.

I thanked the bemused ladies and felt myself walking on air as Miro held my hand and skipped beside me.

I found Michal sitting cross-legged by our tent, hand-sewing new sandals for me. The sight of him, the angle of his head in concentration, his tangible closeness so within my reach caused a burst of happiness within me. I rushed to him and threw my arms around him and kissed him again and again, all the while feeling a barely controllable fizzing inside me.

"Goodness! What's all this?" he pretended to be surprised. Then he laughed and returned my kisses.

"Nothing. I just missed you." I sat beside him with the bundle of rags.

"Anna, if these come out right, if you like them, then my career's made for me! Just imagine all the orders coming in! We'll be rich! Like kings!"

He made me laugh with his excitement.

"I'm already rich! Look what I've got!" I showed him my newly acquired possessions. He looked puzzled. Certainly unimpressed.

"What will you do with these rags?"

"Wash them, and then you'll see!"

I left Miro playing beside Michal, while I dealt with the washing. I shook out the wet, clean-smelling garments and spread them on our tent to dry in the sun, in readiness to pack for the next morning.

Michal finished making my sandals. He placed them at my feet.

"Here, try them on."

They were natural hessian, with peepholes for my big toes, ankle straps and neat wedges. I was astonished.

"Where did you learn to make shoes?" I put them on. They were a good fit. They made my feet look small and pretty.

311

"They look like real ones!"

"Of course they're real!" he laughed.

"Then how?"

He went inside the tent and after a while came out with small torn bits and pieces of leather and canvas, the colour of peat.

"What's that?"

"One of your sandals, remember? They used to be white. Lucky you didn't throw them away. I took one to bits to see how it was made. I found most of the things I needed in my bag of useful things. Good old Frau Lientz! I bless her every time. And the rest…" he tapped his head and spread his hands as if to say modesty prevented him from saying more.

"What other talents have you got hidden away?" I teased.

"Wait and see!" he replied with an air of mock mystery.

That night, when we were ready and packed for the journey the next day, when Miro was fast asleep on his mattress, when all the noises and murmurs from the hundreds of tents around us had died down, and only the chirping of some night birds could be heard in the stillness, we made love.

I was blinded for a moment by the glare from the yellow pavement as we climbed down from the lorry, twenty families such as ours, with small children and babies. Shielding my eyes and holding Miro firmly by the hand, I followed Michal, laden with our luggage to where the group had been directed to assemble.

We were parked on a promenade with palm trees rising from pools of shadows. Surrounding them were raised flowerbeds, which I imagined must have once been tended with loving care. Now, the brickwork was crumbling and the soil was covered in weeds. A line of massive pastel-coloured buildings, with hundreds of windows stretched along the sea road, as far as the eye could see.

This was Riccione. Riccione by the sea. I had never seen the sea. I held my breath as I caught sight of it in the gaps between the empty, unfinished houses, along the beach.

The sea shimmered with all the blues I had been promised, from indigo to azure, from peacock to cerulean. In repetitive motion it ran in our direction, in long, flat, white-fingered waves, then receded forming streaks of foam, like peaked meringues.

"Michal, the sea!" I whispered, excitement bubbling inside me. I picked up Miro and pointed it to him. "We'll go for a swim and play in the water all day!"

Two officers approached us from across the road, from the direction of the massive buildings, which, we later discovered, had been fashionable shops before the war, with apartments above them. Now they were being used by the American, the British, and the Polish military units for offices and officers' accommodation. There was a square nearby with a fountain in the middle and shade-providing lime trees, their beauty obscured by a congestion of army trucks and lorries.

The officers spoke to us in Polish. There was something infinitely reassuring in the sound of our own language being spoken aloud.

"Welcome to Riccione. Come. Follow us. We'll show you to your quarters."

They divided us into two groups. It soon transpired that the empty buildings overlooking the beach were not empty at all. Curious faces appeared over the window sills as we were led past the open front doorways. There were sounds of life inside, appetising cooking smells wafting from within, there were lines of washing attached to the outside walls. It was like something out of a dream in which strange things make sense till you wake up. This was not a dream. This was our reality.

"Here we are," our leader stopped when we reached a house not yet occupied. He stood on the doorstep and faced us. "My apologies it's not a five star hotel," his tentative smile was met with silence. "Believe me, we're doing everything we can. These buildings were planned for holiday accommodation. The war stopped everything. They were never finished…"

"How about some doors and windows?" somebody asked.

"They are on the way."

"What about night time?"

The officer raised a reassuring hand.

"Each building has its own guards. Day and night."

There was a murmur of discontent.

"We've also got night patrols close by on the promenade. It's not all bad news. We've got running water, toilets and showers on every floor. There's a kitchen on the ground floor. Meals will be cooked for you by our very own cooks. There's a small office, as well as a large dining room, which you can use for meetings and other social events."

The children, some in their mothers' arms, some having to stand still with the adults, began to get restless and made fidgety attempts to draw their parents' attention.

"Let's go inside," the officer suggested. "I'll show you to your rooms."

He led us into a rectangular spacious entrance hall, surrounded by doorless empty rooms. The floor was dusty bare concrete, the walls unplastered raw brick. A wide concrete staircase rose up to the upper floors.

Each family in turn was taken up to their allotted room. Ours was on the first floor, overlooking the beach and the sea. Its size was impressive. You could have held a dance on the floor space.

"Don't get too excited," the officer's tone was wry, "There'll be hundreds more refugees coming soon. We've got to find room for them all, somehow. And one more thing," he fingered the empty socket space by the door frame, "We'll issue candles later on."

He left and I let go of Miro's hand. Like a bird freed from its cage, Miro ran around in wide circles, his arms spread out, his head thrown back, his lips parted in joy.

This room, like the rooms downstairs, was in its raw state. There was a centimetre gap between the walls and the perimeter of the floor, exposed rafters lined the ceiling in rows, and a framed square hole was waiting to be glazed. Michal dumped our bags in the corner of the room where three mattresses had been laid out with folded army blankets, sheets and pillows. He danced towards me with exaggerated steps and throwing his arm around my waist he carried me off in a waltz around the room.

I began to laugh. Miro stopped being a bird and watched us, baffled, his fingers stuffed in his mouth.

We picked him up and sat him on the wide ledge of the paneless window, our arms protective around him, and comforting around each other. Below us was the beach, and beyond the breathtaking sea. I hugged Michal to me. He kissed me on the lips, on my forehead, on both my cheeks.

"Isn't this great!" he said. "This makes you feel as if things are really going to get better!" His face was bright from the whiteness off the beach. He turned towards the room. "The size of it!" he marvelled. "Never lived in a room this big! Just imagine Anna, if we stayed here for real, there's space for everything! Beds, a table, chairs, wardrobes!"

"And..." I added, laughing, "ten families besides. Before you get carried away with your grand designs, let's just sort out the door first."

In his bag of useful things Michal found a few nails. Frau Lientz had also given him a small hammer. Miro was reluctant to withdraw his head from Michal's sack of treasures, but then watched us with wide-eyed, all absorbing curiosity, as I held up one of the blankets and Michal nailed an edge of it above the open entrance to our room. Now our space was exclusively our own.

Soon, Michal was helping other men from the adjoining rooms to do the same, while the women took their children for a wash before our late lunch.

I waited my turn on the landing with another woman, who had a girl of about four and a baby in her arms. I was glad Miro was out of nappies.

I tickled the baby's cheek and he turned his round eyes at me and his dribbly mouth formed an instant smile. He had one tooth showing through the lower gums.

"How do you cope with two?" I asked the woman.

The woman stroked her little girl's head.

"They are good children. Had to be where we were. They'd have been taken away if they misbehaved. Halinka knew that from the beginning."

Halinka looked up at us with large mournful eyes and clung to her mother's thigh.

I lowered myself to her level.

"We'll have fun here," I promised. "We'll play on the beach. We'll swim in the sea. Miro and you can be friends."

Miro, taking instant cue from me, stroked her arm, as he used to stroke the chicks and the lambs. Halinka studied us intensely, her expression fixed, then she hid her face in the folds of her mother's skirt. Miro patted her on the back.

Downstairs, in the dining room, two long tables had been set out with places for sixteen adults and some of the older children, like Miro. There were also eight babies, now wide awake and making themselves heard. It was noisy. It was jolly. It was like a big feast day with all the family gathered together.

The soldier cooks produced a three course meal with oranges and tangerines for dessert. The vegetable soup with bread was filling enough. This was followed by a salad made up of lettuce, ripe sweet tomatoes, olives and cubed cheese and served with pasta in tomato sauce. Miro's discovered novelty of sucking in long strings of spaghetti left him with red spatters around his mouth and down his front. The oranges and tangerines were juicy and sweet. I could have eaten a crateful of them. My only experience of such delights at home had been the occasional treat at Christmas.

After lunch there was one thing I simply had to do, and that was to wet my feet in the sea. Michal was just as keen. We fetched the towels and swinging Miro by his arms we ran with him across the beach. It was totally deserted in the intense heat of mid-afternoon. Even the breeze was like the breath from a hot oven.

We kicked off our clogs, slipped off Miro's pearly blue shoes and stood on the edge of the lapping, cooling water.

"He needs a hat," I said, pulling out a square piece of white rag from my pocket. I tied each of the corners into a knot and shaped it to fit on Miro's head. He did not object. He was too absorbed picking up the pebbles and the shells.

"First item on my list of things to buy when we get rich, Anna," Michal promised with a dreamy look.

We waded further into the water and enjoyed the coolness of the waves breaking up against our legs. I could not take my eyes off the sea. So much water, so self-contained, so dark in the distance, mysterious, yet here, at our feet, so transparent, so light and playful.

"In my wildest dreams," I said to Michal, "I had never imagined being by the sea. And here we are, and it's all ours and it's all free. Amazing, isn't it?"

He too had that far-away look in his eyes.

"It is… They'll never believe us at home. All the places we've been to, and all the things we've seen."

I felt the sun burning my shoulders through my dress.

"No wonder there's no one else about. They must think we're mad. We'll have to come back when it's cooler," I said, picking up Miro. He kicked and punched the air in protest, but we enticed him away from the water with his favourite game of swinging him high in the air.

Close to our building, Michal said, "Go ahead Anna, take him up for a nap, and I'll just ask around if anyone's seen or heard anything about our friends."

He came back twenty minutes later, when I was about to doze off next to Miro.

"I've found Lilli!" His words were like a splash of cold water. I was awake in an instant.

"And Franek?"

"No. He's in the army. Lilli's on her own with Stefan. Well, not on her own. Go and see for yourself. Five houses down from ours."

I counted five houses down and found a woman sitting on the doorstep, in the shade, with a baby asleep in her arms. I asked her about Franek and Lilli.

"Yes, I know Franek Dobosz. They're in the room next to ours."

She got up and beckoned to follow her upstairs. The rooms around the landing had screens for doors like ours – old curtains, sheets, blankets – behind which sounds of voices suggested more than just a few people.

"Lilli!" the woman called through the blanket screen, "you've got a visitor!" She walked away and the noise died down for a moment, then the hubbub resumed, the screen was pulled back and Lilli stood before me. Her eyes smiled above the gauze scarf that covered her face and we fell in each other arms and hugged each other and laughed softly, aware of a listening audience behind the screen.

"Anna! We feared we'd lost you!" she whispered in my ear in German. I could feel her bony thinness through her clothes.

"Come inside," she invited, "see how we live."

She held back the army blanket, but I did not step inside. There was no floor space to stand on, except for the narrow pathways running between the mattresses that were spread across the room, wall to wall. People were sitting or lying down on them, most of the children asleep in the oppressive heat. I counted six family groups, with only two men among them, soldiers on leave.

"We can talk outside," I suggested.

Lilli looked over her shoulder to a mattress by the wall, where Stefan was sleeping, his pale hair like a patch of sunlight on the pillow.

"Yes. He'll be asleep for a while yet."

Outside, we sat down on the sand, in the shade of the house, from where we could see the promenade, and the town buildings beyond, with not a single sign of life anywhere.

"Lilli, how do you cope with all this?" I asked her in German. Here, out of earshot, we did not have to whisper.

"It's not going to be for long," she answered brightly. "The men have all joined the army. It's mainly the women and their children now, and the odd visiting man." I knew she was smiling by the almond shape of her eyes. "Franek's so happy, Anna. He's driving lorries. He's their mechanic. He does what he likes doing best. Michal must enlist with him. In the same company!"

"When shall we see him?" I asked.

"Most probably tonight. Though nothing's ever certain. Depends if he gets back to the base before nightfall."

"And the others? Where are they all?"

"They are all fine! They've all joined the army. Bazylka and Tomasz work at the hospital nearby, but with their changing timetables and night duties, we don't see them that often. But Ludwik and Maryla come over most evenings. They work in one of the administration blocks further along the promenade."

"And Bruno? Dorota?"

"They're at a different camp altogether. They've gone with the people they knew from my father's farm."

My curiosity was satisfied, now that I could picture them all in certain, definite situations, but that did not temper my acute impatience to see them all again that night.

"Tell me about yourself," Lilli said, "I want to know everything. It felt as if you had been gone for months!"

"I know," I sighed, "it felt like that for me too."

I described my hospital stay in Udine and all the people I had met there and during my search for Michal and Miro. We talked for a long time, and when I checked my watch, we agreed to get back to our children and to meet on the beach later in the evening.

It was peaceful in our empty, darkened room. I took off my dress, laid it flat on the floor and lay down on the mattress next to Michal and Miro. Before long, like them, I was fast asleep.

When I opened my eyes Michal was propped up on his elbow and looking down at me.

"I didn't mean to wake you," he spoke softly.

"You didn't, it's the heat." I wiped the sweat off my face. "We could do with a good downpour. To clear the air."

"Don't speak too soon. We need some doors and some windows first. Anyway… I've been thinking… I'll enlist tomorrow, with or without Franek. The sooner I do it the better for us, Anna. You'll be all right, won't you?" His concern craved reassurance.

Yet again, separation. My whole being resented it, refused it, resisted.

"I'll be all right," I said, "I won't be alone. I've got Lilli and this house full of people."

"And there'll be more," Michal added with a small smile of relief. "You'll have so many lodgers you won't know what to do!"

He sat up and pulled over his bag. He dug his hand deep, right down to the bottom and brought out the handgun.

I recoiled, leaning back on my elbows.

"Don't be silly, Anna, it's for your own safety, while I'm away."

"What's the point, when it's not loaded?" I tried obvious logic.

"Nobody knows that. Keep it under your pillow at night. As a deterrent. Just till the others arrive. All those holes everywhere, no windows, no doors… I hate leaving you like this…"

"There's a guard downstairs," I reminded him.

"Please Anna, just take it," he insisted.

The idea was crazy, but to refuse was to add to his concern. I took the gun from him, this heavy, metal object that I could hardly bear to touch, and I hid it inside my bag.

"You will get it out at night, won't you? For Miro's sake?"

"Oh Michal! You're a tyrant! This is blackmail!"

In response, he drew me to him and kissed me all over my face.

CHAPTER 32

There was no queue for the showers in the late afternoon. The only sounds of life on our floor were soft murmurs behind the drab screens hung over the door frames. The cold water took my breath away. I felt energised, glowing. While Michal washed Miro, I washed our clothes, rinsed out the sweat and the grime and spread them out on the wide windowsill to dry.

Refreshed and changed, we went for a stroll on the promenade before the evening meal. Our recently recovered freedom was still a novelty. I found it strange not having to report our every move to anyone.

It was peaceful on the promenade. There was hardly anyone about except for a few keen sun-bathers striding towards the beach with towels rolled under their arms. Americans and their girls.

A light breeze was ruffling the crowns of the palm trees, whose long shadows made a regular pattern of stripes across the yellow pavement. The shops on the sea-facing front were shuttered, most of them with that appearance of having been closed down for some time, their faded peeling signs a nostalgic reminder of better times. *La Bella Donna. Valentino. Spirito di Gioventu. Bambini-Angelini.*

There was just one open shop. It seemed to sell most things; clothes, linen, towels, fabrics, haberdashery. The sheets of tissue paper thrown over the items on display and intended to shield them from the sun, were torn, yellowed and crumpled. The plaster-cast mannequin with its ill-fitting shoes and missing finger tips wore a dress in such dull colours, that I could not imagine anyone being tempted to buy it.

We walked towards the square, swinging Miro in the air, much to his delight and shouts for more.

The emptiness around the sunlit fountain was deceptive. In the shade of the linden trees that surrounded the square, the locals were going about their business. Here all the shops were open: the butcher; the grocer; the baker; the vegetable shop with its display of ripe red tomatoes, oranges and lemons; the newspaper and tobacco kiosk. The women, all dressed in black, gave us long unabashed looks. Suddenly, I felt conspicuous in my tale-tell clogs and fraying, patched-up clothes.

"I feel like a freak here," I said to Michal.

"Me too. Let's go!"

Two old men sitting at a table in an open café waved to us and laughed. I gave them a timid, uncertain smile, feeling my cheeks burning. We walked briskly across the deserted fountain square back to the promenade. A man, selling oranges and freshly squeezed juice off his little push-cart, said something to us and smiled to Miro.

"I've got a few liras," I said to Michal, "from the English ladies."

We bought three oranges and sat on the steps leading to the beach. I peeled and divided one orange between us. It was sweet and juicy. Miro wanted more. I peeled the second orange. When that was eaten Miro put his sticky hand inside Michal's pocket and brought out the third orange.

"More," he pleaded, his mouth wet in anticipation.

"We'll save this one for later," I said.

His face puckered and his eyes filled with tears. His grief was immediate and intense.

"I can't stand this," Michal said. "Give him what he wants. He needs it."

When the third orange was gone and Miro had checked all our pockets and was satisfied we had nothing else hidden, he agreed to be led to the edge of the water, where I washed his sticky hands. His mind was already on the sea-shells at his feet. Here, I could have remained for hours to watch the constant movement of the waves, to listen to the crashing sounds of the sea-force against the rocks, to follow the graceful flight of the sea-gulls and watch them swoop down and rest for brief moments on the wavy surface of the water.

"Isn't all this beautiful?" I could not help stating the obvious.

But Michal was quiet, his gaze distant, his manner unresponsive.

"What's wrong?" I asked.

He kicked a pebble.

"I'm just a beggar. That's what's wrong. A beggar! Having to rely on the charity of strangers to treat my own child!"

His anger reawakened my anxiety.

"Michal…" I spoke as if to an upset child, "it wasn't charity. It was kindness. From the heart."

"Charity. Kindness. It's all the same. I'm a pauper, Anna. Nothing noble about that!"

"We're not paupers," I chided him gently, appeasing my own disquiet. "Just look at Miro."

Miro was a seagull. With his upturned face and out-stretched arms he ran around the sand emulating the movements of the birds in the sky.

"We are not paupers," I repeated with some emphasis. "Many would envy us what we've got."

"That is why, Anna, I want better things for him. Not charity from strangers."

He kicked another pebble, before walking off ahead of me.

His mood changed in an instant when he saw Franek. He and Lilli had been waiting for us on the beach after the evening meal, as pre-arranged. The beach was bathed in an orange glow from the sun close to the horizon. Michal quickened his pace; he welcomed his friend with a strong bear hug, with a prolonged handshake, with an unrestrained outburst of laughter.

Franek swept me into his arms and held me close to his tall, thin frame.

"So good to see you Anna! It wasn't a joke, I tell you, losing you on the way like that!"

His hair had been trimmed, his skin was shiny brown, the uniform, though baggy, gave him an air of authority, a hint of importance. I had never seen him looking so handsome before. Lilli's sparkling eyes followed his every move.

Excitement made us talk all at once. Miro and Stefan watched us, puzzled, before turning their attention to collecting pebbles and shells with considered selectivity.

"Michal, you're coming with me tomorrow," Franek declared, when we settled down on the sand.

"Try to stop me," Michal laughed, his previous mood forgotten.

"We'll be driving lorries together!"

Michal laughed again.

"Franek, the nearest I've been to a car was when I used to wash the squire's Polski Fiat at the manor!"

"Manor! Shmanor!" Franek gave a dismissive wave. "I'll teach you to drive in no time! Nothing to it! We'll be partners Michal! And afterwards…who knows? Our own garage…customers… thousands of them."

His enthusiasm was infectious. Lilli and I giggled.

"You sound as if you're planning to stay here for ever!" I said.

His dark eyes flashed orange in the setting sun.

"It wouldn't be such a bad idea! Lovely place. Close to the sea. Great climate. I reckon I could make a good living here. Don't you agree?" He slapped Michal's shoulder. We laughed. "It's all possible, you know," he insisted, then turned to Lilli. "Don't worry. It's just a thought. My head's full of them. What I really want is to go home and take you and Stefan with me."

Lilli's face was soft amber, the scar hardly visible.

"I think," she said, "we can make a home wherever we go."

Ludwik and Maryla joined us later. They stood out as they walked across the sand, their khaki uniforms catching the sky's peachy light, their groomed appearance signalling their newly acquired status. I felt I was watching strangers, but moments later, in their warm, strong embraces, I knew they were my very own old friends.

Ludwik's regiment had been assigned to a rebuilding programme.

"There's work for a hundred years!" he was saying, after we had sat down again. His face was radiant with enthusiasm and his hands, out of habit, were smoothing down his severely trimmed curls. "With American aid we've already made a good start. Plans for new housing estates have been approved. Old historic buildings, they insist, will be carefully restored. Roads and railways too need immediate attention. Everything has become a priority!"

While Michal and Franek showered him with questions, Maryla told us about her work. Her job was to help out with general clerical demands in an office at the Polish headquarters.

"Sounds so important!" I exclaimed in genuine awe. "After the cows and the pigs!"

She responded with a light-hearted laugh.

"Not at all, Anna. I only do what I'm told to do. Girl Friday to everyone. Remember Robinson Crusoe?" In our previous life she would often entertain me with stories from books she had read. I watched her with the tiniest tinge of envy. She looked so glamorous. Her hair had been combed back, rolled on a special rubber-covered wire and formed into a chignon on the nape of her neck.

"You look like a film star!" I said.

She smiled with pleasure at the same time flicking her hand dismissively.

"You can look like that too. Let me show you."

Out of her army-green shoulder bag she took out one of those amazingly versatile wires and a comb. "I'll show you how it's done. What about you Lilli?"

Lilli shook her head then smoothed her pale tresses down the sides of her face.

"I've already got the best style for me. This one."

My wiry, unruly hair proved something of a challenge. Maryla did her best to harness the tangles into a neat knot, but the escaped tendrils around my face bore no resemblance to the simple elegance of her style.

"There," she said at last, her smile apologetic, "trust me, with a little practice…"

"It's great!" I assured her, fingering the knot at the back of my head. "It's just great Maryla, to see you again!" I got up, feeling a wild urge to do handstands and cartwheels. "Let's go, let's dip our feet in the sea!"

We ran across the wet sand, like three small girls holding hands, Lilli's dress and mine billowing in the breeze. Miro and Stefan chased after us, anxious not to miss out on the fun. We stopped at the edge of the water and watched the long-fingered waves curl around our ankles. Maryla wanted to know about my stay in hospital. I gave her a brief account of that and of my search for Michal and Miro.

"It was as if you had all disappeared into thin air," I said, reliving the abject desolation. "As if I were the only one left behind."

Maryla gave me a sisterly hug and it felt like the old times, from all the years we had worked and lived together.

"Let's think about happy times," she said. "Let's think about the future. I dream of going back to finish my studies. I'll be like their grandma when I join the new students. So much time wasted! All those stolen years! What about you, Lilli?"

Lilli flicked back her long hair, at ease with her scarred cheek in our company.

"I loved my work with the nuns," she said, "I too want to do a proper course. But first, I need to spend some time with Stefan. Make up for lost time."

Clouds began to gather on the horizon and rise like a range of black mountains into the lilac sky.

"Looks like a storm's coming our way," Maryla said.

We hurried back to the boys, Miro and Stefan running ahead. All around us people were shaking out their blankets and towels and retreating in haste to their empty abodes.

"Come back with us!" Michal invited everyone.

"Better not," Ludwik glanced at his watch and at the rapidly changing sky. "We'll get drenched if we don't make a run for it!"

"Michal! Six tomorrow morning! Sharp!" Franek called out as we all dispersed.

It was dark in our building, with just a few candles showing the way through the entrance hall and up the staircase, but the house was alive with sounds; small clear voices, whispers, shuffling feet, flushing toilets, showers in use.

Our unplastered, unpainted room was like a cave with its gaping square hole in the wall. There was the faintest glow around its wooden frame picked up from the whiteness of the sand below. Michal lit a candle and placed it nearby on the concrete floor.

"Why is it dark?" Miro asked, crouching at a safe distance from the naked flame.

"Because it's bedtime." I undressed him and tucked him under a sheet on the mattress, together with his Ba-ba. He was fast asleep when the first lightning tore through the thundering sky.

It sounded like a waterfall, the rain outside our window. In the flashes of lightning we could see it pouring inside and the puddle rapidly expanding in our direction.

"I'll get a brush from downstairs," Michal cried, jumping up from our mattress.

There were sounds all over the house; running feet, thuds, urgent voices. I was gripped with anxiety. We had nothing to build a barrier with against the water advancing along our floor.

In the dark I rummaged through our bags. Just by the feel of the worn, frayed material, I knew which were Michal's oldest trousers and my worst skirt. I could not bear the thought of such waste, but at that moment the most important thing was to keep the water away from us.

Michal came back, desperation rising in his voice.

"They've got no spare brushes! They're all being used downstairs. The floor's like a lake!"

We got down on our hands and knees and with our rags we pushed the water back, mopped up and wrung it out over the windowsill, as more water came in and soaked us to the skin. After the heat of the day the water was icy cold and even though I moved fast I was soon chilled through and could not stop my teeth chattering.

This torment went on and on until I could no longer hold back my grief.

"Michal, if we don't drown we'll surely freeze to death!" My tears felt like streams of hot water on my face.

"Not much longer, Anna. It's going!" Michal shouted through the hissing rain, through the crashing of the waves on the beach, through the thunder that made the building shake.

Then, when my endurance had been exhausted to its last drop, when I felt near to collapse with exertion, the rain suddenly stopped, as if cut off with a knife. We dragged ourselves up to the windowsill, our saturated clothes weighing us down, and looked out. The black boiling mass of the sea was simmering down, the storm clouds in constantly changing silver-edged formations, were rushing south, out of view, leaving behind a clear sky with stars and a bright moon. The reflections from the wet sand were like additional light filtering through into our room, giving objects shape and form, our few possessions and a bundle on the mattress that was Miro. Fast asleep.

"I've got to be ready at six," Michal said, stripping off his wet clothes and diving under cover. I did the same, my chattering teeth making my jaw ache, my whole body gripped by a shaking fit.

We huddled together, rubbing each other all over, our breath building up a cushion of insulation around us. Slowly my hands and my feet regained their feeling and I found myself drifting into blissful warmth against the curve of Michal's body.

"I just want a quiet normal life," I sighed.

Michal kissed me on the back of my neck and tightened his arms around me.

"It'll come, I promise."

There was nothing normal about the sight on the beach the next morning. It was strewn with dead birds. The sea had receded and lay sparkling under the opal sky, as if disclaiming any part in this disaster.

"What a waste! They had nowhere to hide, poor things!" Michal said.

We watched Franek make his way towards our building, his long legs, like a stork's, stepping gingerly over carcasses of seagulls, magpies, crows, sparrows and birds I did not recognise, yellow, speckled and bronze We waved to him then Michal kissed me goodbye once more and was gone. I waited to see him come out of the building and join his friend. They were like schoolboys, skipping over obstacles, their arms raised, a faint echo of laughter trailing behind them. Michal, I knew, was driven by his dreams. I turned my back on the death on the beach. I too had dreams of my own.

Miro began to stir. It was time for me to get off my musty clothes. My only garment that was clean and dry, was the one I kept for best, the navy floral dress that had once belonged to Umtraut. I made myself think of a plan for the morning's work. There was that brown dress from the Red Cross to alter; there were those navy cord trousers with holes on the knees to be made into shorts for Miro, and I looked forward to having Lilli as my companion.

All the water had been swept outside on the ground floor and the concrete was drying out fast, when we came down to breakfast. Later, people came out onto the strip of sand closest to the buildings and watched the soldiers with their refuse truck drive along the beach and pick up the dead birds.

I got together with Lilli and we found a sheltered spot close to my building, where it was less crowded. Miro and Stefan played at our feet, but the dead birds proved to be an irresistible attraction to them and our constant reminders to stay away were met with evasive glances and mischievous grins.

Lilli too had brought her sewing and knitting with her. She had a piece of cloth, crispy new cotton, that her mother had bought her, deep blue with tiny red and white flowers.

"Sunday best," I said, feeling the cloth between my fingers.

"A summer skirt, I thought," Lilli said, standing up and holding the length against her side from the waist down, "will take the stares away from my face."

"Oh Lilli, don't say that!" I told her, how we used to envy her, her good looks, her fresh clean clothes, how we used to cringe in our smelly rags at the sight of her on Holtzmann's farm.

"And how things have changed…" her smile was wistful. "Now, I'm like something out of a freak show."

"Franek doesn't think so! None of us do! Lilli, you're among friends!" I said with passion. She shook her head, her silky hair sliding back to expose her scar.

"Some things never go away… Every day when I look in the mirror…"

A shadow fell upon us. We looked up shielding our eyes against the sun. A woman was standing over us. Her hair was tied back with a shoe lace and she had a small child propped on her hip.

"You should be ashamed of yourselves, girls, speaking that hateful language! Is Polish not good enough for you?"

I was so taken aback by the aggression in her tone I did not know what to say. Lilli pushed her hair behind her ears and lifted her scarred face. The woman gasped, her frown dissolving into a sheepish expression.

"I'm working hard on it, believe me," Lilli said politely.

The woman walked away and I held my breath expecting Lilli to be upset, but when she turned round, a small smile hovered on her lips.

"They'd do well to employ me as a night guard," she said.

We worked all morning hand sewing our garments, watching Miro and Stefan, who could not resist the temptation to venture out further and further on the beach, now that it had been cleared of dead birds. The shadow around the building shrank at midday and we were forced to seek refuge from the scorching sun in the cool semi-darkness of my room.

Miro and Stefan threw themselves with reckless abandon onto the floor space and became kites one minute, changing to trains, to galloping horses, the next.

I tried on my newly altered dress. I had repaired the holes underneath the arms with the strip I had cut off the overlong hemline, and I had made a collar and cuffs out of the torn petticoat.

"Mmm...very Sunday best!" Lilli declared. "Now all we need is a grand place to go to."

"The Grand Hotel!" I mimed her mood and we both laughed.

She tried on her blue cotton skirt, with tiny red and white flowers. It had soft even pleats and a neat waistband.

"Lovely work," I said.

Lilli shrugged, nevertheless smiling with pleasure.

"It's just practice. Anyone can do it, as you know."

Was it practice, I wondered, practised acting that made her appear so normal, so even tempered, after everything she had suffered? It was comforting to believe that she had recovered, but to what extent? Questions remained in my mind. How did she cope with the memories, with the loss, with the constant reminder that was her little son? And what about Franek? Was she truly in love with him? After Stefan?

We put Miro and Stefan to bed after lunch. They liked it lying down next to each other on the big mattress on the concrete floor. Before long, the gentle breeze and the monotonous murmur of the sea had the desired effect on them.

While they slept, Lilli and I sat on the wide window ledge sideways, facing each other with our legs crossed, our backs resting against the frames.

"I like pretending this is a holiday," Lilli said, looking towards the sea, her hair gathered back behind her ears, her left cheek exposed, the scar raised in the shape of P. I was glad that she was completely at ease with me. "Just imagine, Anna, before the war this was the place only for the rich. They paid big money to spend their summers here. Now, here we are, ordinary peasants, having it all for free." Her smile was brief, wry.

"I'd change places with them any time," I laughed, "and travel in style. Look how we got here."

Her expression clouded over, her gaze became distant and I had a feeling her thoughts went back to those other awful times.

"For a long time, Lilli," I said softly, "no one knew if you were even alive."

She remained thoughtful and I began to regret my impetuous words, but when she spoke there was no rancour in her tone.

"There are things in your life, you never forget. I've cried such a lot, Anna, I'm not going to cry now." She formed her lips into a smile to prove her point, then taking a deep breath she began, "The day they killed Stefan, my mother and father collected me from the police station and took me straight away to Sankt Veit, to my uncle's house. The burn on my cheek was excruciating, but worse than that was the pain inside me. I wanted to die. I wanted to be with Stefan. My uncle took one look at me and drove me to the nuns. They were wonderful. They gave me a room in one of their cells, but treated me like one of their patients, with daily dressings and medication. Most days, as I waited for my burn to heal and my hair to grow, I lay on the bed and stared at the ceiling. Sometimes I'd wander around their little enclosed garden and stare at the ground." A tear rolled down Lilli's scarred cheek. "I stared at things, but I didn't see them. All I saw was Stefan's broken body at my feet. That image stayed with me day and night, every minute, every second. There was no escape from it, except in death…"

"And the baby? Did you not think about the baby?" I whispered.

She shook her head.

"I know, it's shocking, but I couldn't think of anything else but how to end my torment. Look!" She undid the wide leather watch strap and showed me her wrist. There was a white scar across it.

"What's that?" I did not understand.

"I cut my wrist with a razor blade."

This indeed shocked me.

"I was saved by Sister Clotilda," Lilli continued. "She was a psychiatric nurse. The doctor wanted me transferred to a mental institution, but she insisted I stayed with her, under her supervision, pleading my pregnancy against the usual, accepted treatment."

"And what was the usual treatment?"

"Electric shocks and sedatives."

I had no idea what she was saying.

"They attach electric wires to the patient's head," Lilli explained, "and switch on the electric current for a few seconds. It makes the body twitch and convulse with the shock."

"But that's horrific!" I cried.

"It's supposed to reset the brain to make it forget the things that have caused your depression in the first place."

"And does it?" I found that hard to believe.

"I don't know. I was spared all that. Thanks to Sister Clotilda. She asked for a bed in her room for me. The only medication she gave me were some herbal tablets to make me sleep better. She gave me a nurse's white overall and a silk scarf to cover my head. She made me come to work with her as her helper. I didn't want to go at first, I begged her to leave me alone, but she was adamant, a bit like my headmistress at school. She made me agree to come just for one day. And I did." Lilli took a deep breath, "Anna, I did not need electric shocks! What I saw there was worse than that! Soldiers without legs, without arms, without hands, soldiers screaming with terror at imagined falling bombs, old men clinging to my hand, calling me their angel, begging me to take them to their mother. I was so overwhelmed by it all, somehow, in a strange way, seeing all that suffering around me, took the edge off my own pain. I asked Sister Clotilda at the end of that day, how did she cope with it all? She said she had to. She said she was there for the patients, not for herself. I offered to come with her every day. But she said no. She said I'd already had a fair share of troubles. She said it was time for happiness in my life. Happiness? I almost laughed in her face. But the next day she made me go with Sister Benedicta. To the maternity hospital." Lilli's face broke into a huge smile. "Anna, when I saw the babies, the newly born babies, I knew straight away that this was what I wanted to do. Looking after babies and their mothers. It was a turning point. I realised suddenly, and felt dreadfully guilty about it, that all the while when I'd been wallowing in my grief, my baby was growing all by itself, almost forgotten." She cast a glance in Stefan's direction, where he was sleeping with Miro. "I tried very hard, believe me, to make up for it afterwards. The nuns were good to me. They helped in every way they could. And I enjoyed working for them. I want to do a proper nursing course, when we are out of here, when we start living normally again."

I was glad to hear she was ready to rebuild her life, but I did not want to disillusion her that back at home, further education was not affordable for village folk like us.

As if reading my thoughts, Lilli added, "It was Franek's idea. He reckons he can support us till I qualify."

I gave her hand a gentle squeeze.

"Tell me about Franek."

Her eyes lit up.

"He's a treasure. Before him my life was finished. Then one day, when he was on loan at our farm, and I was at home on my day off, he surprised me alone in the barn. He grabbed hold of my hand and led me to the darkest corner. Before I recovered enough to protest, he began to talk fast. 'Lilli,' he said, 'there's no time to waste, so I'll be brief. I love you. I've loved you for a long time. Tell me, is there any chance for me? Think about it and let me know.' I was stunned. Before I opened my mouth to say anything, he was gone."

"And?" This was such exciting stuff!

She gave me a self-conscious smile.

"All that week I couldn't think of anything else. When I saw him again, I saw him in a different light. I liked him. We met in secret whenever we could. He won me over. Completely. He's so kind to my child…" She paused before adding, "We talk about Stefan. He was fond of him too."

I felt a twinge. A familiar twinge, whenever my thoughts turned to Stefan.

In the late afternoon, before the evening meal, we visited the only open shop on the promenade. Neither of us had much money, but the purchase of one cotton reel would buy us the chance to look around.

Miro and Stefan, regenerated by their afternoon sleep, ran about jumping high, playing a game of 'pink slabs only' avoiding the yellow ones.

It was a great feeling to be able to walk inside the shop as a free person and to look around without the fear of Spitz or Blitz lurking in the backroom, ready to pounce on you. We looked at the few dresses, blouses and skirts hanging on the rack, and from the woman's dour expression we guessed that she knew we could not afford to buy anything. Lilli bought the white thread and we left the shop.

Our attention was caught by two young women getting out of a jeep. My heart contracted with envy at the sight of them. The officer behind the steering wheel flashed them a white smile before driving off. They walked towards us giggling, their arms linked, their flowery flowing dresses swishing around their feet that looked pretty in high-wedged sandals. They wore lipstick and their hair was swept up from the sides and curled on the top of their heads. A haze of scent trailed behind them as they walked past us into the shop.

"I wish I looked like them!" I sighed.

"No you don't!" Lilli laughed. "Don't you know who they are?" She whispered in my ear. I had never seen a prostitute.

"But how do you know?" I was baffled.

"I've seen enough of them at the hotel, where I worked. I can tell them a mile away." Lilli's lip curled knowingly.

"But they are so beautiful! They look like grand ladies!"

Lilli laughed again.

"They've got to be, otherwise no one would want them!"

We led Miro and Stefan to the beach and watched them play from where we sat on a low wall.

"That reminds me," I said to Lilli, "there's no privacy for anyone in our rooms. What do people do when the men come home to visit?"

Lilli shrugged and chuckled.

"We're all in the same boat. We've just got to behave. Or go behind the rocks in the middle of the night. Make the most of your empty room, Anna, before you get lodgers."

"I wish! It takes two to tango!" I joked.

A new transport of people was expected to arrive soon. When we returned from the beach, there was an open truck, laden with mattresses, parked outside my building.

"When are they coming?" I asked one of the soldiers unloading the truck.

"Tonight or tomorrow morning."

In my room mattresses had been already laid down in every corner of the bare concrete floor.

"Pity," I said to Lilli, "I was going to ask you to stay with me tonight."

I wish I had. When it got to eleven o'clock and all the voices and noises in the house and on the beach had died down, and the only sounds around me were Miro's rhythmic breathing and the murmur of the sea beyond the hole in the wall, it became clear no one would be arriving that night.

I was overcome with loneliness. Somehow, watching the distant starry night from my mattress made Michal's absence all the more acute. I tried to imagine his travels with Franek on his first day as a soldier, but my mind kept filling up with images of destroyed buildings, eroded roads, crowded camps, sick children, lorries packed with people, dust and heat and hospitals. Somewhere, in all that chaos, were Michal and Franek.

I slipped my hand under the pillow. Michal's pistol was there, as he had insisted. I hated the damned thing. Why did he have to be so adamant! I checked its hard metal shape and withdrew my fingers and turned my thoughts to my friends.

Bazylka and Maryla had come to see me and Lilli after the evening meal. The setting had felt unreal with its natural beauty of the sea on one side and the outlines of towers and spires rising above the town and lit up by the apricot evening sun. So different from the barns and the stables and the perpetual stench that had been our home for five years. They looked smart in their uniforms. Bazylka's titian hair and her green eyes turned people's heads. She could not stop talking about her work at the hospital. And about Tomasz. I wanted to believe it was like old times, girls having a chat and a laugh together, but I knew, I felt we all knew, that it had been the common adversity that had held us together in a strong bond. I could not help feeling that it was now just a matter of time before our ordinary lives, the normal lives we had dreamed of and desired, would send us all, inevitably, on our separate ways.

I made myself think of happy things. Michal's return. His raised cheeks in a smile, his shining eyes, as he made plans for the future, of somewhere decent for us to live, to marry, to provide Miro with better things.

That night I dreamed we were in a strange town. I was meant to meet up with Michal on the steps of the town hall, an imposing building with huge portals, but Michal was not there. I held Miro in my arms and I searched for Michal in street after street, but every direction I tried took me further away from the town centre, until I found myself on high ground looking down on hundreds of rooftops, towers and spires.

And suddenly, he was back shining a torch into my face.

"Michal, what are you doing!" I shouted.

The torch wavered, and now I was truly awake. The shape outlined against the grey light in the hole in the wall was not Michal.

CHAPTER 33

My hand slid automatically under the pillow and I grabbed the revolver. I pointed it at the stranger in my room. I felt a surge of anger, so strong, it obliterated my fear.

"Leave us alone! Or I'll shoot!" I shouted in German.

He made a dash for the door and disappeared behind the draped blanket.

"Thief! Thief!" I shouted after him. I ran onto the landing and shouted again, "Thief in our house!"

My voice sent echoes through the vast spaces of the building and chased his thudding feet down the concrete stairs. I heard a scuffle below and the guard's cry, "I've got him! I've got the bastard!"

People ran out of their rooms on my floor and from further up, and rushed with me downstairs. There were five men in the house that night. Shining their torches at the intruder they led him inside the office.

"Alert the patrol," the guard said to one of the men, as he held the thief's hands behind his back. The thief was just a boy, perhaps fifteen. He had tangled matted hair, a dirty face and tatty clothes. He kept his eyes down.

The guard scolded him in Italian, then releasing his grip, rapped on the table. The boy began to empty his pockets, as we looked on in a tight circle. A watch, a cigarette lighter, a metal cigarette holder, two boxes of cigarettes, socks.

"How did he get past you?" someone asked the guard.

"Obviously not past me!" the guard retaliated with some annoyance. "It's no great trick to sneak through a back window."

"It's a good job you woke up when you did," one of the men spoke to me.

I was suddenly aware of the gun still in my hand behind my back. Slowly, I slipped it inside the sleeve of my nightgown and held it with both my hands, out of sight. I found myself shaking. Now all I needed was for the boy to give away my secret. But he said nothing, just stared at the floor while the guard reprimanded him in a stern voice.

"It's a scandal!" the man standing next to me said. "The cheek of it! Coming to rob us! Us, who have nothing anyway!"

The two soldiers on patrol came in. They handcuffed the boy and led him away. The men began to disperse. I asked the guard, "What will happen to him now? Where are they taking him?"

"Where he belongs. In the nick." The guard's cigarette glowed red in the dark.

"What will they do to him?"

"What he deserves. A few days on bread and water and a good hiding. That'll teach him!"

Michal's beaten face flashed through my mind.

"He's just a boy," I said. "He's stupid. He didn't steal a fortune."

"We've not got a fortune to steal. Why didn't he go to those who have? Because we are easy pray. That's why. Don't waste any sympathy on him. A little punishment won't do him any harm. It'll make him think next time. It's only fair, isn't it?" The guard drew on his cigarette and exhaled. The smoke rose in puffs like miniature phantoms. He was right, there was no argument in the boy's favour, and yet I felt no joy at the justice done.

Miro was still fast asleep when I lay down beside him on the mattress. I pushed the revolver under my pillow and vowed to get rid of this weapon at the first opportunity as soon as Michal came back to us.

Before then a few changes took place. A new transport of people arrived the next morning. Four crowded lorries. We watched them, Lilli and I, and other groups of women, as we sat in the shade of our buildings, hand-sewing, knitting, mending old clothes, minding our children. We watched the new arrivals spilling out of lorries like an army of ants. There were very few men among them. Children clung to their mothers, babies woken from their sleep cried in protective, rocking arms.

As with our transport, they were met by Polish soldiers, divided into groups and led away to the buildings that were still not fully occupied. I left Miro with Lilli, and followed our new group up the concrete staircase amidst the burst of sounds and activity, reverberating throughout the building. At the entrance to my room, I held back the blanket draped over the doorway for the three women and their children allocated with me. The room filled up, became alive, busy; introductions followed and within minutes it felt as if we were already acquainted.

Lola was the thinnest person I had ever seen. Even her miniature baby Dorotka looked too heavy in her arms, making her mother appear as if she might snap in half at any time. It was a wonder her stick-like legs could hold up any weight at all. The only wide thing about her was the gap between her two front teeth. It gave her smile an impish look. Before liberation she had been a slave worker in a food factory, where stealing was punished by hanging.

Matylda had a two year old, called Filip, crinkly reddish hair and freckles on her arms and face. Like myself, she had been forced to work on a farm in Germany throughout the war.

Iza looked older than the rest of us. She and her husband had been rounded up by the Nazis in 1940 and sent to Germany to work in an ammunition factory near Dachau. Her two little girls, five and three, were called Alicya and Anetka. Iza's husband had died of typhoid a week after liberation. Her face was blotchy and her eyelids swollen from crying. All my own anxieties seemed petty now in the face of such suffering and such irony of fate. I racked my brains for words of comfort and I could not think of anything to say. I picked up her bags and I carried them to her corner of the room. She followed meekly with her two little girls gripping her hand as if they were welded to her. They sat down on their mattress in a tight group and the rest of us set about organising our life in this strange environment.

The serving of meals in two sittings, first and second floors in turn, was decided by the officer in charge of our building. He also suggested that representatives from each room, on each floor, organised rotas for the use of bathrooms and showers. As none of my room-mates relished the thought of this task, it had to be me who met the other three women on the landing by the shower room, to discuss washing arrangements on our floor. We also made out a rota for keeping the bathroom and the toilets clean. All I could hope for now was that this would work in practice and not become a source of aggravations.

Life fell into a pattern around the meals. We filled the times in between with the necessary, practical activities, with attention to our children, with walks on the promenade, with paddles in the sea. Our building was like a noisy school playground in the daytime hours, and as silent as a monastery at night, with just the murmur of the sea floating in through the window-shaped holes.

Freckled Matylda and Twiggy Lola never stopped talking and treated Lilli and me like life-long friends. Iza was withdrawn. All our efforts of enticing her into our group were regularly rejected.

"Take the girls and leave me alone!" was her standard, bristly reply, as she lay curled on her side with her face to the wall.

On the first day Alicya and Anetka, like two little daisies with their fly-away hair, would not be parted from their mother, but wedged themselves inside the crook of her bended knees and held onto her legs.

On the second day, they watched with interest from behind the safe barrier of their mother's hips, Miro and Filip, Matylda's little boy, build towers of bricks on the concrete floor. Shyly, Alicya ventured out. Then Anetka, trailing behind like her sister's shadow, holding onto her dress.

They knelt beside the boys, their eyes following their every move. I spilled our collection of sea-shells before them, and before long, Alicya began to talk to me, her finger tracing the ridges, the convolutions, the spiky bumps, the spiralling centres, as she explained to me her imagined reasons for their being.

In the evening that day the little girls followed us as far as the doorway and stood back against the folds of the drape. We trooped out, Lola with baby Dorotka in her arms, Stefan and Miro holding hands with their new friend Filip, Matylda, Lilli and I. The little girls' upturned faces and their solemn eyes tugged at my heart. I crouched down beside them.

"You can come with us too," I said. "You can play in the sand and your mummy can have a rest. Will you come?"

Anetka looked up at her sister and Alicya looked up at me. Then they both looked at the boys going down the stairs. They placed their hands in mine and I led them away, feeling like their saviour and at the same time like a traitor to their hapless mother who remained on the mattress, staring at the wall.

Michal returned on Saturday night, and a number of other men too, on their weekend leave. Iza's little girls sat at their mother's side and watched silently the men making a fuss of their children, Lola's Pavel cuddling their baby Dorotka, Matylda's Zenon swinging their little boy Filip high in the air, and Michal down on his knees building towers with Miro.

Michal looked smart in his uniform, his hair neatly cut, his brown arms shining like polished teak, his hands strong and capable. My heart swelled with pride and love for him and I longed to have him all to myself, but now was not the time, with a room full of people. He told me only briefly about his week, saving details for later.

After the evening meal the tables in the dining room were pushed back against the walls, making clear a big space on the concrete floor in the middle. One of the visiting soldiers came in with an accordion.

The first dance was a tango. Its enticing, passionate beat was irresistible, and soon the floor filled up with couples, their eyes shining, their bodies giving in to the rhythm, all troubles forgotten, for a short, enchanting while.

Iza came up to us where we stood with her little girls following behind, holding on to her skirt. Miro was beside himself jumping up and down to the rhythm of the music.

"I'm going up to our room," she said, "I'll take charge of all our children, for once. Bring Miro up to me and tell the others to do the same."

I was so surprised I was lost for words. She gave me a wan smile.

"Please let me do this Anna. Trust me. I'll watch them play, and when they're ready I'll put them to bed. This is no place for children. And you have fun, while you can."

We did have fun, Michal and I, Franek and Lilli and our new friends from our shared room. Tangos, waltzes, polkas, shimmies, we danced them all till my legs no longer felt as if they were my own, but attachments running on their own batteries.

"Shall we go outside to cool off?" Michal suggested at one point later in the evening. He was wiping sweat off his face and there were damp patches on his shirt.

"Yes, let's go!" I wanted nothing more than to be alone with him. At last!

The air outside was like warm velvet, the sky was dotted with stars. The white sand gave out enough light to guide us to a formation of rocks about a hundred metres away from the long row of beach huts, that stood silent and discreet, concealing dark secrets that night. We laughed as we ran past them holding hands and pulling each other playfully. We found a spot behind the rocks, level sandy ground, sheltered on all sides.

"Let's have a dip in the sea!" Michal sounded as excited as a child. He stripped off his uniform and folded it neatly on the ground.

He helped me unbutton my dress then we threw off our underwear and ran naked into the waves. The cold water took our breath away at first, but that did not stop us from splashing each other and fooling around. Then Michal caught me in his strong arms and held me so close I could hardly breathe. He kissed me, for a long time, and I felt heat return to our bodies, and even the water lapping around our feet could not quench the intense urgency within us.

We made love on top of my dress, with just the rocks for a screen around us, the murmur of the sea hushing our sounds and a million eyes above keeping watch over us.

Afterwards Michal teased me, holding me like a prisoner in his strong embrace against my impatience to put my clothes back on again.

"What if somebody catches us like this? Starkers?"

He laughed out loud, with undiluted happiness.

"Let them! I've got nothing to hide!"

"You're bragging!"

"Am I?" He kissed me and let me go.

I got my underwear on when distant sounds of voices reached us.

"What did I say? See!" I cuddled up to him and threw my dress over both of us.

The voices got closer. From the woman's giggles and the man's seductive tones it was clear that they had had the same idea as ours. Their two shapes suddenly loomed up from behind the rocks.

"Well, I never!" the woman exclaimed in mock horror.

"Welcome!" Michal called out. "The more the merrier! We've warmed up your place for you!"

"I bet you have!" the man laughed as they walked away.

Michal sat up and lit a cigarette, his face illuminated for a brief moment. Then he settled beside me, his arm cradling my head. I was blissfully happy, having him so close, feeling his skin against my skin, inhaling the scent of cigarette smoke, listening to him, absorbing his fervour.

"Anna, it's all good news! I've been placed with a unit responsible for construction work. Near a hospital in Ancona. They need people like us: bricklayers, plumbers, electricians, joiners. I've been putting tables and chairs together, hanging cabinets and shelves, making wood partitions in barracks and hospital rooms. There's so much work! And I love it all! I feel as if I've returned to normal living at last!" He kissed the top of my head. "We'll be together soon, my dearest Anna. They're already moving soldiers' families to better accommodation, in solid-built barracks with running water and cooking stoves."

It sounded like a fairy tale.

"Believe me," he said, "I've seen the barracks with my own eyes. And another thing," the tip of his cigarette glowed for a moment, "on Fridays I'll be a barber!"

"What!"

"They need barbers badly for our soldiers. I volunteered with two others. Anna, it's dead easy! What with six boys in our family, I've done it for as long as I can remember. Short back and sides. Anyone can do it. I'm surprised there was no stampede for this job!" He kissed me again. "At long last, I really feel that things are definitely changing for the better!"

I described my week to him, saving the episode with the thief till the last.

"I hate that gun, Michal," I said, "please get rid of it."

To my surprise he did not argue.

"All right," he said, "we'll do it together, tomorrow."

When we returned to our room, with the visible square of star-studded sky, like a tapestry rug on the brick wall, Iza and all the children were fast asleep, despite the accordion music rising up the stairwell to the upper floors. Matylda and Zenon, Lola and Pavel were still out, dancing, or no doubt, otherwise engaged. We undressed in the dark, folded our clothes at the foot of the mattress and lay down beside Miro.

The next day was Sunday. After breakfast we all scrubbed and spruced ourselves up for church. It was strange having men in the room, but they each did the honourable thing, and held up screens of towels or sheets, so we, women, could dress in our Sunday best calmly, our modesty well protected. I put on my new brown dress with the beige flowers and the white collar made out of the torn petticoat. I dressed Miro in a shirt that I had made out of an old white pillow case, and new shorts, reincarnated from the blue cord trousers. All this went well with his blue shoes with the pearly buttons.

The men were spared preoccupations with their dress and appearance. They all looked smart in their uniforms.

The army chapel was shared for services between the Americans, the British and the Poles. It was an old Italian church on the edge of the town where the Polish unit was stationed in tents. The neighbouring buildings had been taken over for administration and for the high ranking officers' lodgings.

The church was rapidly filling up when we arrived. We found a space on a bench at the back. I craned my neck and scanned the uniforms and the floral prints for a glimpse of our friends. Miro was mesmerised by the rainbow colours of the stained glass windows, then intrigued by the stone cherubs hovering above the archways to the side naves, and despite my attempts to hush him, commented aloud on their state of undress.

When the priest came out, in his green and golden robes, preceded by six altar boys, borrowed from the parish, and when the organ came to life and the first hymn was sung by hundreds of voices, my spine tingled and my skin covered in goose pimples, and it felt like being at home.

Later, in his sermon, Father Banaszak did not deliver the customary diatribe against our sinful nature, or the warning of hell and damnation, or the call to contrition and repentance. No. Father Banaszak said none of those things. He spoke of bravery, of endurance, of the sacrifice of the Polish nation. He spoke of faith and of hope and of God's love. The end of our enforced banishment was close, he said, and I pictured my mother waiting at the gate, her face beaming as I ran into her arms. Father Banaszak urged us to be patient, warned us about the changes at home. Our Soviet liberators, he said, were our new oppressors now. I felt a coldness seep into my heart.

But then he surprised us all by an unusual announcement.

"I know many of you," he said, "would like to enter into the sacrament of marriage. I am well aware of the fact that circumstances of the war have prevented you from doing so. In the eyes of the Church cohabiting before marriage is sinful. However, when the laws of the oppressing state prevent you from carrying out your religious duties, you are absolved from all blame. To put an end to this unacceptable situation, I have been directed by higher authorities to conduct a joint marriage ceremony during the Holy Mass next Sunday. I urge especially all couples with children to legalise and sanctify their union, so their offspring can bear their father's surnames. All people concerned should see me during the week at the Army Chaplaincy Office, with all their personal documents. We count on your honesty and integrity."

Michal sought my hand, gave it a squeeze and whispered, "Someone up there is smiling down on us."

After the service the crowd spilled out onto the square, surrounded by the shade-giving linden trees. No one was in a hurry to disperse. I left Miro and Michal and searched for Maryla and Bazylka. I found them with a group of their work colleagues. They excused themselves and came back with me, followed by Ludwik and Tomasz. For a brief while it felt like old times – the banter, the laughter, the latest news – but then they had to go back to their duties. A shadow fell on my joy, and I wished I could have taken Maryla back with me, Maryla who had been my soul-mate through the hardest times.

She gave me a sisterly hug.

"I'll visit you during the week," she said, "and then it'll be Sunday! What will you wear for your wedding?"

"Oh, I'll find something in my wardrobe," I joked. "What about you?"

She smoothed down and patted her uniform, a cotton khaki shirt and a matching A-line skirt, tucked in under her black belt that reduced her waist to the thinness of a wrist.

"I'm wearing it already!" she said with a smile. "Saves all that trekking around the fashion shops!"

We dispersed and walked back with Franek and Lilli along the promenade, Miro and Stefan doing sea-gulls around us. The place was busy with Sunday visitors keen for their families to enjoy the health-giving sea breeze and all the pleasures of the beach and the sea water. Milling with them were local people, as well as the soldiers and their women. The city, on our left, with its narrow streets and tall buildings, stood sharp against the crystal-blue sky, the ancient stains on the walls, lost in the brightness of the day.

On our right was the sea, and somewhere beyond it, if I were an eagle, if I flew north-east, I could find my home.

Michal and Franek, behind us, called out to us to stop. There was an ice cream man with his metal square box on wheels. We gathered round him, Miro and Stefan hopping with excitement.

"We've scraped enough liras together," Michal said, "to buy you ice creams."

"And you?" Lilli asked.

"We've got our cigarettes." Franek's smile and tone made out that missing ice cream was of no consequence at all.

But we forced them to taste some of ours, as we sat on the beach, Miro and Stefan totally absorbed in the pleasure of licking their cones. The taste was exquisite. Vanilla. The best vanilla ever. I did not want the moment to end.

In the evening that day, before supper, Michal suggested a walk to the beach behind the rocks, where we could hide from view.

"There's something I want to do," he said mysteriously then laughed at my questioning look. "No, nothing like that, we're taking Miro with us."

He slung his soldier's bag over his shoulder and led us out of our crowded room. The beach was virtually deserted. We walked till we reached the rocks. He bent down and folded back his trouser legs up to his knees.

"Hold up your skirt, Anna, and pick up Miro," he said. "We are going to where the water's a little deeper."

"Why?" I was mystified.

"Patience, my love! All will be revealed in a moment."

I followed him and he stopped where we were completely screened by the rocks, where the sea stretched before us to the distant horizon. I held Miro close and watched Michal. I felt myself tense when he brought out the handgun from his bag. He was solemn and his voice a little gruff when he spoke. "It's been a good day for us, Anna. Let's make a wish that this is the beginning of better things to come. Let's leave all the bad times behind us."

He leaned sideways, then with all the strength of a disc thrower, he flung the revolver into the air. It flew upwards in a wide arc before falling and disappearing in the sea.

CHAPTER 34

We were married on Sunday 17th June 1945. Together with Franek and Lilli; together with Maryla and Ludwik; together with forty-two other couples.

The moment I was awake that morning, I remembered with instant clarity that this was our special day. I lay still, calming the flutter inside me, allowing only my eyes to wander about my surroundings: Michal and Miro asleep beside me on the mattress, laid on the concrete floor; above us, exposed girders; and on all sides rough brick and mortar walls. I fancied that the vivid blue filling in the square hole on the outside wall was made of stained glass, just as I imagined that the sun rising with the promise of another hot, unblemished day, chose to shine especially for us.

There were whispers from Lola and Pavel's corner as they attended to their baby's needs. There were wakeful stirrings from Matylda, Zenon and their little Filip. Iza, in her corner, and her two little girls were fast asleep. There was nothing for her to get up and rush for, nothing to celebrate.

I turned to Michal, to his dear familiar face, the eyelashes blending with the shadows above his cheeks, as he slept, his hair coming to a point just by his ear, a few stray hairs sticking out, their tips catching the light. I was overwhelmed with love for him. I stroked his face with timid restraint. It had been a common understanding that we all respected each other's presence in the shared room, and that all intimate behaviour was confined to the beach huts at night, or to the hidden niches behind the rocks near the sea.

I touched his face with the tips of my fingers.

"It's our special day!" I whispered.

His lips jerked into a smile, his cheeks lifted forming crinkles around his eyes.

"So it is!" he whispered back.

As usual, as any other day, we had to wait our turn for the washroom, making small talk in the queue. I washed and dressed Miro, I got myself ready, and then together with Michal we went downstairs to communal breakfast. We had porridge, scrambled egg and coffee, but in my excitement I could hardly swallow anything at all.

The cook came out of the kitchen, his tall white hat bent like a broken stalk, his white apron loose around his bean-pole body.

"How many of you," he asked with a sad clown's expression, "are taking the plunge today?"

A forest of hands shot up. He shuddered then his face cracked into a smile.

"Good luck to you all, good people! Thank you for giving me a day of rest!"

"What, no special treats today!" someone called out.

He shook his head solemnly, spread his hands and retreated into his kitchen.

Frankly, I could not think beyond the time in church, beyond the marriage ceremony. At home we would have been planning our wedding for weeks, made my dress, my veil, made bridesmaids dresses, got the men to organise the drinks, the tables, the chairs in the village hall, while the women starched and ironed the tablecloths, prepared bouquets and candles, baked and cooked, decorated doorways and windows with garlands of crepe paper flowers.

Here, I could only dream. I just wished time to hurry, eleven o'clock to come, our union to be blessed, legalised, so that I could return home a proud, married woman.

Back in our room, Iza kept an eye on all our children playing in the middle of the floor, while we three couples got ourselves ready for our big occasion. As usual, when men were around at the end of the week, we women dressed behind screens of sheets or towels held up modestly around us. I put on my brown dress from the jumble box at the Red Cross and the canvas sandals that Michal had made for me. I brushed back my hair, smoothing down its crinkly resistance and tied it at the back with a lace ribbon that I had cut off the old, torn petticoat. I adjusted the wooden heart on the leather string at my throat, and I was ready.

Michal looked dapper in his uniform, his beret pulled over his forehead at a rakish angle, a comical sight, paired with his serious concentration over his job of polishing and buffing his boots till they shone like mirrors.

"Have you got our rings?" I reminded him.

"As if I'd forget!"

He fished them out of his breast pocket and held them out on his palm for me to inspect. Two silver rings, the smaller one that he had bought off the good Frau Lientz with all the odd jobs that no one else would have done for her, and the larger one that he had recently acquired from an American in exchange for his wrist watch. The American had examined it, laughed and to Michal's dismay, had thrown it into the sea. For good luck, he had said.

We left Miro playing with Iza's girls. She offered to look after all the children that morning. We left the others behind, Matylda and Zenon, Lola and Pavel, grooming themselves, checking details in the cracked mirror that somebody had propped up on the bare-brick windowsill.

We called on Franek and Lilli on the way and walked together along the promenade, its pink and yellow pavement blindingly bright in the morning sun. The town looked sleepy and staid, as if oppressed by the scorching heat. The sea lay calm, its surface glittering silver over its indigo depths.

Franek ran up to the nearest flowerbed, overgrown with weeds, and picked some wild flowers. He made two bouquets of daisies, poppies and dandelions and presented us with one each, pleased with himself as if he had found a sack of gold.

"Now, we've really got everything!" Lilli exclaimed. There was no derision in her voice. She was beautiful in the blue dress that deepened the colour of her eyes. Her freshly washed hair had the shine of silk and covered cleverly the sides of her face. I was glad for her, really glad that her terrible times were over.

At the entrance to the church, arched like two palms held in prayer, we were greeted by two officers and two elegant women in uniform. The women held small ornate baskets, one filled with white rosettes and the other with white bows.

"Bride and groom?" one of the officers asked.

"Both couples," Michal and Franek replied at once, standing to attention, chests out.

The officers shook hands with us all and the women pinned rosettes to our dresses in place of corsage, then the bows on Michal and Franek's breast pockets.

Inside the church's dark interior the benches were rapidly filling up. We got split up from Franek and Lilli. We sat together, a little squashed, but I did not mind having Michal close to me, aware of his every move, of his anticipation bubbling inside him. I listened to the gentle rise and fall of the organ music, and as I looked around it felt like being a part of a tapestry, with floral prints and ribbons and rosettes embroidered on a sage green background. The air was pungent with whiffs of cheap soap and cologne, mixed with the scent of orange blossom floating in from the square outside. I rested my wild daisy bunch in my lap, encircling it loosely with my fingers, giving my hands a chance to cool down.

I still could not believe that the moment we had been waiting for so long, had finally arrived.

The entry of the priest with his entourage of borrowed Italian altar boys was heralded by a sudden fanfare from the organ. When the music died down, there was a sound like a shower of rice hitting the marble floor, as the congregation stood up to sing the rousing hymn of "Gaude Mater Polonia", Mother of God keep watch over Poland.

When silence fell, the priest turned from the altar to face us and made a sign for us to sit down. The crowd packed in the side naves and at the back of the church could only remain standing. The priest looked magnificent in his cream and golden vestments worn only on the most important occasions in the church's calendar: Christmas, Easter, Pentecost. And our wedding. His voice, when he spoke, carried to all the corners, to all the recesses under the domed roof.

"My dearly beloved, I am much uplifted by the sight of so many of you here today, on this very special occasion. A long service is ahead of us, therefore, I shall waste no time, but get down to the business straight away." He smiled. "During the week forty-eight couples have paid me a visit and forty-eight marriage certificates have been prepared in advance. All they need now are the signatures of our illustrious witnesses, Lieutenant Voklinski and Captain Garczynski. This will be dealt with later on today.

To marry each of the couples separately would take a few hours. I have obtained a special dispensation to conduct a joint marriage ceremony, and only at the end, I shall ask each couple to come up to the altar to be individually blessed. Let us begin. Please stand up and face your partner."

A murmur of movement swept over the congregation. Michal and I faced each other. He looked so serious I could not help a nervous little smile.

The priest said, "I shall speak to the men first. Will you take this woman, your chosen one, to be your lawful wedded wife? Now, altogether…"

"I will!" the men's strong affirmation resounded round the church. Michal's eyes crinkled as he repeatedly whispered, "I will! I will!"

"Now, all the women," the priest instructed. "Will you take this man, your chosen one, to be your lawful wedded husband?"

"I will!" the female voices carried like a note of a song. "I will," I repeated, clasping Michal's hand.

The priest spoke again.

"If anyone knows of any impediments why any of these couples should not be joined in Holy Matrimony, he must speak out now!"

Silence fell upon the congregation and I held my breath as I clung to Michal. After a short pause, there was a commotion and three couples walked out.

"I couldn't be that brave," I whispered. "Not after all the years of waiting."

The priest resumed.

"Please get your rings ready and repeat after me. Men first. Start with the name of your betrothed…"

Looking into my eyes with that familiar earnestness, Michal spoke his vows together with forty-four other men.

"Anna, with this ring I thee wed, for better for worse, for richer for poorer, in sickness and in health. Let this ring be the symbol of my constant love, forsaking all others, till death us do part. So help me God."

He slipped the ring on my wedding finger. It was the women's turn. I said my vows and gave Michal his ring.

After a pause the priest instructed again, "Now, just as if you were coming to take communion, row by row, I want you to come up to the altar each couple in turn."

Our bench was three-quarters of the way down the main nave. It was going to be a long wait. We all sat down. Michal and I held hands and listened to the concert of church music and songs, evidently practised in advance especially for us. A female soloist sang "Ave Maria" which made my spine tingle. The male choir sang a succession of hymns, one of which was so moving, I had a job keeping my eyes dry. Later, I discovered it had been composed by someone called Verdi, and it was a song of the slaves.

Our turn came and we walked up to the altar in a slow moving queue. I pitied the serving boys, no older than ten or eleven, who had waited for so long and so patiently. And then, at long last we were at the altar, the priest leaning towards us, his attention exclusively ours, as if, for that moment there was no one else in the church.

"Take your bride's hand in yours," he instructed Michal. He wound his stole twice around our clasped hands. "What God has joined together, let no man put asunder. I pronounce you man and wife. With God's blessing go in love and peace."

And so we walked back down the isle, officially man and wife.

At the end of the long service, after the priest's final blessing, Lieutenant Voklinski came up the altar steps. He was a tall, slim man with an elegantly restrained bearing.

"Congratulations!" his face beamed goodwill, "this is a very special day for all of us here. The army could not let it pass without celebrations. A wedding feast has been arranged for you at the Albergo Grande. I invite you all to walk the short distance from church."

A spontaneous applause, like the sound of a hurricane hit the vaulted ceilings. He raised his arms and waited for the noise to die down.

"Our boys will pick up your families and bring them round to join you at the reception."

Michal slipped his arm around my waist and held me close. I did not trust myself to speak for a moment or two.

"One final thing," Lieutenant Voklinski announced. "A group photograph. Please remain on the steps of the church until everyone's gathered together."

Outside, as we filed out, the square was filled with laughter and excited talk. Lilli and I hugged each other, Franek and Michal shook hands. Maryla and Ludwik appeared beside us with Tomasz and Bazylka close behind. There were more shouts of joy, bear-hugs and handshakes. Maryla and Bazylka looked exceptionally pretty in their uniforms. A month in the Italian sun had turned their skins peachy, their smiles white and their hands soft and shapely. Real ladies' hands. If only Elise could see us all now!

"Isn't it good to be together again, like this?" I said, feeling nostalgia creep up on me. "Once we were inseparable, and now we need big occasions to bring us together…"

Bazylka placed her arm over my shoulder. "Don't fret Anna, this is just the beginning. There will be other times. When Tomasz and I get married…" She smiled to him and he had eyes only for her.

"And when will that be?" I asked.

"When we return home."

"We'll drink to that!" the boys chorused.

There were calls for us all to gather on the steps of the church.

"Come on, all you married people! Don't keep everyone waiting!" Bazylka moved us on. She stood with the photographer and bossed and directed everyone till the group condensed to fit within the camera's lens. Tomasz's gaze followed her with amusement and admiration.

The interior of the Grand Hotel, the grandest, the most fashionable in town, was breathtaking. It was as if the war had passed it by, unnoticed.

"Used to be the Germans' headquarters, now it's the British," Bazylka explained.

The entrance hall was like a ballroom with a marble floor, marble walls, a marble staircase, all shiny surfaces reflecting light from the hundreds of bulbs on the chandelier that hung over the central patterned walk, leading onto a number of rooms beyond. With our heads turned upwards, we kept bumping into one another as we made our way through slowly, overwhelmed by the opulence surrounding us, such that I had only ever seen on films.

The room prepared for our reception was equally dazzling with its size and splendour. Soldiers directed us to our tables that had been set out around a parquet floor above which rose a domed, stained-glass roof. The walls were covered with glossy pink marble, the edges decorated with elaborate rich carvings. At the far end there was a raised platform on which the army orchestra was already in place. A pianoforte dominated the stage. There were violins, trombones, trumpets, accordions. My brain was dizzy coping with so many impressions coming in all at once.

We were seated together, at our request, Franek and Lilli with us on one side of the table, and facing us, Maryla with Ludwik and Bazylka with Tomasz. The tables had been covered with white sheets and cold food platters placed on them in advance; the Italian "antipasti".

From that moment on it was as if our fantastic dream became reality that got better with every hour. There was no shortage of food, hot or cold, no shortage of wine. An army of attentive waiters hovered around us incessantly, sensitive to our every requirement, refilling our plates, topping up our glasses. And all the while the music flowed: Viennese waltzes, Argentinean tangos, American jazz, Neapolitan songs. But better than all of those things was the company of our friends, the banter, the jokes, the feeling of belonging, the strong bond of shared experiences in the recent past. How I wished that these things could have remained unchanged for ever.

A little later our children were brought to us by their childminders and the accompanying soldiers. Miro was glad to see us, but after perfunctory cuddles, his attention was back with his playmates, Stefan and Iza's little girls. The young PSKs from the Polish Women Corps allotted to the task of minding the children that day, gathered them together and led them outside into the enclosed gardens of the hotel. Through the open door behind us, I could view pathways flanked with tall, slender cypresses, interspersed with fountains and statues, flowerbeds bursting with colour, arbours overgrown with roses. Someone had lovingly cared for and preserved this garden from the ravages of war.

We made room at our table for Iza, and though she fretted and appeared uncomfortable with our requests for her to stay, I filled her plate nevertheless and Michal poured a glass of wine for her. He gave her a brotherly hug saying, "It's a special day for all of us. Please be our guest. Your husband would have been pleased to, wouldn't he?"

Iza's eyes reddened and became moist.

"Thank you," she said, and after a while she took a sip of wine.

There was a break in the late afternoon. Most couples and their wedding guests came out into the hotel gardens, giving the staff time to prepare for the evening celebrations and the ball.

Our group stayed together. We collected the children then walked down to the wrought-iron gates, as tall as a house, at the end of the garden. Here, wide marble steps led down to the beach.

The beach was busy with Sunday people making the most of the sea air and water before the working week began.

We found a spot, sheltered by the rocks and spread ourselves on the sand. The children – Miro and Stefan, Alicya and Anetka – were immediately caught up in collecting sea-shells and pebbles.

"It's all so incredible, isn't it?" Franek said, reclining against the rock beside Lilli, folding his long thin arms to cushion his head. "A month ago we were in another world. This is pure fantasy. I get scared believing it."

Assenting nods and murmurs went around.

Ludwik added, "I catch myself all the while looking for hidden threats in all situations. But today," he allowed himself a wide happy grin, "today, I think it's all real." He drew Maryla close to him.

"There's just one thing missing," I said. "Home."

A collective sigh expressed agreement.

Tomasz's friend, Olgierd, who had tagged along with us, said, "Things have changed at home. Just listen to this!" He pulled out a folded piece of paper from his breast pocket and opened it out. "A letter from my cousin at home," he explained, then read, "I beg you Olgierd, don't be in a hurry to return home. Those who couldn't wait have paid dearly for their impatience. The NKVD, Soviet Secret Police, arrested them immediately on their return, denounced them as traitors for 'collaborating' with the Nazis and have packed them off to labour camps in Siberia. Stay away, I beg you, until it's safe to return."

There was a moment's shocked silence then we all talked at once. How was that possible! Was there never going to be an end to bad news?

Olgierd waited till the outburst calmed down.

"There's no need for my cousin to write lies," he said. "He's had this letter smuggled out and posted to me from Sweden. He's gone to a lot of trouble to warn me. I'd be a fool not to heed his words."

We all fell silent with our own thoughts. Only the children chirped and laughed with joy at their found treasures. Disappointment constricted my throat, sat heavy on my chest. All those years of waiting! How I longed to go home!

Tomasz spoke first, his dark eyes burning in his thin ascetic face.

"I don't dismiss your warning, Olgierd, we've already discussed it before, but I need to get back. How else will I complete my medical studies? I've already lost five years! Besides, I've got to find out what's happened to my family."

Bazylka listened to him quietly, resting her head on his shoulder.

"Mine's exactly the same problem," Ludwik said, plunging his fingers into his hair, smoothing back the curls, "I've got no choice."

"You have," Olgierd replied, "you can both enrol at universities here."

"For how long?" Ludwik argued. "I'd have to learn Italian first. What guarantee have we got of a long-term stay? Who knows where they'll be shunting us to next? How many more beginnings? No, I need to settle down. In one place. At home." Maryla nodded in agreement with him.

Olgierd would not let it rest.

"Listen to General Anders," he warned. "Now there's a man who knows something about Soviet prisons and labour camps. He's got no intention of going back until the Soviets leave our country."

I could not bear to listen to this.

"So where are we supposed to go?" I asked.

He shrugged. "England, most probably. Or America. Neither will be dancing for joy at this turn of events. But they are stuck with us. After Yalta."

A shadow fell upon the happiest day of my life, a shadow that stayed with me through the evening festivities, the dancing, the chatter, the laughter.

We left the Grand Hotel at eleven, together with Lilli and Franek. He and Michal had to be up at five the next morning, to drive to their base near Ancona. We bade them goodnight at their windowless, doorless house, with the night guard on the doorstep.

It was good to be together, alone at last, after this long eventful day. Miro had been taken off our hands and with other children put to bed by Iza hours before. We were free.

"Michal," I said, as we strolled along the promenade, our arms linked, "it's been a great day! But for one thing."

"I know what you're going to say." He stopped and looked around. He led me to a low wall that held in the overgrown flowerbed. "Let's sit down and talk about it before we turn in."

The promenade was deserted, the pink and yellow pavement greyed in the dark, the vast starry night stretching over the town, over the sea beyond the horizon. The absolute quiet, but for the murmur of the distant tide, induced us to speak softly.

"I want so much to go home." I put my arm around his waist. His shirt smelled faintly of tobacco and cologne.

"I know," he said, "but hey, don't be sad. Not today, Anna! Everything will be all right in the end, I promise."

He held my face in both his hands and kissed me. I felt the current of his liveliness, his energy.

"Really, Michal, really? How can you be so sure?"

He let go of my face but kept his face close to mine, a pale triangle with two sparks in deep shadows.

"Because, my dearest Anna, it's time for our luck to change. And it has. Already. Don't you see? We're free. We've got Miro. And we've just got married. I've got a feeling, I believe that it'll get better still."

His buoyant optimism made it appear so simple.

"But when? When will it change?" I persisted.

He was silent just looking out towards the sea. He spoke after a while.

"I've been thinking, Anna, if things don't work out in Poland, if we've got to make a new start elsewhere, would it really be such a bad thing? We've got each other. And Miro. Our home can be anywhere!"

"But..." My longing to go home, to see my mother, was like an ache.

"Anna," Michal hugged me, "just hear me out. First of all, there's our own safety in question. If we return now, straight into a trap, we'll be back to square one. And what about Miro? We'd never forgive ourselves. But if we stay with Anders and go with him to England, we've got a chance of a fresh new start. I want stability for us both. For Miro. I want him to do well at school. I dream of a better life for him. Once things settle down, perhaps even change completely in Poland, then your mother can visit us as often as you wish. We'll be of no use to anyone, packed off to some remote Siberian labour camp."

Such fears had indeed crossed my mind, but immersed as I was in my misery of home-sickness, I had only one burning desire: to return home, to my family in Poland.

"But... England's so far away..." I found it hard switching my thoughts of my imagined home-coming to an alien, distant land.

"It's not that far...only a different direction. We'll be safe there, Anna. And Miro."

"My head's in a muddle…" I said, pressing my palms to my forehead, "I need time to think, to get used to this idea…"

He hugged me again.

"Nothing's going to change overnight," he said. "You've got weeks, probably months to think it over. Let's go, get some sleep. Early start tomorrow."

As we walked to our lodgings, to the unfinished building with its gaping holes, my feverish jumbled thoughts began to form a vision, foggy and vague at first, then with every step, becoming clearer, bolder. I pictured a house just like our home in Poland, with a garden full of summer flowers, a green patch in the middle, and sitting on it, my mother, my sisters, my brothers, Michal and Miro enjoying an apple cake that I had baked for them. I felt my heart lift and light flood my soul.

"I wonder if their summers are as hot as ours," I said, clasping Michal's hand tightly and thinking of England.

Author's Note

In May 1945 Europe was celebrating the end of the war. There was no joy for the Polish nation. Their country "liberated" from the Nazis by the Russians was now under Soviet rule and oppression.

Thousands of displaced Polish families arrived in Great Britain seeking refuge. It took another forty seven years before the last unit of the Red Army left Poland in 1992.

Anna was sixty-nine that year and still living in England.